THE

TOWN SLUT'S

DAUGHTER

Heather Haley
©2014

HOWE SOUND PUBLISHING
Bowen Island, BC V0N 1G1
www.howesoundpublishing.com

ISBN 978-0-9938813-0-5

Printed and bound in the United States

For Corona

girls with guitars

CHAPTER ONE

The girls shoved their way in through a huddle of punk rockers. Fiona thought they looked like soldiers, uniforms of black leather weighted with chains, safety pins, buttons, and badges. Strolling the length of a long hallway, tall murals pulsating with ghastly, contorted faces, she was more startled by her own reflection, eyes gleaming in a glut of mirrors. She looked like a wimp all right, a honey-blond, bell-bottomed puffball floating too close to the spikes and big black boots; so close to the stench of dyed hair, she thought she might puke. Backing up, she grabbed Shannon's arm.

"I don't belong here."

"Okay, so where do you belong?"

"I don't know!"

Shannon sighed.

"Oh, all right," said Fiona, "let's go."

A rising wave of guitar distortion crested and blasted through double doors, a shock of spazzing centipede legs creeping up the base of Fiona's skull. *Music*? Loud! Fast. So fucking LOUD her spine stiffened. A voice wailed.

"Is that English?"

Shannon laughed. "That's DOA."

The girls groped along the back wall, sonics thundering, Fiona wobbly. Shannon pointed to the towering hulk in a plaid lumberjack vest as they headed toward the stage.

"Joey Shithead."

With two fingers under his nose à la Hitler's moustache, Mr. Shithead threw his right arm into a Sieg Heil salute. "Fascism suuucccks!"

The names cracked her up. Chuck Biscuits manned the

drums. Randy Rampage fiddled the head of a Fender bass slung low past his knees.

Shithead scowled. "Fuck tuning!"

"PLAY!" roared the audience.

DOA played. DOA ranted and railed in mega-decibels. Various and assorted jerks fought for the microphone stand, slamming it into Shithead's face, whacking his lips repeatedly. Shithead growled, blood and sweat slinging off his big bear head, pitching in time to some inner tic. Sneering, stick-fisted Chuck pummelled the tom-toms. Rampage moved like elastic, sproinging back and forth across the stage or throwing himself onto his knees and crawling, his raised guitar a sabre.

Head-shorn boys feverishly jumped up and down in one place, arms held stiffly at their sides. Fiona noticed a tall, flaxen-haired Adonis latched on to a humungous speaker like a lecherous hound humping a human leg, his head shoved inside the woofer.

"Who is that?"

"That is Dennis Jeklin."

Dennis Jeklin jumped off and swarmed the room; pit bull in a china shop, snarling, charging, crashing into tables, climbing onto the stage to cavort before flinging himself into the audience. Upraised arms snatched his body, tossing it until Dennis reached the back of the room without touching the floor.

Fans hurled bottles, beer, saliva.

"Eeeuuuuhh! What's with the spitting?"

"Gobbing is difficult to explain," said Shannon. "Later, okay?"

"Okay. How about much later?"

Three songs. *Already*. Hard, furious. Shannon and Fiona glanced between dodging bodies, ramming torsos. Crowds creeped her out, and this crowd was verging on a mob. A core of four goons thumped longer than the rest; Bowery Boys apparently, Dennis decidedly a member.

Shannon clinked Fiona's beer bottle with hers. "To us!"

"Yeah!" She bussed her girlfriend's cheek with a kiss.

2

"Happy reunion!" Fiona looked around. "I gotta pee."

Shannon pointed to the back. Though nervous, Fiona fought the throng all the way to the ladies' room. She opened the door to cackles and squeals, two girls perched on a wet counter, smoking and passing around a mickey of Canadian Club. The littlest one in a striped T-shirt and denim jacket was tomboyishly cute, an orange curl in the middle of her forehead.

"Wanna snort?" She shoved the bottle under Fiona's nose.

"No thanks."

Overflowing toilets crammed with feces and vomit, paper towels and tampons forced Fiona to tamp down her gag reflex. She found the last stall door shut, two pairs of blue suede, thick-soled-shoe-clad feet visible. Fiona leaned against the tiles to wait, everyone staring.

"I don't look right, do I?"

Giggles. "Hey, you're cool," purred the girl with the curl, handing Fiona the whisky. "Kinda look like a hippie though."

Praying they wouldn't slag her, Fiona grabbed the bottle. Turning around to peer in the mirror, the rye steadied her as the light became a little less jarring. She realized the girl with the long black bangs was talking to her.

"Sorry," yelled Fiona. "What did you say?"

"What do you think of the band?"

"Ah well . . . they're interesting."

They laughed. Bangs Girl came to Fiona's aid. "Well, at least she didn't say, 'They're loud'."

Curl Girl sidled up. "I'm Oona. This is Jade. She's in a great band! The Dishrags. What's your name?"

Just as Fiona opened her mouth to speak, the music died to the sound of loud shrieks and whistles. Jade opened the door a crack, a frown marring her pretty, pale face.

"Fuck! It's the pigs."

Groans, screams. "Let's get outta here!" Oona drained the bottle and flung it into the garbage can. "It's a raid!"

They tripped over each other scrambling to get out. *Now what?* Fiona decided to hide her underage ass. She remembered the four legs in the third stall and went over and pounded on the door, the banging and screaming in the club becoming louder, closer. Fiona climbed the neighbouring toilet, leaned over the top to zero in on two girls. The one leaning against the wall, eyes shut, was statuesque with a haystack of dirty-blond hair; the other, a petite Asian, occupied the throne, hunched over a needle resting on her upturned arm like a mosquito. A jolt travelled the entire length of Fiona's body, her knees buckled.

"Hey! It's a raid!"

Leaning Girl lifted her head with a huge effort, gazing at Fiona's head as if it were floating. She returned to her nod. "Okay. Get busted. Why should I care?"

Fiona opened the bathroom door a smidge, squinting at the bright overhead lights, rear fire doors framing a paddy wagon that idled in the alley, back yawning wide open. *Where is Shannon?* At least Fiona could keep her cool, a vital skill for one born to a hysterical mother. Jeanette would run around like a headless chicken, her youngest hollering instructions: "Mom, call an ambulance! Mom, stop the bleeding."

Barking orders, the Vancouver police herded people into queues with their nightsticks, shoving them against the walls, demanding ID. Any kid who got mouthy was handcuffed and hauled off. An awful lot of kids were handcuffed and hauled off. The stall door creaked open, both girls falling forward to stand and blink.

"Let's go." Heroin Girl couldn't, or wouldn't, make eye contact.

"Aren't we better off here?" said Fiona.

"Nah," she replied, the voice of experience.

The two covered their eyes—see-no-evil monkey style—and heaved their high selves out the door. Fiona peeked through her fingers, watching in amazement as they breezed through the melee. *Guardian angels? Patron saint of junkies? Would that be St. John, protector of the sick? Fuck that! What am I gonna do?* Fiona paced. *Jesus Christ! Junkie Girl might be stoned, but she's right. No place to hide. Oh please God, don't let my head get bashed in.* Fiona exited, flitting across the floor strewn with broken bottles, ice, upended tables and chairs, spying a pair of tortoiseshell glasses, lenses streaked

4

with blood. *Should I get in line or try to slip by?* Fiona resolutely headed toward the front door, hovering close to the wall. *Wish I could blend in with those hideous murals.* She watched a girl be dragged by her fluorescent pink hair to the paddy wagon and hurled inside, poor thing landing on top of an unconscious boy. Fiona ducked under a counter. *There's Oona!* Cop grilling her; Oona snotty, naturally, refusing to show ID; probably doesn't have any. She can't be more than fourteen. No one could hush her. Oona talked back once too often. The cop cuffed and dragged her outside to a patrol car. Slamming Oona's head against the hood, he kicked her legs apart, roughly frisked her tiny body, and handily tossed it into the paddy wagon, Oona pitching off the walls until she face planted on the floor.

"Psssstt!"

Startled, Fiona turned around to see a tall woman with close-cut hair peeking out from behind the bar, waving.

"Come here!"

Fiona ran over, ducked down, and squatted next to her. "Come on, I'll show you how to get out."

The woman lifted a trap door and pointed to an oily wooden staircase. Fiona scrambled down, stench of rotting fish wafting up. Two young men lurked in the basement. The big bald bruiser explained she was now under the Ocean Pearl restaurant.

The skinny bucktoothed guy introduced himself: "Spooner. He's Mad Dog. And you?"

"Fiona." *Wish I had a cool name.*

"Fiona." Spooner pointed to a dark passageway. "Let's go."

She looked at his red conversed feet and wondered why she should follow him. He showed her to a door that opened to the parking lot, another paddy wagon skulking in the alley like a hearse. Spooner pointed as a pretty blue-haired girl peered out from behind a pillar and turned back. She directed Fiona to a path leading to the front of the building. A small but formidable group of punks loitered in front of the club, police cruiser circling like a vulture, cop leaning out the window.

"You better get out of here! We'll haul your asses in too."

They turned their backs on him. *There's Shannon!* Hoping the

5

police had met their quota, Fiona crossed her fingers and emerged from the shadows.

"Fiona!" Shannon ran up and threw her arms around her. "Are you okay? I got out right away, but I couldn't find you! Fucking pigs! These busts have been happening a lot lately. I should have warned you."

"Fucking pigs!"

Shannon grinned. "Come on, let's go. There's a party at the Squat."

She pulled Fiona into the crosswalk, where they met her friends Jimbo, Laura, and the big swirling brute Dennis. Jimbo sheltered Laura in his voluminous tweed coat. Both had brown eyes and short blue-black hair.

"Can you believe that bullshit tonight?" Laura rested her head on Jimbo's ample chest. "They keep trying to shut us down, but we are not going away."

Shannon introduced Dennis as a poor little rich kid; a Beverly Hills escapee/transplant. Dennis blushed. Fiona wondered what he needed to run away from. He had the attitude down though.

"Going to the party?" He hopped over and stood next to Fiona.

Soon, much confusion ensued. They couldn't find a ride and their other friends had scattered. Shannon insisted on hoofing it. They walked briskly, chatting amiably as they passed vacant cars, porches, and churches, Dennis stopping frequently to serenade them with his air guitar. *What a goof.* Usually no one rated a smile from Fiona, but she flashed him one.

She felt the house before she saw it. Gusts of guitar squall busted out of a dilapidated, two-story wooden lean-to at the foot of the Georgia Street viaduct. Dennis took Fiona's hand. She pulled away. He grinned and she returned it. They crossed the street, dashing inside before she could change her mind.

Packed tightly with night people, the place had been gutted. The walls looked charred, but up close, Fiona could see the house's framing had been painted black. Laura and Jimbo headed toward the homemade stage. Dennis brought Fiona and

6

Shannon beer, then ran off to join his Bowery Boys. Shannon pointed up at the all sorts of musicians she called Rude Norton. Chuck Biscuits sat below a pair of heavy, wooden scissor beams. The singer resembled a psycho Sinatra—Speedo goggles, choke chain collar, and jeans pulled down to his knees as he bellowed into a microphone, neck veins bulging.

"That's Wimpy," yelled Shannon. "He's in the Subhumans."

Fiona pointed to his pale, hairy thighs and grimy jockstrap. "He's grossing me out!"

Wimpy wrapped the mic cord around his knuckles, punched the guitar player in the arm.

"Rude Norton's a fuck band."

"A what band?"

"A fuck band. People from different groups play different instruments. Drummers sing, singers drum, et cetera."

Fiona watched Laura screech into a mic while straddling the boom stand like a pony. "Groupies get onstage?"

"Laura is not a groupie!"

Fiona pointed. "I thought you said Jimbo is a bass player."

"Yeah, well, there aren't any rules, okay? Anybody can play anything they want. And they only do covers."

"You just said there aren't any rules."

Shannon glared at her.

Fiona laughed and formed a cross with her fingers, holding it up in front of her face, mocking a shield.

"Hey, what's upstairs?"

Shannon led Fiona to a staircase seemingly tacked onto the house, Dennis suddenly on her ass. Tapping Fiona's left shoulder, he deposited his chin on her right.

"Hi," he peeped. She had to laugh.

The room was cold despite walls throbbing with graffiti: A circled A for ANARCHY, WHITE RIOT, HOLIDAYS IN HELL, FUCK THE WORLD, NO BEATLES! EAT THE RICH! SHE WOLVES WERE HERE, NAZI PUNKS FUCK OFF, DISCO SUCKS! KILL YOUR PARENTS, CASA LUNA LOCO and ESCAPE ROUTE over the door. It formed quite the backdrop, punks milling about making conversation, less intimidating to her with each passing hour. A few even had long hair; one guy a beard. Shannon hadn't changed much, and like she said, "Who can afford a leather jacket anyway?" Fiona felt a pang of envy for all the things Shannon had done during the past year and a stab of regret for all the things she had not.

Three girls sat on a couch next to a young man with a Cheshire cat smile, his eyes concealed behind dark lenses. Fiona recognized Art Bergmann, recalling that he'd cruised around their hometown of Cloverdale in an old red Jaguar, big woolly dog Bernie in the back seat. Her ex-boyfriend had played guitar in his band, the Shmorgs. He greeted them warmly.

"Art's got a new group," said Shannon. "The K-Tels."

Apparently, he was only part of a Surrey contingent that had fled the burbs to Vancouver; John Armstrong and Bill Scherk played in Active Dog, Gord Nicholl in the Pointed Sticks, and Jim Cummins in I, Braineater.

Talk about the dragnet at the show was the buzz going round the room; Joey Shithead, one of the first arrested, was beaten unconscious. Twelve others were arrested in the lobby of the cop shop while trying to get their friends out. All were being held in the drunk tank, even though most were sober.

Fiona spotted a fatally handsome fellow across the room. Noticing Fiona's interest, Shannon leaned in and announced, "That's Trent Radislovich. He's an artist."

"He's a hunk."

"He's a queer."

Fiona thought of her uncle, Stephen, the only queer in all of Matapédia; how the family shipped him off to Toronto at the tender age of fifteen, homosexuality a sin too sinful to hide.

So many cute guys! She marvelled, gazing around the room, deciding there were two types—the raunchy, rowdy, leather and chains stud-punk and the four-eyed, nervous nerd-punk. All cute. Except the one before her now. Shannon introduced Spooner.

"We've met. Thanks for saving my butt!"

He hooted, right in her face. Spooner was the kind of guy you partnered with in science class because he got the best

8

grades; the kind of guy who got beat up a lot.

Shannon raised her hand. "Hey, everybody! She just moved here. My best friend Fiona."

"Jeez, you don't have to make an announcement."

They all hailed like a cheerful kindergarten class. "Hi, Fiona!"

She waved, blinded by the radiance of their smiles, then sat down, bass and drums rumbling at her feet, leaning in to hear the conversation.

"So, the people living here, they're not making a statement?" Art's girlfriend, Jenny, challenged a lanky young man with round, horn-rimmed glasses and a matching John Lennon countenance. "They're just bums?"

"That's Angus," whispered Shannon.

Skewing his expression, Angus replied, "That's not what I mean. But why should they make a statement? 'Only the rich can afford principles.' Are you familiar with the Shaw play *Major Barbara*?" Angus paused for a long drag on his cigarette, casting a hooded look at Fiona. "In London, people squat because they have to. Because they have no place to live."

Jenny shrugged. Grinning, Trent moved over to the group and asked if they'd ever heard of Marx's *Whatever It Is, I'm Against It*? "Groucho Marx, that is."

Titters from everyone except Angus.

"I'm just saying that poverty helped create rage, and it's that rage that created punk rock."

Shannon feigned a yawn. "Set it to music, Angus."

Angus' ears turned red.

"Disenfranchised youth?" said Trent. "It's that simple, is it?"

"Fuck it," muttered Art.

"Yeah," chimed Jenny. "All I care about is music."

"New blood!" Spooner pumped his fist into the air. "I was pukin' on all that pap they force-fed us. Not to mention twenty-minute drum solos."

"Okay," said Jenny. "Let's not mention twenty-minute drum solos."

Dennis cocked his hand like a gun. "Let's kill all the old farts. Smash the status quo!"

"Did you know that Fleetwood Mac took almost two years to record that fucking-piece-of-shit album, *Rumors*," Angus said, "and spent half a million dollars on it?"

Spooner rolled his eyes. "Baw—ring!"

"God bless Charlie Manson." All heads turned to Angus. "He killed off the hippies! It was such a reality check, the Tate–LaBianca murders. The end of an era. Peace out."

"Hey, Angus," said Trent, "ever read *Animal Farm*?"

"In high school," he huffed.

"Well, there is the real danger of the oppressed becoming the oppressor. The Machiavellian principles—power corrupts, you know."

"Yeah, well, what do you replace the status quo with?" asked Shannon.

"This!" Jenny pointed, indicating the din downstairs.

"Nothing," deadpanned Trent.

Shannon scowled. "Nothing is right!"

"It's not about nihilism," said Angus. "Despite the media hype, punk's about renewal. Regeneration." He picked at the label on his beer bottle. "Besides, destruction resembles creation, and creation, destruction. Floods, avalanches, forest fires, tornadoes; they tear things up, but they sow new seeds. New life, up from the ashes, et cetera."

Shannon shook her head. "The world according to Angus Tucker."

Fiona heard a loud bang and a strangled cry, and watched as Dennis' pals dragged him toward the door. "No, I don't wanna go!"

"Come on," said Mad Dog. "We gotta do a beer run. We're almost out! You're the only one who knows how to get in."

Dennis forlornly surveyed the regiment of dead soldiers standing guard on the tables. He looked to Fiona. She shrugged.

Angus chuckled. "Those goombas go down to Carling's and steal flats of beer. Dennis used to work there."

Art continued to hold court without saying much, as Trent and Spooner carried on discussing Britain and its wretched, hypocritical class system. Angus sat down next to Fiona.

10

"Well, Fiona, where were we?"

He remembered my name. She pointed to a corner nearly black with graffiti. "That is sickening. Are you guys Nazis?"

"You're kidding, right?" He paused for a big swig. "But you know, the swastika's universal. Ancient. Hindu actually, but then the Nazis appropriated it, unfortunately, and maligned it for all time."

"That's not all they appropriated."

"It's just a symbol."

"But symbols are powerful."

"Precisely why we use them; especially the swastika. Pure shock value. No need to get hung up on it. It's actually quite beautiful." Angus showed her one of his pins; a silver eagle with spread wings and muscular chest, like a man's, its huge talons clutching a swastika. "See, the arms rotate in the same direction. Like the rays of the sun."

You're the one hung up on it, she thought. Angus inched closer. I wonder if he has a girlfriend?

"Have you read Joseph Campbell?" he asked. "The mythologist? He wrote *The Hero with a Thousand Faces. Star Wars* is based on it."

"Is that what you are?"

"I think we all are. On a journey. A quest."

"Me too?"

"I'd say that's obvious. Gender doesn't matter."

"Do you really believe that?"

"I'll be right back." Angus needed another beer.

Soon Fiona watched him talk up another girl. *Maybe I'm a pain in the ass. Maybe I'm just not cool enough.* She spotted Shannon observing them. *Fuck him. He's not that cute. In fact, he's a jerk, with all those opinions he shoves down your throat.*

Shannon came over and sidled next to her, Fiona happy to lie low, but Art suddenly asked, "So when are you going to start a band?"

"I've never been in a band."

Jenny smiled up from the throne of Art's lap. "You don't have to be perfect, you know."

"Most songs are made up of only three or four chords," said Spooner. "The good ones."

"That's reassuring. I guess."

Shannon grinned. "It's not as if you have nothing to say."

"You make it sound simple."

"You always say music is your saving grace. And you know what else? The girls around here don't just hang around being groupies."

"Damn straight!" Spooner flashed a wide load of teeth. "They start their own bands, write their own songs, even play their own instruments. I know a drummer."

"You guys have lots of experience performing," said Fiona. "I don't."

"Sure you do. "Remember choir? All those Christmas pageants?" Shannon laughed. "You can do it."

"Beer's here!" shouted Mad Dog, setting off a stampede.

Dennis poked his head in the door, scanned the room, and waved. Fiona groaned. Shannon smiled. He charged over, parked his butt between the girls and put his arm around Fiona's waist.

"Hey!" She quickly extricated herself.

The beer didn't last long, and soon people began to drift out of the house.

Trent yawned and stretched as he slowly stood up. "And lookee here, the sun also rises. Where did everybody go?"

Fiona bid Trent and Angus adieu, wondering whom Angus would bed, relieved it wouldn't be her. Ditto Shannon, who told Fiona they'd had a thing going until Angus unceremoniously dumped her.

"Ah ha! That explains the grilling you gave him."

"He's an asshole."

"He is an asshole."

Fiona walked out with Shannon, Dennis, Art, and Jenny, into the woolly light of dawn, stretching her arms upward and blurting, "Damn! It's good to be alive."

A hiss of steam escaped from a McGavin's Bread truck as it rumbled past. Dennis skipped, while singing in a raspy voice

Elvis Costello's "The Angels Wanna Wear My Red Shoes."

Shannon glanced over her shoulder, then poked Fiona in the ribs. She turned around to see a police car creeping up on them, two cops inside. They pulled over and approached.

"Hey, Sid," said the young one.

"Sid?" whispered Fiona.

"Oh," said Shannon, "the little wiener thinks he's cool 'cause he knows who Sid Vicious is."

"What have you kids been up to?"

"Not much," replied Dennis.

"Oh yeah, and what does 'not much' include?"

"Oh, you know, the usual quaffing of blood," replied Jenny with a smirk.

Fiona wished she'd knock it off. The fat cop was twirling the handlebars of his moustache, the kids cast their eyes to the ground as the rookie eyed them.

"What's your name, miss?"

"Fiona." She looked the cop in the eye, which was difficult, as she was at least four inches taller.

"Can I see some ID, please?" Fiona fished out her driver's licence and handed it to him. "Beautiful British Columbia. You fit right in, I must say."

Her friends fidgeted and coughed, suppressing their laughter. *Shit. Been dodging heat all night, now this.* Recalling what happened to poor little Oona, Fiona fixed a smile on her face.

He bore into her with a stare. "Where do you live?"

"I just moved to Vancouver."

Shannon offered her address. "We live with my parents."

He returned the driver's licence, his right hand lingering on Fiona's. "There you go, mademoiselle."

Shannon clamped her hand over an explosion of giggles as Fat Cop ordered them to go home.

"What a twerp!" said Jenny, watching them pull away in their cruiser. "That cop was flirting with you."

"Eeeuuuuhh! I hate cops."

Art squinted at the morning sun warming the sidewalk. "Well, they like you."

"I'm relieved," said Shannon. "At least they didn't haul us in on some lame-ass, bogus charge."

"Ah, let's face it," said Dennis. "We live in a fucking police state."

They all headed off in different directions, but not before Dennis leaned in and kissed Fiona, square on the mouth. She cursed and shoved him off.

"What's with that guy? He's so touchy-feely!" Fiona complained after they were safely seated on a bus bound for Commercial Drive.

"He's an American. He just likes you. Dennis is good people."

"Well I just met him. I don't like being pawed."

They got off at Adanac and strolled through the still chill of morning to Shannon's house.

"Hey," she said, "by the time you hear 'Anarchy in the UK,' the back of your brain's already been scorched by DOA."

They laughed. Shannon rustled up some crackers and cheese and threw on *Never Mind the Bollocks*.

"Fuck it. There's no point unless we can play it loud. Tomorrow. After Mom and Dad go to work."

"You mean today."

"Yeah." Yawning, Shannon sat on the couch and put her arm around Fiona. "Did you have fun?"

"Fun is an understatement!" Fiona was greatly relieved to discover that their separation was a mere blip on the screen. "I missed you so much."

"Me too. I hated Vancouver at first, but now everybody's moving into the city."

Fiona reported that things were horrendous in Cloverdale with Bill and Jeanette; parental units from hell. "Non-stop drinking. Fighting. They can't beat on us anymore, we're too big, but they're at each other's throats constantly. The RCMP knows us all on a first-name basis. She cheats on him all the time. Christ. I wish they'd break up and get it over with. I just wanted to kill myself!"

"You had every right to split. And you're welcome to stay

14

here as long as you want." Shannon gave Fiona a pillow, a blanket, and a goodnight kiss, then trundled off to bed leaving her on the couch.

Fiona could not sleep, worrying about the two older sisters she'd left behind. *Oona's right*, she thought. *I do look like a hippie*. She got up and looked around for a pair of scissors, eventually settling for a butcher knife. She went into the bathroom and began to hack away. Daring a peek in the mirror, Fiona thought, *Jeez, I look about as tough as Tinker Bell*. She chopped off more chunks and took another look. *More orphan than anything*. Fiona continued cutting, closer and closer to her scalp. *Shit. Now I look like a prisoner of war*. She decided to like it.

Fiona returned to the living room, picked up her guitar, sat down, and quietly churned out a few chords. *Maybe I can write songs*. After a few false starts, the melody was just there, words coming in a rush. "I Am Not a Nice Girl." She'd love to throw that in her mother's face. *Maybe I don't want to be nice. Maybe I don't want to be Laura Nyro or Joni Mitchell either.*

I Am Not a Nice Girl

I am not a nice girl
Nice never enough
I am not an ugly girl,
That's how this world makes me feel

You say I'm so selfish
You say I'm so ambitious
You say I'm so angry
All I can say is . . . So what!

I am not a nice girl but boy
Am I real. I will not behave
The way you think I should
I will not become what I mean to you

Wired, Fiona's brain would not shut down. *I was hiding behind my hair. Why? I have nothing to hide. And why would anybody want to be known as a shithead?* Fiona forced herself to lie down and closed her eyes. *I forget, what was once bad is now good.* She conked out at last, to the refrain of a new song.

The next morning Fiona stood at the window watching Dennis ride up the driveway of Shannon's house on a bicycle. Beaming, standing on the pedals, he waved, bum never touching the seat. *What a goof.* He bounded up the steps and whammed on the door. Fiona vaguely regretted inviting him. He snapped photographs with an ancient Instamatic all the way to the diner: a mangy, stuffed grizzly in a pawnshop window, treetops reflected in puddles, luminous pink clouds, and her ass, she suspected. They entered Dot's Café, silencing the patrons. An old war-horse of a waitress whinnied at the sight of Dennis. She showed them to a booth and wrote down their orders, wildly flirting.

"Christ. She's old enough to be your mother. Is that Dot?"

"Sue."

"What happened to Dot?"

Dennis shrugged. Fiona had more questions. Nineteen years old, Dennis was born in Vancouver and raised in L.A., his dad a film producer. "I'm sixteen," Fiona told him, mother's in Surrey, father's up north working. Welding, I think. He's a jack-of-all-trades. Or, more like a jerk-of-all-trades."

Dennis grinned. Again. Some more. "Divorced?"

"I divorced them. Took my mother's maiden name 'cause I hate *Koretchuck*." Fiona held her knife and fork in her fists, pounding the table like a convict in a prison movie. "I'm starving!"

They searched for their waitress. Sue hollered. In short order, the cook slammed two burgers under the orange heat lamps, which she delivered with a flourish.

"Don't buy that crap from Angus," said Dennis between

bites.

"What crap?"

"Angus is a dilettante. Drop him off in the underground for a few months and he thinks he's Cerberus."

"Angus thinks he's our watchdog? I know who Cerberus is. Know what else I think?" Fiona leaned over the table to poke Dennis in the shoulder. "You're trying too hard."

He slumped. Looking to the heavens, he confessed, "Okay. I'm trying to impress you."

"I can see you're intelligent, even if you are a maniac." Dennis smiled. Battered boots and baggy sweater disguised his good breeding. "But if you're such a strong individual, why wear the uniform?"

"Same reason you do." Dennis indicated Fiona's hacked-up hair, black duds.

"Yeah. Guess I'm adopting the dress code. But it feels right. I'm starting to believe anything's possible. Even some style."

"Oh, is that what you call it?"

"Ouch!"

"I'm kidding. You're beautiful. You'd be beautiful if you were bald." Dennis tousled what remained of Fiona's hair. "But don't get any ideas." He grabbed her hand, they locked eyes. "And quit acting like you're nothing."

"What's that supposed to mean?"

"You're a bright girl. You should be in school."

"Right now I have to find a job. And a place to live."

Dennis washed dishes at Romano's and would inquire for her. He had more questions.

"No, I don't have a boyfriend. I don't want a boyfriend."

"Why not?"

"Christ. You know, the thing I hated most about puberty wasn't losing my virginity. It was losing my freedom. I didn't have any at home, that's for sure, but at least the playground was a level playing field. I ruled! Then all the rules changed. I had to be a 'nice girl,' even to the boys."

"Is that so hard?"

"When we didn't have to be 'nice,' we all got along just fine.

My sisters and I played war games, kick-the-can, baseball. We went exploring, skating, and rafting with the boys. It didn't matter. We were just a bunch of little savages running around having too much fun to worry about sex."

Laughing, Dennis called her a tomboy.

"Yeah, and it's not just a phase. I hated it! Kids start passing notes, whispering behind your back about who likes who, and which girls wear brassieres. Everybody had crushes and parties and played Spin the Bottle, but only if you were invited. Christ. I've been on shaky ground ever since."

"Until now?"

"Yeah! Until now."

CHAPTER TWO

Rory, Fiona's eldest sister, called to inform her, a tad gleefully, that their mother was fed up with Bill, about to leave him and move to Vancouver.

"She won't do it. She'll never leave her comfort zone. And let her be mad. We shouldn't feel guilty about anything anymore."

"Easy for you to say. We're the ones who have to take care of her."

"What about all those times I walked her home from the bar?"

Jeanette practically lived at the beer parlour when the old man was away; flirting, playing shuffleboard, consuming lakes of ale. On nights she didn't retire with some guy, the bartender at the Clydesdale Inn called the girls to come collect her, Fiona invariably elected. Several times she refused, several times Jeanette got lost, banging on the neighbours' doors, screaming, "Fiona!"

"You could call her once in a while."

"Whatever you say." Fiona would say anything to get off the phone, deciding she hated the phone and wasn't going to answer it anymore.

There was always a palpable sense of relief whenever Bill was absent. No more rules, ambushes, dirty looks, or silence at the dinner table. No more dinner table, for that matter, with Jeanette at the bar. What was there to miss about the cranky black cloud of Bill's reign or Jeanette's blustering rages? The sisters were left to their own devices and a bare fridge, Bill's exceptional wages rarely manifesting in a stocked pantry. He liked to play the ponies. Ditto Jeanette. The girls subsisted on ketchup-slathered dried bread or eggs the landlord bestowed. In summer they raided the neighbours' gardens, hiding out in their pup tent built of blankets, gorging on carrots, corn, and peas. During their incessant roaming, the girls prowled for bottles, which they exchanged at the general store for penny candy, comic books, and pop. One Easter, the sisters collected so many bottles they were able to celebrate the resurrection of Christ with heaping baskets of pastel jellybeans and chocolate bunnies. When Bill did send cash, the girls feasted on fried baloney, wieners and beans, hamburgers, and sugar sandwiches.

Fiona recalled waking one night to a commotion in her parents' bedroom. She sat up, startled, wondering when her father had returned, then realized the male voice belonged to Mom's "friend," Bud. Fiona listened to the blood pounding in her ears and Jeanette's pleading. Bud asked about her girls. Jeanette ignored the vital question, continued wheedling and speaking of her love for him. At age ten, Fiona knew exactly what the guy was after and it wasn't shacking up with Jeanette and her three brats. Fiona pitied her unsuspecting father. Ornery as Bill was, she loved him fiercely and though her family wasn't exactly normal, couldn't imagine life without him. She fell asleep thinking what a ninny her mother was.

Things could get hairy with no supervision, like the time they razed the house. The girls were cooking supper, a long summer day cooling as they ran outside to play. Ten minutes into their romp, they stopped short at the acrid smell of smoke, turning to see black plumes billowing and flames leaping from the kitchen window.

"Mo'o in there!"

Rory tried to run inside, but Fiona pulled her back. The girls dashed to the Wilsons' trailer, grateful to find Gerry, though they were frightened of the brooding, brush-cut muscle-man great-white hunter. He ran over, ducked down low, and entered the inferno without hesitation. Rory and Fiona stood bawling as they listened to Gerry coughing, calling out, "Fiona!"

"Everybody mixes us up!" Fiona stood trembling until Gerry finally emerged with Maureen on his shoulder, a seething fireball on his tail.

Next day the chief of Cloverdale's volunteer fire department reported that someone had left a tea towel on the stove and asked, "Where the hell were you?"

Jeanette dodged the question deftly. No one called it neglect back then.

They were inclined to wing it, Fiona and sisters, blessed with the wondrous grace and resiliency of childhood, though still desperate to be rescued. No one but Gerry Wilson had the daring or any inkling why.

Off to meet Ms. Rita Vanoverschot, Spooner's drummer friend. Fiona endured an interminable bus ride to the Royal City of New Westminster, renowned for its pawn shops, pool halls, and booze cans. Her hopes were high, even as a heavy black cloud blanketed the horizon. Fiona tried in vain to paste down her cut-up curls and cowlicks as people stared, or pretended not to. She pressed her forehead against the window, wondering where her father was. Fiona could recall a photo of the young, tough Bill on Cambie Street; a real ace in a leather bomber jacket, aviator sunglasses, and white silk scarf. *Hard to imagine Bill was ever cool.* Fiona harboured a few fond memories: fishing and hunting trips, her father happiest in the woods, in his element. He used to make them drop everything to run outside and watch the Canada geese fly over, to marvel at their perfect V formations. He used to call her a slut. Charming in public, Bill was a grouchy, miserable bear at home; busy snoozing when he wasn't cuffing his cubs or berating his mate. And Jeanette kept taking it, kept taking him back. They'd rather be miserable together than who knows what, alone.

Fiona wondered what music they were going to play. Rita had a PA and gear set up, hated paying for rehearsal time, she said. Fiona hopped off the bus, winter nipping her anklebones until she found Rita's spooky Gothic house at the top of the hill. She rang the antiquated bell, half expecting Lurch to answer. A dog barked and a female voice commanded, "Quiet." Rita threw open the door and stuck out her hand, plowing through awkward first impressions. Rita wore jeans, a black turtleneck sweater, no makeup, and was tall; taller than Fiona. An Amazon.

"Hi! You don't recognize me, do you?"

"Should I?" Rita invited Fiona in with a sweep of her arm.

"You helped me escape. At the club the other night. The raid? I was terrified! You came out of nowhere. Like a guardian angel."

Rita shooed the notion away with a wave of her hand. "I'm a mere mortal, believe me. I'm glad you're okay though."

Not sure I am. Fiona shivered. *It's like a refrigerator in here. Guess Rita doesn't like to pay B.C. Hydro either.* Rita offered tea. Fiona followed her into the kitchen to the inviting warmth of a wood-burning cookstove. Rita motioned to a chair and asked Fiona how she liked Vancouver.

"Anything's better than Cloverdale. How do you like Vancouver?"

Rita plunked down the teapot. "Vancouver's a unique place. It has such bounty, I think it must be a vortex. The natives have always known that." She poured.

Fiona held her cup of oolong close to her chest, warming her hands, breathing in vapours like a flu-ridden child, impressed to learn that Rita had recently returned from a stint in commercial fishery.

"Just a lot of hard labour," said Rita. "So, to the matters at hand. What are your musical influences?"

"You first."

"Well, let's see. When I was thirteen, I started saving my babysitting money to buy records. I graduated from the Monkees to T-Rex, Mott the Hoople. Oh, and I was a Bowie freak."

"Me too!"

"The very first album I ever bought was Jimi Hendrix's *Are You Experienced?* at Kmart, where I ran into some of the popular girls from school. 'Jimi Hendrix?' Rita squealed, mimicking her nemesis. 'What kind of music is that?' I told her, 'If you don't know, I can't tell you'."

Fiona laughed.

"Oh, and the Velvet Underground, especially the *White Light/White Heat* album, that song, 'The Gift,' about the guy who mails himself to his girlfriend? Have you heard it? Spoken word, really. Edgy stuff."

"I love Elvis Costello!" said Fiona. "His lyrics are poetic. I like how he says he's driven by revenge and guilt. I can relate to that."

Reggae freak Rita rattled on about The Clash and The Slits. "The first all-girl band. A lot of DJs played reggae 'cause there was hardly any punk rock on vinyl back then. Anyway, we can talk later."

They went up to the studio; Persian rug on a hardwood floor, PA, guitars, amplifiers, and a drum kit.

"Wow!" said Fiona.

"I'll show you something I'm working on, okay?" Rita picked up the Stratocaster and played a vaguely bluesy chord progression. "Maybe you can come up with some words. Got any songs?"

"Sort of."

I've never played electric guitar. Should I admit that? "I've never played electric guitar."

Rita passed the Strat and handed Fiona a pick. Cradling it like a baby, she strummed a chord, producing a loud blast.

"Hey, this is great! Like the feeling I get from a new pair of boots. Real shit-kickers in fact."

"Don't play it like an acoustic. Why don't you fool around for a while? Get a feel for it. I'll practise."

The noise gave Fiona a chance to experiment; to wank. So much more forgiving than an acoustic, the guitar's neck was slim, nearly fretless, smooth back, solid curvaceous body, friendly. If she didn't hit the chord exactly right, it still sounded good. Well, good enough.

"Like it?"

"Are you kidding? Wow! No wonder everybody plays so fast."

23

"And loud," said Rita. "Rage isn't just an angry young man thing."

Fiona worked up the courage to show her "I Am Not a Nice Girl." Rita liked it. Soon they were nailing down an arrangement.

Suddenly, the lights flashed on and off. Rita stopped playing in a lurch. A tall, corpulent young man in paint-splattered overalls stood in the doorway, grinning, hugging a six-pack.

"Henry!" yelled Rita. "What the fuck are you doing?"

"Hey, sis. How's it going?"

"Fine. Until now. This is Henry. Give us a beer. And quit leering."

He backed up, shaking his head, no. "Who is this sweet young thing? Your new girlfriend? She's pretty cute, for a dyke."

Rita fixed him in her crosshairs and moved out from behind her kit. Henry veered from the doorway, sniggering.

"You'll have to excuse my brother. He thinks my sexuality is a big joke."

"You're a lesbian?"

"Sort of. I haven't even been with a woman. Yet."

"Well, I hate to say this, but Henry's a jerk."

"Yeah. Henry the jerk and Rita the latent lesbian. We're quite the pair."

After a few long weeks of bus rides and Henry's ogling, Rita convinced Fiona they could find a house big enough to rehearse in. The rickety, albeit cozy East Van stucco monstrosity was that and more, a bargain at four hundred dollars a month. The new roommates enjoyed sitting around the kitchen table talking, often bitching about their parents.

"Our home was bereft of imagination," said Rita, "and so were they."

"I can relate. My old man hates music. How can anyone hate music? We'd have to wait for him to go to work so we could play our records."

"Well, we've both moved beyond our backgrounds. That

takes courage Fiona."

"You know, there were no books in our house, but I always loved to read. Jeanette would lie on her big belly reading *True Confessions* magazines, pigging out on Coffee Crisp. My music teacher wrote on my report card once, 'Fiona has a flair for euphony.' They didn't know what it meant!"

The new bandmates spent a week converting the basement into a rehearsal space. Inspired by their shared feminist ideals and the Dishrags, the two set out to form their own all-girl group, eventually placing an ad in the *Buy & Sell*. As they wrote songs and practised, they received nothing but crank calls until Jackie Danyluk and Dolores Rudeloff, two girls from Trail, got in touch.

Next day, blasting into the house, Rita yelled, "So where are these Ukrainians?"

"They're late."

"Great. Well, now we know they're flakes."

"Hey, Rita, you're late too. It's Lotus Land remember? Everybody's late."

Rita squatted in front of the open fridge holding a jar, ripping leaves off a head of romaine, dipping them into the homemade dressing and shoving them into her mouth. She slammed the fridge door, and bolted upstairs. For such an intelligent woman, Rita could be a dingbat, tearing around in a tizzy, scouring the house for her keys or wallet. Fiona could hear her cursing, slamming doors and drawers. *Christ. I hope she hasn't lost anything, or else I'll have to take a boo. Again.* Rita charged down into the basement and began banging away on her drums.

Startled by a hearty knock at the door, Fiona got up and peeked out the window. *Trendoids.* A pudgy, perky girl, mousy brown hair inexplicably worn in a bouffant, sported a pink shirt, striped vest, fake silk pants, and a leather Moroccan shoulder bag. Her girlfriend was gorgeous; blue eyes and coal-black hair, also teased. At least she left the frosted pink lipstick at home. Fiona warily opened the door. They apologized profusely. Gnawing on a great wad of gum, Dolores introduced herself.

"And this is my best friend, Jackie."

Jackie stepped out from behind Dolores' girth, flipping back her long hair like Cher. The girls smiled, walked inside in sync, and sat and lit cigarettes, sharing a red Bic lighter. Obviously, they'd shared a childhood and more than a few secrets. After a tour of the house and a lot of oohing and aahing from Dolores, Rita emerged, unable to conceal her disappointment. The girls were too fluffy, too girly.

"We're not the Runaways," she hissed at the back of Fiona's neck.

"We've been best buds since kindergarten," announced Dolores.

Cheeks reddening, Jackie fluffed her bangs.

"What are your musical influences?" asked Rita.

Settling into herself, Dolores adjusted her bra strap. "I'm a total Stones freak. My idol is Keith Richards."

Jackie reddened again. "But now we like The Clash, Buzzcocks, Bay City Rollers, Sex Pistols."

"Are you kidding? The Bay City Rollers?"

"I know they're bubblegum, but we like them."

Fiona declared the Avengers as her favourite band. "Their lead singer Penelope, she's like a beautiful Viking goddess!" Fiona turned to Dolores. "You should hear their version of 'Paint It Black'."

"So," said Rita, "back to the agenda. Do you write? Any objections to playing our songs?"

"Of course not. We wanna play original music."

They went down to the basement. Rita and Fiona exchanged glances as their new song "Let's Play House" quickly came together. *Holy shit. They're good!* Still, Rita couldn't imagine being in a group with "those twits," which she reported as soon as the girls departed.

"We can't wait forever, you know."

Rita thumped her bass drum a few times. "Well, maybe if they get rid of those awful outfits." She laughed. "And those hairdos! They're straight out of a John Waters film."

"Let's invite them back. We can pull a Dr. Doolittle on them."

Sighing, Rita looked to the ceiling. "You mean Higgins. Mister Higgins, Professor of Phonetics, from *Pygmalion*. She was Eliza Doolittle." Rita tightened the nuts on her snare. "They might not be so malleable, you know. Especially Jackie."

It was as if the jolly neon Buddha blessed you every time you entered the Smilin' Buddha Cabaret in the belly of Vancouver's Downtown Eastside. Igor, the hulking Slavic doorman gave everyone a hard time, though the club wasn't too picky about ID, and when they were, people would manage to sneak in somehow. It was like a *Punch and Judy* show with all the bashing, slamming, and garbled dialogue, air thick with the odor of mould, sweat, and stale beer. Pink satin drapes obscured the grime, scenesters swilling gin and tonics, glowing like fireflies beneath the black lights. Everybody hated the place, but everybody was always there, even paying the three-dollar cover charge when they weren't on the guest list.

"Hello?"

"Fiona?"

Great. She's tracked me down. Hang up, quick! "Yeah?"

"Fiona! Oh baby, I've been worried to death! Are you okay?"

"I'm okay. How'd you get this number?"

"One of your sisters. Why are you putting me through this?"

Because that's what you deserve, you old hag. "I'm not putting you through anything. I've been busy, that's all."

Jeanette tsked and tutted. "I don't care. You should have called me. I'm still your mother, you know."

"Yes, Jeanette. I know."

She'd ceased calling them Mom and Dad shortly before fleeing. *They should name a hurricane after my mother, a crashing, roaring, smashing-dishes, chucking-tobacco-tins-at-Dad—or Bill—hurricane,* thought Fiona. Jeanette routinely levelled her daughters with her body, pounding them systematically, one by one, TV on, dirty laundry airing in its blue light. Sometimes she used a belt, most of the time, her fists. Fiona sobbing in the corner, cold pee of fear trickling down her leg.

"I'll give ya somethin' ta cry about! If one of ya git's a beatin', yer all gittin' a beatin'."

Jeanette invariably ran out of wind, washing up on the plaid La-Z-Boy. Panting, shaking, bawling, she'd scoop up one of the girls into her arms, rock her back and forth, crushing Fiona or Rory or Maureen's little head against her jumbo breasts so hard the child could barely breathe. As if to assuage guilt, Jeanette regaled them with horror stories, how her mother, Riva, threw knives and forced her to do all the housework. Desperately poor, their father had died in Hong Kong, a prisoner of war. Then Riva got cancer and Jeanette had to quit school at age twelve to care for the family. Her daughters had heard it all a million times.

"Go ahead," screamed Fiona, towering over her mother that last day. "Hit me! Kill me, why don't you? I wish I'd never been born!"

Simultaneously dropping her swing and lapsed Catholic jaw, Jeanette screamed, "Blasphemy!"

She never hit Fiona again. Jeanette lost her grip that day, spiraling in a boozy tailspin ever since, daughters expertly delivering payback: skipping school, drinking, smoking, staying out all night and dragging boys home to fuck right beneath her nose. A burlesque of family. Fiona tried to slash her wrists a few times. She took off for Vancouver at the first opportunity. No one called it child abuse, and there are worse things she could call her mother.

Jackie and Dolores sang from the stoop, "Hi, Fiona! Hi, Rita!" They went everywhere, did everything together, and were soon dubbed The Twins from Trail.

"One is definitely a clone," said Rita. "And I've stopped

trying to figure out which."

"Jesus H. Christ, they're an hour late, again!" Fiona threw the door open. "Can't you get here on time?"

"Yeah well, we have to take a bus all the way across town," replied Dolores, wearing a Party 'Till You Puke T-shirt. "All you have to do is roll out of bed."

The twins were eager to move into the extra rooms. Though determined to rent them to non-band members, Rita was eager to get their act together, and she was softening on the issue. After she relented, they moved in with a vengeance. The four young women began writing songs in earnest, in pursuit of a set. Dennis hung around a lot. He always brought beer or milk for their tea and made himself useful setting up the PA and moving gear. Up in her room, Fiona serenaded the North Shore Mountains with a slew of new songs. *Melody*. It had become a dirty word to Jackie and Dolores, along with arty. Apparently, Fiona's guitar playing wasn't cutting it, though she was the most likely candidate to front the band.

"You gotta be like Johnny Rotten," suggested Dolores, more than once.

"Hey, I never said I was hard-core."

"Fuck that," said Rita. "If Fiona's going to emulate anyone, she should emulate Janis Joplin."

Dolores gasped. Jackie spit up her coffee. "Janis Joplin was a fat hippie!"

"Janis Joplin wasn't the stereotypical beauty, but she was a star." Rita slammed her skillet down on the burner. "She had style. Soul."

"So, what does that make me?" wailed Fiona. "A scared, arty wannabe?"

"Well, I for one," sniffed Rita, "abhor discussing our image ad nauseam. Our sound is what counts."

"Yeah, well, Fiona gets it," said Dolores.

"Hey, that doesn't mean I wanna look like a skank." Fiona was not about to turn herself out with the slutty schoolgirl persona Jackie and Dolores now favoured: dollops of eyeliner, plaid miniskirts, fishnets, and stilettos. *Who's going to get the irony if we just crank up the prevailing fantasies?*

"Who you callin' a skank?"

Fiona was tailored where others were tattered. She loved the clean, sharp lines of Mod, her favourite shirt a black and white pin stripe with wide lapels and elongated cuffs trimmed with tiny, round pearl buttons. She loved the sleek style of Emma Peel. *Suits.* Fiona felt most female decked out in men's clothing. Men noticed. Though the leers and wolf whistles were excruciating, Fiona always tried to look her best, relieved she'd missed the sixties' Mama Cass muumuus and flouncy, flowy trash. *I wanna kick ass.* Dressing in layers allowed her to take cover when necessary, but lately Fiona was feeling ready for anything; fighting, fucking, touring, singing.

"I agree with Rita. I'd rather concentrate on our music."

And to that end she twiddled, making up chords much to Rita's wonder, and melodies, humming them into a tape recorder, while Jackie and Dolores skillfully polished things up. Sometimes the band batted around the head—a riff—until the body—a song—surfaced. Fiona liked to tape rehearsals and finish writing the lyrics on her own. The more songs she wrote, the more she detested rich, conceited wankers like Genesis, and Emerson, Lake & Palmer. It was simple, once you found the resolve.

★ ★ ★ ★

"Look who's on TV!" Rita pointed to Joey Shithead on *The Vancouver Show* with Pia Shandel.

"Ha!" hooted Fiona. "She looks like a Pia Shandel."

Joey handled bubbly Pia with aplomb. Fiona threw down three tickets to the St. Valentine's Day Massacre emblazoned with *Hit Someone You Love.*

"Great!" said Rita. "What's with all the misogyny? I thought the scene was supposed to be so egalitarian." She grabbed the kettle. "Well, I suppose it is if you happen to be young, white, and male."

"Maybe we shouldn't go."

"Maybe we shouldn't. Who is Transformer Productions, anyway?"

"I don't know. Never heard of them. But it's a great bill. Rabid, Pointed Sticks, Subhumans, K-Tels." Angus was a hero for digging up a new venue, O'Hara's, a derelict nightclub on the pier at the foot of Main. "I wanna go. We gotta see the K-Tels."

"Okay, okay. We're doing our bit to fight sexism, right? We play electric guitars."

The next night, Fiona, Shannon, and Rita drove down to the show, a near riot on by the time they arrived.

BAM! THUD! WHAM!

"Hey," said Fiona, "just like Batman."

Entering cautiously, they noticed a riser to their right and looked up into the scowling faces of thirty or so long-haired bikers and fat, bearded yahoos, greeting them with upraised chairs and benches. A table whizzed past their heads, crashing against the wall, but when the girls advanced, like a sea parting, the bikers moved aside to let them pass.

"I guess we don't pose a threat," said Fiona, "or maybe they're sparing the girls."

"Ha!" said Shannon. "As if they have policy."

They found the K-Tels soldiering on through "Automan," bassist Jim Bescott and green-haired front man Art so on the beat, they deftly dodged an assortment of projectiles. Fuming, Rita sidled up to a big greaser and grabbed him by the arm, just as he was about to launch a Labatt can.

"Hey, asshole! Those are my friends."

He nearly choked on his tongue. Rita stood guard until the frustrated hit man left.

Like hyenas tracking a herd of wildebeest, their tormenters plucked the youngest, sickest, stupidest kids from the crowd, methodically pummeling all attitude out of them. Simon and the Bowery Boys were on rodeo clown duty, goading the creeps, pulling them off their friends, and throwing in a few punches of their own.

"This is nuts!" shouted Fiona. She waved at Oona and Spooner across the room. They dashed over. "Are you okay?" she asked.

"Yeah," sputtered Oona. "What the fuck is going on?"

"I dunno, it's bizarre," said Spooner, glancing nervously about the room. "Every biker and greaseball in the Lower Mainland must be here. I heard they're even coming up from Bellingham."

Is a mob the sum of its parts? Fiona could see no eye contact with each other or their prey. No motive, no reason. No head. No heart.

Shannon surveyed the pandemonium. "Well, if it's Valentine's Day, this must be hell. Where's security?"

"Maybe this is security," Rita said grimly. "I'm having visions of Altamont."

"What?" asked Fiona.

"The Rolling Stones famously, stupidly hired the Hells Angels as security. Tons of violence, one guy got stabbed to death."

They exited at the first opportunity. Fiona saw Dennis wrestling a particularly nefarious biker. She beckoned, afraid for him, but Dennis waved, calmly ducking a punch, then springing up like a jack-in-the-box. POW. He neatly plowed several teeth down the guy's throat. Before the biker, blubbering blood, could plop down onto a spindly, wooden chair, Dennis smiled and pushed it over with his foot. He pointed and laughed at the biker lying like a beetle on its back, legs and feet paddling the air, then ran over to Fiona.

Arms linked, Dennis, Fiona, Shannon, Rita, Oona, Spooner, and Simon marched out. They encountered more thugs leaning against the railings, hooting, howling, grunting.

"Oohhh baby. Nice tits. Nice ass!"

"Hey, little girl, come on over here and suck my cock!" The biggest, in a Judas Priest T-shirt, grabbed his crotch. "Come on, ditch those faggots. You need a real man."

Fiona turned, gave him the finger. "Go fuck yourself."

The pier trembling was the next thing that registered, then feet thumping, bikers on top of them within a matter of seconds. Spooner was thrown to the ground first—all 135 pounds—punched and kicked while in the fetal position. Desperately holding on to his head, Spooner was kicked in the ribs. When he lowered his arms, they kicked him in the skull. One of the bikers grabbed Rita by the elbow and spun her around.

"It's a girl!"

He turned and punched Simon in the face instead. Fiona jumped on the biker's back, yanking on his greasy hair, attempting to pull his colossal bulk down. Her efforts were in vain. He flicked her off like a fly. Then Rita pounced. He swung round and pinned her arms behind her back. Rita whacked him in the shins with her boot heel. Cursing, he tossed her to the ground. Simon was down next, legs thrashing against a beating, Dennis trying to get to him, but up to his eyeballs in fisticuffs with another greaseball.

"Leave them alone!" screamed Fiona. Shannon screamed, Oona screamed, they all screamed. *Jesus H. Christ, where are the fucking cops when you need them?*

"Get off him, you prick!" Rita managed to pull one of them off Spooner, though not for long.

Snorting and laughing, the bikers continued their gleeful pounding. Then, sirens. *At last!* The bikers were relentless though, refusing to stop until the patrol cars' red and blue lights were flashing across their faces. They scattered, leaving bodies splayed the length of the boardwalk, including an unconscious Spooner. Dennis hauled a bruised, but okay Simon up off the ground. Oona ran over, crumpling at the sight of Spooner spread-eagle. Shannon crossed herself, Fiona following suit. *Christ! Don't let him be dead.* Dennis and Simon ran to search for a paramedic, girls hovering as Rita checked Spooner's pulse.

"He's breathing."

Thank God! Rita loosened his collar and positioned his head so the blood drained out of his mouth.

"Spooner. Spooner," whispered Oona, like Wendy to Peter

Pan.

"Maybe we should just take him to the hospital ourselves," said Shannon.

Rita didn't want to move him. "He might be bleeding internally."

It felt like forever, but help finally arrived. There were many casualties, and more chaos ensued as they prepared to move Spooner's broken body. He was attended to with oxygen and seemingly revived by sleight of hand. Spooner blinked, friends screaming his silly name as he came to. Oona was permitted to ride in the ambulance with him.

Fiona slapped Dennis on the back. "Hey, Grasshopper." She mimed punching and kicking. "Martial arts training?"

"A little karate."

"Black belt?"

"Nah. My parents tried to prepare me, that's all."

"They did a good job. You're still slumming though."

"So are you."

"No. I'm going sideways. You're lowering yourself."

"Why? Because I can defend myself?"

"Because your folks want to pay for stuff like that. Because they're even aware of it."

Dennis shrugged, as if spitting out his silver spoon. "And next time just back down. Flight, not fight. That's the best defense."

"I'm sorry!"

Fiona sopped up the last of her oyster stew with a fist full of sourdough bread, wishing the rain would let up, the Only Seafood Café about as cozy as a bus station. It reminded her of all the greasy spoons her mother had worked in. Still, Fiona enjoyed hiding out in the tall wooden booths painted a putrid shade of green—sea green—watching the regulars captain the wobbly stools. Besides, the food was cheap.

"Hey, what's a girl like you doing in a nice place like this?"

"Oh. Hi, Simon. Sit."

He was not alone. Oona and Mad Dog popped out from behind his coat. They ordered Cokes and rehashed the previous night's attack of the killer beer bellies.

"They managed to put dents into just about everybody!" Oona's eyes were an even deeper blue, framed by wet, oxblood curls.

Fiona grabbed the salt shaker before Mad Dog could loosen the lid. "Well, I bet Angus changes his attitude after seeing his friends get the snot beat out of them."

Simon threw a match into the tank crawling with crabs. Fiona got up to leave, holding on to her jiggling tummy.

"I'm outta here before you manage to get us kicked out of another dive. Come on, Oona. Let's go."

Simon and Mad Dog trained their puppy dog eyes on Oona. She slammed down the last of her cola. "Okay, let's go." The boys moaned.

Fiona popped open her umbrella, putting her arm through Oona's, inviting her under. The girls strolled down Hastings.

"What do you want to do now?" asked Oona.

"I don't know, but I'm freezing and my mascara's running. Let's go somewhere."

"Hey, I know! Let's get a mickey for Spooner. For medicinal purposes."

"He'll probably get plastered. He doesn't drink much, you know."

Dennis had blamed the incident on Fiona, her big mouth and loose middle finger. She felt bad.

"Those guys were gonna kill us!" said Oona. "They would have come after us no matter what."

They found Spooner limp and pasty as a noodle, gasping at the sight of his purple shiners. He waved them in, puffy lips curling into a crooked smile.

"I am so sorry, Spooner!"

"Forget it." He propped his pulp-face up with a pillow. "No use crying over spilled blood." Oona pulled the bottle out of a paper bag. "Thank you!" he squeaked.

Fiona handed him a straw. Spooner winced and sucked on the Scotch hard and fast. He grimaced, pouring some of the whisky into a saucer on the floor to share with Walter, his pet pigeon. The bird bent over and, much to their delight, actually imbibed.

"Hey, Walter's a real party animal!" said Fiona.

Walter cooed and squawked for a little while before toppling over. They howled with laughter, Spooner rolling back onto the bed, holding on to himself.

"One more drink and Walter will be under the host!" said Fiona.

"Don't make me laugh!" groaned Spooner, cradling his ribs. "It hurts!"

Spooner was feeling no pain by the time they left, though Fiona was acutely afflicted with remorse.

Rita, in cat's eye sunglasses, basked in some rare November rays, eating with a pair of red plastic chopsticks. Grabbing a can opener, Fiona fixed herself a meal and sat. Rita's nose wrinkled.

"What the hell is that?"

"Sardine stew. I just put a can of sardines into some Campbell's mushroom soup."

Rita mimed gagging. "Yuck."

"It's nutritious. And economical. I like seafood."

"That is not seafood. That is tinned fish."

"It's no worse than that brown rice, soy crap you eat. Which makes you fart, by the way."

"Here, have some salad." Rita slid a wooden bowl at Fiona. "You don't eat enough vegetables. Or fart enough. So, Factory Girl, what are you going to be doing at your new job?"

"Shipping clerk. Some warehouse."

"Nice of Dennis to put a word in for you."

"Yeah, I guess. Now he can keep an eye on me all the time. It's three doors down from Romano's."

"You could do worse, you know."

"I know. You keep telling me that. It's not gonna happen. You know what he does? He jerks the steering wheel so he can drive through the puddles. 'Better than gumboots!' He's a nut!"

"I know, but he's a sweet, magnanimous, lovable nut."

"Yeah, well, I must be allergic."

★ ★ ★ ★

"One-two-three-four!" yelled Rita, sticks high in the air.

"Wait!" said Jackie. "We should practise that part."

"No," said Rita. "Let's play it from the top. One-two-three-four!"

Rehearsal. Forever. In a little hole in the ground. We are the damned, thought Fiona, condemned to play our songs over and over and over again. Her feet hurt, sore from standing all day, packing shit in a friggin' warehouse. Fiona stared at the clock, straining to sing half-recalled lyrics for the hundredth time. As if anyone's listening.

"Why do we have to rehearse so fucking loud?"

"I don't even know if I'm in tune," said Jackie.

"Well, do you think you could turn it down a little? Then maybe you could tell. I'm gonna get nodes!"

Dolores reluctantly lowered the volume on her amp. Fiona watched Dennis, his perpetual grin. *How can he be so enthralled with these tedious rehearsals?*

"Let's put him to work," was Jackie's suggestion. "He can roadie."

Naturally, Dennis was thrilled with the job offer. How would she ever be rid of him?

"One-two-three-four!" Rita lowered her sticks and off they went, though not exactly together, stopping every few bars to argue.

During the next lull, Fiona mouthed slowly, "Dy-nam-ics. Ever heard of them?"

Dolores cupped her hand around her ear. "What?"

She had to laugh. "We can't play everything cranked up to eleven!" said Fiona.

"Why not?" Dolores reached for her cigarettes. "I think we should get some Bose monitors and mount them on our heads."

"Gawd. You're not going to light up again are you? You haven't even finished that one." Fiona pointed to a butt burning in the ashtray.

"Oh." Dolores hot-dogged it and cracked open another beer.

"You need a muzzle. You have an oral fixation, I swear."

"Fuck you, Fiona. Fuck you and your armchair psychology."

"Maybe you'd lose some weight if you didn't have something—or someone—in your mouth all the time."

"Look who's talking!"

"Settle down!" yelled Rita. "Okay? Now . . . One-two-three-four!"

"Wait!" said Dolores. "Rita, maybe you should play a little more on that last bar? You know? It's in the geometry of the song."

"Christ, Dolores! Are you still high on 'shrooms?"

Rita had made tea out of the psilocybin magic mushrooms growing in the front yard. The band members got thoroughly wigged, the high a form of pure torture for Fiona, who was terrified and hid under a sleeping bag until Shannon burst into her room.

"Are you stoooned?" The question ricocheted around Fiona's skull as if it were the most hilarious thing anyone had ever said, and she laughed until she was sure her face was falling off.

"One-two-three-four!"

Fiona leaned into the microphone. *Zzzzzzzsssstt*. A sustained arc of electricity snapped round her head like a strand of spaghetti, snaking through her ear canal. She collapsed in a heap as the other girls gaped.

"I got a fucking shock!" Fiona held on to her singed lips, biting back tears.

Dennis rushed over. "I'll ground this thing for ya." Fiona sat numbly staring at an abandoned cobweb, while he scooted around the basement searching for his tool box.

"Once we get to that E chord, really hit it hard!" Jackie

demonstrated for Rita with a thwack on her bass. "At the end we come out of the E and go into a B. All right? Rita, take it away!"

The band was soon cranked back up to ten. They nearly made it to the last chorus when an earsplitting CRACK emanated from Dolores' Les Paul. She sprang back as if shot.

"Oh man. I broke a string!"

Rita threw her sticks down. "It's a conspiracy, I swear! We never get any work done."

Dennis examined the Les Paul's neck. "You're winding them too tight."

Dolores fingered the string. "It's me. I'm wound too tight."

"Too loose is more like it," said Fiona.

Dolores evil-eyed her, plopping down on an amp to light a joint.

Dennis worked on the broken string. "Hey D, don't Bogart it."

"She's murdering it." Jackie snatched the spliff from Dolores' mouth.

"Ow! That hurt. You ripped the skin off!"

Jackie toked long and deeply, then passed the joint to Fiona.

"So, hammer it in the chorus, then lie back in the verse, right?" said Rita.

"Right! But really get behind the beat in both. Okay?"

"Let's play a different song!" pleaded Fiona.

"Whaddya mean, play a different song?" Rita straddled her drum stool. "We can't even play this one yet. One-two-three-four!"

★ ★ ★ ★

"I got us a gig!" announced Rita, charging into the basement. "Opening for the K-Tels."

"We're not ready!" shrieked Dolores.

"Let's get ready." Rita maneuvered around the amps to her kit. "Let's practise."

"What are we going to call the band?" asked Jackie.

"Yeah," said Rita, "they're putting out a flyer."

"Shit!" said Fiona.

"No. I don't like it. Too smelly."

"Besides," said Dennis. "I bet there's already a band named Shit."

"I have an idea," said Fiona. "How about Vagina Dentata?"

"Vagina what?" cried Jackie.

"Vagina Dentata!"

Dennis' ears pricked up. "Did you say vagina?"

"Yes," said Fiona. "Va-gi-na Den-ta-ta."

"That's disgusting," bleated Dolores.

"Freudian, isn't it?" said Rita. "He talks about castration anxiety, but a lot of myths refer to that male fear of having less than when he entered. How during intercourse the male fears the vagina has teeth that will bite down and sever his organ from his body."

Hands flying to his crotch, Dennis doubled over laughing.

"What do you think?" asked Fiona.

"I'm not afraid of women," replied Dennis. "Or fucking. You should see me in bed."

"No, I shouldn't. And you're not afraid of anything, no point in asking you."

"Hey, if men can secretly be afraid of intercourse, does that mean they're afraid of fellatio too?" Rita pushed her cheek out with her tongue. "That involves real teeth. Or could."

"Well," said Dolores, "this is all very interesting, but I don't want to be in a band called Vagina whatever."

"Why not?" said Fiona. "I thought you were hard-core."

"It is reminiscent of The Slits." Rita stood and stretched.

Dennis held up his hand. "It's moot. There's a band in L.A. called Vagina Dentata."

"Shit."

The Virgin Marries emerged for their debut at the Smilin' Buddha Cabaret. The twins weren't crazy about the name but could provide no alternative. Fiona favoured it for the same reasons as Rita; her Virgin Mary collection, which included a magnetized Mother Mary on the dash of her Volkswagen van and a freaky, plastic glow-in-the-dark Virgin of Guadalupe statue in the bathroom. Rita found religious iconography fascinating, but it was the pagan goddess worship angle she relished, theorizing that Mariolatry was a sneaky way for people to hold onto a female deity.

"I'd love a Bloody Mary right about now," said Dolores.

Twins giggling in the back seat, they headed north along Victoria Drive. Fiona was beginning to feel at home in the city laced with water, Burrard Inlet teeming with salmon and orca not so long ago, according to Rita.

Hooting and hollering, Jackie and Dolores stuck their heads out the window. "Virgin Marries ruuule!"

Fiona followed suit. Rita suddenly realized that she'd forgot her drumsticks on account of nerves. Cursing, she turned the car around.

"We'll just be fashionably late," said Jackie. "That's what divas do, you know."

After much agonizing about her attire, Fiona had gone half-glam, half-cowgirl, wearing shiny patent leather gloves, a silver mini dress, and ankle-high western boots. Righteous or ridiculous, she wasn't sure which, but Rita said she looked pretentious.

"Of course I'm pretentious! How can an artist not have pretensions?"

"Well, excuse me. I didn't realize you were an *artiste*."

Since it was the night of their first gig, Fiona refrained from telling Rita to fuck off.

A widely grinning Dennis was waiting in the alley behind the Buddha when they arrived. Fiona delighted in telling doorman Igor that they were there to play. Igor grunted.

They set their gear up quickly, then sat, nervously chattering. Rita bought their first round, though she made them swear to a one-drink limit before this and future shows.

Fiona realized the stage was just a riser. No wings. No

curtain. Twenty minutes later, the twins sought refuge behind their guitars, Rita's drums like a fortress. Stomach churning, Fiona shifted her weight from one foot to the other. People moved up front to check them out.

"Rowdy diesel dykes," reported Jackie.

Fiona had to pee. Ignoring the band's protests, she darted through the crowd, shoved the door open, and bolted into a stall. The polyester dress was sticking to her. She tried to take a deep breath, to will her muscles to relax. Finally, a little tinkle. Fiona checked her boots for toilet paper, then went to the sink where two members of the dyke party hovered; one in leather, resembling a biker, the other in denim overalls, a tree planter.

"What's the matter?" said Biker Dyke. "Nervous?"

"Yeah! It's our first gig."

"We heard," said Tree Planter. "Came down just to see you."

"Thanks for your support." Struggling to reign in sarcasm, Fiona touched up her lipstick.

"You sure do have pretty hair." Tree Planter cackled as Biker Dyke leaned over to grab a lock of Fiona's tresses, giving it a little tug.

"Hey!" Fiona recoiled, heated blood rising.

"I liked your head shaved."

"Yeah, well, I didn't." Glaring, Fiona imagined her eyes were boring a hole between Biker Dyke's. "Am I supposed to look like you?"

They glanced at Fiona's shaking hands and backed off to the exit, laughing. "Break a leg!"

Dennis frantically ushered her to the stage. The air was thick with fear. Or smoke? The milling crowd now a chanting crowd... VIRG-IN MARRIES! VIRG-IN MARRIES! Fiona clambered onstage. Rita sat with her sticks poised, looking tough in a striped orange shirt and black stovepipe jeans. The twins beamed serenely. Before Fiona could reach the microphone, she slipped on a giant, gross gob of spittle, nearly landing on her ass. Faint, knock-kneed, ham-handed, Fiona thought, people are just here to spew beer on our equipment. Piss on our music! She stood still, for the longest time, as did Jackie and Dolores.

Dennis pantomimed strumming at them.

"Play!" yelled a voice in the crowd.

The Virgin Marries played. Up went the cheers. Catcalls. *Goddammit! What do I do with my hands?* Gobs. Gobbing. *Yuck! Every face so hard to look at. Where do I look?* Fiona spotted a lethally handsome young man in the corner, staring at her like Kaa the snake from *The Jungle Book*. Lanky. Slavic. Exceptional lips. She forgot her lyrics. *Keep singing! Gawd. Who is that guy?* First song. Over already. *Wow. Clapping!* Many hands clapping. Next song. *Why am I doing this? What is the next song?* Fiona bent down to the set list on the floor soaked with beer. *No room to move!* No way to dodge Biker Dyke and her gals' gobbing.

Rita threw her sticks down. "You stupid cunts!"

They responded with a shower of spittle.

"Fuck you! Nobody spits on me."

They jeered. Dennis strode into their midst. They circled. He gestured "Play!" at the Virgin Marries. The Virgins played. *That guy, he's drop-dead gorgeous! Wow. We're actually keeping it together.* Practise, practise, practise. *Paid off, I guess.* "Edie's Gift" dragged a little, but they sounded good. Fiona couldn't hear her voice in the monitors though. Singing without a net. Screaming without a net. *Oh, he finally moved.* Mr. Cocksure, directly in front of her. *Wish he'd stop staring. I can't concentrate! Ah, what the fuck. Band's so loud who can hear the words anyway?*

Set over at last. *What do we do now?* Four blank looks, crowd clamouring for more. There was no more. They played "Guns and Guitars" again. The band exited stage left to a roaring wave of applause. Dennis tackled Fiona with a sweaty hug. Kisses, kudos all around, Virgins bouncing off the walls, screaming until hoarse. Shannon squeezed Fiona's hand. They bumped foreheads, mock glaring at each other, bellowing, "Aiiieee!"

A few minutes later the hunk appeared at Fiona's elbow, smiling. He handed her a cocktail and gestured to a table. They sat, sipping Cuba Libres, the cola gritty against Fiona's teeth. *He's so quiet.* Deep or dumb? She thanked him for the drink.

"You're welcome."

"Oh, so you do speak," she said, genuinely relieved. "Are you in a band?"

"I play keyboards for Bluto."

Ooohh, the local new wave band teetering on the edge of fame and fortune, off to London to record with Nick Lowe. The keyboardist for Bluto pushed a pack of cigarettes at her.

"Thanks," she said, glad to give her hands something to do.

Clocked by Cupid, Fiona admired the big fists mapped with veins, long, sturdy fingers wrapped round his tumbler of rum. *I can see those hands on my tits.*

Her guitarists ran over, Jackie shoving cleavage in his face, cooing, "Hi! I'm Jackie." He said nothing. *Must be a leg man.* "When do we get paid?" she asked.

"Well, if we get paid, it won't be until way later."

Dolores gave Fiona a sly smile and a thumbs-up as she trotted off arm in arm with Jackie.

"Let's go for a drive," he said, rising.

"I don't even know your name."

"Emmett Hayes."

Emmett Hayes gathered up his things, asked her name, responding inaudibly. *Where is Shannon?* Dennis was starting up the van. Fiona downed her drink and followed Emmett Hayes out the door. He motioned to a white Porsche parked right out front.

"Wow!"

Channeling Cinderella, Fiona climbed in before turning back into a bumpkin. *I must be out of my mind. Oh well, the belle of the ball always leaves escorted by the charming young prince.* They stretched out their legs. So close to the ground. Emmett put the key in the ignition and turned it slowly. Engine purring lowly, he leaned over to take her chin in his hand and brushed her cheek with a delicate kiss. *I think I shall faint.*

They tore off, top down. Soon, they were climbing Mount Seymour, the little sports car that could concealed in a beard of mist, clinging to each curve in the road, a sudden mizzle diluting the spiny perfume of spruce. They reached the crest and parked in a clearing lit by the waxing moon. Emmett retrieved a pair of chilled Heinekens from the trunk.

"Wow!"

"Hashish?" He smiled, passing her a soapstone pipe.

Fiona put it to her lips and puffed cautiously, leaning back and stretching, gazing at the city lights below. "Doesn't it feel like gravity's collapsed?"

"Come here."

Her pulse quickened at the command. Emmett pulled her into his arms, smashing her mouth with a kiss, the quickening in his jeans poking at her thigh. Fiona pushed him off, staving off panic.

"I feel like talking."

Slightly sulky, Emmett put together a few sentences and soon became animated while describing the desert.

"My utopia would be self-sustaining, a house built into the side of a hill, twin cooling towers. A windmill powering everything."

"Let's go find Captain Beefheart!"

"Really? You wanna go? William Burroughs lives in the desert too. I wanna buy one of his shotgun paintings."

Soon they were grappling over the stick shift, Emmett guiding her hand to his hard-on, while fumbling with the hooks on her bra. "Hang on."

He leapt out of the car, ran to the trunk, pulled out a Hudson's Bay blanket, and spread it under the low branches of a cedar, Fiona stifling giggles. *Men are so funny when they're horny, and they're always horny.* Emmett scurried back and opened the door, taking Fiona's hand as if ushering her to nirvana. She kicked off her boots before lowering herself onto a bed of cones and crackling needles. Her head hit a rock. His pupils pinned. *Who does he see as he's peeling off my stockings?* She wanted to be kissed. He wanted her dress up. Off. *How many girls has he screwed on this blanket?* Fiona unzipped Emmett's jeans, stroked his cock. *Look at my skin glowing in the moonlight. It's beautiful! Why can't he say so? Why can't he say anything?* Emmett shoved his cock into her face. *Visual elements turn men on. Yeah, right. The sight of my lips wrapped around his cock, that's all he needs to get off. Then he can come all over my face.*

"Hey!" Fiona heaved him off. "Slow down."

"Sorry!"

Trembling, Fiona fought back tears.

"I'm sorry! Really. I got carried away."

He held her close to his chest like a nestling, sowing Fiona's eyelids with tiny kisses, the blood pounding in her temples easing.

He placed her hand on his penis, pricking up again. She bent down, ran her tongue up and down the shaft, slid it all in, nearly gagging. *Blowjobs are no big deal as long as they don't take too long.* It helped to close her eyes, pretend she was an infant suckling at the teat. Emmett came quickly. Quickly and quietly. She spit out jizz, hoping he didn't notice. *Guys are so weird, like the more cum you swallow, the sexier he is.*

Time for a beer. They sat a while, puffing on hash. Soon he was hard again. "Condoms?"

"No. I wasn't planning on getting laid."

"Hang on." He dashed to the car. Across the meadow, two giant Douglas firs stood vigil like brothers. Trees appear so human, she thought, benevolent somehow.

"What a good Boy Scout you are."

Grinning, Emmett tore open the package, squatted, and rolled the latex down over his erection. He climbed on top, pulled down Fiona's panties, and probed. He found her vagina and inserted his penis, grinding away for a long time, which was supposed to be a good thing, but she'd never had an orgasm; had given up on the idea. Shannon advised her that older men made better lovers.

"Eeeuuuuhh! It'd be like doing it with your father."

"It's like doing it with somebody who knows what they're doing."

"Turn over," said Emmett.

Fiona turned over, resting her head in her forearms as she raised her ass. Grabbing her hips, Emmett pulled her to him and shoved his cock in to the hilt. *Okay, this I can feel, anyway.* Spine arching, he leaned over and cupped her tits. Fiona listened closely for his climax. Emmett leaned back onto his haunches

46

until his cock flopped out.

Soon flat on his back, Emmett mumbled a few words, turned over, and passed out. Fiona pulled on her clothing, now heavy with dampness. She wrapped her arms around herself, huddling inside her jacket. Staring at the clouds, roving, revealing the brilliance of a billion stars, Fiona squinted, studying the man in the moon, as remote as the boy lying next to her.

★ ★ ★ ★

Caw. Caw. The fluttering of many wings pushed air across Fiona's face. Flapping. Squawking. She flailed at the ravens in her hair. *What?* Pulled herself up. A swarm of feuding jays and ravens flitted in and out of the trunk of the Porsche. She shook Emmett Hayes. He rubbed his eyes, but refused to open them.

"What's all that noise?" Emmett sat up. "Fuck!"

He bolted, zipping up his jeans while running to the car, cursing the rocks jabbing his bare feet. Emmett threw stones at the screeching birds and they soared away, one raven with an orange lanced upon its beak, the orb promptly falling to the ground with a thud. Laughing, Fiona stumbled over to join him as he wiped mushy bird doo-doo off the fenders with a handy rag. He shook his fist at the sky. Paper bags of provisions and produce were strewn about the ground, winged bandits determined to carry off their loot had even marked the grapefruit.

"Not very appetizing anymore, are they?" Fiona pitched one into the bushes.

Emmett grumbled as they salvaged the canned goods. "I knew I should have gone home." *Ouch!* "How the fuck did they get in the trunk?" Emmett found a loaf of bread reduced to crumbs.

"What do you think? The birds popped it open?"

"Natives call the raven the Trickster, you know."

They started at the sound of gravel crunching beneath an RCMP cruiser entering the clearing.

"Great," she muttered. "Heat. What is it with this town?

Don't they have any real crime?"

A constable pulled up slowly, parked, and got out. "What are you two doing up here? Can I see some ID please?"

"I was just showing my friend some of the sights, sir."

The cop turned to Fiona. "And now you've seen everything, right?" He eyed Emmett's driver's licence. "Well, well," he deadpanned. "A Sagittarius. My wife's a Sagittarius. Really loves to suck cock. How about you?" Smirking, the cop looked up and levelled his eyes at Emmett. "You like to suck cock?"

Is that what punk means to this pig? Apparently he was just filling out his uniform and, in short order, let them go.

Fiona endured silence all the way down the mountain, last night drifting further and further behind them. Ah, the morning after. Talk about anticlimactic. They pulled up to her house, which was spectacularly shabby in the early morning light. Emmett was not about to open her door, or usher her anywhere anymore. Fiona said goodbye and got out.

"Bye," he replied, shoving a map inside the glove box and slamming it shut.

"Nice meeting you . . ."

Emmett gunned the engine. Fiona turned and walked toward the front door, choking down a rush of shame-scorched tears. Rita was in the kitchen pouring coffee that smelled so good she felt like bathing in it.

"My God! What happened to you? I've been worried sick."

Opening her mouth to speak, Fiona emitted a sob instead and toppled into Rita's arms. "I'm sorry!"

Rita held her tightly, wiping away the mascara streaking her face. Fiona sat and gave her the lowdown as Rita scuttled about, flipping eggs, buttering toast. She set down a plate.

"You just disappeared! Don't ever do that again."

"I won't. I promise. These are the best eggs I've ever tasted."

"That guy is bad news." Rita poured a glass of orange juice.

"Yeah, so, what does that make me?"

Rita glared. "Talented. Beautiful. Intelligent. Most of the time."

"I don't feel beautiful."

"You have to be more discriminating, Fiona! There are a lot of assholes out there."

"Don't worry. I won't be hearing from this particular asshole again."

"Well, that's his loss."

"Christ, Rita. You are so good to me."

She smiled. "By the way, Jeanette called last night. And no, I didn't tell her anything."

"Shit! Thank God. That's the last thing I need. Jeanette armed with enough ammunition to come out to Vancouver and rescue me."

"Like a good mother?"

They laughed. The twins came downstairs, full of concern.

"Yeah," said Jackie, "that guy leaves a bad taste in your mouth." She cleared her throat. "That's what I heard anyway."

Dolores giggled. "Hey, Fiona, sounds like you drank too much panty remover."

"I'm too tired for this bullshit. I have to lie down."

Fiona fell into bed wishing for a cradle. She clutched her pillow and stared out the window at the Lions to the north. *Wish I were still on top of a mountain.*

Post-nap she found Dennis standing at the foot of the stairs. He handed her a glass jar.

"Tiger Balm. For your neck."

"You know my weak spots, don't you? Thanks." She cracked the seal, breathed in a deep shot of menthol. "It's clearing my head."

He padded after her until she yelled at him to leave her alone or get out.

The Virgin Marries were hot, the group engaged for Rock Against Racism with DOA, Rock Against Prisons with the Subhumans, Rabid, AKA, Devices, Tunnel Canary, and the Zellots, and Rock Against Radiation with Private School and Perfect Stranger.

"Why can't we rock for something?" said Jackie.

They were excited about playing the Smilin' Buddha with the K-Tels. A secret admirer had been leaving roses in their vehicle after nearly every show.

Rita laughed. "I think they're for me. Only a lesbian would do something like that."

Randy Rampage joined them backstage at the DOA show, good-naturedly instructing Jackie on bass. She preferred to use a pick, God forbid, and played her instrument at waist level.

"See. Like this!" Randy tugged at the guitar strap and lowered Jackie's bass to her knees.

She smiled and cooed, playing it low and dirty, retreating to her regular stance for the Virgin Marries' set.

Camaraderie and a strong feeling of goodwill prevailed among the musicians who shared rehearsal space, PAs, vans, billing, door proceeds and of course, beer.

Rita drove cautiously through black puddles and thin white air, the city as cold as a witch's tit, as Jeanette would say. Fiona could hear a foghorn and a train whistle, both stirring melancholy. The house lights were on as they pulled up. Rita groaned.

"Who told those boy-crazy social butterflies they could have a party?"

"Sweet Jane" blasted from the basement window. "I can't believe they're plugged in down there!" cried Fiona. "The neighbours must have called the cops by now."

They charged inside, Rita surveying the damage. "Great. An entire herd of party animals."

With the twins nowhere in sight, Fiona and Rita dashed down the stairs to find Rabid and friends bashing away on the Virgin Marries' instruments.

Jon Doe looked up and grinned. "Hello, girls!"

Rita threatened to pull the plug. Sid Sick shoved his face into Rita's. He's brave, thought Fiona, or drunk. Rita grabbed him by the dog collar, pulling his face to hers. "Wind it down."

Terry Fernandez, bassist for San Francisco band Third Rail, landed on the veranda, peering through the slat of door window above his giant, face-splitting grin. Fiona had a huge crush on their devastatingly handsome lead singer-guitarist, Harlan, and sought him out among the crowd. Terry announced that the band was in town to record an EP for Quintessence, emphasizing Vancouver and San Francisco's cross-fertilization: Brad Kent in the Avengers, Zippy Pinhead in the Dils, Dead Kennedys' Jello Biafra, practically an honourary "cheesehead."

The stereo blasted X-Ray Spex, people yelling to be heard. Every room was socked in with smoke, every inch of counter space occupied with empty beer bottles. Fiona cracked open a couple of windows, grabbed a beer, and got the latest dirt on DOA from manager Ken Lester.

Sneering, peroxide-blond Mary Jo Kopechne in her *Reform School Girls* T-shirt danced maniacally. Mary had a lot of guts, though got her nose broke after calling Randy Pandora a faggot one too many times. Chuck Biscuits slapped bright yellow Crime Stoppers stickers on every conceivable surface, including skin. Jenny sat on Spooner's knee, whispering, while Fiona wondered if he ever got laid. *Where's Harlan?* She found Jackie in the living room in an overstuffed chair, rocking some guy's world. Dolores was in the kitchen admiring Brad's guitar playing. *On my acoustic!* Randy Rampage and Karla Du Plantier were having a discussion about her old band, the Controllers. Exotic in more ways than one, Karla, a black lesbian drummer from L.A., sported cowboy boots and a do-rag. A border guard had called her Mister.

She'd flipped. "Hey, I know you've probably never seen a black person, but I'm a girl!"

Her nickname was Maddog. Meeting Vancouver's Mad Dog, Karla informed him he'd have to find a new name. There were two John Does as well: John Doe of L.A.'s X and Jon Doe of Vancouver's Rabid. Great minds? Notorious for trashing her drums, and anyone who got in her way, Karla complained about the cold and wet; missing L.A., but not her folks. She laughed.

"I'm the black sheep of the family."

Where is Harlan? Fiona's mystery man, mutual attraction too strong to be denied. So charming and chivalrous, escorting her to the Cozy Corner grocery last week so she wouldn't have to navigate the Downtown Eastside alone.

"My pleasure," he'd drawled.

Fiona could sense his presence before laying eyes on him, and then could only gawk along with all his other admirers. Harlan looked up, lazy brown eyes meeting hers. *Please come over.* He smiled and waved. An interminable thirty minutes of cruising each other was required before getting in close proximity.

"Let's go to my room," she whispered.

At the first lull, they snuck up the stairs and ducked into her bedroom, laughing. Fiona had wanted him so bad, for so long, she couldn't believe he was there. In her room. With her. They drew their faces near, kissed, fumbled, groped; Harlan's lustrous locks still cool from the night air. He nipped her earlobes, huffing tendrils of heat against her neck.

Suddenly, he stopped, a wave of trepidation travelling the length of Harlan's long body. "I have to go. I'm sorry. I have a girlfriend."

"Oh." Spell ending as sharply as an elevator lurch. "Why did you come up here?"

"I don't know. I really like you, Fiona. I'm sorry. I should go," he whispered, halfway out the door, looking both ways. Harlan, secret agent man.

Fiona bit her tongue rather than begging him to stay.

"Take care," he said, shutting the door with far too much finality.

"Fuck you, Harlan!"

I wish. Lying down, woozy, she stared at the window, blind in the darkness, piecing together a face. *Why did I think you were different?*

Harlan? Voices penetrated her dream state. Fiona sat up and peered at the clock face. Five a.m. *Voices? My God! Where are they*

coming from? She opened the blinds to see Dennis, Simon, and Mad Dog—Vancouver's Mad Dog—through the mist, sitting in the oak tree, chatting nonchalantly as if reclining on a couch. Fiona pulled on a sweater and marched downstairs.

"We're waiting for the buses to start running," explained Dennis.

"It's freezing out here. I can't believe you're still drinking!"

"Breakfast beer." Simon saluted with his bottle.

"Are you crazy?"

Dennis nodded, happy as a squirrel with a knothole of acorns.

"Good night! Or should I say, good morning?"

Fiona turned on her heel, turned off the lights and stereo, and examined a thick patina of grease on the stovetop. *Yuck.* So that's what that smell is. She opened the freezer. *My lamb chops. Gone. Goddammit!* She ran outside to find the tree bare. *Those buggers! They are dead meat!*

Emmett finally called. Fiona had just wrapped her mind around the idea of a one-night stand; a farcical one-night stand. Surely he timed the call according to his agenda. You don't phone a girl too soon; you'll come off as eager. She abhorred mating games but a glut of relief swamped her body as they made small talk.

"So, you coming over?"

"Sure, why not?" *Because Rita will kill me. I'll hurt Dennis' feelings. Screw 'em. It's my life.*

Talking on the phone and fucking soon became the extent of their relationship.

"I wanna lick you. Right on that kitchen table."

"Oooh! Sounds delicious."

After an hour of teasing, Fiona's ear was sore and her vulva ached. With only one roommate, they found it convenient to meet at Emmett's, invariably winding up in a sexual frenzy, Fiona falling off the bed mid-fellatio once. She usually left just before sunrise.

"You gonna go see Devo?" he asked. "Pointed Sticks are opening."

"Those guys in the jumpsuits and goggles? I saw them on *Saturday Night Live*. Man, I thought we were being invaded. Are they ever weird!"

"We are being invaded. By the Spud Boys of Akron, Ohio."

She suggested they go together. Emmett shook his head no and placed a Graham Parker album on the turntable.

"Fuck Elvis Costello. This guy's a much better songwriter."

Emmett was so cutting-edge. As if it mattered he only smoked Gauloises and watched "films." As soon as a band became mainstream, he threw it out with the bathwater.

"Why can't they both be good songwriters?" she asked, primarily to annoy him.

He moaned. "Come here."

She moaned. "Don't moan, Emmett! Moans are contagious. I gotta go."

"That's what you get for having a job."

"Hey, some people still have a work ethic."

"Fuck that," he said, displaying his penis cocking up. "Work this."

She'd never had a guy talk to her that way. *Christ. It turns me on.*

He didn't conform to the crowd and it wasn't just the sports car. Emmett was the consummate Casanova, screwing every girl he could get his hands on, going against the punk scene's anti-sex and romance edicts, while taking it as licence to be cruel. Fiona feigned indifference. How could she care for such a self-absorbed letch, though she'd engaged in her share of heart stomping, proving she could be just as cold and callous as the next guy. *Ah, maybe he just reads too much Henry Miller.* He'd given her a copy of *Tropic of Cancer* like it was a bible. The guy may write with his dick, but she loved Miller's bombastic style. It had become a guilty pleasure.

Nauseated, sore all over, Fiona fled and caught a bus, not quite fitting in with fellow East Van residents, though she resembled an Italian widow in her black hosiery, dress, gloves, platinum spikes, face concealed by a black scarf. Still, everyone stared. *Nobody fucks with me though.*

You never knew what he would do next. Often witty, or merely creepy, Emmett loved to create a disturbance, everyone a target, everything a prop. At London Drugs he made faces, sniffing a box of tampons marked "with applicators."

"These must be for the girls so repulsive they can't bear to touch themselves. Hey!" he yelled at the clerk, "got any used tampons?"

"Emmett. Do you have to be so rude?"

"People are staring," he replied indignantly. "That's rude. Why not give 'em a good story to take home to the wife?"

She once found him drawing lingerie onto the women's bodies in his porno magazines, "to make them interesting." He told Fiona, "Our meeting was fated," after ignoring her all night. She knew Emmett was afraid of his emotions, of being vulnerable, blah, blah, blah, and found little solace in knowing. He liked throwing her off guard. Apparently, there was also no depth of feeling between them and, "Licking your pussy is like licking stamps."

Emmett wasn't truly capable of the malice he spewed forth so readily. He was desperate. Pathetic really. Still, it hurt.

CHAPTER THREE

Pacing nervously at the corner of Main and Hastings, Fiona waited for her mother and sisters. Supper together, something they hadn't done in over a year. She lit a cigarette and shoved her hand into her pocket, hoping she looked tough. Shaking a paper bag, a gangling girl teeter-tottered toward her, squinting through eyes purple with fresh bruises.

"Wanna buy some shoes?"

"No thanks." Fiona stared straight ahead.

A few seconds later another chippy clomped up in a pair of plastic cowboy boots, waving a curling iron, also for sale.

"Jesus Christ! Do I look rich?"

Cursing Fiona out, she scurried off. *Guess I am rich compared to them.* Maureen's Jeep pulled up. Relieved, Fiona ran to the vehicle to find the doors locked. Maureen shook her head and folded her arms. Rory giggled.

"Your sister doesn't want to get out of the car," reported Jeanette.

"Oh Christ. Come on, Mo! It's broad daylight."

Maureen set her face harder. Fiona persuaded them to go to Chinatown. They cruised a few blocks, lucky to find a parking spot. Strolling down Pender past bustling seafood and vegetable stands, Maureen recoiled at gooey ducks and sea cucumbers floating like bull penises. Fiona showed them the narrow Sam Kee Building with its glass block sidewalk, the tunnel below allowing Chinese to escape opium den raids. They held their noses while passing a dumpster caked with dried fish guts. Fiona pointed to a storefront kitty corner to the Shanghai Barber Shop, yellowed newspapers lining the transom.

"There's a gambling club in there. They bet on mahjong."

"Yup. Chinks love to gamble." Jeanette laughed. "And they're really superstitious."

"Yeah, right. Unlike the Irish."

They couldn't agree on a restaurant, Fiona finally dragging them into the Ho Ho. Rory and Maureen fidgeted, Jeanette in her element having worked so many eateries. Fiona recalled stopping off at the Twin Dragon on her way home from school to be loaded up with toilet paper, eggs, and frozen peas.

"But, Mom, it's stealing."

Apparently it wasn't because they needed it more than Jimmy. Jeanette's boss Jimmy Wong always invited them to a huge Christmas feast and Fiona always felt guilty, even as she stuffed her face. She pointed to a corner booth and led the charge of hungry Koretchucks. The waitress tossed menus on the table. Jeanette ordered Cokes.

"I don't think you need one."

Jeanette was jazzed, skin glowing, eyes lit. Generally, Fiona only thought of her mother as grotesque, but today Jeanette was almost pretty. She wore a dab of lipstick now and then, and despite packing on a few pounds over the years, saw herself only as gorgeous, proud of her "big tits." Jeanette often strutted around the house naked, much to Fiona's horror, barefoot, a short, curvy, wavy-haired brunette she-monster, green eyes flashing. Mother and daughters all blessed with bewitching eyes, Maureen's were the most striking. Jeanette called them hazel; green, flecked with gold. Maureen most resembled their mother, all three girls grateful they hadn't inherited her nose, which was odd; rather bulbous, like WC Fields'. If Jeanette was beautiful, it was definitely an offbeat beauty. Fiona was well aware, however, that men found her mother extremely attractive.

They ordered the usual: won ton soup, chicken chow mein, pork fried rice, egg rolls.

"I can't believe you still don't know how to use chopsticks," said Fiona.

"I can't believe you're still such a pain in the ass," snapped Maureen.

Fiona leaned over and tried to pinch her sister's cheek with her chopsticks.

"Now, girls, don't start."

Fiona thanked Jeanette, passing the bill with chopsticks, depositing a peck on her cheek.

"Yeah," said Maureen, "don't spoil the family reunion."

Fiona stuck out her tongue. "I didn't say it was a reunion. Anyway, let's blow this pop stand." She rose. "Gotta get over to the Buddha."

They drove around until everyone agreed the closest lot was two blocks away. They piled out of the Jeep, locked it securely, and walked up Hastings toward the club. Jeanette put her arm through Fiona's, as Rory and Maureen clung to each other. A catfight in the Sunrise Hotel spilled onto the sidewalk, two fat slatterns clutching fistfuls of the other's hair, hunched over in a deadlock.

"I'll knock your teeth down your throat, you bitch!"

"Let's get out of here!" Maureen grabbed Fiona's arm, as the stench of stale beer and urine assailed their nostrils.

"Why don't they go back to the reserve?" Jeanette pointed to a "drunken Indian," leaning against the wall of the Balmoral Hotel, one leg tucked under him like a crane.

"My mother, the bigot." Her mother ignored the remark.

Maureen's face pinched at the sight of Dawn and Miss Mustard hanging out in front of the Buddha, cheering at the sight of Fiona. She complimented Miss Mustard on her latest dye job and led her tribe inside. They showed their ID to Igor, who haggled with Fiona over the guest list. He grunted and reluctantly anointed their hands with red stamps. They found a relatively clean table and sat, but not before Maureen inspected her chair. Jeanette bought a round of drinks. Maureen in her hockey-mom perm and Rory in her tight Vanderbilt jeans and sequined T-shirt were rather conspicuous, but nobody paid much attention. Jeanette rummaged through her purse, looking for a match. Maureen lit her mother's cigarette.

"Ta."

Rita loped over. "Rude Norton is outstanding tonight," she

shouted as the band bashed out a pickaxe murder version of the *Green Acres* theme.

"How about another round?" Fiona hollered into Jeanette's ear.

She smiled and passed her old purse. Fiona headed to the bar with it, packed with Doublemint gum, bingo chips, wadded tissues blotted with lipstick, and Jeanette's trusty travel-size Taboo perfume. *How does she find anything in this mess?* Fiona opened the bulging, beat-up wallet, faded photographs of Jeanette's angels plopping open, the girls seven, eight, and nine years old—Catholic triplets—Jeanette never blessed with the son she so desperately yearned for, so broken-hearted, she nearly left Fiona with the nuns. Some idiot doctor that opened her up for the cancer surgery informed her that Fiona was a boy, then tied her tubes. Jeanette refused to touch her youngest daughter for days. *Was it called postpartum depression back then?*

Fiona carefully set down four rye & sevens. Maureen sipped a dainty sip. Rita beckoned Fiona from behind her drums.

Jeanette grinned. "Good luck, sweetheart!"

Fiona climbed onstage. *I can't breathe. Damn! Am I always gonna feel this way?* When it was good, Fiona could lose herself, but tonight she was a mess. *I can't focus. Every song too fucking fast!* She glared at Dolores. "Slow down!" Dolores pointed at Rita. Fiona scanned the crowd, searching for a friendly face. There's Ma, Queen of the Blarney, surrounded by Shannon, Dennis, Oona—all her friends—Jeanette beaming, surely boasting about "my baby." She'd always called Fiona "the baby," much to her sisters' ire. The Virgin Marries slogged through their set, Fiona fuming, hugely relieved when an eternity onstage finally came to an end.

"You were great, honey!" Jeanette jumped up with a hug.

Fiona sat down, but couldn't remain still. "What did you think?"

Rory gazed past her. "It was fine." She returned to flirting with Dennis.

Maureen scowled. "It's so loud!"

Fiona threw up her hands. "It's supposed to be loud." She cursed them under her breath. "Oh, why don't you just go back to Cloverdale?"

Jeanette's eyes welled.

"Oh Christ, Ma! I'm sorry."

Next day Fiona and Shannon burned up the phone lines with a post-mortem. "It was great seeing your mom last night."

"What's so great about the old bag?"

"Look, I know she was hard on you."

"Was? You have no idea. Your parents are normal."

"Try to see the positive," said Shannon. "It's a fresh start, for both of you. She's always going to be your mom. Might as well try to get along."

"I don't care, as long as she leaves me alone. She wants to move to Vancouver so we can live together. So she can live through me."

"Jeanette? I've always thought of Jeanette as independent. Doesn't she have to be, with your dad gone so much?"

"Independent? Why do you think she sleeps with all those men whenever he's away? She can't live without a man telling her what to do."

Fiona hung up, ran outside, and jumped into Rita's van for coffee with Shannon at Calabria, then rehearsal. At Commercial Drive, they heard the din of blaring horns.

"What the fuck?"

Rita slammed on the brakes as a man wearing red, white, and green face paint darted into the street. They encountered more pandemonium in the next barricaded block. Fiona surveyed the street party.

"What the hell's going on?"

Rita smacked her forehead. "The World Cup! I forgot. Italy's playing."

Rita turned around and headed east to the next clear intersection. Shannon suggested walking down to the Drive. They left Rita's van parked on the street and the three wound their way through numerous huddles of drunks, Calabria proprietor Lorenzo's face brightening at the sight of Fiona and friends.

"Ah, *buon giorno, bella*! Please. Sit down."

Lorenzo shooed his sons away from a table by the window, where a parade of high-on-soccer humanity was weaving past. The girls ordered espressos. A van stopped, sliding doors yarded open, a swarm of football louts tumbling out, nearly impaling passersby on their Italian flags. Lorenzo returned with a tray and set down four liqueur glasses filled with a clear liquid. Fiona sniffed.

"Sambuca. To the glory that is Italy!" Lorenzo clinked their glasses, sun glutting the room with a golden light. "May the gods shine upon us!"

The cafe's denizens broke out with cheers and boisterous backslapping.

"Everybody's Italian today!" shouted Shannon. She pulled her chair closer to Fiona. "So how are things going with you and Emmett?"

"Emmett who?"

"Come on, don't be coy. Everybody knows you two are an item."

"He doesn't want everybody to know."

"Christ. Sometimes I think he's a closet case. Compulsive sex addicts often are," said Rita. "Desperately trying to convince everyone they're straight. Especially themselves."

Fiona threw back a shot. "Not everything's about sexuality. I do think he's disturbed. His dad took off when he was just a little kid."

"Well there you go. Father hunger. Your affliction as well."

"Christ, Rita! You think you know everything."

"I do. At least, I know more than you."

"Well that's not saying much, is it?" Shannon laughed. Fiona smacked her playfully.

Lorenzo brought another round. "I see you girls are getting into the spirit of things."

"Thanks to you!" Shannon lifted her glass. "To victory!" She drained her Sambuca and slammed the glass down, gagging.

"You keep seeing him," said Rita, "because you think if you can convince that asshole to love you, warts and all, everyone else will. That you're worthy."

"You have warts?" sniggered Shannon.

"He's a feckless narcissist," added Rita. "Too shallow to love anybody but himself."

"He's damaged," said Fiona.

"You know what? There aren't enough keyboardists in this town. That's the only reason anybody puts up with him."

Shannon grabbed Fiona's chin. "Warts? Where?" She reared back, nearly falling off her chair, recovered, and lifted Fiona's arm. "Show me!"

Fiona swatted her, then asked, "So, did you sleep with him?"

Shannon recoiled and looked down at her lap. "A long time ago," she mumbled, wrestling with her napkin.

"He has fucked every girl in this town!"

"Not me," said Rita.

"You should go out with Dennis!" said Shannon.

"Dennis is no saint, you know."

"He knows what matters," said Rita. "And he's the only guy around here that can take the heat in your kitchen." She tossed back her Sambuca. "Emmett's going to dismantle you."

"Jesus Christ! Get off my case, will you?"

Five drunken yahoos stumbled past braying "Volare!" "Whoa, whoa, whoa, whoa, Volare! Whoa, whoa, whoa, whoa."

Lorenzo brought round after round, the girls serenading each other until hoarse.

"To providence," said Rita, raising her glass as she stood. "Come on, we gotta get to rehearsal."

Fiona groaned. The trio managed to stagger out the door and catch a bus, singing all the way. Upon reaching the house, they bumbled down to the basement, twins snickering at the turned tables. Rita could barely balance on her stool. The bandmates got into the usual arguments concerning roles and skill levels.

"Scream Fiona," said Dolores. "Snarl! If I were you . . ."

"You are not me! Okay? You don't get it, do you?" Fiona poked Dolores in the shoulder. "You are not me!"

"Okay, okay, Miss Thing. Back off!"

Shannon pulled her aside. "Why don't you take it easy?"

"I'm sick of being bombarded with unsolicited advice! Nobody appreciates what I do."

"Humour her. Humour them. Nod your head. Agree. Tell 'em what they want to hear, then go ahead and do what you want. Okay?"

Fiona smiled. "I never thought of that."

"Obviously." Shannon squeezed her hand. "You don't have to go for the bait, you know."

"You're so smart."

Fiona stood at Emmett's door in a deluge. She looked down at the WELCOME mat and laughed. *He's going to be so mad. Fuck him. He can start treating me with respect or I'm outta here.* She worked up enough gumption to knock. His bandmate and roommate Donald answered and directed her upstairs.

Fiona found the bedroom door ajar, Lene Lovich on the stereo, Emmett in the shower. She stared at the symbols of his character. *Or lack thereof?* On the wall, a neon Heineken sign, movie posters, flyers for No Fun, Bluto, Exxotone, UJerk5, and on the bureau, a silver Zippo lighter and roach clips rested in a Penthouse Club ashtray. Listening to the water running, Fiona felt free to snoop, noting that his collection of framed photographs depicted no people, just cars and motorcycles.

She moved to the bed to examine a jumble of sheets. A ripped condom package fell to the floor. Fiona winced, conjuring an image of Emmett's Ideal Woman. Beautiful, of course, but petite, weighed down by a mane of long raven hair, like the actress from that Truffaut film, *The Story of Adele H.*, the one Emmett fell in love with when he was sixteen. *Isabelle Adjani, that's her name. Everything I'm not. Continental. Sophisticated.*

Fiona felt guilty sneaking around; didn't want to startle him, so called out. Emmett was in good cheer. Or drunk. A twenty-sixer of rye sat on the bedside table. Fiona downed a long, hard swig. He called her into the bathroom. She opened the door cautiously.

"What a pleasant surprise!"

"Do you mean that?"

"Can't you tell?" Emmett pulled back the shower curtain, exposing a huge hard-on.

Emmett was devoted to his body and its parts. Like most guys. Amusing, the relationship a man has to his penis, often honouring it with a nickname. *Wouldn't that be like christening your nose?* Their joy at having a penis was the only thing Fiona might envy, but surely it's a disadvantage to have such precious cargo dangling right out in front, especially considering how much they like sports. Female bodies are streamlined. Her pussy, or cunt—Fiona still struggled to find a term she could embrace— was as much a part of her as her fingers, elbows, toes. And she feared she might never understand the male of the species.

"What are you doing here?"

"I need to talk to you."

A BOOM of thunder shook the house. Lightning bolted across the yard and the lights flickered, honeycomb tiles disappearing in the ensuing blackout. Fiona grabbed onto the sink.

"Holy fuck!" cried Emmett. "Did you see that?"

All Fiona could see was what appeared to be golf balls hammering the roof. "It's hail!"

The room was charged, nearly dark. "Why don't you join me?" he said, grinning. "You're all wet anyway."

"No. You're all wet."

"Come on."

Fiona heard a loud CRACK, saw a flash, and looked down at his outstretched hand. Empty. Biting her lip, Fiona fought back tears and some sort of craving, wondering what she was doing there. Gingerly, she stepped forward and bumped into the curtain rod. A sharp current travelled the length of her body, roosting in her wisdom teeth. Fiona gasped, hesitating a long moment. *Oh, what the hell?* As if galvanized by the shock, she peeled off her sopping clothes, flung back the curtain, and climbed in. She grabbed a tuft of Emmett's hair in her fist, tugging his head toward her. Gripping round the small of her back, Emmett parted her lips with his tongue, darting in and out, snakelike.

"Ah, you have such a lovely, long neck," he said, peppering her throat with pert, rapid kisses.

She swooned. He'd never said anything like that before. Fiona reached down to grope his cock and squeezed. *God, he's huge.* This used to alarm her, but lately she was only relieved to find it so hard and heavy. Another flash of lightning lit the room as the power went out, along with the lights. Emmett bent over his unwieldy erection to turn off the faucets.

"Holy fuck!" he yelled, riveted to Fiona's skin prickling in the cold air.

He pawed her tits, rolling a raised nipple between his fingers to squish, squelching her sob with a kiss. They got out of the tub. He grabbed her by the waist.

"Turn around."

"Let's go to bed."

"No. Right here. Right now."

"What if Donald walks in?"

"Fuck Donald."

"No. I wanna fuck you."

She offered herself up, heels of her hands braced, knees cradled in a pile of wet towels, Emmett gripping her flanks, cock parting petals of flesh, vengefully, she thought. He reared up from his knees to thrust, jabbing at her cervix.

"You're making animal sounds," he said.

There are no words. Just a warring winter sky, a trance, a black and white blue movie, lovers ferried beyond flashing white strobe lights. They got off the floor, rushed to the bed, under the covers. *Ah to be under his skin.* Emmett drew lines down her belly with his tongue, burrowing his nose into muff furrows, a big Lab lapping at pussy. He teased her clit till it was swollen. She needed to fuck. Long legs straight up, Fiona rubbed the back of his head with her toes. Taking her foot in his hand, he kissed the instep while moving inside her in a wide, slow spiral, a sustained moan stemming from some place low in her gut. Emmett came, tumbled off, laughing and groaning. Fiona dragged her body upright, bumping into the headboard, dopey, feeble.

"You bruised my tailbone!"

Emmett laughed and dove under the blankets, pulling them up over their heads like a tent.

"You drive me out of my skull with that thing." Fiona coiled her leg around his thigh, stroking his cock.

"You mean I fucked your brains out?"

She had to laugh. *No words.* It's only lust. Emmett was happy. Don't say anything. Don't ruin it. Nuzzling her neck, he rested his chin on her shoulder, caressed her hair. Must be the negative ions she thought. Another white flash, then a loud BOOM jolted the bed.

"I'm getting tired of this. The storm, I mean."

"I love storms!" Emmett threw the window open, gusts of fresh air sweeping away the funk of sex. "Natives believe thunder is the gods fucking."

"I feel like a god. Do you?"

"Zeus! When I'm fucking you."

She didn't trust it, this sudden wooing, near joy. He was even insisting she stay over. "You can't go home in this." Emmett lit a candle. "My God!" he said fiercely. "You look like an angel in this light."

I think I shall faint.

"Ethereal." He stroked Fiona's cheek with the back of his hand. "Such fair skin."

That look. The look that said it all. The look that rattled around in his skull. He opened his mouth a few times.

"What, Emmett?"

"I didn't know how special you were."

"Oh. And now you do?" cooed Fiona.

He nodded.

"Guess you haven't kissed the right frog."

"*Mon cheri.* I feel connected to you, girl."

Before she could respond to that bombshell, Emmett

grabbed an envelope off the dresser and flashed Clash show tickets. "Let's go!"

She leapt up from the knot of sheets. "Yay!"

Taking turns serenading each other, they passed his acoustic back and forth. Fiona was surprised to discover an equally rural B.C. Emmett, growing up in a Chilliwack doublewide with his single, welfare mom. A gifted mechanic, Emmett had worked hard to acquire his posh car.

"But I wanna focus on my music for a while. Try to make it as a professional."

They fell asleep to the sun rising, curling their bodies into each other, snug as a pair of played-out pups.

Does he do this? She wondered; conjure up last night, the things we did, feel an after-shudder? Waiting to see Emmett Hayes was agony! Fiona couldn't eat. Or think straight. *Gawd, I hate this!* Half an hour late. Again. She diddled her guitar, scanned a book, traipsed back and forth to the fridge, swinging wildly between anger and anxiety. *Why doesn't he call? That dink!* She could have gone with Rita and Shannon. She could have spent her hard-earned cash on something besides a new silk bra and panties. *That bastard.* Then, still cursing, Fiona heard his obnoxious Porsche engine out front and relief coursed through her limbs. She barely resisted the urge to run to the car.

"Sorry I'm late," he mouthed, The Clash's "I Fought the Law" blasting from his Blaupunkts. "Did you hear? The Clash came out and played soccer with us!"

"Yeah! Who won?"

"They did, of course. My shins are covered in bruises."

Emmett yarded on the gears, pinball-wizard style. Soon they were pelted with fat raindrops. He pulled over immediately to put the top up. They cruised the block repeatedly, in search of the safest parking spot for his precious steed of steel. At last, they entered the fading art-deco grandeur of the Commodore Ballroom, Emmett waving tickets at the doorman, breezing by security like a diplomat. *Christ. He must have been left under a cabbage by mistake.* Emmett surveyed the room, refusing Fiona's hand.

"Fuck! Look at all the poseurs."

Fiona spied Dennis across the room, her stomach tilting at the reproach in his face. A young woman in a booth flanking the stage sat sneering.

"Emmett, who's that girl glaring at us?"

He ignored the question and wandered off, Fiona following.

The Clash had an excellent DJ, spinning a killer mix of ska, punk, reggae, and dub. Fiona waved to Shannon and friends. The place was jammed with every diehard in the city, slam dancing on its famous ballroom floor, originally designed to make any clodhopper hoof it like Fred Astaire. The Commodore had character all right, and it was the perfect size. Fiona hated arena shows. The Dishrags opened. She loved watching fellow females wailing on guitar. They closed with a blazing rendition of "London's Burning." Next up, Bo Diddley. Emmett told her The Clash brought the old guy along as a way to pay homage to one of rock and roll's originators.

Fiona shrugged. "I'm too young for nostalgia."

Unfortunately, the Powder Blues were his pickup band, old fart guitar god wannabes and though playing with a legend, forced everyone to sit through a long, boring wank session.

"Fuck this. I wanna see The Clash!" Fiona was not alone in her sentiments.

Shannon walked over and pulled her aside. "See that girl? That's Electra. One of Emmett's girlfriends. He told her he was bringing her tonight."

"Electra! Sounds like an Italian scooter."

"She's weird. Really mad. Says she's gonna beat the crap out of you."

Laughing, they walked over to Emmett. He lowered his drink and deigned to look at them, insisting he hadn't invited anyone but Fiona. Clouds of tension were gathering on the dance floor as well, burly security guards manning the barriers. Finally, The Clash emerged, a tidal wave of bodies surging forward, the band opening with "I'm So Bored with the U.S.A.," Emmett off the hook. For now.

Beer: you only rent it. Fiona ran to the bathroom between songs, in and out of a stall quickly. Electra appeared, strutted over, and squinted up into Fiona's face like a Pekinese.

"Hey, bitch! Keep your paws off Emmett or I will kill you."

Looking around, Fiona laughed. "Where's the hidden camera? Hey, Eeeelectraaaa. I think you'd better stay away from Emmett."

"Wanna fight about it?"

"Hah! I could squish you like a bug. Fuck off! This ain't junior high, you know."

What Electra lacked in size, she made up for in attitude, fuelled by four-inch stilettos, garters, fishnets, and a black leather mini skirt, all of which had nothing to do with punk and everything to do with Emmett.

Electra spit at her. Missing her target—Fiona's face—the gob splatted onto her clavicle. Fiona looked down. Nearly blind with fury, she handily hoisted Electra up by the lapels. Shannon barged in. Fiona slammed Electra into the wall, back of her head banging the paper towel dispenser. Electra yelped.

"You bitch! You fucking whore!"

Shannon grabbed Fiona by the arm. They walked out, dogged by the undaunted Lilliputian. Fiona barrelled over to Emmett.

"What were you thinking?"

"I told you! I didn't ask her. She just assumed."

Wee Electra was at the bar again, glowering.

"Get lost, you skanky broad!" Emmett hollered at her.

Snotty pose pierced like a balloon, Electra flumped away, people laughing in her wake.

"God, Emmett, you're an asshole!"

"Hey, I brought you. What do you care?"

"I care because it's the same way you treat me. Like shit!"

"Fuck this!" He walked away in a huff.

Fuck this, all right! Fighting tears, determined to revel in this night to remember, Fiona formed two fists and shoved her way through the crowd, jabbing, elbowing, bashing. She glanced back. Emmett had gone. Naturally. Though the faces on the floor were familiar, the horde formed one huge alien, reeking of stewed leather and body heat, The Clash so loud they cloaked the clamour of thumping heart, roaring blood. Fiona was rammed. Hard. She heard the wind blast from her lungs, body boxed about as if by bulls. She slipped, nearly going down, floored by the vision of her fractured skull being ground into the boards by dozens of tightly laced combat boots. *I am too black in the heart to fall!*

She carved a line out of the crush to the foot of the stage, and stared up at Simonon. He was perfect—angled cheekbones, long, lean muscles, mouth gaping open like a Lego-focused kid. An art student apparently, before hitching up with The Clash, he couldn't play a note till Mick Jones taught him. Like John Lennon. Must be a British thing, that link between art school and rock. *So why did I let Trent talk me out of art school? Oh my God. Simonon! He's looking right at me!* Got a girlfriend, according to Shannon, some tart who writes for *NME*.

Strummer strained against his Telly, snaking the mic stand with his body. Tossing his guitar onto his back, he leaned over the crowd, ranting, railing. Loose-kneed Mick Jones was running, leaping and boinging all over the stage, carving out notes with an axe; his golden Gibson Les Paul. Goofy booster Dennis vaulted onto the stage during "Career Opportunities," ricocheting off amps and various Clash members, security goons giving Keystone Cops chase. Strummer even let Dennis commandeer the mic and bray out the chorus with him, Fiona feeling a twinge of envy.

Several encores later, Shannon and Rita caught up with her, the usual confusion about the after party location ensuing. Fiona felt a tap on her shoulder and turned around to face Emmett, his eyes trained on the floor.

"Wanna go to the party?"

"Not with you."

He threw his head back, looked up at the ceiling. "Kee-rist! Get over it, will you?"

"Where's Eeellectraaa?" Fiona couldn't say it with a straight face. "Emmett and Electra. Electra and Emmett. Has a nice ring to it, don't you think?"

"Look, are you coming or not?"

"Oh, all right."

Rita couldn't disguise her disdain. Shannon watched as Emmett tried to open the car door. "You're drunk," she said.

"Hey, I'm the best drunk driver in the world. Just kidding. I'm not drunk."

"I'll be fine." Fiona waved at Shannon and Rita. "I'll see you at the party."

Emmett handles his car the way he handles everybody, she thought; knowing exactly when to switch gears, drop the hammer, brake.

No stars. No moon. They stopped at a light. Fiona watched a man buy a bouquet of roses at a Chinese grocery. *I wonder who they're for? Lucky girl. Or guy.*

"Hey, do you know where the word anathema comes from?"

"No, but you're gonna tell me, aren't you?"

"Aren't you interested?"

"No. But I am interested in history, theology, philosophy."

"This is beyond theology. It's goddess worship. God was a woman two thousand years ago."

"Pagan."

"You say it like it's a bad thing."

"I think you've been hanging out with that bull dyke drummer too much."

"Hey! Rita's my friend, you know." Fiona turned to glare at him. "Anatha was the goddess the Canaanites worshipped, the fierce, bloodthirsty goddess of fertility. Of course Zeus banished her. Anathema's the only sign she ever existed. Since then, God has replaced the Goddess, and thousands of women have been accused of witchcraft, burned at the stake, et cetera."

"According to who?"

"Whom. Forget it. You've never heard of them. All you read is porno magazines."

"That's not true!"

"Oh yeah. I forgot. Henry Miller. Misogynistic crap."

Emmett clenched his fingers into a fist around the steering wheel. "I read Nietzsche. Ellison. Philip K. Dick. Kurt Vonnegut. William Burroughs."

"Oh yeah. The junkie that murdered his wife in Mexico."

"It was an accident."

"Like their marriage? Playing William Tell with pistols. Brilliant."

"You're such a bitch."

"You say it like it's a bad thing."

Emmett set his jaw.

"As far as I'm concerned, any woman worth her salt has to be a bitch sometimes. What's the corresponding male term for bitch anyway? Guess what? There isn't one! The closest might be asshole, which is a perfectly acceptable thing for a man to be. It means he's self-assured, determined. A man can bitch all he wants. A woman asserts an opinion and she's an evil hag. Not a nice girl."

He accelerated. "You have me confused with someone who gives a shit."

Engine roaring, Emmett pulled out to pass a little green MG, Fiona's head jerked back, hands flying to the dash. The MG sped up. "Now that's an asshole," muttered Emmett, overtaking the car.

"Yeah, Emmett. Why should you care? You're in the driver's seat."

"And you're not. That's no accident."

"You can't stand that I have a brain! That I might wanna do more with my life than suck your cock."

"You think you're gonna bust my balls!" Emmett slammed on the brakes.

Crash test dummy flung forward, Fiona's head met the windshield with a loud THUD. She saw stars. The moon. The sun.

"Talk about assholes!" A warm, sluggish rivulet of blood trickled toward her eye.

Emmett sat dumbfounded, mouth open, loose as a corn hole. Fiona heaved herself up and out of the Porsche.

"Who the fuck do you think you are?" she screamed, guts churning. "I'll kill you!"

She delivered a mighty boot to the car door instead, turned, and bolted, blundering along a row of cars, blindly seeking the sidewalk, cold air whirling around the base of her spine.

Emmett pulled up. "Get in."

"I don't think so!"

"Come on, Fiona!" His voice strained, containing fury. "I'm sorry. I'm not even gonna get out and look at the damage."

"No! You're not sorry. Any kindness from you is just a fluke, as random as all the cruelty. *We* are not going anywhere!"

Lips curling, Emmett shouted, "Fine!" gunned it and sped off.

Boy, I really know how to pick 'em. Where the fuck am I? Broadway and Main. Mt Pleasant. Yeah, right. Shit! The address of the party forgotten, she wiped her eyes, slinging tears to the rain. *Who can I call?* Stumbling along Main Street, Fiona trained her eyes on the North Shore Mountains, deep blue even at night. Nothing open. *Fucking hick town!* She spied a head full of pink foam curlers in a picture window, in an apartment above a shoe store, and wondered what it must be like to live above a shoe store. A woman on a couch. Maybe some guy stood her up. *If only.* The lights were on in a restaurant across the street. *Yes!* A Ukrainian restaurant. *Hah!* She peeked in and saw the staff sitting at a table. Face smeared with blood and mascara, Fiona entered. She hated to ask.

"May I use your phone, please?"

A hulking, meaty fellow and the cook, a large, seasoned woman, frowned. *His mother?* She reminded Fiona of Grandma Koretchuck. *They must think I'm crazy. I must look crazy.*

"We're closed."

"It's local."

The cook shot Junior a no through narrowed eyes. They argued in Ukrainian. He grunted, rose, and led Fiona to a red phone on the bar.

"Thank you."

They sat in their white uniforms, staring as she dialed home.

Yeah, better watch out. I might steal something or run you through with a butcher knife. No answer. Everybody's at the party. Having fun. With The Clash! She considered calling Rory. Forget it. She goes to bed with the chickens. *God, this place stinks. Trying to make it look fancy, but what's fancy about peasant food?* Fiona recalled Grandma Koretchuck, always miffed that her daughter-in-law, the French Mick Jeanette, cooked better cabbage rolls than she did. Of course, her mother's were weird. They weren't bland, greasy little green turds stuffed with sticky rice. Jeanette improvised, using an entire cabbage leaf for a single roll, roasting them under a pork rind with tomato sauce. *Yum. God, I'm starving!*

"What do you put in your pirogies?"

The old woman stared blankly. Fiona felt like saying, "Take your precious pirogies and your precious red phone and stuff 'em up your big bohunk ass, lady."

Bohunk. Jeanette loved calling her father a bohunk. He called her frog or pea souper. *What a pair! Nice family. No wonder I'm so fucked up.*

She walked outside and down the street, passing a derelict dance studio, a deli with checkerboard tiles beneath a shiny, papier-mâché bull's head, snout painted on. *Oh well, it's closed too.* She stopped at a crosswalk. *What a fucked-up neighbourhood. No one around. What am I gonna do?*

Fiona found a dollar bill in the pocket of her jeans, and an open diner. Relieved, she sat at the counter, ordered coffee, and tried to figure out her next move. A pockmarked, mocha-skinned man with a black eye sat fondling a young woman. Dying for a cigarette, Fiona leaned into his smoke. The man grinned and offered her one, flashing rings on nearly every finger.

"What's your name, young lady?"

"Fiona." *Shit. I should have lied.*

"Hello. Perry Kashkouli." Perry was Persian. He neglected to introduce his girlfriend, who was gone anyhow, swaying, nodding off, lit cigarette in one hand, pretending to read the menu.

"So what's a nice girl like you doing in a place like this?"

"Are you serious?" Fiona realized he was as serious as the audaciously wide lapels and gold medallions gracing his furry chest. "How'd you get the shiner?"

Perry brightened. "Why, defending the honour of a damsel in distress."

"That one?" Fiona pointed to the high young woman about to fall off her stool.

"Oh, she's just taking a break. She's a good girl. So what's a lovely maiden doing out all by herself?"

"Oh, just taking a stroll." Fiona leaned over an ashtray and wrung the rain out of her hair. The matronly waitress came over and topped her up. "Where's Victoria Avenue from here?"

"East. About twenty blocks."

"Can I walk it?"

"I don't know." The waitress sighed and set the coffee pot down. "Can you?"

"Hey. We leaving," said Perry, rising, smiling. "We can drop you off."

"Ah, no thanks. I'm fine."

"No, really. It's no trouble. I insist."

"Leave her alone, Perry," said the waitress sternly.

He smiled and bowed, handing Fiona a business card. *Shangri-La Escorts.* The waitress snatched his bill off the counter and motioned him to the till.

"Call me anytime," said Perry. "I'm always hiring." He gathered up his mohair coat and the girl.

"Here," said the waitress, grabbing a handful of change out of the tip jar. "Go over there across the street, catch a 25 bus to Kingsway, then transfer to the 20 Victoria."

Fiona read her name tag. "Thanks, Joyce!"

"I've got a daughter your age. At home, where she belongs."

Fiona paced for twenty minutes, happy not to be in a car with that pimp and his junkie whore. *And thank God for weary old waitresses.* She was relieved to find everyone out when she finally arrived, house cold and black as a cave. Icing her bump, Fiona huddled under a blanket in front of the TV, wondering why she took shit from anyone anymore.

★ ★ ★ ★

Biology is destiny. It seemed so, as Fiona moped in her room. *I hate it! Thanks for the ride. Fucker! Am I always going to be the last stop on a power trip?* Famished, Fiona mopped up her tears, hoisted herself off the bed, and determined to track down a chocolate bar, nearly collided with Donald at the foot of the stairs. Emmett sauntered in, plowing straight into her heart, which jackhammered so loudly she was certain everyone could hear it.

"Bluto has to borrow some equipment," explained Rita.

Donald gloated. "Yeah, we're opening for the Buzzcocks! Short a few mic stands and cords and shit. We wanna sound great tonight."

Emmett said nothing. Fiona looked him directly in the eyes, could see no anger, just a man on a mission. The last time she kissed him, he made a face, annoyed at having to remove the cigarette from his mouth. *The last time I kissed him. I will never kiss him again. I will never fuck him again either!* She clutched the railing, throat throbbing. *Say something. What is there to say? Why can't he say something?* Fiona wrenched herself free from his gaze to bolt into the living room.

"My God!" said Rita. "You can taste the sexual tension in the air."

"I think that's dread, Rita. It's over, you'll be happy to know."

"Are you okay?"

"No! I'm not. Feel like I've been run over by a truck. A truck named Hayes."

CHAPTER FOUR

The I-5 might be the most expedient route to California, but it was *Grapes of Wrath* bleak, Fiona dissuaded from the Pacific Coast Highway every time they toured, even after revealing her scheme to go to Big Sur to meet Henry Miller.

"Henry who?" asked Dolores.

The Americans built their superhighway on a flat strip, running straight through the middle of Washington, Oregon, and California. With the exception of Mount Shasta and Grants Pass there wasn't much scenery, even if the van had windows. The epic battle over seating raged on. Rita and Dennis did the driving, Fiona banished to the back with the equipment and the twins. The band pulled into a Denny's after much debate.

"Yuck." Dolores slammed down her glass. "Why does this water taste like a swimming pool?"

Rita sniffed it. "They have to use a lot of chlorine. Get used to it. Culture shock, I mean. The differences between Canada and the U.S. may be subtle, but they are very real."

Fiona had discovered that pissed meant mad, not drunk, and was royally pissed when the waitress brought her a bag of Frito-Lays after she ordered chips instead of French fries.

"When do we get to River City?" said Jackie.

"Less than two hours," replied Dennis. "Hey, did you know that Portland sits right next to a dormant volcano?"

"You know what I like about Portland?" said Rita. "The audience isn't big on spitting and slamming, at least with girl groups."

With audiences that did relish spitting and slamming girls, their roadie became their bodyguard. Dennis the Menace was handy with a mic stand and harboured no qualms about ramming its base into the chest of any yahoo that gobbed or grabbed the girls' feet.

Ever the protector, he once bestowed Fiona with a choke collar.

"What's this for? We don't have a dog."

To demonstrate, Dennis had hooked Fiona's keys onto the large ring, grabbed the chain by the opposite end, and spun it in a lethal circle.

"It's like driving into a postcard!" shouted Fiona.

The Golden Gate Bridge spanned San Francisco Bay against a cloudless sky, distant foothills barren as moon rocks.

"But the bridge is red not gold!" squealed Dolores.

Fiona found it a little disconcerting, to suddenly be in a place she'd only ever seen depicted in photographs or movies. Dennis pointed out a set of cement ruins on the seashore, site of the old Sutro Baths. They drove streets adorned with Painted Ladies, row upon row of Victorian houses. A cable car went clanging by, girls tickled by the Chinese housewives and suits hanging off the poles. Back home, they'd strap you in, or on, all the while lecturing about safety and rules. With several shows slated, including the Mabuhay Gardens, Berkeley Square, and Temple Beautiful, the Virgin Marries were prepared to couch surf in the Bay area for a couple of weeks before heading south to L.A.

Okay, so the band's hummin' and ready to go, when Jackie abruptly reeled around to face the audience and WHAM, whacked Fiona square in the bull's eye of her forehead with the fat end of her Fender bass. Suspended in a ceiling of pain, Fiona could hear tweety birds, and nearly passed out. She latched on to the mic stand, trying to staunch the bleeding.

The zaniness didn't end there.

"Hi. You were sensational!"

"Thanks." Fiona yawned.

"You're even more beautiful up close. You look like Artemis."

"How do you know what Artemis looked like?"

"I know. Can I bring you a beverage? What does such a fair lady favour?"

"Beer."

Gawd. Nose like Cyrano's, long wavy hair down to his bony shoulders, Mr. Guy jacket, penny loafers. *A dork who knows of Artemis? Hmm.* He returned with a longneck Bud. Fiona swigged.

"Gawd! I swear American beer tastes like piss. I like these bottles though."

"By the way, I'm Maurice Carter," he said, lobbing his name, grenade-like.

"Hi, Maurice Carter. I'm—"

"I know who you are. Fiona Larochelle. You're famous."

"Ha! Infamous is more like it."

"I've heard so much about you, I had to come down and see for myself."

"Oh yeah? Was it worth it?"

"Oh yeah."

What a goof.

"I can't believe you're going out with that goof!" hooted Dolores.

"We're just friends. He's kind of interesting, into some radical stuff actually."

"Jazz," she said, holding her nose.

"And Luis Buñuel. Haida art, myth. André Breton. Man Ray."

"Man who?"

Maurice and his neo-surrealist friends did hold some strange notions. Why flog a dead movement? Fiona tried to point out the often-touted parallels between dada and punk, but Maurice and his pals were content to reside in the past. They did provide an amusing change of pace, with their salons, clove cigarettes, and Coltrane. Invoking Paris circa 1922, they gathered to puff and prattle, composing exquisite corpses, moon glowing beyond the gauze curtains of Paul and Sun Hee's railroad apartment. Romantics, and Fiona was secretly a sucker for romance.

"I'd rather go to The Clash show," she said on the way to their gig at the Fab Mab.

"We can go to the Target Video party later," said Dennis. "They'll be there."

The Virgin Marries loaded in. Fiona was beginning to realize sound check was a complete waste of time. Acoustics during performances never reflected the pre-show sound check. Dennis tried to placate her, claiming it was a good way to tame pre-show jitters. Still, they managed to play a good set.

A big fan of their slack, thundering dirges, Fiona was thrilled to meet Bruce Loose of Flipper. He talked about his pet rat and the best way to roast a chicken. Loose had a reverence for food, if nothing else. Soon East Bay Ray of the Dead Kennedys sidled up and hit on Fiona. American men were so direct they often caught her off guard. They required far less deciphering than Canadian men who were loath to admit they might desire someone, and worked hard to conceal it. So sophomoric; like knowing a boy likes you because he slugs you in the arm.

The girls approached Target Video. Fiona saw Mick Jones and Paul Simonon leaning against a car, smoking, and chatting away like regular blokes. Rita struck up a conversation.

"Hey, I like your pants," said Paul.

Fiona looked down at her olive green White Stag ski pants, one of her most prized thrift store finds. She pulled her gaze back to take in all of him.

"I like your pants too." *Gawd. I must sound like an idiot.* "I saw you guys play in Vancouver. Amazing show!" *What is he holding? His bass. He must think I'm staring at his crotch. Oh my God! I am staring at his crotch.* Mortified, Fiona mumbled goodbye and bolted.

Rita apologized. "Don't mind her. She's high."

Mick and Paul nodded sagely. Once the two guitarists entered the building, gropers and groupies buzzed like flies on dog poo. An hour later, Fiona was latched on to a column.

How to stop the tilting? I'm losing it! Nail me down. Please. Christ, why did I take acid? I hate hallucinogens. Who gave me acid? Wish I was straight. Some stupid acidhead with a sheet of pretty tab paper. Just stand here, next to all these clubby, Clash-y people, watching a throng of inky, nefarious cutouts prancing against a wall of orange flame, deejay spinning Madness. Ah, 2-Tone—the black and white of it all. Ska against racism. So, who let the skinheads in? Hats as horns, fingers curling into fists, Zoetrope right around the corner. Thunder and napalm in the morning. If ever I pray to God again. Fiona clung harder. *Man your station in life. Feel the light flare, flutter, snuff out. Don't tread on me! I am already dead. Please. Gawd. I wish I was straight! Those people. They're staring. Hey, I can rock. Rock and roll. Fuck you! Fuck the world. Up yours with a wire brush. I better walk out of here backwards. Might get screwed. Pierced. Shit! I lost an earring. Full of holes. My whole life story. What am I doing here? Fuck this shit!*

Fiona strode directly toward Joe Strummer and tapped him on the shoulder. *In front of everyone.* He turned around smiling, equally startled by, and drawn to the well of despair in her eyes.

"Hey, Joe. What makes life worth living? This band? Does it make you happy? Playing music?" Fiona yelled above the din. "Why haven't you killed yourself?"

Strummer rested his hand on her shoulder. "I know it's hard." He lowered his cigarette, waved his hand as if to banish angst with smoke. "But you can't give up."

Strummer flashed his famous British working-class teeth. *They aren't so bad.* Soon, he was snatched away by several dipshits shoving a bong into his face, casting a look of regret over his shoulder. *Or is it relief?*

Ah, here comes Rita, Dennis right behind her, he who takes the bullshit by the horns. "She seems to have snapped out of her funk."

Rita shook her head. "No. Her attitude is worse."

"How do you know?" said Fiona.

They dropped their shoulders, relieved, preferring an ornery Fiona to a petrified, tweaking Fiona.

"Hey, Dennis, where was Adam when Eve was being seduced by the serpent? What did he expect, leaving his back door open like that?" *Did I say that?* "Where are we going?"

They escorted her to a tiny Mexican restaurant in the Mission, replete with wooden booths, balls of blue glass, and fishing nets hanging in the doorway.

"Are we having menudo?"

"Maybe we should," said Rita. "They say it cures hangovers."

"LSD hangovers?"

A smiling señora greeted them and showed them to a table. Rita ordered chicken tortilla soup and crab tostados. Fiona lunged at the chips and salsa. Rita smiled.

"She gets atavistic around food."

Dennis nodded. "I've always been attracted to her appetite. Or appetites."

"Hey!" said Fiona, "Quit talking about me in the third person. And I'm not that bad. Dolores is way worse. At least I can show some restraint, when required."

Fiona buried her nose in Dennis' coat, redolent of misty Vancouver. Persuading the señora to sell them a bottle of tequila, he set up shots, which they knocked back pronto. Lips recoiling, Fiona shuddered.

"I think it's straightening you out," said Dennis.

Rita gestured at the window. "Hey, the sun's coming up."

Fiona groaned. "Dawn of the Dead. Are we sleeping at Target Video again? I can't take that cement floor," she whimpered. "I wanna go home."

Dennis and Rita took pity, allowing Fiona to sleep in the van as they ventured inside to weather the twins and chilled rooms. Fiona slept fitfully; acid flashes and brilliantly hued Rorschach blots pulsing across her eyelids, waking on the hour, tear-soaked, ashamed, unsure why.

Next day, she couldn't stop talking about him. "I love Strummer! He's compassionate. A foreign concept these days. It takes courage to be kind."

"He probably thought you were crazy," said Jackie.

"No. He recognized a kindred spirit."

Maurice was indignant. Offended that Fiona refused to fall in love with him. Instead, Fiona caught herself intently watching Sun Hee and all that she did: whipping up a batch of noodles, scolding her fiancé, Paul, twisting her lustrous hair into a chignon secured with black, lacquered chopsticks. And Sun Hee thought Fiona was exotic.

"I was born in Quebec, not Paris."

"That's okay," said Sun Hee. "I'm Korean. Not Japanese."

A lithe, ginger-chomping vamp with teal eyelids, fiery, foul-mouthed Sun Hee was a wonderful cook. She fed their friends bean paste soup and *pulgoki*—barbequed beef—and demonstrated how to crisp up a sheet of seaweed over the flame of a gas stove.

"See." Sun Hee ripped off a piece and shoved it into Fiona's mouth. "Better than chips!"

Sun Hee attended Virgin Marries' shows and picked fights with the punks. She worked as a cocktail waitress at the Hyatt downtown and shanghaied a small fortune in tips every night. After dinner, Sun Hee sprang forth from her kitchen, requesting that Fiona go to the corner store with her to buy cigarettes. The two left in the middle of a raging debate about original sin and who really wrote the Bible, Maurice's Adam's apple bobbing up and down in his scrawny throat. Sun Hee whooped as they hit the street.

"Let's go for a walk!"

"North Beach is an excellent neighbourhood for people-watching." Fiona grabbed Sun Hee's hand. "So, are you a Dadaist?"

"No! That's Paul and his boys."

"Boys is right."

"*Doltaegaris!*" growled Sun Hee.

"What's a *doltaegari*?"

"A moron."

"I wonder if that's where the word dolt comes from?"

"Haven't you noticed? I'm the one who plays Devil's advocate."

"I have noticed the conversation heats up whenever you're around."

"Yeah." Sun Hee grinned. "Must be all that kimchi, huh?"

"What are you then? Besides a hot head?"

"A poet. No. The muse. I'm the muse."

"Is that why Paul's so in love with you?"

"Yeah. Plus, I give good head."

They laughed.

"You're a poet. You've got all the qualifications. Crazy and gifted."

With no interest in Vesuvio's or City Lights—Sun Hee was not a Beat either—they crossed Columbus, dodging taxis and a pair of traffic-stopping transvestites.

"There's Ru Paul!" yelled Sun Hee, pointing to the black person wearing a blond wig and towering fuck-me heels.

"Who is Ru Paul? Or maybe I should say, what is Ru Paul?"

"Never mind. I forgot, you just came out of the deep freeze. The Great White North."

The barker from Carol Doda's pounced on them, Sun Hee flipping the bird as they strolled by. Aromas assailed: espresso from Savoy Tivoli, pesto pizza from Golden Boy, basil and rosemary from Bozzini's bakery. Tendrils of slinky jazz slipped between the saloon doors of a club on the corner of Grant and Vallejo, marijuana smoke signalling from the alleyway.

"I'm not sure I appreciate being led around the streets of San Francisco like your bitch."

Sun Hee approached a leather bar. "Come on. It's fun watching them sling their rump roasts around." She opened the door with a grunt. A pair of bare buttocks in chaps gamboled across the dance floor to Abba's "Waterloo."

"I hate Abba."

"What? Fiona, if you hate Abba, you hate music!"

"Hey, Sun Hee, opinions are like assholes. Everybody's got one."

She laughed and pointed. "Especially in there!"

A poker-faced urban cowboy holding a black leather rose bumped into them as he entered the club, peering at them through Lina Wertmüller frames as if they were lunatics.

"Are you some kind of fag hag?" asked Fiona.

Sun Hee tossed the notion away like a soiled hankie. "No. It's just that straight men are so boring."

"Men are boring."

Sun Hee smiled waggishly. "And predictable. Let's go have a drink!"

It seemed the most natural thing in the world, tossing back Rusty Nails, Fiona's hand between Sun Hee's thighs, stoking their ardour under the table, stealing kisses.

"Hey, girlfriend!" A big foghorn of a transvestite blew in and plunked down at the next table. "DOA plays the Mab tonight," the HeShe announced to an irritated friend. Fiona's ears pricked. "Just left Joey Shithead standing on Castro. Not much in the way of queer bait. Hey! I wanna go to Mass. Come with me. You're the only Catholic I know."

"No way. I'm on my knees half the time as it is now."

Fiona and Sun Hee suppressed giggles. A bloated, middle-aged man in a cheap business suit leered at them.

"I don't think women should be allowed to be lesbians," he said, "until all the men have wives."

The girls howled. "But, we're not lesbians." Sun Hee smiled sweetly. "And your mother has a bald pussy."

Laughing hysterically, the girls waved goodbye and hauled themselves out of the booth. They staggered onto the sidewalk and plodded up a hill. Sun Hee pulled Fiona into the entrance of a round, sunken courtyard, ringed in patches of manicured lawn and rusty oaks. She opened the gate, darted in, then slammed it in Fiona's face. Kissing through the steel bars, Fiona begged to be let in.

"What's the magic word?" demanded Sun Hee.

"Please?"

"Wrong."

"Coochie?"

"Wrong."

"Sun Hee?"

"You win!"

They sat on a stone bench, groping and kissing, Fiona big and clumsy. It's like playing with a doll, she thought. Sun Hee unbuttoned Fiona's shirt and heaved out her breast.

"They're so big!"

"No one's ever said that before! Guess they're Grand Tetons compared to these," Fiona teased, squeezing Sun Hee's tawny nipple.

"You biittchhhh."

Fiona pulled her head back by her mane. "You love it," she said, crushing her mouth with a kiss like a boy.

The night ebbed. Time to escalate or move on. "Is there some place we can be alone?"

Sun Hee began to cry. She had to go home. They could suspend reality no longer. Paul must be worried.

"Fiona, sometimes I'm so afraid. I don't think I know how to love anybody."

"You? Afraid? You love him. I can tell."

Fiona believed it, but, as she made soothing sounds, wondered how Sun Hee would ever be sated. Sun Hee was on fire. Fiona dried her tears, walked her home, like any other pedestrians. They shared one last woeful kiss before Sun Hee dragged her feet up a gloomy stairwell, Fiona nearly overcome by the throbbing between her legs.

"I kissed a girl last night."

Rita turned with stunned expression. "That beautiful Japanese girl?"

"Korean. Does that mean I'm a lesbian?"

"I don't know. I doubt it. You still like men, right?"

"I hate men."

"I mean sexually. Sometimes you like women."

"I did fall in love with my first grade teacher, Miss Young. When I was nine, I used to take baths with my best friend Nancy. We'd draw letters on each other's backs. When I was twelve, I remember lying in bed next to my best friend Christine at a pajama party, aching with lust, only I didn't know that's what it was."

"You're bisexual. Bi. "

"Shit. I don't want to be bi."

"You don't. Everybody hates them, bi phobia rampant. It confounds."

"Well that appeals to me."

"Hets think they're promiscuous, blame them for AIDS, and some gay people deny they even exist. You know what?" mused Rita. "I think there should be four genders. That's what the Navajo believe."

Fiona sighed. "Why can't I be normal? I've ruined my friendship with Sun Hee."

Band in van tooling down the freeway to L.A., buffeted by a hard rain, but bolstered by the aural raunch of Flipper. "I'm sure gonna miss my Frisco squeeze," announced Dolores.

"Oh yeah, Tom, the rocket scientist."

"He's a bike messenger. Hey, he keeps me warm at night."

Rita leaned over to lower the volume on "Love Canal."

"Aw!" said Fiona, "that's my favourite song." It had effectively drowned out the roar of rain pounding on the roof. "Always gotta have your mojo workin', right, Dolores?"

"Look who's talking!"

"You'll get over it," said Jackie. "You always do."

"But he's so . . . good."

"Dolores," said Fiona, "he's from Arkansas, for chrissakes."

"Let me just say this. They grow 'em big in Little Rock."

The Virgins emitted a collective groan. "Hey, it's not the meat, it's the motion." Rita extended her middle finger. "This is all the man I need."

The twins recoiled. "Puleeze!"

A touch of vertigo hit Fiona as the van began hydroplaning. She gulped, leaning against an amplifier until she could feel the rubber reconnect with the road.

"Shannon says the guitarist from the Heaters has a bent dick."

"No!" cried Jackie. "Miguel Henderson?"

"Yeah. She said it looks like ET's finger."

"Eeeuuuuhh! Gnarly!"

"That's hilarious!" said Rita.

"Shannon is hilarious."

"I wonder if it was circumcised?" said Jackie.

"Yuck. I hate those uncut ones. They look like sausages." Fiona glanced at Dennis. "Good thing our roadie can't hear us."

"Men are too squeamish for girl talk," said Rita.

Jackie nodded. "You know what I hate? Men who won't kiss. You know, deep, soulful kisses?"

"Yeah," said Fiona. "They kiss in the beginning, then get complacent."

"Women are the best kissers anyway." Rita looked out the windshield, checking on Dennis' progress.

"But how do you have sex with a woman?" asked Dolores.

Rita rolled her eyes. "That's a whole other Pandora's box, isn't it? Honestly, I think most straight men are closet cases."

"They will fuck anything that moves!" said Fiona. "Did you know VD was an animal disease? Some lonely shepherd screwed the sheep and passed it on to the rest of us. And you know that shepherd was a man 'cause they get all the really good jobs."

Rita raised her hand against a squall of laughter. "And at the same time they're uptight, homophobic hypocrites."

The twins didn't share their disdain for the opposite sex. "Your friend Sun Hee is still getting married to a man," said Dolores.

Fiona shrugged. "Yeah well, nobody's perfect."

She woke abruptly from a nightmare of talking drums and roaming equipment. It was excruciating, fearing that at every stop a hundred-pound Fender Twin amplifier might plow into her cranium. Body aching, Fiona hauled herself up and squinted through the windshield.

"Yay! We made it."

"Shhh," said Rita. "Don't wake up the twins."

The city's mute neon glowed, Fiona feeling like a six-year-old with a secret.

Dennis laughed. "Every time I'm on the Hollywood freeway, it's like I never left. It's a time warp, I swear."

I'm in Hollywood. "Hey, I'm in Hollywood! This is Hollywood," said Fiona, as if a tongue mauling would make it real. "Look, there's Frederick's of Hollywood!"

Housed in a purple building with pink awnings, Fiona recalled their ads in the back of Jeanette's romance magazines, scantily clad women in pink baby dolls and high-heeled pom-pom slippers.

They passed taco stands, psychic readers, tattoo parlours, adult book-head and leather shops; storefronts shielded with black steel gates. Craggy scrawls of piss on the sidewalk implicated winos huddled in vestibules. Dennis pointed out landmarks, delighted to play tour guide. They cruised past the Capital Records building, the Frolic Room, the Dianetics Store—Scientology headquarters—Musso & Frank Grill and Grauman's Chinese Theatre. Fatigued nearly to the point of delirium, they headed to their L.A. crash pad, Fiona watching Dennis' pensive expression in the rear-view mirror.

"Real people live in Hollywood," he said, "just like any other place. Only difference is, filmmaking's the cottage industry."

"What are you saying?"

"I'm saying it's not Mecca. It's just another neighbourhood."

"Ah, don't burst my bubble! It might as well be Oz. The end of the rainbow."

A place with enough muscle to flood a small B.C. town—the entire world—with visions of Mickey Mouse and singing cowboys, Fiona's first movie theatre experience, *Mary Poppins.*

Jeanette claimed her youngest clutched the armrests, mouth agape, throughout its entire one hundred and thirty-nine minutes. Fiona and her sisters loved engaging in an odd ritual, singing *"California here I come, right back where I started from,"* when they rode in the car. No one knew why. Surely they saw it in a Saturday morning cartoon. *And here I am! Let them rot in all that miserable rain.*

Elegant giant palms lined both sides of Beachwood Canyon Drive, a wiggly Dr. Seuss vista. Fiona admired the stately, Spanish Colonial homes with their balconies, red tiled roofs, gardens of eucalyptus and jasmine perfuming the night. Arriving at their destination, they roused the twins and went to the door. A stroppy, bespectacled Beaver Cleaver peeped out at them.

"We're friends of the Controllers," said Dennis. "Didn't Karla tell you?"

The young man shook his head, assuming they'd leave, but Dennis pushed past him, Virgin Marries in tow.

"Hey!"

"Hey, we're desperate, get used to it." Everyone but their hapless host laughed. "Don't worry, dude. We'll be outta here tomorrow."

Hollywood Boulevard in the morning was a most rude awakening. Beneath the spotlight of California's ruthless sun, Fiona could see past the stars to the dope fiends, hookers, and bag ladies. They headed east on Sunset, through Silver Lake and Echo Park.

"Where are we going?" asked Rita.

"Sound check. You're playing the Hong Kong Cafe tonight."

Dennis passed tickets. *The Virgin Marries. The Gears. Friday, March 5. Show Continuous.* Fiona was surprised to find L.A.'s Chinatown much smaller than Vancouver's.

"The hard-core bands play here." Dennis pointed to a building across the courtyard. "The new wave sucks play over there at Madame Wong's."

"I don't care," said Fiona. "I don't want to play either of 'em."

The club was a long room with a low ceiling, tiles painted gold, walls of rice paper silkscreened with dragons and butterflies, claustrophobic, even with a row of windows.

"The sound is shitty." Dennis winked. "Don't expect much, and bear in mind, it isn't you, it's the room."

Dennis was a capable road manager, and he and Rita had appointed themselves de facto Mom and Pop. Dolores plopped down on the shallow stage with her guitar.

"The place is packed. This is great! Our L.A. debut."

"They must be out to see Kidd Spike's new band, the Gears," said Fiona. "He was in the Controllers with Karla, you know. They had a huge following."

The girls were in trouble with the club because their guest list was too long.

"How can our guest list be too long?" asked Dolores. "We don't know anybody."

Jackie pointed at Dennis. The locals greeted them all warmly, Virgin Marries thrilled to be introduced to Craig Lee of The Bags, KK, drummer for The Screamers, Margot, bassist for the Go-Go's, and, crème de la scum, Darby Crash of the notorious Germs, whom Dennis had known since he was Bobby Pyn.

The Virgins followed Dennis down the stairs into the back alley to unload their equipment. A silver convertible Bentley screeched to a stop, cargo of pretty girls bouncing up and down. The driver, slinky and Chinese, threw her arms around Dennis. He introduced the Virgin Marries to Chloe Chan.

"See you inside. I gotta park this monster."

The band hauled their amps up a long flight of stairs. "So, Dennis, where are your friends now?" grumbled Rita.

They ran through a cursory sound check, went for a walk, and found Dennis' Beverly Hills brats in a tiger-striped upholstered booth in the First Empire bar. They were awfully friendly, ordering the Virgins a round of drinks, Fiona, a farmer's daughter next to their sleek urbanity. Soon their claws were out, tongues lashing the L.A. scene between sips of their martinis and Pimms Cups; Chloe, Misty, Melanie, and Michelle quick to inform the girls they grew up with Dennis, their folks all film industry types. They'd be eaten alive in Vancouver with their slick hairdos and designer duds, thought Fiona. All snooty and flawless, aspiring models or actresses, except Melanie, who wanted to be a photographer. Rita whispered that it was the best way for a groupie to get backstage, citing rich girl Linda McCartney. Chloe and company prided themselves on consistently getting backstage passes, but they were not groupies. The topic turned to the Go-Go's. Melanie ordered another drink, demanding the waitress to hurry.

"They're getting signed! To Sire."

"Cute." Chloe mimed gagging. "They're so fucking cute, with their polka dots and capris."

Michelle concurred. "Yeah, even the porkers in the band are cute porkers. Can you believe Belinda was in the Germs!"

Rita shifted her weight forward. "I thought these people were your friends?"

You'd think she'd cut one, the way they looked at her in utter astonishment.

"Well, we can hardly wait to see you girls play tonight," cooed Misty.

Chloe smiled. "We'll have to introduce you to Cecil."

"Who's Cecil?" asked Jackie, blowing smoke rings, feigning nonchalance.

"Cecil Zavaroni. Big-time record producer. He's got a real thing for girl groups." Chloe applied lipstick sans mirror. "And anything British."

"We're Canadian," said Rita.

"Oh. I thought it was the same thing."

Her girls giggling, Chloe blotted full lips on a matchbook. Fiona and the twins downed many free drinks, Rita scowling. Melanie looked Fiona up and down.

"You should be a model."

With such high cheekbones, Fiona wondered if Melanie was native.

Dennis came to collect them. Fiona downed her drink and

stood, sort of, hurling her body forward through a tangle of bare limbs. She dragged her feet upstairs in dread. Maybe not dread. Dread had another meaning, since Rita and reggae. Struggle definitely, learning everything the hard way. *What does Misty struggle with besides a blow dryer?*

A motley stew of humanity awaited: surfers, rockabilly cats, preppies, Mexicans, blacks, queers, nerds, queens, punks of all nations, and even a few hippies and people over thirty, all expecting the Go-Go's, *and the Go-Go's, we're not.* Skittish as a stray Doberman, Fiona ran to the bathroom. She couldn't pee. Pent up, cranky, Fiona headed for the stage, audience a gauntlet, *and me, sacrificial virgin.* She climbed up and grabbed the mic stand. Lately, Fiona liked to pretend it was her dance partner, but without much success. *How did I get myself into this? Who do I think I am?*

"Now! All the way from Vancouver, Canada, The Virgin Maaarrrries!"

Rita counted in. *Can they tell how scared I am? Christ. I'm no actress!* Fiona trained her eyes on the beer-soaked Astroturf. *There's a reason I'm up here and you're down there. Why can't we come in together? Jackie late this time. Some eye contact would help. This fucking band! Never look at me, except when I screw up. No support. Nada. Goddammit! I can't breathe. Faces. I know what they expect. Too much! At least people aren't gobbing, bashing, some even listening.* Chloe placed four beers on the stage. *Uh oh. Now we're in trouble. They like us.* Their "96 Tears" cover went over well, but the audience didn't seem to relate to Wire's "Fragile" as much as Fiona. "Lambert Kidd" was well received, ditto with "Let's Play House," the chorus a sixties girl group parody.

POW! POW! POW!

Gawd! Now they're taking pictures. Fiona watched as her new friend Melanie—bittersweet, Nikon-armed Melanie—climbed onstage. A teasing, flitting damselfly, she reached out and placed her hand between Fiona's thighs.

No.

Appraising each other through the lens.

Yes.

Melanie moved her hand down the back of Fiona's leg, the length of her boot, audience going berserk. She sprawled on the stage to shoot, thick tresses fanning out over the wet floor. Fiona spread her legs wide, planting one foot on either side of Melanie's hips, singing, *"There's too much to swallow, too much to choke down."* Fiona leaned down, lunging toward Melanie's belly, breasts, as if branding them with the microphone. Hoots! Hollers. Howls! Melanie rose. The girls twisted, turned off each other, colliding Apache dancers. Hanging from the pillars, dangling from the beams, the crowd crawled over each other to gain a better look. *"Everything gets in your mouth."* Glancing up from guitar tempest, Dolores exchanged glances with Jackie, Rita pounding out exact meter. Tossed to the top of the sound swell, hit by a WOMPF of air, Fiona fell to her knees. *"She tries to touch colour, she tries to kiss truth."* Crowd, going gaga, rising up into a horde. *"But it just gets in her mouth."*

Out of film. Song finished. Set over. The crowd would not stop, Virgins chanted back onstage for an encore. "The Great Indoors" again, then a new song, "Coral Aggression," too soon, Fiona was certain. No one noticed. Finally allowed to exit, the girls leaned against the wall, panting, gloating, Jackie and Dolores slapping Fiona on the back.

"You were great!"

"We were great!"

Chloe, Misty, and Michelle brought more beer, offered to put them up. *Why are they being so nice? They must think Canadians are blue bloods, or French, or Eskimos. They don't know how boring we are.*

Chloe introduced Fiona to Tom Saltzman, publisher of *REJECT* magazine, a chunky man with massive arms, roomy cheeks, and unwavering smirk. He peered at her through tinted aviator glasses, handing her a copy. She held it by the corner as if it was covered in dung. *Smut for vampires, judging by the cover.*

"Wow," he said. "It was like watching Iggy Pop. Are you French?"

"*Oui.* Canadian. I was born in Quebec. Les Québécois."

"Ooh-la-la. Hey, I wanna interview you."

Dennis yelled, "Rampage is here! He just put his fist through a plate-glass window."

What the fuck? They ran downstairs. "Holy shit!" yelled Fiona. It had been a bakery. Huge plates of glass sheeted the sidewalk, an alarm blasting the alley. "He must have frapped his hand!"

A van pulled up and screeched to a halt. They observed a shock of black roots and peroxided hair as Randy scrambled to get in.

"He had a fight with his girlfriend," said Jackie. "She was taking off with some guy."

"Who's his girlfriend?"

"Melanie Bowman."

"Chloe's friend?" asked Fiona. "The Indian princess?"

"Yeah. The one who was crawling up your leg. He's crazy about her."

Chloe got the twins, Rita and Dennis drove off to his cousin's place in Pacific Palisades, and Michelle got Fiona. With both parents being doctors, Michelle's house was high up in the Hollywood Hills. How do these girls sleep at night, wondered Fiona, so far from the train tracks? Hunger. Fear. Well, they're free. Freedom their birthright. Why not mine?

Squared away in the solarium, Fiona woke surrounded by a sky of glass. Ah, linens, duvet cover embroidered with roses. Ensuites with Mexican tiled tubs and gold faucets. Tiffany lamps, fresh-cut flowers, crystal vases, wall-to-wall carpeting, the thick, plush cream-coloured kind, nothing shaggy or orange about it. *I am liking this.*

Fiona wandered around the library, perusing volumes of Austen, Faulkner, Wordsworth. *Great name for a writer. Picasso!* Sketches mostly, nudes and Minotaurs. They must have been tossed off, but still, so vital. And he is so dead. *How sad is it that we all die? Even Picasso.* Fiona wondered about Michelle's parents. Are they in love with the arts and each other too? She headed to the terrace with a volume of Yeats, hummingbirds hovering over fuchsia bougainvillea. Her stomach lurched at a whiff of bacon drifting up from the kitchen. Fiona heard her name. Michelle entered, her mother following. *What was I expecting? Joan Collins in a lab coat?* Stout and frowzy, Daphne fussed about, apologizing for the towel shortage and the maid not coming in.

"Oh, Mother," moaned Michelle.

They invited Fiona to breakfast and left her to dress. Hearing whispers, she put her ear to the door.

"When is she leaving?"

"Oh, Mother!"

Michelle gobbled down a bowl of Cheerios and ran off to school, Fiona vexed by a cramp of envy. Patriarch Dr. Rosen gave her a ride to the store in his Mercedes. She prayed they had Rothmans. *American cigarettes are so stinky. Saltpeter, yuck.* They engaged in a lively discussion about the Eastern Bloc, Václav Havel, and Charter 77. Dr. Rosen, a semi-retired radical, leaned back and looked her over.

"Well, Miss Larochelle, you're certainly well informed. Wish my daughters would read something besides *Vogue*."

Guess they're the reason he's had to compromise his principles. His daughters ducked in and out of the house all day, eyeing Fiona, hoping to catch her stealing the silverware. She did lust after Michelle's cowboy boots, closet lined with every colour and texture imaginable. *Très chic* when paired with a floral print frock, apropos for the rockabilly, cow punk, neo-bluegrass, or western swing scenes so popular in L.A. Wild West indeed.

Fiona gorged on Brie, Gorgonzola, lox, smoked turkey breast, and black forest ham with hot mustard on rye bread. *No wonder they're so fat. Michelle must be adopted.*

Darby Crash surprised her with a visit, directing a scowl at Judy, the eldest, who scurried off.

"That one got knocked up on purpose. Just to see if she could! Stupid bitch had an abortion."

"Some people have too much time on their hands. And money."

They chatted, Fiona vainly explaining her perceived differences between Canada and the U.S. "We have a social safety net. We take care of our sick and elderly."

96

Darby pulled Coronas from the fridge and handed her one. "I'd rather be a fascist than a communist."

"We're not communists. A lot of us may be socialists."

"Same thing."

She laughed and changed the subject. "I didn't know San Francisco and L.A. were so different."

Frisco people were arty, into heavy drugs, listening intently to edgy, cerebral British bands like PIL and Magazine. A lot of LA punks scarfed down Quaaludes like candy, boozed and worshipped Sid Vicious. Though menacing, they could be benevolent as individuals. The Germs might be one of the most dreaded bands on the West Coast, but there in the kitchen, Darby was just a kid with a skateboard and skinned knees.

"I have noticed people in this scene are pretty smart," said Fiona, "especially about music; really into their rock and roll heritage."

Darby nodded. "We're nationalists. Fucking British invaders. Beatles, Rolling Stones, Bowie. They ripped us off. Wankers! This is where it all started. The good ole U S of A."

"Maybe I have landed in the right place, the birthplace of jazz, R&B. Rock and roll. Screw London. Maybe we should move to L.A."

Fiona felt right at home with Darby and all the other misfits, aliens, ex-pats, and transplants. A lot of snowbirds resided south of the border as well.

"All the smart Canadians leave," she said.

On the other hand, Fiona didn't belong in L.A. either. No one did. It was a desert, for chrissakes, a desert sucking the Owens Valley dry, as portrayed in *Chinatown*, a whole other can of worms she and Darby dissected the rest of the waning afternoon.

"Wow," said Fiona. "Disneyland and opening for X all in one day!"

Dennis warned the Virgin Marries to dress down. "You

won't get in with florescent pink hair. They will very politely refuse you entrance because you don't meet the standards of their unspoken dress code."

"Guess we look un-American, eh?" said Fiona.

Dennis argued with Rita over her trail mix and canteen of water. "You can't bring in your own food."

Rita bitched about how we're all consumers, not citizens, how corporations, not democracies rule the planet, but she calmed down and they all played innocent long enough to get in.

"Wow. Disneyland! I'm in Disneyland."

"Okay, Fiona, you can cut with the awestruck adolescent bit."

"Okay, Rita, I've only been dying to come to Disneyland since I was five years old."

"It's an amusement park. Okay? Run by a bunch of fascists."

"Well, if it's good enough for Khrushchev," said Dennis, "it's good enough for me. Yeah! He came over in '59. They wouldn't let him go to Disneyland. And he was pissed! Asked why it was so dangerous. Did they have rocket launching pads in the Magic Kingdom?"

"Okay, so we're in. Now what?" asked Rita.

"We walk," said Dennis.

And walk they did, the whole day and the whole length of the Happiest Place on Earth. They strolled down Main Street, U.S.A., with its animatronic President Lincoln sitting out eternity, Disney's in-your-face patriotism tickling their Canadian funny bones. All tight on cash, the girls chose their rides carefully, Fiona lining up for Mr. Toad's Wild Ride and Magic Mountain. Dolores was dying to go through It's A Small World and persuaded the Virgins to ride in the little boat with her. They immediately regretted floating between papier-mâché mountains, and being blasted from all sides by a hideously saccharine melody. Rita feigned puking into the shallow moat.

"The Virgin Marries Do Disneyland!" Dennis photographed them in front of Cinderella's Castle. "We have to go on the bucket ride, so you can get a look at the whole park." He pointed to the brightly coloured orbs gliding overhead. Once aboard, Dolores and Jackie began dropping gobs of spittle onto the people below, cackling and jeering.

"Don't," said Rita. "They'll kick us out. We're under surveillance, you know."

The girls looked to Dennis. He nodded.

"Creepy." Jackie pulled her head back in.

They consumed huge quantities of hamburgers, ice cream, and candy, but not without Rita griping about prices. Exiting Fantasyland, Fiona noticed a Snow White concealing a walkie-talkie. She elbowed Dennis.

"I can't believe you used to come here high on acid!" Several hours later Fiona whined, "I must be sprouting little black mouse ears by now."

She was tired, begged to leave. They argued about the Main Street Electrical Parade, Jackie and Dolores pleading until everyone agreed to stay. Dennis asked if they'd like to play Dead at Disneyland while they waited. He seemed to harbour a morbid fascination with the park's death toll.

"Five guests and one cast member have been killed on Disneyland rides. No one's ever been officially declared dead on Disneyland property."

"What's a cast member?" asked Fiona.

"Those guys." Dennis pointed at a passing Goofy.

Jackie took the bait. "So, how do you play Dead at Disneyland?"

Dennis dropped to his knees, clutching his chest and keeling over, adding a slight, spastic head-jerk, nearly hitting a lamppost. People gasped, paused, then moved on, nervously glancing back. Dolores abruptly turned into a puddle in the path of several tourists. Then Jackie tumbled down some fake stairs and slumped into a flowerbed. A father with two frightened children chuckled at Dennis lying face down on the flagstones. A Country Jamboree Bear approached and stooped over Dennis, gently prodding him. He might have been saying something, but who could tell with that inscrutable cartoon grin? Then, to everyone's surprise, the bear straddled Dennis and sat on him. Fiona couldn't decide if he was an entertainer or a cop. People laughed, but others were upset, more suspicious and annoyed than concerned.

"Please follow me." Busted. A security guard dressed as a tourist flashed his ID.

"Christ," said Rita. "Should have known we couldn't go to Disneyland without an incident."

He led them to a station house on Main Street, through a door to an office. White-shirted Disney henchmen quickly surrounded them. Dennis was unusually quiet throughout their lecture on responsibility and good citizenship. Soon, they pulled out photographs.

"Look," shrieked Dolores. "Here's a good one of you Jackie!"

The tallest White-Shirt raised his voice. "We have to call your parents."

"No, Steve," said the boss gravely. "I think we better call the police."

"Go ahead," said Dolores.

Fiona poked her in the ribs. *This is getting out of hand. Why doesn't Dennis say something?* "Dennis!" She stamped her foot. "Do something."

"You'll have to call long distance," he informed the boss. "Their parents live in Canada."

The Disney staffers glanced at each other, then abruptly escorted the Virgins out the door to the main gate, but not before scolding them again.

Jackie let out a hoot. "Why did they let us go?"

"They're worried about bad publicity," said Dennis.

"That's right," said Rita. "They're not about to let their precious public image be sullied, or perceived as unfriendly to tourists."

The Virgins were startled by signs posted at Club 88 warning that by entering they were consenting to be part of Penelope Spheeris' documentary, *The Decline of Western Civilization*, small

100

corner stage made smaller by the film crew's klieg lighting. *Part of, not featured in.* Disappointed, Fiona was equally annoyed when forced to use the production company's strange, bulky studio mic, which she thought resembled a dildo.

Dennis introduced the girls to L.A. legends Exene Cervenka and John Doe. Wasp-waisted queen bee Exene addressed people as Dear, Dennis just one of the many strays the X clan had adopted. Fiona got up to perform, feeling as if she were playing for her life, Virgins thrilled when John and Exene later reported their approval to Dennis.

X launched their set, clobbering them all with murder ballad "Johnny Hit and Run Paulene," followed by "Los Angeles," an in-your-face rant on racism; something Canadians are too polite to discuss or admit to, despite having fucked over native, Chinese, Ukrainian, Japanese, and other peoples. Exene ripped at her hair, pitched her small body about. Grinning guitarist Billy Zoom commanded the stage like a rockabilly gunslinger, wearing cuffed jeans and a silver leather jacket. Drummer DJ Bonebrake lived up to his name and charismatic John Doe looked like a cross between James Dean and Li'l Abner. "Intelligent sleaze," but hardly hard-core enough for a lot of the locals. Fuck that, she thought. X is original. It takes guts to be original.

The girls were invited to a tar beach party in Silver Lake after the show, the twins swiftly filching beer from the fridge. Dennis entered one of the bedrooms, then quickly re-emerged looking dazed.

"What's going on in there?" Fiona peeked over his shoulder. "Oh my God!" *Hieronymus Bosch.* All she could see was a squirming pile of naked bodies grabbing, poking, slithering.

Dennis smiled sheepishly. "Orgy."

"This is El Lay," said Rita.

Dennis laughed. "Melanie and Michelle are in there, asking for the Virgin Marries."

"Tell Melanie to come out here," said Fiona.

"Ahem. I think she's busy coming in there," said Rita.

At that moment, some joker put "Group Sex" by the Circle Jerks on the stereo.

"Like I said, porn capital of the U.S." Rita shook her head.

Dennis laughed. "When in Rome . . ."

Fiona downed her beer. "I think I'll go. I'm tired."

X songs ricocheted through her skull during the drive. "I wanna be Exene! Empowered. In control."

"Ha!" snorted Rita. "That's presuming a lot. How do you know she's not struggling just like everybody else?"

"What? You think she's fake? A poseur?"

"Persona. I think it's a persona. Fake implies deceit. A persona is more like an alter ego. That's Exene up there all right, but a larger-than-life version of Christine, her real name."

"She's so tiny."

"She does possess an Édith Piaf quality. The sparrow, tiny but tough. Abiding."

Waiting on the man, the nefarious Tom Saltzman, Dennis and Fiona watched a young couple glide by, man on a bicycle tugging a woman on a skateboard.

"Why do married people look alike?"

Dennis laughed. "How do you know they're married?"

"They act married."

Dennis didn't like Tom Saltzman. Nobody did. He was strange, even by L.A. underground standards. A car approached. Saltzman emerged with a tall, skinny, helmet-haired Ric Ocasek doppelgänger, introduced as his photographer, Don. With only a vague notion of what to shoot, Don suggested the police academy down the road.

"You like a man in uniform?" asked Saltzman. He pointed to the Elysian Park men's washroom. "Hey, there's some radical graffiti all over the tiles in there."

"No way!" said Dennis.

"A bit cliché, don't you think?" asked Fiona.

Saltzman raised an eyebrow. "Got any piercings?" he asked, scanning her up and down.

"I like this light," said the photographer, "under these old palms."

They framed Fiona against a giant cross-hatched tree trunk.

"Do I look tough?"

Dennis laughed. "You look like you just lost your ice cream cone."

They tried a few more locations and poses, shooting two rolls of film. Saltzman waved Fiona over to a picnic table, pulled out a tape recorder, brushed away some bird shit, and set it down.

"So, are you a virgin?

This is gonna be fun.

"Say something in French."

"I don't speak French. I wish I did, but we left Quebec when I was little."

"Too bad. That would turn me on," said Saltzman, invoking a lame impression of Gomez Addams.

Fiona stared at him coldly.

"You like Los Angeles?"

"I did. Until someone tried to rip off our equipment last week. But, yeah, I still like L.A., it's just weird."

"It is weird. One of its charms. So, Fiona, what kind of men do you like?"

"I can't say I 'like' men." She wondered, should I just be honest and direct, or fuck with his head too? "I thought we were going to talk about the Virgin Marries?"

"We are. How old are you? You're not jail bait, are you?"

"Two things my aunt says you never ask a lady: her weight and her age. I'm sixteen."

"And no lady, right?" Grinning, Saltzman peered at Dennis over the top of his glasses. "Got a boyfriend?"

"No. Why not interview the whole band?"

"I don't interview girl bands. You can't get a word in edgewise. So, Fiona, wanna be famous?"

"I'm not dying to be famous. Just wanna rule the world!" She smirked.

"Oh, yeah. Like being on top?"

"I like having artistic control. And I want to write songs

about something besides love."

"Anti-love songs. Gee, that's never been done. Are the Virgin Marries copying the Go-Go's?"

"Hey, we never even heard of the Go-Go's until we got to L.A.! You saw us play. You know we don't sound like the Go-Go's."

"Okay. So, what are you reading lately?"

"Anaïs Nin."

"The erotica?"

"The diaries."

"That haughty Parisian twat. Far too precious for my taste."

"Obviously."

REJECT was lying on the table. Besides music features and intriguing anti-fashion, its marginless pages brimmed with grotesque depictions of lepers, mutants, Saran-wrapped mugwumps, and flesh-eating disease victims.

"Do you do drugs?" asked Tom.

"Sometimes. Nothing heavy."

"Define heavy."

"You know, heroin, cocaine."

"Just say no, right? Got a single out?"

"Not yet."

Saltzman angled his head away from Dennis, whispering, "Will you go out with me?"

She was thinking he was too old for her when Dennis jumped to his feet. "Okay. That's it. Interview's over. Come on, we've got a mare to foal."

The photographer looked to Saltzman. Saltzman shrugged.

Fiona waved as they got into the van and pulled away. "What's this about a foal?"

"Mom called this morning. My favourite mare, Shalimar, is leaking colostrum. She's about to foal."

"Leaking what? No. Don't tell me. I don't want to know."

"And Mom wants to meet the Virgin Marries."

 ★ ★ ★ ★

They collected the Virgins and headed up to Dennis' folks' place near Santa Barbara, Fiona excited, insisting on a visit to the Santa Barbara Mission. The weather was glorious, their world a blue sphere; sky of sapphire, ocean of turquoise. She noticed a fantastic tree hanging off the cliffs, pistachio wood peeking out from peeling cinnamon bark.

"Madroña," said Rita, planting her big feet on the dash. "They're called arbutus in B.C."

Jackie and Dolores skulked and sulked. *Jackie is prettier.* She should have been interviewed, photographed.

"It's not surfing season, is it?" Fiona pointed to several zinc-nosed hangdogs trying to catch a wave.

Rita laughed. "It's always surfing season in California."

A kaleidoscope of kites whirred above Santa Barbara's tidy, expansive pier, gumbooted locals lazily fishing. Mottled pelicans waddled by, begging for tidbits like dogs. Kamikaze gulls zeroed in on the girls, one snatching Dolores' hot dog. She nearly cried.

They reached the pink adobe Queen of the Missions, situated in a natural amphitheatre, carved by the coastline and the Santa Ynez Mountains. They strolled past crumbling tombs, cactus gardens, and a lion's head stone fountain spitting water. Fiona gazed up at a looming crucifix—thorny crown, sunken gut, ragged loincloth, spikes driven through hands and feet of clay; Christ, so beautiful in his magnificent suffering. I am not a good Catholic, she thought. Fiona was good at ignoring martyrs and victims, whether Jesus, Jeanette, Dennis, or herself. The twins mimicked the strung-up Son of God and hugged the statues. Inside they found ten cubicles for praying to Christ, the Virgin of Guadalupe, and any number of saints.

High noon. Time to go; countryside arid inland. It seemed everybody drove a pickup in and out of the oak groves and hills carpeted with poppies and chaparral. Dennis waved to a local yokel in a Sunny Country 102.5 FM cap. Soon they pulled into a long driveway and headed toward several big barns and a huge, yellow Victorian house festooned in white gingerbread.

"Hey!" cried Dolores. "It's just like 'The Big Valley'."

Jeklins' Champion Arabians. Dennis had made it sound like a

hobby farm. He pulled into the yard and jumped out of the van, swooping his mother up into a big bear hug. More blonds. More Jenkins barrelled toward him, pouncing on his chest with glee. Dennis introduced his mother, Louise, and adolescent sisters, Tina and Nicole. The property was overrun with goats, geese, ducks, chickens, calico cats, Labrador dogs, and Elvis, the potbellied pig; the only beast rating an introduction and aptly named, propelling himself forward primarily from the pelvis.

They walked to the main barn, Fiona recognizing the horses as the breed in *Black Beauty*, one of her favourite childhood books. Her tail held high, Shalimar pranced in a circle around the paddock, pawing the ground. Louise explained that Arabians were exotic, hot-blooded, and bred strictly for show.

"She's gorgeous!" gushed Dolores.

"Horses are beautiful," said Fiona, "but I have no urge to ever mount one."

Louise smiled. "We love them. For their courage. Their spirit."

Dennis communed with his broodmare. "She's colicky. A couple of hours, I'd say. Monitor on?"

"Yes," replied Louise. "Let's hope she stays away from the wall."

"The wall?" asked Rita.

"Sometimes a mare tries to push the foal out by lying down with her butt up against the wall. We have to go in and relocate her. It's never easy and always annoying."

"Stupid," Fiona told Dennis under her breath.

"You're afraid of their magic." He pointed to a horseshoe tacked to the wall. "Their power."

"It's still a dumb animal."

Dennis threw up his hands. They left Shalimar to her labour, strolling back through tea roses and foxglove. A towering, barrel-chested man emerged from the house; Doug Jeklin, as blond and good-looking as his son. They embraced.

"Been on the phone all morning, he has," groused Louise.

Doug smiled and shook their hands. "Just bringin' home the bacon, honey. And I have to get back to work. I'll see you all for

106

supper."

Friendly enough, thought Fiona, but unlike Dennis, very low-key. Strong, silent type? Why is the wife always the extrovert? On the home front anyway.

Louise showed them to their rooms and, most importantly, the shower. Downstairs later, Fiona found her setting out a pitcher of lemonade. They chatted, Fiona chomping ice cubes until Louise informed her it was bad for her teeth. They went outside to a gigantic herb wheel.

"Did Dennis tell you he quit law school?"

"Law school!"

"He was enrolled at UCLA School of Law. He was going to be an attorney."

Dennis sauntered over, so funky Fiona could smell him through the lavender. A familiar odour, after all their miles together on the road; a comforting odour, the way her father's had once been. Fiona held her nose.

"She's gathering intelligence, isn't she?" Dennis pointed to his mother.

Louise rose and turned to him. "Your father's going to grill a leg of lamb. You'll have to help him with the coals. Doug takes his role of barbecue chef very seriously."

Dennis nibbled on some chives. "He's gonna rake me over the coals."

Louise sent him inside to shower. Rita ambled over, the three chatted amiably. Dennis soon emerged from the house scrubbed, shirtless, ready for anything in a well-blocked cowboy hat. He motored across the compound to the van and retrieved a shiny blue and gold hibiscus shirt.

"Hey, dude!" shouted Fiona. "Wait till Dolores gets a load of you. She'll think she died and went to heaven!" *Or Hawaii.*

"Everything about him is loud, isn't it?" said Louise.

"A real upright guy though," replied Rita.

Louise smiled. "And highly motivated. Even if he has 'dropped out'; something his father doesn't understand."

Dennis pointed to the barn. Rita caught up to him.

"Still, he's lucky to have such supportive parents," said

Fiona.

"We've only done what any parents would do."

"Not any parents. 'Parent' was never a verb to mine. I disowned them."

Louise regarded Fiona with pity. *Now she'll say she's sure my parents are worried. That I should go home, back to school, blah, blah, blah.* Fortunately, Rita emerged from the barn and beckoned.

"I'll stay here," said Fiona. "No foaling mares for me, thank you."

Chuckling, Louise handed her the basket of herbs. Fiona joined the twins on the veranda, smoking and gabbing. Louise returned shortly after, Rita and daughters in tow. The women convened in the cool kitchen, redolent with cumin and cucumber. Louise assigned tasks: chopping vegetables, stirring sauce, grating cheese. They watched Shalimar on the monitor, throwing her head back at her stomach, nuzzling and licking herself.

"What's she doing?" asked Dolores.

"She's in pain." Louise tied her hair back before lopping off the top of a red bell pepper.

Jackie stared. "Poor thing."

"You have no idea. Still, they have it easy, compared to humans."

Tina giggled and pelted Nicole with a carrot peel. Nicole bonked Tina on the head with a radish.

"Girls. Settle down." Louise's daughters flashed crossed eyes at one other. "The human pelvis isn't wide enough for childbirth, due to our bipedalism. Which is why we have year-round estrus, to up the odds of infants surviving."

Jackie and Dolores exchanged glances, unnerved by Louise's earth mother routine, as Tina and Nicole calmly diced and peeled.

"Fifty-two hours of labour with Dennis, twenty-seven with Tina, and twenty-two with Nicole."

Rita put down her knife. "Fifty-two hours!"

"Oh yes!" Louise laughed. "All weekend. Nine pounds, four ounces. I refused the Cesarean. The drugs too. I wanted to be lucid. Own the experience."

"At least it got a little easier," ventured Jackie.

"Every pregnancy's different. They cannot be controlled, as much as the obstetricians would like you to think."

"I'm never having kids," said Fiona. "My sister Maureen had a baby, then fobbed it off on our mom, the same mom that messed us up so bad."

"I hope that means you practise birth control. And never say never, Fiona. You don't know how you'll feel ten years down the road."

"Ten years! No. I can't imagine. Ten years. Gawd!"

Rita patted her on the head. "Fiona is prone to all-encompassing statements."

Louise coordinated an incredible meal: pinto beans, corn tortillas, chips with homemade salsa, a tray of enchiladas and another brimming with peaches and watermelon, and Doug's killer rosemary-seasoned and aromatic leg of lamb to top it all off. They feasted in twilight beneath a grape arbour, bluebottle flies bobbing in zephyrs of mesquite. Doug lit TIKI torches.

"You have the coolest parents on the planet," said Jackie.

"I've never seen such a sexy old guy," whispered Dolores, giggling.

Louise appeared with fresh strawberries and shortcake, whipped cream flowing lava-like, everyone moaning, protesting they were too full to eat anymore.

"But you have to. They're from my garden."

Wish Louise was my mother. It was obvious where Dennis got his generous good nature.

"But she doesn't take crap from anybody. Including my dad."

Doug removed his Top of the Food Chain apron, sat down and handed Junior an Anchor Steam. "All right then. And what are your plans, Son?"

Dennis sighed. "Later, Dad." His gaze fell on a monitor. "Shalimar!"

A stampede to the barn ensued. Fiona and the twins remained sitting, content to smoke and drink under the stars, well clear of the blood and guts.

"All right. Well, I'm going to sit down." Louise flopped into a chaise lounge, put her feet up. "I need a break."

Jackie raised a glass to her. "You certainly deserve one."

Louise gulped her Chardonnay before glancing at the monitor and doing a double take. "Uh oh."

"Uh oh, what?" asked Fiona in dread. Dennis had told them about a mare once killing a foal by slamming its head against the wall.

Louise peered at the monitor like a doctor inspecting an X-ray. "It's going to be a long night! Rosie's water just broke. Tina's mare. She wasn't due for another week. I'd better go alert the crew."

"Jesus H. Christ!" yelped Fiona. "Is it a full moon or something?"

Fiona and the twins sat back to watch, both mares down, Louise in one paddock with Rosie, Doug attending to Shalimar in another, Dennis running back and forth. As predicted, Shalimar was flush against the far wall, refusing to move. They coaxed, cajoled, and yelled in vain. She refused to budge, the foal a bulge under her thick hide. *Must be part mule.* Finally, in desperation Doug yarded on Shalimar's tail and heaved her far enough away from the wall for the foal to slither out. A blast of cheers shook the barn.

"*A la vida!*" Fiona and the twins toasted the newborn, Rosie's foal feted a few hours later after a long struggle to push past its shoulders.

As morning dawned, wine bottles were replaced with coffee and croissants. Dennis walked over from the barn, an odd expression on his face. Surely the horses were fine after all that effort and TLC.

"Darby's dead." Dennis collapsed into a chair. "They just found him. OD'd."

The trip back to L.A. was moist; a blur of tears, mourning giving them licence to drink more than usual. Germs blasting, Rita navigated the 101 South, Virgins and an inconsolable Dennis bawling throughout an impromptu memorial. Fiona wept, not just for Darby, but for herself, for all of them having to live with such cold, hard facts of life, their cheap mortality the hardest fact of all.

"I like it so loud, my ears bleed," she said to Dennis. "Volume can be a kind of silence, you know? Nothing can penetrate. You don't have to listen. Or think. And silence is golden."

Dennis nodded glumly. Golden boy, she thought. Darby too. Punk Peter Pan, stirring up shit his primary purpose in life. Rumour had it he drove out to the desert, wrote a note, then shot himself up with a lethal dose of heroin. What a romantic.

Dennis kicked Jackie's Ampeg. "I should have seen it! I shoulda been there for him."

"Hey, he's immortalized in Penelope's movie," offered Dolores.

Dennis smiled. "Everyone drawing on him with felt markers. Remember?"

"A martyr to the cause," said Jackie.

"What cause?" Rita stared them down in the rear-view mirror. "He was suicidal. Mentally ill. I'm amazed he earned as much credibility as he did. Always so drunk onstage."

"Charisma!" Jackie yelled at the back of Rita's head. "He had charisma."

"He was really smart too." Dolores turned to Dennis. "I liked what he had to say."

"Who cares what he said! The fuckin' words don't matter."

Fiona nudged Dennis' shoulder and offered half her apple. He cupped it in his palm, a tear plashing onto its snowy flesh.

"They matter to me," she said. "They mattered to Darby. They matter 'cause we matter. It's just so fucking sad he was more afraid of life than death."

Saltzman arrived in a woebegone white Cadillac Eldorado to

pick her up for their outing. Fiona refused to call it a date.

"Hey, Trashmeister. You look tired."

"Couldn't sleep."

"Darby?"

"Nooo. I could see that coming. Colitis. Kept me up all night. Old man's disease. And I'm not that fuckin' old."

"Thirty-two? That's old. So, what's colitis?"

"Your intestines flare up and you bleed from your asshole."

"Yuck! Ah, you just drink too much beer."

"You're right," he said, coolly navigating L.A.'s sprawl. "I think it's interesting Darby did it in a car. It's so L.A., using our cars for everything. Cars instead of communities."

They arrived at Saltzman's apartment, television droning, "Look, it's Cal Worthington and his dog Spot."

"Wanna meet Howard?" Saltzman opened a cupboard, revealing a can of Hormel tamales and a bottle of Tabasco sauce. "My pet roach." As if on cue, a huge cockroach scuttled off of a box of sugar cubes. "Don't worry, he won't bite." Saltzman leaned in. "But I might."

"That is so gross."

"Yeah, well he's been around so long, I don't have the heart to exterminate him."

"Hey, Saltzman, it's not a dog. It's a bug. Let's go."

"Yeah sure, soon as I have a snack." He cracked open a can of Colt 45 malt liquor and handed one to Fiona.

She downed it quickly. "Where are we going?"

"To see my friend Aaron."

"Who's Aaron?"

"A friend of mine."

Asshole. "Is he a musician?"

"Yeah, actually, he is. Plays guitar. Leads a western swing band."

They walked to the car. "So, what's Canada like?"

"Big, beautiful. Untouched, mostly."

"Sounds like you."

Fiona groaned. "You know, the only wildlife I ever see down here is dead. Roadkill."

"And that upsets you?"

"I can't believe how overrun this country is. There's no wilderness."

"Go back to Canada."

"I would, but I'm so frustrated when I'm there," said Fiona. "It may be big, but it's small, you know? Lot less gun violence though."

"Yeah, well, people kill people, not guns."

"That's bullshit."

"Ever heard of free will?"

"Hey, accidents will happen."

"You're right. If someone's too stupid to handle a gun, he'll probably shoot himself in the foot, when it would be better to shoot himself in the head, to no longer pollute the river of life. Very Darwinian." He picked up speed. "I find the effect of a loaded firearm intriguing. Know this guy who gets a hard-on every time he thinks about the .45 in his glovebox."

Fiona glanced at his glovebox. *Ah, this guy's no gangster.* He's a wuss, a wannabe, about as dangerous as a kid pouring salt on a slug.

"You should join the Beverly Hills Gun Club. Maybe Chloe can get you in."

"Look, my father's an outdoorsman. He taught me how to shoot. But we killed ducks. Which we ate. I hate handguns. They only have one purpose."

Saltzman pulled into some shady, wooded grounds, Fiona commenting on the dismaying number of homeless in Los Angeles.

"Why don't you just think of them as urban outdoorsmen?"

Asshole. They drove past an institutional building and neat rows of white crosses.

"What is this place?"

"Veteran's Administration."

"What are we doing here?"

"Visiting Aaron."

"Aaron's alive, right?"

Saltzman laughed as he pulled into a parking space. "For the most part."

"Is he a Vietnam vet?"

"Nope. Just a powder monkey."

They trudged across a green sea of lawn, landing upon a group of Confederates who were chatting and puffing Marlboros. "Where's Aaron Goldstein?"

"He's a Yankee this year." The toy soldier pointed to a big swarthy man across the way, who was cursing and yarding on a rusty wheeled cannon.

"Hah! He must be pissed! He so relishes playing a Dixie Jew."

"Which battle are they re-enacting, dare I ask?"

"Gettysburg. I don't know about the rest of these crackpots, but it's a good way for Aaron to get his ya-yas out."

They walked over to the union army headquarters, a tiny pup tent. Pointing to the administration building, Aaron tossed Saltzman a uniform and told him to go change.

"It's too far."

"I don't care. If you wanna fire this cannon, you have to be in uniform."

Saltzman pulled it on over his clothes, much to Aaron's mortification. They loaded the cannon, sweat from Saltzman's hands foiling the fuse. After much frustration and finagling, they managed to force a lame-assed BOOM from the decrepit old thing.

"Yippee!"

They jumped around, slapping each other on the back between pulls of Budweiser. *Boys will be boys, and men will be boys too.* The three dined in the cafeteria; Kraft cheese slices on stale Wonder Bread, Campbell's Tomato Soup, and Fiona feeling like lunch, dead centre in the sight of every whiskered, wheelchaired, drooling old geezer.

"Hey, I really know how to show a girl a good time, don't I?"

Aaron shook his head. "Saltzman, you are such a jerk."

Wearing goggles and a leather flying helmet, Aaron took Fiona for a ride on his vintage Indian motorcycle. She loved watching the people watch them. *Go ahead. Look. I'm so glad I'm me and not you.*

She smoked opium with Saltzman the following week. "Chasing the dragon," he called it. Loafing on his mattress, they droned in and out of a pleasant dream state, troubles drifting away in a stream of silver smoke.

Rita was appalled. "That's heroin!"

Saltzman was soon on the offense, dumping Fiona because "The sex isn't so hot." *He can't get it up, but it's my fault.* Then, another kick in the teeth: the review came out. Shannon reminded Fiona that he did put her on the cover, and that there was no such thing as bad PR. Furious, Fiona called him.

"No wonder everybody hates you!"

The Virgin Marries
Like the name, lead vox Fiona Larochelle is a fiery and fetching Lolita hailing from Matapedia, Quebec. That's in Canada. Ah, virginal, nubile, skin like alabaster. I thought I was in love. Until she opened her mouth. Won't talk French to me, dresses funny, no tattoos, and missing a hymen, far as I can tell. Pretentious. Trivial. Anne Murray has more to say. Am I dismissing them? No. The group, Larochelle in particular, has great potential. Whether she can transcend her white-bread roots to produce anything original remains to be seen. And rest assured, the Virgin Marries are not copying the Go-Go's.

Back at the Smilin' Buddha, Vancouver gossip was nasty. Emmett accused Fiona of stealing one of his songs as she was coming off stage. "Yeah, I love you too, asshole!"

Band meeting at the Railway Club.

"We don't get any respect in this town." Dolores slammed down her beer. "And I do mean town."

Again, Jackie suggested moving to L.A. "Dennis has so many connections!"

"No way." Rita pulled herself up from a slouch. "Let's go to

London."

"No. We could get stuck there," said Fiona. "I've heard horror stories. It's really hard to find a job. We could work under the table in L.A."

Dennis grinned. "Yeah, you can be snowbacks."

"What's wrong with L.A.?" said Dolores. "We always have fun there."

"Sure we do, but that doesn't mean I want to live there." Rita wagged a finger in Dolores' face. "Besides, you have fun everywhere. Let's move to Toronto."

"Too cold!" replied a chorus of Virgins.

"We should make it here, then go down to the States."

"That's completely bass ackwards," said Jackie. "Who cares if we make it up here? All the people are down there. As in audience. Money."

Dolores threw her arm around their roadie's shoulder. "And we'll have Dennis to protect us. Right?"

"Right," said Rita. "And who's going to protect Dennis from the Virgin Marries?"

No matter how many times they moved, Bill and Jeanette managed to find another shack, the latest a long, low rancher in Langley. Jeanette was homesick, longing to return to Quebec despite how wretched life there had been. Would she ever be free of the past, the fear that Sister Ann-Marie might come along and yank her pigtails or rap her on the knuckles with a wooden ruler?

Relieved that her mother had taken up crochet, Fiona still worried she might hurt herself again. Fiona didn't find too many empties, though all the crappy old furniture was covered in ugly, acrylic afghans. *Why can't she use real wool?* Bill had gotten her a pet; a little wiener dog she dubbed Schultz, after the character in *Hogan's Heroes*.

"Why couldn't you get a real dog?"

"He's a dachshund. He's a tough little bugger! Full of piss

and vinegar. Just watch him."

The little bugger dragged in a giant field rat. Jeanette cheerfully tossed the carcass into the garbage, explaining the goddamned things chewed through her telephone cables. She mopped up the blood as Fiona watched Schultz chase down more vermin, his sturdy little body parting a sea of tall grass.

"They were bred to go down badger holes." Jeanette deftly shuffled cards, machine-rolled cigarette dangling from her lips. "You know how mean a badger is?" She dealt out a hand of solitaire, Fiona relieved she wasn't badgering her into gin rummy.

"Shultz doesn't know how little he is." Jeanette gloated. "He takes on any dog that crosses his path. He wriggles under, goes right for the jugular."

"Well, they say pets resemble their owners. Or is it the owners that resemble their pets?"

Jeanette laughed. "Yeah, we're tough."

Fiona once watched her mother evict a drunk twice her size and half her age by the seat of his pants. Her rent had been reduced in exchange for unloading and stacking bales of hay, feeding and watering the landlord's horses.

Jeanette admired the animals through slats of a wooden fence as Fiona perched on the top rail. The thoroughbreds' hot breath moistened her collarbone as they nudged her for carrots. *Funny, I'm not scared when I know what they want.* Jeanette pointed to the pinto.

"Indian Joe. They just gelded him."

What was left trotted round the periphery, stallions shadowing him, nipping his neck and flanks. He snorted and kicked wildly, but the stallions were ruthless, tormenting him until he ran and cowered under a hemlock. Fiona quickly clambered down, Jeanette grabbing her by the arm.

"Fiona. No! What do you think you're doing?"

"He needs help! Why don't they leave him alone?"

"You're too young to understand."

"I am not!"

Jeanette ground her cigarette butt into the fence post. "Do

you understand that he's a freak? Spooking the studs."

Fiona stared at the pinto, stranded in his altered state. Jeanette shrugged. They headed back to the house, Fiona informing Jeanette that she was moving to L.A.

"Aw, no!" gasped Jeanette. "Don't tell me that!"

"I have to go. We wanna get signed. All the major labels are down there."

"But, I'll miss you!" Looking to the ground, Jeanette began to cry.

Go for the jugular, Ma. "You can come visit."

They both knew that was fiction.

"Why won't you let me be your mother? You're just a baby! My baby."

Fiona vehemently shook her head and Jeanette winced. Schultz, the wonder wiener, was yipping and dogging horses, inches from hooves the size of his head. Pointing, she nudged her mother. Jeanette's eyes rounded at the mutt's antics.

"No badgers, but he's happy as a pig in shit, isn't he?"

Laughing, she whacked Fiona across the shoulder blades, nearly knocking her into the knee-high muck. Two days later, the Virgin Marries moved to Los Angeles.

CHAPTER FIVE

My dearest, darling Shannon,

Que pasa! I miss Canada in general, Vancouver in particular, and you, specifically. We're all fine in spite of the fact that I landed in Los Angeles with only a hundred dollars, in the middle of *les jours caniculaires*. But I'm not complaining. I love the palm trees, Hollywood bungalows, and most of all, the people. They're wacko.

Rita and I are working under the table at a movie poster shop, Kater Litho. Jackie and Dolores need to find jobs. Their parents still send them cheques! And they're still inseparable, always going on about the "musical magic" between them. Gag me.

Hey, I'm sitting on a stone bench under an olive tree, reflected in and reflecting by, Douglas Fairbanks' reflecting pool. We've been adopted by Chloe Chan, who feeds, instructs, introduces, and chauffeurs us around. We are now officially "living like Mexicans," five of us in a one-bedroom apartment near the Hollywood Cemetery. Last week, two Armenian families had a shootout in the parking lot of Vons, a few blocks away. Oh well, this is just a crash pad. When we aren't rehearsing or playing, we're at The Whiskey, The Starwood, or Blackies. Chloe gets us on the guest list every night. The girl that works the door at The Whiskey hates the sight of us. Hah!

It's amazing here, Shannon. I'm soooo inspired. Been writing tons. There are so many bands! My faves are X, Black Flag, The Plugz, the Alley Cats, the Weirdos, and get this, Catholic Discipline. Their front man, Claude

Bessy—Kickboy Face—is the editor of *Slash* and a francophone I can relate to. But what is it with critics starting their own bands? Like Lester Bangs and Birdland. Isn't that kind of like asking for it? 2 Tone bands are playing The Whiskey lately. We decked ourselves out in black and white and saw the Selecter's, Pauline Black looking killer in a trilby and trench coat.

Going to see Gang of Four on Thursday. There's a real audience for punk rock here, whole contingents— Hollywood punks, skate punks, Valley punks, beach punks. They're the ones with the sunburns. (Then to confuse the issue, there's a band called Surf Punks). Talk about hard-core. They all wear Knuke the Knack T-shirts and absolutely despise mod, new wave, and power pop faggots.

KROQ's deejay, Rodney Bingenheimer, plays lots of great music. Have you heard Wall of Voodoo's "Ring of Fire?" It's hilarious. Should play it for Jeanette. She'd die. I'm getting a real education, especially regarding roots music. L.A. is one big roadhouse! There's so much revivalism, it's like a roots-rock movement, a religion with these guys, going on about Howlin' Wolf, Joe McDowell, Carl Perkins, Chet Akins, and Robert Johnson. It reminds me of summer in Quebec. Remember that trip round the Gaspé? Every little fishing village had a bandstand. Blues mostly, but lots of folk, bluegrass, even storytelling. I really like psychobilly, bent, twisted roots bands— hybrids—like X, The Unknowns, The Cramps, The Gun Club. The Blasters DO blast you out of the room. Los Lobos! Gawd. I LOVE Los Lobos. Your body has to move.

You know what else is interesting about the Mexican thang? They're bilingual down here without it being much of an issue. They coexist. It's not like there aren't problems, but language isn't the only line in the sand.

Please call. I know we're hard to reach, but I'm dying to share some seriously sick stories. Did I tell you that I

120

miss you? *Adios Chiquita!*

xoxo,
Your best girl, Fiona

Dennis found the Virgins some rehearsal time in a decrepit building on the corner of Hollywood and Western, an area crawling with pimps, prostitutes, and drug dealers. The Virgins entertained themselves during breaks by tossing wads of pink bubble gum onto the johns' heads as they were getting blown directly below their window. Or spittle. The hookers put their hands out, palms up, and looked around to see if it was raining. It never rains in California and they never thought to look up.

"Hit it hard," yelled Jackie. The band played a couple of bars of their new song "When the Earth Was Flat." "That's not it." Jackie slowly and loudly banged out the chord progression. She had to; Legal Weapon was rehearsing next door. *Americans really are fixated on guns.*

"From the top," yelled Rita. "One-two-three-four!"

They managed to play an entire verse before a grinning Dennis walked in, a six-pack under his arm. "Guess what? My illustrious producer friend Dan Foley wants to produce an EP for the Virgin Marries!"

"Yay, Dennis!" Dolores slapped him on the back and grabbed a beer. "The Virgins on vinyl!"

"The price is right. He's donating his services and we can record during downtime. For half the cost. And get this, the studio's in Malibu!"

"How many tracks?" asked Rita.

"Twenty-four."

"I hope we use eight."

Costs would come directly out of their hides. They might argue incessantly, drive each other crazy, but the Virgin Marries agreed to share songwriting credits, and someday, God-willing, royalties. *We are a band.*

121

★ ★ ★ ★

Vons. A huddle of black kids speaking loudly and gesturing, slowly moved closer. *Too close.* Low laughter, the glint of a knife blade. *Dammit! Don't look back.* Fiona looked back. *They are following me!* Floor tilting, stomach pitching, she stalled at a magazine rack, cursing under her breath, watching as they sauntered out of the store. Fiona strolled down a few aisles before going to the till, where she counted change slowly, her pulse pounding a beat on her eardrums. She exited. Nearing the corner, Fiona sensed skulking, heard whispers suspended in the breeze, adrenaline floating her bones. She dashed back inside the store, ignoring the gawking clerks as she exited the rear door. *What should I do? Call the police? Yeah. Right. They'll just deport me. Where are those little buggers?* Fiona ran for it, through the parking lot and onto the sidewalk. *Oh my God! There they are!* Three of them running abreast on the opposite side of the street. *I'm dead!*

"Hey, white girl!"

"Hey, bitch! Hey! You fuckin' freak!"

Ditching the paper sack of groceries in a hedge, Fiona pulled out her choke collar key chain. Charging headlong into traffic, she forced a long convertible to a screeching halt, which placed her on the same side of the street as her tormentors. *Oh my God. I'm dead!* Lungs burning, the last few feet to the apartment building stretched into miles of slow mo. Thank God, the super was in the lobby. She blasted in.

"Lock the door, Mr. Sapprovich!"

THUD. His German shepherd Soldier growled gutturally. CLANK. The kids slammed into the glass doors, banging, yelling, jeering.

"Get the hell out of here!" Mr. Sapprovich raised his fist.

They laughed until he let Soldier off the leash. The dog bared its fangs and lunged, smearing the glass with froth. The kids blanched, turned, and ran.

"Goddamn niggers! Good thing they're afraid of dogs."

"Thank you, Mr. Sapprovich!"

Guts roiling, Fiona ran up to the apartment, threw open the

122

window, and snatched a big gulp of cool evening air. She gripped the frame and leaned out, her eyes slowly focusing on the boulevard's pedestrians. *Is that them?* She vaulted into the bathroom and vomited.

Fiona had to lie down, numbly watching moonlight stream through the balcony's railing, striping the wall with shadows. She made a phone call and Karla came over, cringing at the sight of Fiona's raccoon eyes of smeared mascara. They hugged, Fiona blubbering and burying her face in Karla's frizzy curls, warm, coconut pomade smearing her cheek.

"Why would they do that? Were they gonna kill me?"

"Because you're white," replied Karla, rankled. "You're pretty. And you're weird. What's not to hate?"

"Christ! Do they think I'm rich just 'cause I'm white?"

"Maybe. Maybe not. They probably think you're better off than they are."

"I'm not! I'm total white trash. Grew up poor. This is fucked! I don't hate black people."

Karla smiled. "Maybe you don't tell nigger jokes, but come on, you've got your prejudices, just like the rest of us."

"Well, I admit I find their . . ."

Karla narrowed her eyes.

". . . *your* behaviour strange sometimes, but it's just culture shock." Fiona collapsed on the couch. "Oh, everybody's a racist. It's tragic!"

"Hey, you don't go around wearing a pointy hood, and I feel no urge to kill Whitey. Okay?"

They drank beer, talking until Fiona's blood cooled and her hands warmed.

"So, why do *some* black people wear that big comb in their afros?"

Karla laughed. "Oh, that's so yesterday. Just dumb niggas."

"And you can say that?"

"Yeah, and I can say dyke too."

"So, I shouldn't take it personally? I'm just some white chick to them."

The two walked downstairs and said goodnight at the door.

Mr. Sapprovich peeked through a crack in his curtains, eyes growing wide at the sight of Fiona embracing a "nigger."

Dennis drove them to Boylston Heights to shoot a series of sexy apocalyptic shots for the record cover. Ankle-deep in detritus and crumbling foundations, their backdrop a sheet of white noise rising from the Harbor Freeway, the Virgins posed in relief against a row of palm trees, trunks evaporating into the haze, tops floating like shrunken heads. How naturally it all came, vamping, writing, performing, as if subconsciously they'd been watching, learning, preparing all their lives.

"More like we've been programmed," said Rita.

Heading to the studio, they wound their way along the curves of Pacific Coast Highway, past sunning sea lions, surfers bobbing at Point Dume, and shithawks—seagulls—bombing the pier. Fiona watched Dennis ogle a busty brunette riding bareback on a Palomino stallion, galloping through roiling surf.

"You can see the grey whales during migration." He told them smugglers used to run liquor, opium, and Chinese labourers through the area.

The studio sat under the lee of the mountains, a veritable citadel by the sea. The massive foyer, a circle of mahogany pillars, opened teepee-like, rays of sun warming the slate floor.

"Hey, Virgins, it's your first time!" joked Dennis. "In a studio."

Dan Foley ambled in, gently gruff in a Recovering Catholic T-shirt, black jeans, and lizard-skin cowboy boots. He sat while the Virgins arranged their bums on a bank of white couches.

"All right then. What kind of production values are you going for?" he asked, voice like sandpaper.

"Don't you know?" Jackie clung to her guitar case.

"It's your music. You tell me."

Fiona knew. "Raw. Gritty."

"Right," said Rita. "And we want it tight."

"Monster bass!" said Jackie. "I play bass like no one,

melodically, but with a lot of guts."

"Describe your sound. As a band, I mean."

Gawd. I wish we had a manager. "We sound like the Virgin Marries. Our drummer is a walking, talking, sonic boom! Our bass player *is* an original. Dolores plays her Les Paul like a band saw. It rips! We write excellent songs. The singer can actually sing. I have great stage presence. We all do. Right, girls?" They nodded. "We're talented. Fucking brilliant, in fact."

Dan feigned ducking, as if to avoid a blow. "All right then. We have a band in the studio. Who's responsible for the arrangements?"

Dolores groaned. "Arranging is for wimps. We don't *arrange* our stuff."

Rita brandished her drumsticks. "Yes we do! We don't want a ton of effects, LinnDrums, or a million overdubs."

"No cowbell!" said Fiona. "I fucking hate cowbells. Let the farmers have 'em."

"Or synthesizers," said Dolores.

"I hate saxophones almost as much as I hate cowbells," said Fiona. "And flutes! I hate the flute. It reminds me of beatniks. And hippies."

Dan stood at the window, looking out over the mist-shrouded hills. "Okay, so you know what you don't want. I will venture to say that I think you need a clean sound. Organic. Unrestrained. Untainted."

"Organic?" bleated Jackie.

"Yeah. Organic, as in authentic. Virginal. Pure. Virgin Marries, doing what comes natural."

"Er, yeah, okay." Jackie feigned gagging behind Dan's back. "But we are not hippies!"

Pink Sombreros

The cowboy led his horse to water
The horse refused to drink
The cowboy roped a steer one day
The steer was full of sawdust

125

The cowboy saw a sign in the sky
Revolving neon stars

Dudes in white fringes live here now
Dudes in pink sombreros here to stay

The cows are lowing, the myth is dying
This land can break my heart
I have no place to go
Beyond my wild whiskey dreams

"How about piano?"

"Gimme a break! Do you want us to sound like the Eagles?"

Rita glared at Fiona. "We couldn't sound like the Eagles if we tried!"

"It is a ballad," said Dan.

"Yeah, it's a ballad," said Fiona, "but it's a cowboy song. I hear guitars."

"Guitar, yes, of course, but this song, a wonderful song by the way, should be played on acoustic. The rhythm parts anyway."

"Acoustic!" yelped Dolores.

"Yes. Acoustic will make it a classic. Showcase the vocals. A little piano in the bridge." Dan levelled his eyes at Fiona. "And another thing: hit songs do not have minor chords."

Let's hit you.

"I thought you were tired of wasting away on the fringe," said Dan.

Dear Mom

How are the Provinces?
No, I can't come home
I have viewed the greatest paintings
But none of them move me
I hear so many voices
But none of them move me

126

I wish he would draw me in

"What's it about?"

"Alienation?"

Jackie thought it sounded derivative. She'd been pulling out the ten-dollar words lately, as if she could compete with Rita.

"It's not very original," parroted Dolores.

Rita was bothered by its overt pathos.

"Christ," said Fiona. "Everybody's a critic."

"Don't worry about being original." Dan sat at the console. "It isn't possible. There hasn't been a new chord written in over three hundred years. Shoot for distinctive. Or better yet, just be your inimitable selves." He shooed them out of the control room. "Go set up."

The twins started each song with a loud thwack on their guitars, Dan wincing. "Turn down, please. We have to get out of the red. At least once in a while."

"It's too crunchy," reported Dolores. "I need more fuzz."

"I love these musical terms of yours. And you're going to have to turn down."

"Come on, Dolores!" Rita rose from her kit. "It's not the same as playing live, for chrissakes."

The twins plugged, unplugged, tuned, retuned, Rita complaining that she couldn't hear herself in the click track of her headphones. *Hurry up and wait.* Waiting for all the Virgin Marries to be happy could take forever; only one reason Fiona was beginning to detest recording.

Everything Gets in Your Mouth

She stops his heart with red lips
I can see him staring
I can hear lies resounding
After each sigh
Sense secret desires

Everything gets in your mouth

127

She tries to touch colour
She tries to kiss truth
But it just gets in her mouth
There's too much to swallow
Too much to choke down
Too much to swallow

They finally managed to piss off Dan by smoking hash in the control room. Dolores and Jackie refused to turn down or play any song more than twice. Fiona found them blowing smoke rings, Jackie sitting queenly on her amp, Dolores leaning against her stack of Marshalls.

"We're on strike," said Dolores, crushing a Marlboro. "I hate the way he's making my guitar sound. It's so wimpy."

"Yeah," said Jackie, "the overall sound is way too thin."

"Oh, so now you're experts all of a sudden?"

"He's not listening to us Fiona! He doesn't know what the fuck we're about. I mean, look at him. He's just a big old hippie."

Dolores the teapot, short and stout, calling the kettle fat.

"He's doing us a huge favour, and you're making Dennis look bad. Besides, Dan's not a hippie. He's a hipster."

"Who gives a shit?" said Jackie.

Dan emerged from the control room, smiling, despite the tension in the air. "Maybe I should pull a Phil Spector on you. He once held the Ramones at gunpoint you know, forced them to play with a string section."

The twins recoiled in horror.

Many hours later, working on lead vocals in the isolation booth, Fiona flattened notes and flubbed lyrics.

"You're coming across hard," said Dan. "Cold."

"Yeah. So?"

"Well you're not hard, or cold, so why do you want to come

across that way? You should be thinking beyond punk, remember? You're writing some heady tunes here, Fiona. At the same time, you're holding back."

"Holding back?"

"Surrender. Learn to surrender."

Surrender what? She was not about to ask. With concentrated coaching, things slowly turned around, eventually leading to a series of superior takes. *Time for a break.*

"Was it good for you too?"

They laughed and listened to the playback as the other Virgins descended for their scheduled tracks, Dolores toddling into the control room, pupils like nailheads.

"We should fire her ass!" hissed Rita. "I hate it when she plays all fucked up like that."

"Yeah, well," said Dan, "she's not playing through the nod on this recording. You'll have to come back tomorrow."

Jackie may have quit smack, but it hadn't dampened Dolores' appetite. She used to follow Jackie's lead, but lately it was one way the twins differed. Dolores represented a deep cavity of vague yearning, but Jackie knew what she wanted and how to get it. They tried to keep Dolores away from the stuff, but the scoring process was nearly imperceptible. As soon as they hit town, any town, it was as if smoke signals went up. Locals ran out, tracked down dope for the guitar player of that all-girl band, the Virgin Marries from Vancouver.

"You're sabotaging everybody's hard work!"

Rita's lectures had no effect. All she could do was warn Dolores not to buy drugs from bikers. Dolores continued playing down the volume of her inside dope, no sleeve long enough to cover her festering itch, once mewling, "I'm just trying to crawl back into the womb."

Fiona went off on her. "Okay, I get it. Supreme bliss. But why does everyone talk about the womb as if they remember? How do you know it's the same way you feel when you're high? I'm so tired of that fucking cliché. It's almost as tedious as a rock-star junkie."

★ ★ ★ ★

Recording wrapped the next day and the Virgin Marries didn't implode. They traipsed to a beer bash a few houses down the beach, relishing hot homemade salsa, barbecued chicken, and a bonfire. The Honeydrippers ambled over to meet the Virgins after playing at a nearby wedding reception, Fiona as equally thrilled to meet country singer extraordinaire, Candye Kane, and her friend, ultra-blond, super-stacked Los Angeles poet, Saint Teresa Stone, radiant in a silk bridesmaid's gown.

An hour later, Fiona snuck away to rendezvous with Dan. She breathed in his musk-citrus aftershave, still pleasantly surprised by his carnal aptitude. He threw a big, powerful arm over her hips.

"So why's the record called 'Mnemonic Device'?"

"Uh, let's see. Because I use them all the time?"

"Will you remember me?"

"You sound sad, Dan. What is this, if not a fling?"

"What is it for you?"

"A fling. With Dan the Man, the married man with children, the married man with a seven-year itch. How's that for a mnemonic device?"

"Very effective, I'm sure. Especially the itch part. Wanna scratch it again?"

She did. He did, placing a series of furtive phone calls in the following few days.

"Dan! It's okay. I have no regrets. I know you care for me."

He asked to see her again. Though sorely tempted, Fiona declined. "I know you don't want to lose your family."

He was not happy.

It seemed no one else was happy either. Next rehearsal, Jackie said, "The mix is way too treble. It doesn't have enough bottom."

"It's too bad," said Rita. "What he calls atmospheric, I call hollow."

"The only thing he didn't entirely fuck up was your vocals," said Dolores, eyeing Fiona with suspicion.

She sighed, determined to view it all as a gift.

Bombing straight up the I-5 yet again for shows in Vancouver, Seattle, and San Francisco, the Virgins were hard-pressed to arrive on time. Dennis griped as they drove past orange groves, windmills, tree ranches, and black Angus cattle dotting hills of red clay.

"You can't see the forest for the RVs!" The monstrous vehicles jammed the highway, along with big rig caravans that invariably boxed the Virgins in. They laughed at a big, beefy trucker pissing on the gargantuan tire of the Mack truck he'd parked on the shoulder.

Shannon and her thing for birds. Fiona stared out the window, wishing her girl could see the hawks pervading the valley sky. "They take our souls when we die," she often spouted, citing as an example the screech owl that showed up at the circus of Gary Gilmore's execution to land on a praying protester's arm.

The band steadily put more highway behind them, along with orchards, junkyards, coulees, vineyards, Airstreams, telephone poles leaning like old soldiers, and bare-limbed trees gnarled with forsaken nests that resembled knots of hair.

Fiona was amused by the small-town names: Yolo, Zamora, Arbuckle, Redding. Miles and miles of interstate. Foothills began rolling into mountains, and Mount Shasta's crest, white as Santa's beard, loomed before them. They crossed the state line and passed through Portland at nightfall, accompanied by a persistent train whistle. Several hours later, the Virgins approached the Welcome to Washington State sign, driving past apple trees draped in moss, ramshackle farms, dilapidated outbuildings, an abandoned sawmill painted rainbow colours, and yards filled with heavy machinery and rusted cars. *Dogpatch, U.S.A.? Ah, the Great Northwest. Must be something in the water.* Fiona conked out despite a stiff neck. White line fever. Several excruciating hours later, she rubbed her eyes, thinking she must be seeing double after days and days of double yellow lines.

Canada Customs. *I declare we are the best band in the world!*
The fucking I-5. It'd be too soon if I never saw it again.

Nearly a month later, the Virgins were back on the I-5 heading
south to Mexico from L.A. Crossing the border was easy, just as
Dennis had predicted. The landscape mutated into Mexico
within minutes, the road growing bumpy and Dennis cursing
potholes. The place looked chewed up and spit out, as if a
hurricane named Zelda had flung her booty across the entire
region; rickety tin shacks, stripped, crumpled car corpses, heaps
of wooden dinghies, satellite dishes resembling black lilies
rooted to rooftops.

Fiona felt conspicuous in the posh RV Dennis' folks were
brave—or foolish—enough to lend them. Ensconced in the
dining nook, a brooding Rita spent more time tuning than
playing Fiona's guitar.

"Hey, what do you call somebody who hangs out with
musicians?" said Jackie.

Dolores looked up from her *Cosmopolitan*. "I don't know.
What?"

"A drummer."

Rita continued plying the guitar, raucous laughter erupting.
Giddy, the twins shoved and wrestled each other to the floor.
Fiona spun around in her seat.

"Will you two knock it off!" She looked to Dennis. "Hey,
when do we go through Tijuana?"

"You don't go through Tijuana. It's more like Tijuana goes
through you," he guffawed.

"I wanna go, I wanna go," chanted the twins.

"Oh, you'll go all right, especially if you drink the water."

Rita insisted they pass on Tijuana. "Let's drive down to
Puerto Nuevo for lobsters, as planned. It's a lot less sleazy.
Right?"

"Sort of. I mean, we're talking Mexico here," said Dennis.

But there was nothing to fear except the Federales, notorious for hijacking tourists, often forcing them at gunpoint to empty their bank accounts. But Dennis spoke Spanish and claimed he knew how to handle them. He persuaded Rita to stop off in nasty old TJ after all, a trumpet blast sounding as the engine died, while *huapangos* flowed from a nearby jukebox. The low buildings reminded Fiona of the barrios of East L.A. *Maybe it's East L.A. that resembles Mexico?* Her Chicano friends liked to remind her they were the first Californians.

Dennis and the Virgins strolled the market, a maze of kiosks, vendors hustling leather belts, black velvet paintings, onyx animals, and world-famous fish tacos. Born-to-shop twins drooled over the silver jewellery. Dolores purchased a pair of deely bobbers; glittering red hearts on springy antennae. Dennis' first acquisition was a handsome rainbow-striped blanket. He placed it in Fiona's arms. Shaking her head, she handed it back.

"I can't accept this."

"Take it," he commanded, then begged. "Pleeease."

"Okay, okay." Fiona kissed him on the cheek. "Thank you." She'd been eyeing the blankets, though it might have been nice to select one herself. "You're so sweet."

"Don't call me sweet. Kind or thoughtful, I can handle, but sweet! It makes me cringe."

"Okay, asshole. Whatever you say."

He laughed, stopping at the next stall to buy a sombrero the size of a stove.

Rita finally smiled. "Like we're not conspicuous enough."

"If there's one place to lose your dignity, it's Tijuana."

We must be a strange sight, thought Fiona, even in TJ, a parade of loco gringos ten steps behind a bouncing goofball impersonating Frito Bandito. At the same time, they blended in with the colour and clamour of the street, smiling locals waving.

Dennis pointed out Hong's, an infamous hangout for American college kids. They found beggars huddled in alcoves with cups and canes, mothers displaying their offspring's blindness, club foot, or leprosy. Dolores noted that she felt sorrier for the baby chimpanzee posing for pictures with tourists at five bucks a pop.

"Maybe he's the missing link," cracked Rita.

It was warm in Tijuana, sidewalks soft, vague stench of squalor stalking their brain stems. A swooning, nauseated Fiona soon stumbled, nearly falling to the ground before grabbing Dennis by the arm. Alarmed, he scooped her up and carried her to the closest cantina. Gently, he lowered her onto a bench and lay her new blanket over her. The cavelike coolness was comforting, but Fiona couldn't stop her teeth from chattering. Rita handed her some bitters she'd acquired from the bartender, instructing her to down them quickly.

"Dennis, she'll be fine. Go find the twins."

He left, reluctantly. Rita handed Fiona a canteen and with effort, she raised her head to sip some water.

"Ah! I swear water tastes as sweet as nectar sometimes." Fiona gazed around the room at the paper roses and hand-painted tiles. "Everything's so bright and cheerful."

"Their optimism is astounding," said Rita, "in the face of all their problems. The Mexican people really know how to live."

Dennis returned, twins in tow. Fiona played the victim for a while, then sat up. "I want a Dos Equis."

The twins were thirsty also, for a pitcher of margaritas. Rita forbade it and insisted on leaving. After a bout of bickering, they got into the RV and headed for Puerto Nuevo. Feeling hollow, Fiona found comfort observing roadside shrines to the Virgin Mary. Steinbeck said, "She is as eternal as our species." Papist foolishness perhaps, but praying to Mary and a variety of saints seemed more efficient than laying all of one's eggs in one God's basket.

By the time they arrived, Fiona was desperately in need of nourishment. Three enterprising street urchins ran up to the vehicle, pleading to be hired as guides. They knew of the best place in town for lobsters. Dennis pressed a greenback into the eldest boy's hand. Jackie protested.

"It's okay," said Dennis, "we'll never get rid of them anyway."

Each chattering boy grabbed a Virgin to drag through the warren of winding streets and alleyways. The restaurant turned out to be Dennis' favourite; a seaside place roosted on a bluff, picturesque with fountains and palm trees, feathery fronds undulating as though underwater. A burly *camarero* greeted them warmly, shooing away the little *muchachos*. He led them to the best table, near the fireplace and beneath an arched, ivy-trellised window with expansive ocean views. Rita consented to a pitcher of margaritas.

Seeing a photo op, Fiona framed Dennis against a massive mural of unicorns, Viking ships, prancing white deer, scowling skulls, and a Christ figure in a jewelled crown. Dennis crossed his eyes and tipped his cap. With sharply angled cheekbones and a sturdy jaw, Dennis managed an air of nobility despite each silly antic. At the moment, he was liking everybody and everything, surfing a wave of *cerveza* and goodwill. Bliss must be contagious, Fiona thought, craning her neck like a heat-ray-seeking daisy each time the sun peeked through the clouds. *I have never been so happy in my life.*

The waiter brought chips and salsa. Rita ordered their meal. Two huge macaws screeched as a mariachi trio strolled over to serenade them. As the bassist belted out a ranchera, Fiona marvelled. *How is he so resonant? Two years of singing lessons and I have one-tenth the power this guy has.*

Their pint-sized guides popped up from behind the potted palms, squealing, mugging for the camera and trying to swipe the Virgins' sunglasses. The lobsters arrived at last, everyone agreeing they'd been worth the wait and the drive. They resembled crayfish, but were incredibly flavourful. The food kept coming, their table groaning under the weight of beans, tortillas, butter and lemon, rice, enchiladas, guacamole, and an array of salsas and hot sauces. Fiona tied her napkin on like a bib and dove in.

Several Americans on the other side of the room stole glances; three men in suits, one orderly with a briefcase, the other two scruffy-looking. Briefcase Man was one slick dude in a leather coat, two-toned shoes, tinted wireframe glasses, and a derby hat, of all things. Well-endowed in the nose department, he was not exactly handsome, but blessed with thick, dark curly hair, and unmistakable charisma.

"Record company executives, I bet," said Jackie. "Or movie producers."

"Drug dealers," said Dennis, scowling.

With each respective pitcher of margaritas, the glances gradually became looks, and before long, the dude in the bronze Italian suit approached to say hello.

"So, where y'all from?"

"L.A." Dolores giggled. "By way of Canada."

"Well, well, well. Canucks, eh?" He winked, made small talk despite Rita and Dennis' unveiled hostility. Ray and his friends were driving back to Los Angeles soon. Would they all like to have a drink together first?

"Sure, why not?" blurted Jackie.

Rita glared. "Unilateral decisions are not acceptable and you know it. We're supposed to go down to the beach."

Ray waved his friends over. Fiona suspected the cocky ones were bodyguards and probably packing. They immediately hit on the twins, Fiona always amused by their desperate need for the attention of men. Any men. And this man, the apparent Boss Man, was decidedly macho, though oddly, equally awkward. His minions grabbed a chair for him. *He is definitely starring in his own life.* His smile revealed pointy canines, sharp as fangs, and a gap between his front teeth.

"Caleb Crowe," he announced, extending his hand. "I could tell straightaway you're not from around here. L.A., I mean."

"How could you tell?"

"You're wholesome."

"Wholesome!"

"Yeah. You've got roses in your cheeks. It's endearing, actually."

Fiona blushed. "Gee, and here I thought I was fitting right in."

"Well, you are, in a way. L.A.'s full of emigrants. I'm from New York."

"So, what do you do, Mr. Crowe?"

"I'm a record producer."

"Oh. Who have you produced?" she asked as casually as possible.

"Tom Verlaine. DNA. Talking Heads."

Wow.

He pulled out a business card. Fiona tucked it into her pocket, Dennis eyeballing them. *Oh, leave me alone. This is business.*

After more margaritas and much confusion, everyone wound up on the beach building a bonfire. Dolores ran back to the RV to get their guitars and soon they were singing round the campfire like renegade Girl Guides, passing a bottle of Cuervo Gold as Dennis and Rita kept time on discarded oil drums. Ray matched Dennis with one joint after another, everyone growing progressively more drunk and high.

Fiona and Caleb managed to slip away. They strolled through snakes of kelp lit by the full moon. He pulled out a small brown vial and a tiny, black plastic spoon, chuckling at her bemused expression. He demonstrated. Fiona followed suit and snorted the white powder.

Wow.

Between a cappella versions of Virgins' songs, Fiona blasted Caleb with a cavalcade of opinions, everything suddenly so relevant. He encouraged her with an unflinching smile.

"I could do this all night!" She shoved her toes into the warm sand. "So loud and limber am I!" Abruptly aware of an odd sound, Fiona stopped to listen. "What is that? Is it raining?"

Caleb looked up. "An aural illusion perhaps?"

"Am I hallucinating? Cocaine doesn't do that. Does it?"

The ground seemed to shift and Fiona reached out to clutch Caleb's sleeve. She looked up and down, and peered around, slowly realizing that they were standing on a rapidly shrinking sandbar.

"Oh my God!" she screamed.

Caleb glanced down. "Holy shit! Come on! We better make a run for it."

Fighting panic, they waddled though waist-high waves, eyes trained on the shore.

"Fuck!" Caleb checked the damage to his shoes.

"Oh no, your Rockports."

He grimaced. "They're not Rockports. They're Rogani."

"Well, excuse me. At least they didn't get washed out to sea. With you in them!"

He laughed. They joined the others and Fiona fetched towels. Dennis soon found them, wet, flushed, giggling.

"Where have you been?"

Fiona motioned to Caleb to go on ahead. "Oh calm down. I'm fine. Nothing happened."

Dennis stalked off. Fifteen minutes later he was stoking the fire, still fuming, surrounded by singing Virgins.

"Uh oh," said Rita in a measured voice, pointing to the three silent, rifle-toting figures that had emerged from the dunes.

Fiona harboured a tiny hope that the Federales would quit their marching and head off in the other direction. Dennis smiled as they advanced. They're short, she thought, and surely must suffer from SMS—Small Man Syndrome. The twins ran to the RV. Rita stood staring, a pillar of salt. Caleb's boys nervously jingled the change in their pockets. The Federales stopped a few feet in front of them, a slow, sugar skull smile spreading across the Commander's face.

"*Buenas noches*," said Dennis.

"*Buenas noches*. No fires after midnight."

"Sorry."

"*Familia.*" Caleb piped up and put his arm around Fiona's shoulder. "*Estamos en vacaciones. Mi esposa.*"

Caleb silently slipped the officer a substantial wad of cash. He pocketed it without examination, and stared inscrutably for a long moment, sweat glistening above his upper lip.

"Have a good night," he said at last, slightly bowing to Caleb. He retreated with his men, much to the group's relief.

Dennis turned to Caleb. "Why did you jump in like that? I was handling it fine."

"No, you weren't, dipshit. He was about to bust our asses. Or rob us."

Dennis lunged forward. "Take your hands off her!"

Caleb's goons pounced, though they had a hard time

grappling a seething, snorting Dennis to the ground. Each time they pinned him, Dennis wrestled free long enough to deliver a sailing fist to a mouth and a nasty kick to a groin. Rita ran up to the skirmish and booted one of the assailants squarely in the ass.

Waiting by the car, Caleb waved to Fiona. "Call me when you get back!"

He climbed into his BMW. The bodyguards counted to three, then released their hold. Ray lifted his foot, as if to kick Dennis in the head. The girls screamed, voices piercing, disembodied. Ray desisted, ran, and clambered into the vehicle.

"Assholes!" hollered Rita, fist in the air.

Better get a pregnancy test. Fiona could not abide limbo.

Nearly every week, she received a call from one of her sisters, complaining about Jeanette's latest escapades. Her parents were finally splitting up, Jeanette moving to a tiny border town in Alberta to be closer to Maureen, who lived out there with her second or third husband. Fiona had lost count. Inebriated nearly every night, their mother had thrown a whisky bottle through the living room window. Fiona's sisters resented her for being so far away for so long. Then Jeanette called, informing her she'd been diagnosed with diabetes.

"Guess that means you have to quit smoking and drinking."

"Ah, I'm too old to change."

Biology is destiny. *Not!* Fiona wondered how many high school students had spawned because of that inane Madonna song, "Papa Don't Preach." *Christ. Knocked up by a married man.* Fiona wasn't feeling particularly ripe. Since her sisters had tattled, she'd spent much of her time arguing with her bawling, Catholic-to-the-bone mother.

"I can't have a baby! I'm too young."

"I'll raise it."

"Forget it!"

"We can help each other, Fiona! You're not having an abortion. I'll call the police!" yelled Jeanette.

"Go ahead."

"You're a minor. They'll send you home."

Fiona pulled back the drapes to watch Dennis tinker with the van. They'd need to score some black beauties if they were going to make it to the Big Apple in three days.

"That bohunk's gone. I'm all alone! I can't take it anymore!" sobbed Jeanette. "I'll kill myself. I swear!" Her mother engendered sympathy as ruthlessly as a March of Dimes poster.

"Go ahead."

"Fiona. Please! Don't do this. Come home and have your baby."

"No."

"You little whore!" shrieked Jeanette.

Fiona calmed her down, said she would visit soon, and hung up. She flopped down on the couch, gazing upon a photograph of herself at the tender age of six, a beat-up accordion strapped on, while she dutifully posed in front of Bill's old Plymouth. The sun was in her eyes and she was scowling. *Hurry up! Take the picture. I wanna play.* Shorts, T-shirt, white socks, Buster Browns. She hated those shoes. She hated the accordion. She hated her mother and her father, at least once a day, if not all day, every day of their lives together. *I wasn't a bad kid.* Fiona peered more closely at the photograph, stunned to notice something she'd never noticed before: the silhouette of her mother standing inside the screen door, directly behind her.

Rita got on her case. "You should tell Dan. The father has a right to know."

What would I do without Rita as my conscience? "Hey, it's my body."

She had a feeling Dan would do the right thing; encourage her to have it. *It, not us. Ruin everyone's lives. It is part of me. Already.* At times, Fiona felt like having the baby. *No! I have to be tough.*

140

Just got my life on track. Why throw it all away to wind up as a welfare mom? Pretty hard to tour with a baby hanging off your tit. Probably a mutant anyway. She felt tired and fat, like a cow. *Burden of sin?* How would she feel in eight months? *I have to do it. Sin. Sometimes the right thing is the wrong thing.* She paid for it with two weeks' wages, leaving her without enough cash for rent.

Fiona bused to the clinic and signed the consent form. They administered a sedative and led her to a small room, explaining the details as she climbed up onto the examining table. D&E. Dilation and evacuation. The doctor held up a vacurette. Performance artist Mark Pauline's anti-functional contraptions sprung to mind, especially Assured Destructive Capability, and Mummy-Go-Round. A nurse guided Fiona's feet into cold steel stirrups, while she stared at a poster of a redwood tree taped to the ceiling, doctor droning on and on.

"This instrument will be inserted into the uterine cavity after dilation of the cervix, thus reducing the possibility of perforation of the uterus and extreme blood loss, minimizing trauma. It's highly effective, resulting in complete removal of the fetal material."

Fetal material. "You just suck it out? How long does it take?"

"You're not far along. Less than one minute."

No, it's taking forever. They lubed her up with icy gel and pried her open. A speculum was inserted to hold the vagina open and secure the uterus—*instrument indeed inserted*—neatly ripping Junior from Fiona's uterine wall. *My uterine wall.* She closed her eyes to what smelled like pickled pigs feet, and the sound of a vacuum blasting. *It's my body.* Fiona abruptly recalled one summer ride on Emmett's motorcycle, their mission as meaningful as their pairing. Sharing courage from a flask, they'd roared past dry docked hulks in a naval barnyard; colossal horses asleep in their stalls. The nurse wiped away a tear sliding down her cheek. *Dammit!*

Counselling? Fiona was given a hot water bottle for cramping, a lecture on birth control, and an assortment of condoms.

"But, I'm Catholic."

If you don't laugh, you'll cry. Fiona saw one of the girls who

141

worked at *LA Weekly* while she was waiting for a cab.

"Hi, Fiona!" yelled Cheryl above the Wilshire Boulevard traffic. "How are you?"

"Oh fine. I just had an abortion." *Sins are more sinful when the whole town knows.*

Cheryl's smile collapsed. Fiona apologized. *Get thee to confession?* She got to a homemade altar instead: paper roses, ivory seashell dish, candy eggs, and a tiny, blue, baby boy doll. Fiona lit candles and prayed, in her fashion, grateful for a little mercy, zealots at the clinic refraining from spitting. *My forsaken particle.* Fiona was proud of her problem-solving abilities and independence, despite feeling guilty. *Unburdened.* Another test of character. Junior in limbo, Fiona going straight to hell.

CHAPTER SIX

New York, New York: a town so nice, they named it twice. Yeah, right. And the city that never sleeps never sleeps because it's rank and sweltering hot, baked sidewalks oozing blood, urine, spit. Neither did things cool after sundown. Still, Fiona loved the city's fascinating, ruthless nightlife and omnipresent skyscrapers.

The Virgins scored a sublet on the Upper West Side, not far from Dakota Apartments, and the American Museum of Natural History. New York City, a peeping Tom's paradise. The Virgins spied on yuppie couples cooking, cleaning crews dusting, and a working girl roosted on her toilet. *There's a fine line between inhibition and exhibitionism.*

The plan was to sojourn in NYC for a month, play shows, make contacts, seek management, and promote the EP. Everybody else liked the record. It got them gigs, which got them press, which got them a European tour, airplay on a string of college radio stations, and big-time booking agent, Brian Kezdy. Most East Coast press coverage was favourable, though Fiona wondered why rock journalists could never come up with at least one original question.

From Canada—Pure Punk—The Virgin Marries
I must admit that I'm a sucker for girls with guitars. At times, this well-built punk thrash outfit from Vancouver, Canada sounds like Bessie the Brontosaurus, pounding the city's pavement. You have to give them credit for being tough and loose, fast and funny, all in a femaleist way, as they steadfastly condemn tanning beds, silicone

implants, and Citibank. The Virgin Marries exhibit the introspection of Steppenwolf with "All I Have Is Me" while "Woman Driver" reveals insights into the female psyche: *A mother, a bride, or a daughter/Now which one will I be?/Forever and ever is a long time/To turn my back on me/My parents ornament the hood/My husband's in the rear-view mirror/My children ride up on the roof/I think I am behind the wheel.* This is a seditious band and these provocative young women are fine, if not frightening, role models.

New York City is not a good place for anyone with a jones for heroin. Dolores swore she had corralled her habit, but Jackie often found her in the bathroom, head in bowl or spike in arm. Rita kept an eagle eye on the band's equipment.

"That's the next step with junkies. They start stealing your shit and pawning it."

"Aw man," said Dennis, "don't call her a junkie."

They should put Dolores into rehab, but Kezdy had them booked to play the U.K. and Europe a month down the road.

Despite a loud Virgin Marries buzz, $150 was the most money they'd ever earned. Friends and hangers-on volunteered to manage the band, but Rita insisted on holding out for someone with clout. They did have a certain breed of chippy coming out for all their shows, new friend Poppy the ultimate fan. Poppy was an exotic dancer; a euphemism for stripper, Fiona learned.

"Poppy is sexually strident, cheerfully malevolent, and a larcenist," observed Rita. "Check her purse."

A huge Plasmatics fan, Poppy had decided that the Virgin Marries were her newest favourite group. "I'd walk through Bed-Stuy to see you girls."

She often left the stage at the Galaxy Club in Times Square, covering her tits and track marks with feather boas before taking a cab to Max's, because "CBGB's is full of bridge and tunnel people now." Poppy spent her tip money on drinks and dope, indulging Dolores far too much. She introduced the Virgins to Dee Dee Ramone, Mink DeVille, Johnny Thunders, and Gordon Stevenson, bass player for Lydia Lunch's band, Teenage Jesus and the Jerks.

They wondered why Johnny Thunders knew everybody, the truth of which soon became obvious. Thunders was a desperate opportunist, hustling anyone who showed even the remotest interest in him. Once Poppy asked Fiona to come by her room at the Chelsea to pick her up for lunch. Fiona dutifully arrived on time and walked in on Poppy giving Thunders a blow job.

"Oops, sorry!" she'd sputtered.

The "living tragedy" looked up. Sort of. Poppy lifted her head of kewpie doll curls, Thunders' dick flying at half-mast. "I'll be right with you, sweetie."

Yeah, right. Too bad you're not getting paid by the hour.

It seemed the entire Isle of Manhattan fancied the Virgin Marries, including John Belushi, who showed up at their shows, entourage in tow. Club and record store owners were bombarded with requests for the Virgin Marries. Major label deal rumours flew.

"Oh man!" said Jackie. "We've gotta get signed to Virgin Records."

Revelling in their run of successful New York City gigs, Fiona sat sipping coffee, reading an article in *The Sunday Times* about John Steinbeck's friend, marine biologist Ed Ricketts, not only the inspiration for *Cannery Row* character Doc, but often Steinbeck's muse. The phone rang. Fiona answered.

"Get over here!" yelled Poppy. "Quick! Jackie OD'd."

"What?"

"Jackie's dead!"

A lump with legs skittering across her innards, Fiona looked at Rita and Dennis eating their breakfast and repeated, "Jackie's dead!"

They sat a moment, staring at each other across congealing eggs until Rita bolted, toppling her chair. Fiona demanded the address, hung up and followed Dennis out the door and down the stairs. They hailed a cab, slamming into each other trying to enter. Fiona stared out the window as they drove to Midtown. *Jackie's the tough one. Jackie's the smart one!* Yelling at the driver, they battled rapids of traffic all the way to their destination and jumped out, frantic. Poppy buzzed them into a trendy apartment gleaming with glass and stainless steel. She led them into the bathroom and crossed herself.

Rita gasped. "Oh my God!"

Jackie, floating in the tub, translucent, stiff. *Already.* Head swimming, Fiona slapped her hand over her mouth. A clock ticked loudly. Dennis fell to his knees, weeping. He lifted Jackie's long, slender fingers from the water, crushing them to his cheek, sapphire ring raising a red welt in his flaxen whiskers. He looked up at Fiona, the anguish in his face triggering a pang in her gut. She glanced away, the tub's claw feet clutching swollen, turquoise marbles; minute bubbles in the glass. Fiona knelt and leaned into Dennis, fiercely pressing her brow to his, clutching the hair at the nape of his neck.

"How could this happen?" Dennis rose with his voice. "Goddammit! What happened?"

Pillow-clutching Dolores huddled on the couch, moaning, face hidden behind her hands. *You stupid bitch.* Dennis went over and put his arm around her, cradling her head on his shoulder. She wailed and heaved with a series of strident sobs, Fiona barely reigning in the urge to smack her.

"Why didn't you call an ambulance?"

"Because you were wasted as usual!" shouted Rita.

"Couldn't you hear her? Couldn't you hear her dying, for chrissakes?"

Dolores buried her face. "Nooooooo! Jaaaaackie!"

The twins had attended a party with Poppy, while Dennis and Fiona went to see *Fast Times at Ridgemont High* and later adjourned to The Golden Harp for a Guinness. Rita had bathed and gone to bed early, as Jackie and Dolores drank crazy sake served with ice in little wooden boxes. Jackie downed Quaaludes; no one knew exactly how many. Several hours later, she passed out, turned blue, and nearly stopped breathing. Some jerk put her in a cold shower and poured coffee down her throat. The party animals got scared and buggered off, leaving Jackie unconscious and choking in the bathroom, where she eventually suffocated on her vomit, while Dolores and Poppy nodded out in the next room.

'Christ! All you had to do was dial 9-1-1. They could have pumped her stomach!"

"Get her out of here." Poppy's composure floored Fiona and Dennis, and infuriated Rita.

They refused to leave, a nasty argument ensuing. Rita called the police, Poppy scuttled off. Rita identified the body. *Jackie's body. Jackie.*

Provocative Virgin ODs. *New Musical Express*, *The Vancouver Sun*, *The Georgia Straight*, and *LA Weekly* called. Then Kezdy.

"You could capitalize on this, you know. Graduate from notorious to nefarious. The ultimate bad girls." He offered to be their manager.

"Asshole!" Rita slammed down the phone.

Fiona sat on a bench in Central Park and bawled, staring down anyone who dared look at her twice.

The girls were questioned by the NYPD, required at the inquest. After the Virgins endured a week of red tape, Jackie's body was sent home. Rita, Dennis, and Dolores flew back to attend the funeral. Fiona couldn't bear the thought of returning, tail between her legs. *Easier to face the press and police.* There was talk of the Virgin Marries regrouping. In the meantime, Fiona would have to find a job and a place to stay. Dennis vowed to come back to New York soon. She begged him not to.

"I just want to be alone."

Three months later, Fiona still could not unearth a viable music scene, but the ever-helpful and repentant Poppy introduced her to movers and shakers Anya Phillips, Bebe Buell, and Anna Sui. Steven Meisel photographed her, but had no luck connecting her with other musicians. Fiona even auditioned for a band, the first and only time. She met the bassist from The Waitresses and one of the guys from The Contortions, but they were far too cool to play music with some small-town girl from Canada. Margot Olaverra, ex-bassist of the Go-Go's, was living in Alphabet City. Maybe she could track her down and they could share rehearsal time. Fiona couldn't afford it herself at twelve bucks an hour.

No fixed address. Fiona slept on floors and couches, even crashing in a shooting gallery at Hotel Earle, waking each morning to walls crimson with blood. Some yob informed her that the copper pipe on the side of the building was worth a lot of dough; she conspired with Poppy to harvest it. Fiona gave blood at the Red Cross as often as permitted, often lingering in front of the bakery next door, as if to extract sustenance from its tantalizing aromas. One windy morning, she chased a five-dollar bill down the street for a block, eventually grateful for a hot dog breakfast. Still, Fiona refused to beg, stealing only when necessary.

She found a few more modelling gigs, but the majority of offers were in rough trade. Poppy sent her to apply for a receptionist position at an escort agency. The telephone rang non-stop and the first thing the proprietor said was, "Take off your clothes," claiming it was the only way he could be sure that Fiona wasn't a cop.

Another Poppy associate offered her work as a hostess in her establishment, which translated into hooker or specifically, dominatrix in an S&M parlour. Fiona went there with Poppy, passing through a series of deadbolted doors to enter a reception area that could have been that of a law firm's if not for the paddles and whips. Madame O, a dead ringer for Morticia Addams, led them into a room equipped with a one-way mirror. A jittery john stood shivering in plaid boxer shorts, next to an apparatus not unlike a dentist's drill. He looked frightened, but Fiona soon realized that's what was turning him on. Poppy kept telling her how benign it all was, that the guy was a stockbroker. Fiona giggled, trying to convince herself she could do it. The money was good and it might even be fun. She fled when she saw the things Madame O did to her client. Poppy declared Fiona a snob, Madame O was disappointed. She thought Fiona was perfect for the job.

"Sorry, it's just not my cup of tea. Looks good on you though."

"That's why we want you. We admire your spunk."

Fiona's spunk was waning. When not contemplating suicide, she thought only the blackest thoughts. Finally, she found a job as a barmaid at the Baby Doll Lounge, a topless joint on White Street. The management kept trying to get her to strip, bribing her with cocaine.

"No thanks, I don't miss the stage that much."

She only had to watch the dancers—what was left of them—flaunt it, appalled that the fat-cat lawyers, CEOs and executives were turned on by such pathetic junkies. *No way I'm going to wind up there.*

★ ★ ★ ★

Everybody's so fucking old in this town! Fiona could find no teenagers. She decided they weren't smart enough to use fake ID, or that they would rather go to the disco. Must explain why The New York Dolls and The Velvet Underground were cult groups; you had to be over twenty-one to see them. *Oh well, the city is as old as sin.*

"Why's this place called Interferon?" she asked Poppy. "Isn't that a cancer drug?"

"It sounds cool."

Cool. New York and its world famous cool. Of course, New Yorkers wore black leather before anyone else. Cool to the point of popsicles, sticks up their arses, and whatever else they could shove up there. Bunch of filthy pervs, into bondage, *Venus in Furs*, Marquis de Sade. Toiling hard in the vice factory; hey, that's what matters in New York City. *Somebody's always trying to fuck you in this town.* Hurrah's, the Peppermint Lounge, and the Mudd Club offered nothing but withered old studs and bull dykes that hit on her the minute she walked in. *Vampires.* Poppy once escorted her to The Anvil, the infamous gay bar. *Fiends!* Sucking the blood and cum out of each other. The girls fumbled their way down a moist, murky gauntlet, while strange hands reached out to grope and snatch them by their genitalia.

Poppy laughed. "They throw you back if you're a girl!"

New York may have been a great city at one time, but its heyday was decidedly over. Then there was the weather: soppy heat in summer, brutal blizzards in winter, inhabitants bitterly cold all year-round. Manhattanites worked as hard at being mean as they did at paying the rent. She heard that stupid, fucking "New York, New York" song everywhere she went, every single day, as if trying to convince everyone that it was all worth it; the muggings, the stench, the cost of living. Yet Fiona saw only misery in the hieroglyphs of graffiti obscuring billboards, in vacant lots littered with winos burning boxboard. After being blown around the city's concrete canyons like a waif, Fiona came to a realization. *I don't want to make it here. In fact, I could die here.*

One of Fiona's few regulars, Filipino Joe, the banker, came into the Baby Doll and ordered a ten-dollar beer. *He'd like to fuck me too, but at least he's polite about it.* He was nice enough to take Fiona to her first Broadway show, *Evita*; her first and last Broadway show. Found out what she wasn't missing; musical theatre, all spectacle, no soul.

"Hey, kiddo, I'm having a weird day. Saw all this Christmas wrap blowing down the street and thought it looked familiar. Then I got home and found the place broken into. Again! That was my wrapping paper!"

"Hey, I got robbed too! They stole my guitar, my camera, everything. You know, I had a funny feeling that morning; almost hid everything, but thought I was just being paranoid."

"Better learn to trust your instincts, kid. Especially in this town. Guess I don't get to play Santa."

"You think that's funny?"

"Like you always say, if you don't laugh, you'll cry."

"I'd rather move, before I devolve into a New Yorker. I don't have the required killer instinct. At first I felt like I had to assimilate. Now I just want to get the hell outta here."

Joe was an expert at blackjack and encouraged Fiona to take her smarts to Vegas. Together, they hatched a plan. He would teach her to count cards, Fiona would quit clubbing, save her money, and take the bus to Nevada, acquiring some serious financing on her way back to Los Angeles.

"Manila has some of the best casinos in the world." Eyes misting over, Joe described the ancient Banaue Rice Terraces, scuba diving, magnificent beaches, and told her he would love to take her.

"Sure, but what about Vegas?"

"Don't be like those losers who never get past the slots. Blackjack's the only game where the player's decisions affect the outcome. Gives you the best shot against the house."

"I have a shot against the house?"

He winked. "If you play your cards right."

They worked out a strategy, going over how to play soft hands and hard hands.

"The dealer deals clockwise." Joe drew a diagram of the seating arrangement on a cocktail napkin. "Avoid pressure; first and third bases, this being your first time. You Virgin, you."

There was no cash at the table, just chips. She was to ask, discreetly, to change colour, please, when her winnings weighed her down. "Let's hope you have that problem." He explained deck penetration.

"Ooh, penetration."

"It's the number of cards the dealer has dealt before shuffling."

Joe told her about the priest who had such superb counting skills that he donated millions to his Jesuit order. Fiona thumped the bar with her fist.

"I'll do it!"

"Of course, no one at the table can know you're counting. Be a hustler, not a gambler."

"But, Joe, you know I'm no good at that. I can't hustle drinks worth shit. I make less tips than any of the other girls. I'm a big joke around here."

"Hardly the same thing. You get to hustle with your brains, not your booty."

"Hey, yeah!"

"Okay, let's review. Don't get cocky. Act your age. Act like a tourist. I know, act like a Canadian. Good thing is they don't expect women to count cards, especially a sweet, young thing like you." He wagged a finger in her face. "The drinks are free. Have a Pepsi. Keep your wits about you. Keep your composure and number-one cardinal rule: quit while you're ahead! Remember, the object of the game is not to get twenty-one. That's what the casinos want you to think. The object of the game is to beat the dealer."

Jeanette was jealous. "I've been dying to go to Las Vegas!"

Mecca. For losers, Ma. Fiona bit her tongue, though she had learned a useful skill from Jeanette after all. It was how she always knew her mother wasn't as dumb as she acted. A card shark, especially at cribbage, Jeanette played so much cribbage she even pulled off a twenty-nine hand once. Eventually, she became a bingo fiend. Bill and his ponies, Jeanette and her bingo. No wonder they were always broke.

Fiona didn't thaw until Utah, finally reaching Las Vegas after a long, lonesome bus ride, working hard to avoid the lowlifes in the back. One in particular smelled like stale beer and B.O., carrying himself as if he'd just murdered his family.

From one extreme to the other, blizzard to heat wave, beautiful loser to fortune hunter, East to West, the Mojave Nirvana, Fiona's tight white fist of fingers unfurling in the sun girl with guitar

CHAPTER SEVEN

Day one of the operation, blasted by 110-degree heat, Fiona checked in and showered. Too wired to nap, she kicked off the first part of her plan by going out in search of the best single- and double-deck games, and blackjack tables in town, increasingly giddy, as if the glut of lights exuded nitrous oxide. Perhaps it was the desert air, or vertigo from teetering on the edge of a new beginning.

Sans makeup, Fiona looked like a nice girl in her floral sundress and ponytail. Going for plain, even homely, would explain her flying solo; casino management was typically on the lookout for pairs of cheats. Not that Fiona was cheating, or that counting cards was illegal.

The Strip. Miles of casinos. She slunk into the Sahara, carpet-muted raucous, whoops of triumph and groans of dread cresting in ceaseless waves of winning and losing. *Ding ding ding.* No clocks, no windows, Fiona's skin tingled in the cool, simulated air. Aware that the casinos piped extra oxygen into their ventilation systems to keep the suckers up all night, Fiona hunkered down, calibrating to the rhythm of the room, man-made and as closely monitored as an aquarium. She passed card sharks and a school of walleyed, white-haired old ladies commandeering banks of slot machines. She found the blackjack pits; six decks, average penetration. *Look for the high rollers; they keep the dealer and pit bosses occupied. Look for bored or sloppy dealers.* Fiona found them to be irritatingly inscrutable.

"Stay away from the Oriental dealers," warned Filipino Joe. "They're company men."

Binion's. Fiona happened upon a dealer with exceptional

penetration and she remained playing for as long as discretely possible. Barbary Coast; double-deck games, one dealer down to less than twelve cards, friendly pit boss. Hit, stay, double down, or split. *More options than I've had in a while.* Up sixty bucks in three hands. El Cortez; shoe games, mixed penetration. *I'm outta here.* Good single-deck games at the Landmark and Horseshoe, though heavily policed. Double-deck games, excellent penetration at Sands, Imperial Palace, and Riviera nearly as good. *Caesars Palace sucks. Six decks!* She'd move to the Golden Nugget next.

First, Fiona had to meet her best girl. She came upon Shannon in the lobby of their hotel, slowly pivoting her head from side-to-side, agog at Sin City. Once ensconced in their room, Shannon opened her knapsack in a flurry, pulling out a big bag of pot, several vials of cocaine, and two twenty-sixers, one a 100 proof Stoli, the other, Kahlúa. Then Shannon heaved a jug of milk onto the dresser, for the vile White Russians she favoured.

"What do you think this is, *Fear and Loathing in Las Vegas*?"

"Hey, Fiona. Yeah! I'll be your attorney, and you can be Dr. Gonzo 'cause it's your birthday."

"Sure you can handle that fat new salary? Anyway, keep that stuff away from me. I can't indulge, or imbibe."

Shannon pulled out the cocaine, laid out lines, and tooted. Fiona paced.

"Shannon. I am so sick of *losing*." Fiona flopped onto the bed. "I just gotta stop the flow, you know? My band. My music. Jackie. Dolores. Rita, the best mother I ever had. Dennis, my sweet Cerberus. You." She got up and bussed Shannon on the cheek. "Or, maybe everybody but you? Dear, sweet, kooky Shannon. I will always have Shannon. Right?"

"Come on, I thought we were gonna celebrate."

Fiona pushed the mirror away. Shannon reluctantly shoved the drugs into a toiletries bag and stashed it under the mattress. She threw her arm around Fiona's waist and waltzed her to the mirror.

"Viva Las Vegas! Let's go unleash our awesome

righteousness."

Shannon lurched forward, wetting Fiona's cheek with a sloppy kiss. She sat down and lit up a joint, toked deeply, and passed it.

"No thank you. I don't smoke pot anymore. Okay? It just makes me paranoid."

"That's 'cause you don't smoke enough. Hey! I have a big surprise for you."

"Yeah? What is it?"

"*Who* is it." Shannon poured three liberal fingers of Stoli. "It's a who." Smirking, she added a splash of milk, glanced around, then stirred the cocktail with her index finger.

"A who? Who is it?"

"Guess." Shannon downed a big swig, bared her teeth, lifted her eyebrows, and smiled broadly.

"I'm too tired for this. Why don't you just tell me?"

"If I told you, it wouldn't be a surprise, would it?"

Fiona groaned. "Let's have supper. There's an all-you-can-eat buffet downstairs for $2.99."

"Are you kidding? No troughs for us. We're going to a real restaurant. I'm buying."

Upon arriving at the Jockey Club and being seated, the two sipped the recommended California Merlot and ordered a pair of sirloin steaks.

"Good," said Fiona. "I have my period. I need the iron."

"I need the vino." Shannon sipped. "Now, what's with this guerrilla gambling?"

"I've been developing a strategy with my buddy Joe."

Composing an expression of good-natured skepticism, Shannon shook her head. "Good luck with that."

"It has nothing to do with luck. I am to play only games that favour me. I am to get out if they don't. I am to count accurately, bet as much as I can, when I can."

"You count cards?"

"It's not that hard. Me and my natural aptitude for numbers. Good memory. Remember?"

"You said they use four to eight decks! A *shoe*?"

"Yeah, well, some casinos do, and that's why; to foil counters. But you're not actually counting all the cards, just keeping track of the high cards. Positive count. Negative count. Betting accordingly. And I have to win without drawing attention."

"I thought we were here for a reunion."

"We are!" said Fiona, throwing her arm around Shannon's shoulder. "But it's not a vacation. I'm here to work the rooms. Hit and run. I told you that. I need to make enough to live on while I look for a job in L.A. I'll need equipment and rehearsal time too."

"L.A.!" cried Shannon. "You're going to L.A.? Why?"

"To start a new band." Fiona sliced her meat. "That's all I care about."

"I thought you were coming home."

"What for? Vancouver's a one-horse town. An outpost."

"We have a real music business now, you know."

"Yeah, right. Perryscope. Quintessence Records. Long & McQuade rentals."

"There's Nettwerk Records! The Town Pump, the Railway, the . . ." Shannon crushed her cigarette. "There's a lot going on!"

"Not according to Art. There's no A&R. No airplay."

"Yeah. Well, did he tell you he just got signed with another record company?"

"Which he described as timid. I'm going to L.A."

"By yourself?"

"In case you haven't noticed, I've been doing everything by myself. For years now."

They ordered lavender cheesecake, small town girls delighting in their doggy bag—a swan—the waiter sculpted from tinfoil. They returned to their room, Shannon braying the birthday song while powdering her nose. Fiona fancied cocaine, and barely summoned enough willpower to resist.

They headed to the Golden Nugget. Fiona spotted a handsome dealer, tall and lanky, prematurely grey, flashing intensely pale blue eyes. He smiled warmly. She decided to like the table, flirting always a good foil, another useful skill acquired from her mother.

"Ooohhh, look at that guy over there." Shannon draped herself over Fiona's shoulder. "He's betting five thousand dollars! Obscene, isn't it?"

The high roller in tux and bow tie sipped his cocktail with Noel Coward flair and leaned over to toss the dice, laughing when they came up twelve.

"You should play your cards right with him."

"Craps. Now there's a game for losers. Hit me," Fiona directed the dealer. "Shannon. Dear. Will you go away? Please."

"Oooh, look at that guy! Doesn't he look like a mobster? Sexy! Sonny Corleone."

"Why don't you go play the slots or something?"

She watched Shannon hover, then plop down onto a stool as soon as one of the blue-haired biddies abandoned her one-armed bandit. *Everybody should have a strategy.* Showing seven, Blue-Eyes dealt Fiona an eight and a three. Pleased to the point of doubling down, she heard Shannon yelp.

"I won! I won!" A river of coins rushed out in a silver racket.

Fiona got an eight, for nineteen. The dealer dealt himself a five and a four. *Yes!*

Shannon trotted over, grinning triumphantly. "I love this town!"

Fiona stared at sixteen; the dealer's ten of clubs. He pulled a jack, the jack of hearts, no less.

"I surrender." Fiona threw her hands up and her cards down. "I meant that figuratively, of course." He smiled slowly. *Oops. Did I blow my cover? It's a lousy table anyway.*

"Why are we leaving?" asked Shannon.

"Because I can't concentrate. Besides, the dealer's a tease. Terrible penetration. Keeps shuffling halfway through the deck."

"That dealer's a hunk."

"What's with you? Suddenly you're this horny little devil."

"I don't know. I must be ovulating." Smiling provocatively, Shannon put the back of her hand to her forehead, feigning a fever. "Hey birthday girl, you having fun yet?"

"Oh sure. Look at this place. Swarming with losers.

Especially me."

"Lighten up. Come on, what do you want for your birthday?"

"I want my life back."

First round, no aces. Restless, Fiona couldn't resist and bet the maximum, two hundred bucks. She received a nice soft hand, a six and an ace, dealer showing eight. Fiona tapped the table for another card. *A four!* The dealer got a four. Then a king, going bust. *Yay!*

Vegas must be a vortex for wealthy widows, like the fussy, bespectacled granny across the way, colour-coordinated in a suite of pearls, clip-on earrings, matching bracelet, ring, and watch. Next to her sat a severely Anglo-Saxon, Sam & Libby-shod couple, obviously just married; thin patrician bride with big gleaming teeth, sipping champagne, young lion of finance groom acutely annoyed by her distractions, raising an eyebrow at Fiona's win.

"I was pushing for the French Riviera, but Rupert insisted on the Colonies," griped the newlywed in a BBC accent.

"You're kidding, right?" replied Rupert. "This is the greatest gaming city in the world."

Fiona was dealt a five and a six, the dealer, an ace of clubs. "Insurance?" she cooed.

Yeah. Right. Do I look like an idiot? Hoping so, Fiona gave her a goofy grin while taking an eight of clubs, dealer going bust after a three, a nine, and a queen. *Yes!* They all beat the dealer. Whooping, the skinny bride high-fived her husband. So much for British reserve.

Next, Maxim's, Fiona sussing out what appeared to be a good table. She bet a hundred dollars. *A ten and a queen!* Dealer got a blackjack. *Shit.* Fiona lost hand after hand as the neighbouring hawk-faced old soldier won, rambling on about high tea on the train with Field Marshal Montgomery, paying no attention to his cards whatsoever. *Lady Luck is such a slut.* Fiona was down nearly five hundred bucks in ten minutes.

"Where are we going now?" groaned Shannon.

Stardust Club. Fiona zeroed in on a promising table, banishing Shannon to the slots. She bet green until the deck got good, then bet black. The dealer shuffled. *Christ. Oh well, I'm still winning. Play with the house's money, like Joe said. Know when to walk away. Get that right and I'll never have to look back.*

Ten minutes later, Shannon came up behind her. "Hey! They're comping us for supper and a show."

"Shit. They noticed my action."

"Are you kidding?"

"My black action. Let's go."

"But it's free!"

"Oh God. Nothing is free, Shannon. Shit! I should have used more camouflage."

"You look like a dork. Believe me."

"Thank you. I mean, I should have made more dumb plays."

"I'm not leaving."

"Do you really wanna see Helen Reddy?"

"Hear me roar. It's not Helen Reddy. It's Siegfried & Roy."

"Oh, now that I want to see; a pair of queens performing S&M on a cage full of big cats. Hear me roar! Look, they're staring. Probably think you're my agent."

"Agent?"

"A cheat," hissed Fiona. "A cheat's partner."

"You're not cheating."

"They don't care. Once they think you're counting cards, you might as well just leave."

"You're paranoid."

"No. I'm well informed. They're gonna back-room us if I keep winning. We have to go. Now!"

"Who are you? Back-room us!"

Fiona gathered her chips as discreetly as possible and exited, Shannon following in a huff.

"Why won't you believe me?" said Fiona. "This is a contest of nerves. You're my best friend. You're supposed to provide moral support."

They cabbed it back to the hotel, Fiona still fuming as they walked through the lobby, headed for the elevators.

"Fiona!"

She spun around, peering ahead. "Dennis?"

His hulk emerged though plumes of tobacco smoke.

"Dennis!"

He gathered Fiona up in a huge hug, quickly kissing her forehead, cheeks, lips.

"My birthday surprise!"

Their bodies drew together every alone moment, as if they'd always been lovers. Must be the pheromones, she thought. Or the heat. Or Vegas. They stopped every few feet to grope and smooch hungrily. Dennis bought her a bouquet of flowers on their way to dinner with Shannon.

"To my Surrey girls."

All three clinked flutes.

"*A la vida!*" shouted Fiona.

"I love champagne!" said Shannon "How it tickles my nose, gives me a distinct buzz."

Dennis honed in to plant a kiss on Fiona's neck. "It's too hot in here. Let's go get naked. Double down."

She grabbed his thigh under the table. "Well, you know what they say, where there's smoke, there's fire."

Dennis touched Fiona's arm with the tip of his finger. "Fzzzzt. Yow!"

They posed with roses for Shannon and her Instamatic, jamming them between their teeth, *à la flamenco*. Dennis graced her cleavage with a sprig of baby's breath. Maddened with arousal, Fiona traced the delicate bumps and valleys of Dennis' outer ear with a velvety rose, then screwed it in.

"Ooh, floranicating!"

Floranicate they did, for hours, while Shannon prowled the casinos, happy for them, but more than a little frustrated.

"Your beauty still astounds, Fiona."

His exuberance was endearing, finesse a revelation, though

their initial attempts were awkward, kneeling like choir mates, banging, bumping, clacking teeth. They hugged and fondled through a long, slow hush, until at last, falling into sync, their kisses said it all: *I've missed you!*

Dennis gazed at her décolletage. "I love the view from here."

"You're such a cornball."

He slipped his fingers under her skirt and pulled down her panties. The bra disappeared next, tits tumbling out onto his chest. Dennis examined her thighs in the sunlight poking through the blinds. Latching on to her nipples, his feverish suckling triggered a deep stirring, as though a filament linked them directly to her clit. *We are wired for pleasure after all, we beastly humans with our non-procreation, purely recreational sex, fucking with our minds, brain a sex organ . . . STOP THINKING!* Fiona stroked his taut belly, drawing slow, wet lines with her tongue down to the tuft of tight, blond curls, flickering tiny kisses up and down his cock, licking the head, teasing its hungry little mouth. *Sex-starved. And I didn't even know it.*

Dennis squirmed. "Enough of that. I'll come too soon." He leaned over, easing Fiona onto her back. She yielded to a barrage of kisses across her eyelids, throat, shoulders, breasts, thighs. He moaned, whooped, yelled.

"I love your ass." He gave it a little nip.

"You bum-biter!"

They wrestled. Dennis loved that she was tall, strong, and agile. Still, he managed to get her into a headlock. "Surrender!"

"Never!" Fiona wriggled free.

"Okay, I will." He crawled under, cupping her buttocks, pulling her down to his mouth and as though staking a claim, lodged his tongue onto her clit. Fiona tried to relax, to ease into a place near ecstasy. *I can't.* She'd never seen a man so willing and able to give pleasure. Still, Fiona could not let go. Willing herself to relax, she leaned her head against the wall, watching, enthralled with his antics.

"I love the way you taste, girl."

"I love the way you taste me."

She straddled him. "Manhandle me."

Dennis gripped her waist, lifting her up and down onto his cock. Hips bucking through a tangle of flying hair . . . *the way things look!* The sight of muscles flexing, swollen pink nipples caught between teeth, tanned, sun-worshipped fingers fanning across mounds of snowy-white breast.

Fiona leaned back, limber, spine elongated. Big as it was, she wound up hanging off the end of the bed, her head down, dangling from his cock, wondering where to put her hands; whether to pull herself up, or place her palms on the floor in a handstand. They tumbled into a heap together, laughing. Exalted, Fiona stretched out her entire being, head to toe, Dennis following suit, plying her little piggies with his. *Christ. It's making him hard. Again.* They giggled. He moved over her, maneuvering his cock inside. A few thrusts and Fiona moaned.

"I love our bodies together."

That sent him. Dennis erupted. "Oh God! Oh God! Oh God," he cried, clutching her tit.

It hit her. Men hoard their orgasms. Well, some; too many of the ones she'd encountered remained silent or emitted a niggardly groan at the moment of critical mass. *My response has been stifled by such miserliness. Emmett. He may have loved humping, but would rather die than bare his soul. Dennis came as wholly, as unabashedly as he lived. Nothing to hide, nothing withheld. An open book. Which is why he's lousy at cards. Why he's scary.*

He caressed her arms. "You move like a jaguar."

"The jaguar was Frida Kahlo's *nahual.* I think mine's the bear. They hibernate, thus they dream."

"You are a dreamer. You resurrect too."

"Yeah. From out of the den, the dark, toward the light. But why do I have to go through it every spring?"

"We all go through it."

Fiona turned on her side, parking her bum in the bay of his loins. They tried to rest, but reality soon reared its ugly head, Dennis frowning when she insisted on returning to the tables. They sat on the bed, nuzzling.

"I love your hair."

She marvelled at how easily she bloomed from the warmth

of his praise. *Oh Dennis.*

"So thick. So coarse." He buried his nose in it. "Luxuriant. Like horse hair."

"Jeez. First a jaguar, then a horse. I think you're anthropomorphizing. And, loony tunes. I have to go."

"Aw." He leaned in to rub Fiona's nose, while fondling her tits.

"Yes. I have to go."

She hunted down a good table back at Maxim's on the Strip, urging Dennis to leave. Dennis preferred to linger.

"Are you betting?" asked the dealer.

"Oh, yeah." Fiona pushed a chip forward.

Grinning, Dennis mimicked fucking with his fingers. The old battle-axe next to Fiona nearly dropped her cards.

"Are you two a team?" asked the player to her right.

She grabbed Dennis by the arm. "I'm thrilled you came to surprise me on my birthday, really I am, but get lost!" She rubbed her body up against his, pinching his bum. "I'll see you soon."

Now, I just have to get back into the blackjack groove I had going yesterday. Fiona found a dealer going deep into the deck at the Frontier. She sat down and lost a hundred bucks in five minutes. Up and down. Proverbial nerves of steel required. *Christ, it's noisy in here. Concentrate!* She could feel the tug of that tender, hard body upstairs. *Quit while I'm ahead? But I just got here. Strange, but the count, high or low, just didn't seem to be factoring in tonight. It's the hardest thing to do, quit. The next hand could be a winner.* She tried another table. Lost. *Better trust my gut. To hell with it.* Fiona returned to their suite, slipping next to him between satin sheets.

Next morning, said lover traipsed around in the buff until Shannon begged him to cover up. Fiona tried to persuade them to do tourist things; visit Hoover Dam, Red Rock Canyon. "I need to focus."

"You don't need to do anything," said Shannon. "Look at

you. You're a nervous wreck."

"You're right. I don't need to. I *want* to! Take on a challenge. Win. Okay? You're acting like I'm stupid or deluded. I won't allow myself to believe either. And I'm not supposed to get emotional about this stuff, so if you can't help me, then get out of my face."

Stricken silent, Shannon bowed her head.

"I have a plan and need to stick with it. Okay? I just want a decent shot at dare I say it? Success."

"You're a success."

"No I'm not!" Fiona slammed down her mug, coffee sloshing all over the *Las Vegas Sun*. "Jesus Christ! We are so trapped. Trapped by the banalities of existence; up at the crack of dawn to punch a clock, day in and day out, just so we can scrape up enough dough to pay the fucking landlord. How do you escape such a fate? I want more out of life than a lousy job. I refuse to be a white nigger."

Aghast, Shannon rose from the table. "Look, I know you want more. You deserve more. We all do. I'm just worried about you."

"Well, I'm worried about you! You start making some substantial money and it seems like all you're doing is blowing it on blow."

Shannon swore she wasn't abusing cocaine, only using it recreationally.

"Good. I've got enough losers in my life."

They gave Fiona the entire day. She was off to an auspicious beginning at the Westward Ho, dealer dealing deep, count going up. Then Fiona got an eight. Hard hand. *Sit tight, see what the dealer's got besides the five. Hit.* A seven. Another hit, a king, and he goes bust. *Yes!* Next, a pair of eights. *Always split eights.* A push. Better than losing, dealer shuffling up every time. *Asshole.* Fiona placed a big bet. *An ace and a nine!* She got a rush each time she saw a hand like that, but soon found herself on the receiving end of a long series of hard hands.

Fiona had to admit she was on a round of miserable dealers. Finally, she found a sweet one at the Imperial Palace. Mavis made the uniform look good—crisp white shirt, pert bow tie against a slender neck—gracefully doling out cards with long, perfectly manicured fingers, chestnut hair twisted into a matronly bun. She looked like a schoolteacher. Dealt deep into the deck, Fiona finally brave enough to sit at first base. Mavis looked under her ten. A six of clubs. *I don't believe it! I can see her hole card.* Fiona doubled down. It looked like such a dumb play that friendly Ed, the world-weary newspaper editor, stared disapprovingly. Mavis dealt her an eight. Seventeen. *Stay.* Forced to play another card, Mavis got a seven, going bust. *Five hundred bucks! Does Mavis know she's flashing?*

Fiona could feign drunkenness when necessary, when the deck went positive and she started raising bets, but the lush next to her would probably be taking off any heat, splitting all his pairs, regardless of the dealer's upcard. He hadn't stayed once, got nineteen and asked for another card, dealer hesitating, pit boss leaning in to advise. She dealt the guy a four. He kept playing that way, losing hundreds of dollars on each hand.

"Waait! I have ta puut on my locky hat." He pulled a crumpled Dodgers baseball cap from his back pocket. "Hit me!"

I'd love to. He blew smoke in Fiona's face. *I should leave. I can't leave.* Mavis had a jack on the table, but a four in the hole. Fiona doubled down. On nine. The drunk went bust naturally, losing another hundred. Fiona got a king. *Stay.* Mavis got a three. *Yes!* A few more rounds and the pit boss returned, leaning into Mavis' ear. She promptly quit flashing. *Shit.* Oh well, Fiona was on a torrid hot streak anyway, careful not to increase any bet by more than double. *I'm winning! Me. How long will it last?* Fiona couldn't sit still. *Easy to see how people get addicted to gambling.* She kept going south, discretely sliding chips into her pocket. In the old days the casino would bring in the resident mechanic to wipe you out in a few hands. The long run? Everything's relative. *This isn't taking long at all.* Mavis' upcard, a seven, count very positive. Fiona doubled down, her biggest bet yet. Split fives, then a jack and an eight. *The advantage is mine, the advantage is mine . . .* Fiona got a three and an eight. *Wow. Breathe, for chrissakes. Shit. Wish I could see the hole card.* Mavis slowly turned it over . . . a jack. *Yes! Okay, now . . . bust card for Mavis, bust card for Mavis, bust card for Mavis . . . Wait!* Fiona hadn't seen many fours go by. *What if Mavis gets a four?* The luck of the draw . . . Mavis takes a hit, slowly turning over . . . a queen! *Yes! A lady for the lady. Thank you, Mavis! Thank you, Dame Fortune!*

Old Stinky plowed into her with his shoulder, running his fingers down her arm.

"Hey!"

"Just hopin' it rubs off, Laaaaady Luck."

She had to laugh. "It's not luck. It's women's intuition."

Fiona noticed a guy hovering. Staring. *Griffin Investigations? Did they see her hole-card play? Nah, I'm just being paranoid.* Paranoia is egoism, according to Joe. *Why should anybody care about little 'ole me?*

"Change colour, please."

'Cause I'm winning. Winners cut into their precious profits. Mavis didn't look happy. Dealers get fired when their table loses too much. *Oh, but I'm sure Mavis will be happy when I leave her a nice, juicy tip.*

Shannon laughed. "Three days in the city of lost wages and we haven't seen Elvis yet."

Fiona scowled. "This place is a dump. First, they can't bring our meals together, then they keep playing Hank Williams, which reminds me of my mother, and third, they overcook my eggs. How can anyone call himself a chef when he can't even cook eggs properly?"

"What did you order?" asked Shannon.

"Over easy. These are rock hard." Fiona picked up one of the eggs and waved it in surrender. "It's simple. You cook the whites and leave the yolk runny."

"Your Cheatin' Heart" came on the jukebox.

167

"Mine are fine. Scrambled."

"That's a good idea, but they never put any milk in them. That's how Jeanette makes 'em; with fried onions and just a little bit of milk. Yum."

Fiona sent her eggs back with the spent waitress, pleading, "Hurry. Please. I'm hungry!"

"Obviously," she muttered.

Bitch. Fiona considered filching the retro green glass salt and pepper shakers. She'd need some for her new digs.

"So, how did you do?" asked Dennis.

Knee bouncing, toes tapping, Fiona rapped the table with the tip of her butter knife. "I did what I set out to do. I tripled my bankroll. Up nearly eight grand."

"Wow!" said Shannon.

"Wish you had some blow left. 'Cause now I can celebrate."

A police cruiser pulled up and parked next to a vintage Nash. Two corpulent state troopers hoisted themselves out of the front seat. *Cops always know the best places to eat.*

"Brilliant!" said Dennis. "You're an amazing woman, Fiona."

"It's amazing I did any wagering with you two around."

"Maybe you should move here."

"A career in blackjack? Nope. It's too nerve-wracking! Easier to earn it. I am not a loser. Know when to quit. I was lucky too."

"And skilled," conceded Shannon.

"Why, thank you! You know what? I did play well despite the odds against it."

"That's not surprising. You have the tenacity of a pit bull," said Shannon.

"Okay, I'm gonna take that as a compliment. Besides, I couldn't live in this town. It reminds me of New York. Everybody on the make."

"Not like L.A."

The waitress slammed Fiona's plate down, then bolted. *Okay, bitch. No tip for you. Pennies maybe. Covered in spit.* Fiona tucked in.

"Goddammit. These eggs are *still* not over easy! They're gross." Fiona pushed the plate away, flashing a look that could kill.

Shannon disparaged L.A., "Tinseltown", for being just as rampant with wannabes and starlets as Vegas. "Waiters who are really actors, limo drivers who are really screenwriters."

"Yeah, there's that element, but you know what? I rarely encountered it. I was much more involved with the underground. I met one actor the entire time I was in L.A. It's not just the music scene that's happening, it's video art, spoken word, new music, electronic art, performance art, aspects of L.A. people don't even know exist. You tell me where to find that in Vancouver and I'll go back with you."

"It's there! All that stuff. Western Front. Video In. At least go back to New York."

Fiona glared. "You know what? L.A. has this cross-pollination between disciplines. Painters hang out with musicians, bands play at gallery openings, performance artists work with dancers, writers create videopoems. Everybody works with video. The place is wide open. Unlike Vancouver or New York."

"Canadian artists do tend to be cliquish, elitist, but . . . "

"Besides all that, I can go see Monets and Gauguins at LACMA's Impressionism show, actual Frida Kahlos at a little gallery in Boyle Heights, et cetera."

Shannon scoffed. "New York is where you go for visual art."

"Yeah, right, but I'm not a painter, and who can afford to live in New York? I found that out the hard way. In L.A., they help me find digs. Gigs! Everything's more accessible, including art. That doesn't happen in New York. They're vicious. Territorial."

Shannon directed her gaze at Dennis. "So why are you moving to L.A.?"

He blushed. "I told you. I have a job. I'm going to work for my dad."

"Which you said you'd never do." Shannon squeezed Fiona's hand. "Look, I miss you, that's all, and I'm being transferred to New York!"

"Great timing! I'm going, you're coming."

Shannon jumped up. "I have a plane to catch! Let's go."

"Hey, girl, wherever you're going, I hope you get laid."

"Fuck you." Shannon chuckled. "No, you're right. Fuck me."

Shannon was going places. Just what she needs, a bunch of snotty, blow-snorting Manhattan yuppies. *Maybe I should go back with her. What is it about L.A. anyway?*

Dennis convinced Fiona they had to visit Joshua Tree National Monument on their way to Los Angeles.

"I want you to see the real desert. This is the best time to go. Spring. Everything's in bloom."

They stopped for gas, kitty-corner to the Oasis of Love Wedding Chapel. Dennis pointed to an uneasy and checkered queue of couples lining the block, clad in black and white.

"Let's get married!"

"Are you crazy?"

"You still need a green card, don't you? Isn't that the best way? Marry a U.S. citizen?"

"You mean you?"

"Why not?"

"Because, green card marriage or not, you'll take it seriously. Besides, I'm too young to get married. You're too young to get married."

"What am I to you?"

Fiona groaned. "You're a friend, Dennis. One of my dearest friends. A friend with privileges. Take it or leave it."

I am such a bitch. A mile down the road, she slid her hand between his legs, stroking the denim taut over his balls. Moaning, Dennis pulled the van over. They did it in a plume of red road dust.

The lovers gradually eased into *au naturel* mode, more serene with each mile of desert highway kaleidoscoping past. They motored through gorges and coulees, vaguely familiar, like a Road Runner cartoon, Sidewinder Cafe, Borax, Lost Horse Mine road signs riddled with bullet holes.

The Mojave Desert was a shock of alien beauty, teeming with

life. *In bloom, indeed.* They stopped, got out, waded through bellflowers, asters, and fuchsia sand verbena, beavertail cactus sporting coral red blossoms like hats. Dune primroses reminded Fiona of the Alberta wild rose. Dennis laughed at her wide-eyed gaping mouth astonishment.

Finally, they reached Joshua Tree. She'd been expecting a phallic wonder rising off the desert floor, but realized Americans used the word monument when referring to a park. Dennis photographed her in relief against a horizon of softly sloping stone hills, sporting her new circa fifties flying saucer straw hat. She struck a pose beneath a Joshua tree, which was not a tree at all. Lightheaded and languorous in the balmy air, Fiona stretched out movie star-style hands on her hips, looking directly into the lens, studly paramour documenting their euphoria for posterity.

They came upon a thick stand of bigelow cholla cacti harbouring nests of sage sparrows.

"The balls of their spine break off and stick to your skin like a magnet," warned Dennis. "Don't get too close."

The yucca produced strange fruit, its clusters of pale blossoms exuding a warm, waxy scent, but the most sublime desert plant was the ocotillo; a tangle of towering, quivering green stalks resembling tentacles, gilded with scales and topped with scarlet arrow tips.

Dennis' sharp eyes spotted all manner of lizard: banded geckos, iguanas, chuckwallas. They saw silver spotted grasshoppers, and a walking stick suspended from a Mormon tea branch.

Further down the road, they were forced to stop the van, agog at the sight of thousands of kamikaze caterpillars crossing the asphalt in a shuddering river. Dennis bent down to examine the freaky fetid stew of yellow, black, and lime.

"Man! This was a wet winter. This only happens every seven years or so."

They climbed Jumbo Rocks, huge boulders suggesting rising dough or granite buttocks of sleeping elephants. At the crest, the rock face resembled scarred skin, lined and pockmarked. Up close, the surface was pebbled, and filled with cracks and crevices. Elated, Fiona photographed Dennis beneath a large, round boulder as he mimed Atlas supporting the earth. He snapped one of Fiona standing inside the huge eye socket of a rock skull. They nearly fell into sinkholes, perfectly rounded basins carved into rock by water. Dennis invited her to sit.

"What about scorpions?"

"Nocturnal. We probably have more to fear from rattlesnakes. Just don't put your hands on any ledges you can't see."

They sat, nestled together, gazing across the valley of saltbush and smoke trees. Dennis pointed to a jet etching contrails upon a gradient blue sky. Cap Rock jutted from the horizon, a visor of stone.

"You can see all the way to Mexico from here."

"It's easy to see why this place became sacred." A breeze cooled Fiona's skin, prickly from too much sun. She turned. "The air up here is making me randy."

"It is?" Dennis was hard in an instant. Panting.

"Yeah." She avoided his eyes, resting her chin on his shoulder as if studying the lengthening shadows. Fiona allowed a few seconds to pass, then stroked the length of Dennis' cock, relishing the teasing, never having felt her powers quite so absolutely. "Should I have my way with you?"

"Please do."

"The sun's going down. Maybe we should head back?"

"It's okay. It won't be dark for a long time."

"What if somebody sees us?"

"Who? The birds?" He winked. "The carpenter bees?"

Dennis always smelled so clean, so pure, she thought, plying his neat, compact balls, smooth, hairless, cool, even in such heat. She squeezed. He gasped as Fiona scaled his erection with accelerating kisses. Eyes closed, head thrown back, Dennis balanced his weight on his palms, Fiona nibbling, licking, the hollow of her mouth soon filled with a moan. *Uh oh, he's going to blow.* She stilled her jaw. One second, two seconds, three . . . then depth-charged with her tongue down so low her lips were gripping the base of his cock. Dennis groaned. She found the presence of mind to slow down enough so that she was able to suckle them both into a trance, adrift as tumbleweeds. Slowly, almost imperceptibly, gentle, primal suckling escalated into feverish thrusting. Dennis came. She took the sperm, swallowing most of it, allowing a dab to dribble down onto the warm rocks.

Hot Mama, you're the devil's sister! A heavy metal dirge started up, scuttling across the valley floor, bouncing off the distant wall of the Orocopia Mountains. Fiona looked up to see Dennis, blissed out against a blind of clouds. *Why ruin it? It's funny, in an absurd way, but how can you listen to anything but the sky out here?*

They set up camp. Pitched a tent, built a fire, flame-roasted a supper of hot dogs and marshmallows.

"Look at the stars!" The constellations leapt off a velvet drape of deep purple. "They're positively glowing." Fiona opened her mouth and craned her neck, as if to drink in the air. "It tastes! I swear the air has a taste."

Lolling about the fire, Dennis suggested strip poker.

"No cards!"

They laughed. He retrieved her guitar from the van, enthralled the entire duration of their two-song concert. They retired, Dennis as excited as a Cub Scout, zipping their sleeping bags together. Fiona laughed. *You'd think it meant we were engaged.*

They didn't get much rest. Finally, exhausted from the hiking and extended lovemaking, the two passed out. Fiona slept fitfully, caught up in sordid dreams, one about a small, black, bleeding bear, stomach sliced open, ear lopped off, tongue dangling serpent-like from its mouth. She woke, lying motionless, listening to coyote howls, imagining psychos and snakes. *Dennis said scorpions are nocturnal. Oh, there's nothing to worry about. What's that noise?* Right in her left ear. Some kind of animal just outside, snuffling about. *Oh, it's just the air mattress rubbing against the tent pole.*

In the morning, Fiona woke, startled to see Dennis gazing down at her. "I dreamt you were singing. It was the voice of an angel."

"I'm no angel, you know better than that. How do you know what an angel's voice sounds like anyway?"

173

"I can imagine."

"Yes, you can. You do. That's what I love about you."

"Love?"

"Dennis, you know I love you. I'm just confused. I can't get serious about anybody."

"Do I make you happy?"

"Yes! You make me happy. But it's not that simple. Besides, it's not your job to make me happy. It's mine."

"Fiona. It is that simple! I love you. You love me. Why can't we be together?"

"We are together!"

They argued.

"I don't care what you think! I know what needs to be done."

"Love, Fiona. What else is there? Friends, family. Love. Right?"

Yeah. Right. People. That's who I write all these bloody songs for. Fiona shuffled through her funny black feelings.

"I'm on a different path, okay? I'm just a white trash harpy, hell bent on a happy childhood. Better late than never."

CHAPTER EIGHT

Ah, the intoxicating aroma of a clean slate. Time to chalk out a new life. Again.

Beyond punk. Like Dan said. Fiona had to move beyond rock, explore her musical heritage, finally embrace her roots; the folk and country music Jeanette raised her on. She discovered The Chieftains. Her mother listened to The Clancy Brothers and The Irish Rovers, but The Chieftains were innovators. Drawn to the McGarrigle Sisters, Fiona suspected she'd been spawned in the same Gallic/Gaelic gene pool. She hunted down a bodhran through the bulletin board at McCabe's in Santa Monica. Though a sixties relic, the club hosted an eclectic concert series: Meat Puppets to Mojo Nixon, Allen Ginsberg to ex-Pere Ubu front man, David Thomas, whom she adored.

No more pandering. The Virgin Marries thought they were so radical, but were just aping the Buzzcocks or The Clash, like everybody else. *My life, my songs.* She'd have to have faith in her songs, and allow them to be simple, accessible, universally appealing. She'd tried so hard to be special; a survival tactic remnant of a rotten childhood. Fiona could see more of herself in others all the time.

No more all-girl band. She'd been painted into a corner with that concept. Male or female didn't matter, character and talent did. *I must choose my allies wisely.* What would it be like to work with a real *collaborateur*? Could all the energy expended on power struggles be directed toward developing a distinctive sound, a successful band?

Fiona looked up old friends; the ones who hadn't succumbed to overdoses, AIDS, or ennui. Dennis was still a godsend, hooking her up with influential people; Brendan Mullen, founder of The Masque, currently booking Club Lingerie, and David Trachtenberg, record producer of renown, though he made it clear he was currently too busy to take her on.

Dennis gave her a California Republic flag bearing two red stars and a brown bear.

"For the dreamer," he said. "Let's get a place, hang it."

"In your dreams, buster."

Fiona adopted a tortoiseshell kitten, naming him Evinrude because he purred louder than a boat motor. She moved in with Virgin Marries fan and rock photographer Kaye Shutter. Fiona delighted in their quintessential Hollywood apartment, courtyard with its shady palms, luxurious pool, and formidable gate to keep out the riff-raff.

"Try keeping the coons out," said Dennis, pointing.

A family of roly-poly raccoons ambled by, looking both ways before crossing the street to plunder several garbage cans. They removed the lids as capably as any sanitation engineer.

Fiona laughed. "My dad says raccoons always leave one egg when they raid a nest. If only humans were capable of such restraint, eh?"

Fiona bought a Fender Twin and an elegant, ivory Telecaster. She rented rehearsal time at a studio, placed an ad in *Music Connection*, and started auditions. Bam Bam, slow-eyed, slow-handed guitarist of the defunct Formidable Foes, was limited to playing bar chords.

Moving his finger up and down the fret board, he asked, "Is this it?"

"No. It starts with a G."

Bam Bam slid his finger down. "Is this it?"

"No," said Fiona, stifling giggles.

"Hilarious," said Dennis, after Bam Bam's departure. "And those guys had a hit record!"

They tried out a tall, tight-assed Swiss émigré who extolled the virtues of digital keyboards and drum machines, especially the Oberheim. Gerhard "constructed" drum tracks, and "programmed" songs. They auditioned a married couple, stunted transplants from New York City who regaled them with exploits of their supposedly famous group, Toxic Shock. Hubby played keyboards, wifey guitar, Fiona amused by her whiny voice and Brooklyn-ese accent, referring to Fiona as "a sing-ger."

"You have to take us both," explained her spouse. "We have a symbiotic relationship, musically and otherwise." He winked.

Gag me. "See, that's what marriage does to people," Fiona told Dennis later.

One evening, she auditioned a bass player named Thor. Dennis was working and Kaye had gone out. The guy seemed okay despite his name, so Fiona let him in. She was not impressed. Everything he played sounded like ska, which explained the dreadlocks. White guys in dreadlocks look ridiculous, and though she liked ska, this wasn't ska. They made small talk, Thor's favourite subject being Thor. Fiona put the teacups in the sink, hoping he'd take the hint and leave.

"Wanna hear my new demo?"

"No. It's okay. Thanks."

Fiona heard chair legs scraping across the tiles.

"I have to get up early in the—"

He was on her. Kaye's vintage Donald Duck mug crashed to the floor. He yanked her arms back and locked them into a solid hold, one hand reaching down to squeeze her ass.

"Hey!" She broke free and spun around.

He grabbed her face with both hands, hissing "Shut up bitch!" and thrust his tongue down her throat so hard she choked. He slammed her hips into the counter, ground his pelvis into hers and shoved her T-shirt up, his hands fiercely groping, twisting a nipple so hard that Fiona cried out. She heard the fall of footsteps and a screen door groaning, neighbour Betty returning home.

"Help!"

He clamped his hand over her mouth so tightly her incisors sliced her lips. Fiona tasted nicotine, and the tin of blood. *I can't breathe!* Desperate to get his stinking hand off her face, Fiona willed her jaw into a vise and chomped down on his finger.

"You fucking cunt!" He pulled his fist far back and clocked her in the temple.

Fiona blinked, shaking her head as if putting her brains back.

"You want it. You want it!"

He shoved her to the floor. Panicked, struck by a whiff of pine cleaner below the kitchen sink, Fiona fought for what seemed like eternity. Outrage and hope crushed to piecemeal by each blow, a precise, absolute extinguishment of defiance, seeping narcotic-like, yet driving terror through her bloodstream. *He's going to kill me!* She ceased fighting with a loud exhalation, let him rip off her panties, force her legs apart, and ram his fingers in. He whipped his pants down, positioned his cock—hard as a bat—and thrust. Fiona shut her eyes, rumbling helicopters as loud in her ear as the low moan from the back of his throat. He grunted, rolled off.

"What are you crying about? You wanted it. Admit it!"

Fiona looked down at her arms and legs, seared with welts. *Scarlet letters.* A rank spiral of sperm dribbled down her thighs.

"Just leave. Please!"

The creep left, with her panties. A trophy, apparently. Fiona dared not use the "R" word. What was the correct response? Appropriate behaviour? Now that she was a statistic. *Shhhh.* Fiona would refuse to discuss it. *What is there to say? I screwed up? I'm stupid?* She'd always been leery of men and still, it had happened. *To me. Control, all illusion.* She longed to confide in Shannon, but if she let this hit her, she'd be right back where she started. *Christ. Don't let me be pregnant! I'll have to get tested for AIDS. Goddammit!*

Fiona bawled for a day, wondering how the creep's renegade cells had managed to root in her gut, suffuse her muscles with dread. It made life sweeter—the rape—same as a brush with death.

Harmonies. She'd nearly forgotten how, but Fiona's new guitarist, Ted Orchardson, had a great ear. *Salvation through action.* Afraid the mighty Thor might return, angry that she had to feel afraid, Fiona considered moving. Unable to sleep, she secured her door by jamming a butter knife between the frame and wall, one of her mother's tricks. Fiona immersed herself in the single-minded pursuit of career and music.

Introduced by a mutual friend, Ted and Fiona found they shared sensibilities and immediately got to work writing and arranging songs. Ted had a four-track set-up, ideal for experimentation. It was a luxury to record without the clock ticking, playback illuminating flaws like an X-ray. Ted was a bit of a pothead, speaking non sequitur at times, but Fiona was grateful to have such a talented guy in her corner. He was a rare breed, a native Angelino.

An astute musicologist, Ted was hard-working and genteel, devoted to his beautiful Chicana wife, Yreina, family, friends, and music, in that order. A swanky, stylin' dude, he was a changeling, and on this day, decked out like a cholo cowboy, wearing wraparound shades and a bandana beneath his straw hat. He liked to tease Fiona, addressing her as "Chief" or with, "Yes ma'am," but did not hesitate to give her the what-for.

After she'd whined about the pain of playing an F chord, Ted placed her much longer fingers against his.

"I've always hated my big, peasant hands."

"Turns out they have a purpose," he said, executing scales on his Martin-like Segovia. "Look, we have some real simpatico here."

"I agree. Our stuff is sublime. Slightly askew. You think?"

"I do. Let's keep writing until we get the rest of a band together." Ted chuckled. "I was just a dingus you know, pouring out all my lonely teenage angst, holed up with a guitar 'cause I couldn't get laid."

Along with Ted, Fiona had acquired her own personal couturier, Yreina, who fervidly sewed stage wear for both of them. An aspiring designer and Manuel apprentice, Yreina needed the experience. Fiona needed to refine her stance onstage and she envied Yreina. A fashionista with a penchant for silver crosses and suede, Yreina could wear anything and often did; goofy horn-rimmed glasses, navel-revealing snakeskin halter tops, zebra-striped silk gloves, vintage beaded sweaters, and ballet flats.

They decided to cultivate a chic, urban cowgirl persona. Yreina designed a neo-mariachi suit with a short-waisted black jacket, silver balls and chains adorning each side of a short, black muslin skirt, which Fiona wore with a bolero hat and ankle-high boots, the straight, simple lines accentuating her long legs.

"If you've got it, flaunt it." Yreina checked a seam.

"I'm kind of afraid to flaunt it."

"Why?"

"I dunno. I cover up."

"I've noticed."

"Men. Their oh-so-keen response to my body. It overwhelms me. Being desired does not make you powerful. I know lots of women who think it does."

"You make You powerful," said Yreina. "You are powerful! I'm surprised. You seem so in possession of your body. Yourself."

"It's all a facade. I am no Madonna, believe me."

"The world doesn't need another Madonna. Don't equate sleazy with sexy."

"A singular stance. Like my voice. I hope. And bearing. Those are more important than sex appeal."

"I agree. But they don't cancel each other out."

Kaye had put in a good word for her, Fiona relieved to find employment as a receptionist at independent label, Lost Angels Records, boss man Leo Feldheim extremely familiar.

Dennis reassured her. "Hey, it's a good way to learn the music business, meet people, make contacts."

Who did Fiona meet? Pearl Noonan, Leo's personal assistant,

fatally charming southern belle from Mississippi. Fiona marvelled at how men fell over themselves at the mere sight of Pearl. Pretty, but oddly frowsy, with a questionable ability to coordinate accessories. Rubenesque Pearl with her fluttering brown eyes, long chestnut curls carelessly tied back with a rubber band, tittered, speaking to the guitar gods and record executives in a deliberately soft voice. They in turn talked down to her, blind to the flashes of irony in her persistent smile.

A close friend of both Kaye and Pearl's, former Bags guitarist and esteemed rock critic, Craig Lee, resurfaced in Fiona's life. In fact, Pearl introduced her to a bevy of musicians, including John Curry, Suzie Gardner, Donita Sparks, Shelly da Cuhna and Keith Levene, who turned Fiona onto a group named CAN and graciously answered a myriad of questions, waxing eloquently on the Fairlight synthesizer and digital sampling. Ted claimed Levene was PiL, and that U2's The Edge ripped off his guitar sound.

After months of searching, Fiona and Ted hit it off with a rhythm section, a pair of brothers from Louisiana; Acadians, no less. Drummer Kit and bassist Floyd Doucette were antipodes. Beneath wild hair and a copious, furrowed unibrow, Kit alternated between somber and sullen; "a real grooveologist," according to his brother. Floyd was good-looking, risible, vainglorious, and as loud as his brother was quiet. Both relished pushing their sibling to the limit of his abilities. Ted started calling them the dynamic duo from Dixie.

"Hey, that's where rock was born!" Floyd set them straight.

The Doucettes weren't too thrilled about backing up a girl, but appreciated Fiona's Gallic roots. "And we like your material." Though mercenary and condescending, she felt lucky to have found them.

Lolling about on her futon after a thorough and resounding romp, Fiona groaned and threw her leg over a prone, panting Dennis.

"So does your new band rock you half as good?"

Fiona laughed. "Yes! My new band rocks me, but I have to rock them, or I'm dead in the water. You know?"

Dennis gazed down at her through a beatific smile. He leaned over toward the water glass on the floor, stopping mid-reach to take her nipple in his mouth.

"Now behave. I have to get to rehearsal."

She kissed his forehead. They traded sips, kisses, lying back, sighing, one after the other.

"I love you," said Dennis.

"Stop that."

Dennis imagined an all-consuming love, heavy-handed as a bear paw, Fiona uncertain she had it to give. *He wants one thing. I want more.*

"You have to stop dropping by unannounced."

"You and your precious freedom. Some day you're gonna wind up all alone with a bunch of smelly old cats."

"Better than taking care of some broken down old coot."

"So hey, what's the difference between a magician and a chorus line?" said Floyd. He waited a beat. "One is a cunning array of stunts and the other . . . well, you know."

She knew it would be like this, the only girl in a band. Cars. Chicks. Equipment. It's not as though she ever got a word in edgewise anyway. Fiona sorely missed girl talk, female energy, the level playing field the Virgin Marries had provided. Then there was the time spent refereeing.

"Come on, you guys. Do you know how irritating guitar solos are?"

The boys in the band howled at such a ludicrous statement.

"We were just jamming," said Ted.

If she pushed too hard she was a bitch, but Fiona had to speak up or otherwise feel miserable, so she bore the Doucettes' resentment. Thank God for Dennis, and though Ted could get caught up in backslapping male bonding, he constituted the group's core with her. Fiona tried not to dwell on frustrations.

Ted examined the set list. "'Look Within' and 'Woman of the World?' They're both in F. Let's go out with 'Lambert Kidd' instead."

Ted played mandolin.

"Show-off," said Fiona. "You get to go out flashing the fact you're a multi-instrumentalist."

"And multi-talented."

"It's a great song to go out on," said Kit. "He makes like Hendrix on that one."

"Yeah!" said Floyd. "It's slicker than deer guts on a doorknob."

Their Club Lingerie debut was quickly approaching. They were to open for funky punks Radwaste and the fierce Minutemen. It had taken nearly a year, Fiona worrying they might flounder in their amniotic sac forever.

Priming his amplifier, Floyd scrutinized the set list. "Isn't it *The Friendly Ghost?*"

"No. No. *The Friendly Giant.* I used to watch this show on CBC called *The Friendly Giant* when I was a kid." Floyd shrugged. "The Canadian Broadcasting Corporation. Kind of like PBS, only really boring, and painfully earnest. Like Canadians. Or, at least it was. I'm sure they're doing their best to be hip and current. Anyway, this fake drawbridge would come down, the doors opened and you'd be inside a castle in front of a fireplace. Then a big hand would come down and pull up a teeny, tiny rocking chair—'for the one who likes to rock'—and oh man, did I ever want that chair! Then the camera would pan up to Friendly and he'd say in a big, booming baritone voice, 'Look up. Look waaaay up.' I loved it! Especially the music."

The boys exchanged looks.

"I swear *The Friendly Giant* could be a metaphor for Canada. Polite, morally superior, and huge. Plus, he was the only positive male role model I ever had."

★ ★ ★ ★

By the time the night of their inaugural gig had arrived, Fiona felt ready for anything.

"Please welcome the former lead singer of the Virgin Marries, Fiona Larochelle, and her new group, Fiona LaBand!"

The brothers Doucette were such a muscular rhythm section, they capably guided Fiona and her guitar playing to a place where she was able to keep pace with Ted. And Ted was brilliant, so deftly executing eloquent picking and blistering barnburner guitar licks that Fiona got goosebumps. Her singed, sultry contralto ricocheted off the walls of brick facade, the immense toe-tapping audience listening intently. *Smile.* It was getting easier. Ted and Floyd assisted with between-song banter. *Look Ma, no thrash. Wow, playing with skilled musicians! It's like a magic carpet ride. Could really take me places. Places I've never been.* They received round after round of rousing applause, Fiona's fingertips raw by the end of the set.

She found working at Lost Angels Records so entertaining it made the necessity of a day job bearable. Fiona fit right in, staffed as it was by an odd assortment of kooks, artists, and musicians. Each employee displayed a bulletin board overflowing with treasured pins, flyers, photos, and memorabilia, none very useful or work-related.

Kaye roosted beneath a large poster of actress Karen Black, crossed eyes crossed out with a felt marker. Kaye was smart, svelte, and Marsha Brady-perky, though preoccupied with all things supernatural, lately absorbed with stigmata. In addition to her freelance photography work, Kaye played keyboards in some arty band whose name Fiona could never seem to recall.

With an MFA from CalArts, Kaye's best friend, art director Evelyn Mintzer, was overqualified and underpaid at Lost Angels. Witty, mercurial Evelyn favoured Peruvian ponchos and fingerless gloves. Fiona didn't believe her at first when she invited her to a Jell-O moulds party at the Otis Art Institute.

"I'm not kidding. The categories are Archeological,

Futuristic, Beauty, Homestyle and Architectural Fantasy. I was thinking of making a mould of my tits, but that's so cliché. Got any ideas?"

Fiona was reluctant to venture any, Evelyn being her boss, though it was likely an unfounded fear.

Then there were the boys. Or boy. Guitarist, singer-songwriter Bradley Waite in promotions was an effeminate, square-jawed, stiff-haired Ian McCulloch clone, reeking of Vetiver and seemingly Pearl's surrogate brother; most people in the office solicitous toward her.

One summer afternoon the lot of them got into a heated debate about the politics and überaggression surrounding a Henry Rollins and Lydia Lunch performance piece, wherein people were lured into a room to be humiliated and abused verbally, even physically.

"Sounds like Aristirde Bruant and the cult of abusive derision," chirped Evelyn. "Or the Situationists."

"Or, some situations are fucked up," said Fiona. "Christ! I like performance art, but you could commit murder and call it performance art."

Kaye had only heard about the piece and decided it was brilliant. "Art is violent. Exultant and violent."

Fiona suppressed a retort of "sycophant," replying instead with, "Easy for you to say. Bet you've never been beaten for spilling your milk."

Still, Fiona thought she worked with a highly stylish, savvy crowd and actually looked forward to going into the office.

"The devil is a Jew from New York."

Boss man Leo, the biggest kook of them all, enjoyed baiting his staff and gauging their reactions. Though Leo cut them a lot of slack and paid the union rate, he viewed his employees as proxy children. Leo confounded; a New York City snob secretly in love with Los Angeles, a New Age hippie popping vitamins every morning after prowling the clubs all night. An avid amateur psychologist, Leo loved grilling the female employees. Inordinately curious about her relationship with her father, he once asked Fiona to rate her rage on a scale of one to ten. She chose six.

"Nah, you're more like an eight."

"Now that pisses me off!" She had to smile before Leo got the joke.

The gang liked to congregate at their favourite watering hole, the Red Lion Tavern, a local *ein gasthaus*. Huge platters of bratwurst with sauerbraten and mighty steins of draught Warsteiner were served by nimble blond Fräuleins in scandalously low-cut blouses and lederhosen. Short lederhosen. Hot pant lederhosen. An old codger played accordion, jukebox crammed with Sinatra, Perry Como, and Rosemary Clooney. The LAPD must have enjoyed the cleavage in Sensurround too, as they regularly commandeered a table upstairs. The cops seemed amused by the antics of the Lost Angels crew and left them alone, though it wouldn't have been difficult to bust them for drunk driving. It amused her to think their camps were bonded by a love of beer and big bosoms.

The office was abuzz: Lost Angels act Bullet Proof was nominated for a Grammy for Best New Artist.

Fiona grumbled. "Nobody signs the right bands."

"Ah, the Grannies are a joke," said Ted. "Album sales. Not much to do with artistic merit."

Leo was even buying ads in *Billboard* and *Rolling Stone Magazine*, enlisting everyone to work late, ensuring the promo got out in time, speed and cocaine provided as incentive. One night in particular would require more of his employees than dedication. Paged by the beeping microwave, Pearl had just returned with a big bowl of popcorn, the aroma warming the room, when there was a screech in the circular driveway below. Survivor antennae up, Fiona peeked out the window, spotting three Latino males brandishing huge handguns, bandanas over their faces. Motionless, she strained to hear, the night air on her bare arms suddenly cold. Alarmed shouts erupted, then loud bumps, banging, and "Oh my God!" screamed through the hubbub in the foyer below, reports of "robbery!" shunted up the stairs like an ill wind.

Everyone froze, embracing their desks as if delegates at a trade show. Everyone except Fiona. Commanding her legs to move, she bolted through the office, down the long, narrow hallway. She rammed open the back door and darted down the stairs, nearly tripping over her feet, pushing off the railing at the bottom as though to achieve flight. *Don't look back!* Pupils swelling at a dizzying rate, blundering, peering into the murk of a moonless night she heard, *"Parada! Señorita, parada!"*

No way, José! Fiona felt the gunman gaining, her burning lungs pumping like a bellows. *Where do I go?* She could see nothing. *Where is that bastard? He's gonna shoot me! Christ! I must be in his crosshairs.* She was a moving target, and so despite feeling foolish, ran in a zigzag. For her life. *Uh, oh. Dead end?* Fiona encountered a tall, rickety board fence. *Where is he? Fucking fence! Must be eight feet high!* She jumped and, extending her arms, grabbed the top, flesh of her palms punctured by crags of rotting plank. Mustering every ounce of strength, Fiona hoisted her body upward. Teetering for a few long seconds, she searched for the source of the footsteps that were growing louder. *Still can't see him!* Infuriated, neither could she see the ground, or the stinking dumpster, her toes bumping wood damp with dusk. Fiona breathed deeply, then hurtled both legs over, pitching her body. She landed, knees smashing concrete, taking most of the impact. Wincing, squinting through tears, Fiona hobbled across Sunset Boulevard, dodging hookers and traffic to get to the pay phone. Dial 9-1-1.

She looked back and stared in disbelief at the frenzied thugs emerging from the building, beast-like, burdened with electric typewriters, adding machines, appliances and Leo's safe. They scrambled into a cab, yelling, cursing, dropping the microwave. *Oh my God! What if they see me?* Fiona sank down into the booth, yelling at the dispatcher. *Oh my God! Pearl. I left Pearl in there!*

All the old venues—Blackie's, The Starwood, The Whiskey—
were over, but Fiona LaBand successfully cultivated an audience
and played regularly. She booked the gigs: Al's Bar, the Lhasa
Club, Anti-Club, and the Cathay de Grande, opening for Faith
No More and the Red Hot Chili Peppers at the John Anson
Ford Theater. Dennis helped with promotion, gleefully
documenting her name up in lights for the first time at the
Palomino Club: Fiona LaBand, Jimmy Lauderdale, Beat
Farmers.

Pearl's tiny apartment housed a rumpled hodge-podge: dusty
houseplants, tiki head vase, paper daisies, red gingham curtains,
a muddle of books, and a ceramic Portuguese rooster crowing
from its perch atop the fridge. Pearl claimed kinship to Flannery
O' Connor and displayed a large collection of family photos.

The Lost Angels tribe, still decked out in costumes after a
round of hullabaloos—Halloween far more significant a holiday
in Hollywood than Christmas—had convened at her place for a
nightcap, strains of Édith Piaf emanating from Pearl's ghetto
blaster. Aptly turned out as a princess, Pearl sat in a cloud of
white satin and organza furbelows. Feline Fiona had painted her
face with orange and black stripes, employing Evinrude as a
model. Evelyn was decked out as the consummate witch, replete
with long wonky nose and hair protruding from a bulbous chin
mole. She passed a spliff around, revellers talking, or yelling
simultaneously. The landlady above banged on Pearl's ceiling.

Evelyn cackled. "Sounds like she rides a mean broom."

Pearl turned down the music. "You guys! You're gonna get
me evicted."

"Yeah, shut up!" commanded Evelyn. She picked up an *LA
Weekly*, Prince on the cover, and placing it over her face like a
mask, pretended to pick his nose with her index finger, which
caused Pearl's guests to roar with laughter. "Or you will be
banished to the barrens of Minnesota to listen to *Purple Rain* for
the rest of your natural lives."

Bradley the human condom laughed. "Is that a hex?"

Vampire Kaye vainly tried to squelch giggles. Soon they were snapping Polaroids, Evelyn etching designs onto the film as it developed. Kaye slurped her gin and tonic.

"Pearl! You look like one of those toilet paper covers. You know, those dolls people stick on their toilet tanks. Old ladies knit them."

"Gee, thanks," replied Pearl, above peals of laughter.

"Hey, yeah!" said Bradley. "I know what you're talking about. Is there a name for those things?"

Kaye laughed. "Yeah, piss elegance."

Bradley fell to one knee at Pearl's feet. "She looks like a beautiful bride."

"She looks like the wedding cake!" Evelyn dipped a finger into Pearl's organza icing and popped it into her mouth.

Pearl fluffed her stacks of tulle and played "I Put a Spell on You."

"I love Screamin' Jay Hawkins!" Kaye flung her cape over her shoulder, invoking the showman they'd seen in concert earlier.

"The flaming coffin!" cried Bradley. "I loved the flaming coffin!"

"Well, you are a flamer," said Evelyn.

He ignored the remark. "And the bone in his nose!" Bradley sweated profusely despite discarding most of his plastic costume. "What a brilliant performer! I had no idea."

"Alice Cooper stole his shtick, if you ask me." Kaye rose, stretched, and repositioned her fake fangs. "Hey, I'm getting out of here before sunrise."

Fiona drained her drink. Pearl asked her to stay a little longer. One by one their co-workers filed out. Fiona washed off her face paint as Pearl removed her tiara and crinolines with a sigh of relief. Bathrobe-clad, she lit sandalwood incense and beeswax candles, and settled down next to Fiona on the couch.

"Mmm. You smell good."

"White Rabbit." Pearl lifted her wrist to Fiona's nose. "Rose essential oil, actually."

They discussed Irving Azoff's purging of thirty-nine acts from MCA's roster, Pearl's potential for promotion, and gender politics.

"There aren't many female-friendly labels out there," said Fiona. "Look at Lost Angels. The roster is almost completely made up of guys."

Their bodies inched closer together. "Women are making inroads," said Pearl. "I know some female executives."

"Probably the same executives I naively targeted with my demo tape, thinking they might identify with a woman's voice. So much for sisterhood."

"They can't do anything unless they're in A&R."

"Yeah, right. And the A&R people can't do anything because they're afraid of losing their jobs."

"There are more independent labels than ever before in the history of popular music."

"Okay. Airplay. How about that? A whole other Everest. All the program directors are male. They won't play more than one girl singer an hour." Fiona emphasized the point by banging her Corona down on Pearl's prized black lacquer and mother-of-pearl inlay coffee table. Her eyes widened. "Sorry!" Fiona quickly placed the beer on a coaster. "But it's true. The music business is a male preserve."

"Look at you. You're a sign of the times."

"Yeah. Right. And it's a real bitch. You have no idea how tough it is for a woman to have control over her career in this business."

"Get a manager. Dennis is a great guy, but you need a real manager."

"Easier said than done. At least Dennis is in my corner. I need all the help I can get. I'm sorry. I'll quit whining. At least I finally have a repertoire I'm proud of."

"I'll tell you a secret." Pearl lowered her voice. "Leo's going to offer you a recording contract. But you can't say anything! He's waiting 'til next quarter."

"Wow! A recording contract! All right. Maybe I won't spend the rest of my life answering telephones."

190

They toasted her good fortune, edging onto the middle cushion together, body heat registering. They discussed parents, how Fiona's father, as much as she resented him, had always encouraged her.

"He said I can do anything a man can do. So put me to work weeding, mowing, cutting down trees, stacking wood. We went hunting and fishing together. Thought he could turn me into Annie Oakley."

"I think it affects your performance. I love the way you carry yourself."

"Really?" Fiona shifted sideways, marvelling at Pearl's pert titties, wide cradle of hips, luscious bottom. "Well, I love it when you bend over the Xerox machine."

Pearl straightened up, turning to face Fiona, feigning shock. "You do?"

"Oh yeah. Casting your pearls before swine though."

"My God! What can you see?"

"I can't see anything. But it's hard not to look."

An instinctive smile slowly spread across Pearl's lips. "Fiona! I didn't know you cared."

"Oh, you did so. Don't be coy."

Tittering, thighs touching, their shoulders met. Gnawing on a fingernail, Fiona could think of nothing to say, but eventually mustered, "I find you very attractive."

Pearl smiled. "I love your Canadian accent. It's sexy."

"Pshaw. Your drawl. Now, that's a turn-on." Fiona took her hand. "Pearl," she said in a lazy voice, in imitation. "You don't tell a platonic friend she's sexy."

Squirming, Pearl lifted her eyes to Fiona's, scrutinizing, questioning. Fiona contemplated her choices. *Our choices*. She is not about to give anything away. Pearl's willing; just won't say it, much the way she picks at her food when people are watching, but digs in when they're not. Fiona bent her head toward Pearl. They kissed. Fixing her eyes upon Pearl's, Fiona slipped her hand under her shirt, onto her breast. Pearl gasped and capitulating, thrust her tongue into Fiona's mouth.

★ ★ ★ ★

My darling Fee, come to me. Please? I need to talk to you.
Meet me in the ladies' room. Okay?
Your precious Pearl.
xoxo

Pearl loved sending love notes and buying gifts: chocolate fortune cookies, dried hummingbird fetishes, fluted silver earrings. Every night she invited Fiona to dinner and every night begged her to stay, the intensity of Pearl's amour disconcerting.

"I don't need to be needed," Fiona told Shannon on the phone.

Pearl complained they didn't spend enough time together and greatly resented Dennis. Fiona protested, but was always aroused by the sweet nothings Pearl cooed to her in bed. They spent nearly as much time in her exquisitely tiled walk-in shower. Dennis had been alarmed when Fiona divulged the new developments, though relieved she wasn't doing it with a guy.

"You sexist," she said.

"You slut," he said. They laughed.

"Hey, I never said I was a nice girl."

Fiona was so elated she felt no guilt or shame, doubly hot for Dennis in fact, their sexcapades euphoric.

"Look!"

Entranced, she pointed to their silhouettes undulating on the wall, everything in life just as startling and wondrous. Things were beginning to happen; good press, band about to get signed.

"Think my ship is finally coming in?"

"Hey, you can always swim out to it," said Dennis.

"I love you."

Dennis was flabbergasted. Lately Fiona loved everybody. So many humans, so little time.

★ ★ ★ ★

Farrah Fawcett, Clark Gable, Deborah Harry, and Sammy Davis

Jr. Seemingly every L.A. hair salon, coffee shop, parking lot booth, and bar proudly displayed framed eight-by-ten headshots of both their well-known and unsung celebrity patrons. The legendary Formosa Cafe had one of the most impressive collections, spanning back to the thirties. Fiona and Pearl sat in the railroad car lounge sipping martinis, Pearl dutifully inspecting the signatures on the portraits.

"I'd rather look at The People of Los Angeles," said Fiona. "Daniel J Martinez's holographic portraits. Have you seen them?"

"No. But yes, there are real people in La La Land." Pearl kissed her cheek. "People like you."

"People like us."

The two were giddy from the swirl of gossip and innuendo, and indeed constituted an odd couple. Pearl bore the shape of a woman, a voluptuous woman, developed in adolescence. Fiona's frame was that of a gangly girl, slowly filling out. A late bloomer.

"You know, I'm not comfortable with either term; woman or girl."

"You're a woman. A beautiful woman."

"I bet you say that to all the girls."

Pearl chuckled.

"Hey, how is a martini like a woman's breasts?" Fiona waited a moment. "One is not enough and three is too many. And I think you've had enough."

"But, not enough of your breasts!" Pearl lunged.

They grappled and giggled as a hard-assed, white-collared barfly intruded upon their tête-à-tête with a cold, steady stare. Fiona kissed Pearl and he looked away. Holding hands usually created an effective barrier, though they relished flaunting the fact they were lovers. Men are not easily deterred, however. Most were intrigued, some hostile, many condescending, asking rude questions like, "Which one of you is the boy?" The hardcore Casanovas tried to pick them both up. Beating them to the punch wasn't difficult.

"I know, a ménage à trois is your favourite fantasy, right?"

It was usually amusing. When it wasn't, the girls downed

their drinks and departed, often at Fiona's behest, since Pearl was always so nice. One night Pearl couldn't remember where she'd parked her car. They walked in circles for ten minutes, Pearl in short skirt and high heels brimming with vim, Fiona fuming.

"Oh Fiona, shhiiilll out." Pearl wobbled "You are so—hic—paranoid."

"Paranoid! This ain't Hattiesburg, ya know. You're putting me in danger too."

Pearl shrugged.

Leo "surprised" Fiona with the recording contract over lunch the next day. Despite the expense, she hired Glenda Gutierrez, an upstart entertainment attorney friend of a friend. After several interminable weeks, the young lawyer advised Fiona to agree to nothing.

"Unless you want to sign away your first-born male heir. Lost Angels may be an independent, but this is more Faustian bargain than the major label contracts."

"Dammit!"

"I know you feel desperate, but you should probably keep vying for a major label. You've got the talent."

"Yeah. Right. What I don't have is a career."

Fiona asked Glenda to speak to Leo again. Half-hearted negotiations went back and forth for several more weeks after which Glenda insisted the options were still too binding. Fiona agonized over the decision and seriously considered going with Leo and Lost Angels anyway, just to get a new record out. Finally she turned it down, offending Leo and disappointing her band. She'd have to find a new job and prayed the boys would stick around.

Operating on Dixie Time, Pearl caused endless arguments about punctuality, or the lack thereof. She arrived late and missed most of the Billy Bragg concert, as with the Sam Shepard play *True West*. Both Quaid brothers made it onstage, but Pearl didn't show up until halfway through the last act. She couldn't be bothered to attend most of Fiona's shows and was tardy when she did. Pearl was even late meeting Fiona at her own apartment. Feeling entitled, Fiona snooped through Pearl's cupboards and drawers. *How can anyone eat candied yams?* She found a thong and wondered why Pearl hadn't worn it. *That bum of hers would be rendered even more beguiling in that thing.*

Pearl called, purring, "Hi, sweet thang! I'm on my way. There's some killer brie in the fridge. I got it at that little French shop on Hyperion, just for you."

"Pearl. I will kill you if you aren't here in fifteen minutes. I'll leave. I swear!"

Fiona paced, trying in vain not to seek the clock face every five minutes. *That little bitch! She's doing it on purpose. Isn't she? She's with somebody. I just know it! I can see her dangling those pretty tits of hers in that degenerate Bullet Proof guitarist Ron's face, draping them around his cock. Why does she do this to me?*

Pearl arrived at last, venerating Fiona's indignation. "I'm sorry! Let me in. Please!"

Fiona scowled at her through the peephole, Pearl's calculated fragility magnified by the fish-eye lens.

"Let's see now, how many times have I heard that before?"

Fiona unbolted the lock. *Have to take what I can get.* Pearl threw herself into Fiona's arms, unsullied skin smelling faintly of gardenia. *Maybe she is guileless.* Pearl bestowed her with a black velvet belt amid a frenzied shower of kisses.

"Isn't it darling?"

"It is. Thank you."

"Are we in love?"

"Pearl! Slow down. What's your hurry?" But by the end of the night, it was Fiona who was clutching, and murmuring into her neck. "I love you, Pearl."

Tttcchhh. Tttcchhh

"What the fuck was that?" Fiona jumped up.

Tttcchhh. She peered out the little window above Pearl's bed to see pebbles hitting the glass.

"Muff divers!"

She looked down at a swaying sot howling in the moonlight. Fiona poked her head out.

"What! Men can't go muff diving? You outta try it sometime, Ron."

"You lezbos having fun?"

"Yeah, especially with your little dick in your pants where it belongs."

Pearl pulled her head out of her slumber. "What's going on?"

"It's your idiot boyfriend."

Pearl clambered atop several pillows to look out. Ron was leaning down, about to pick up a large rock.

"Ron!" she scolded in a levelled scream.

"Hey, Pearl! Ain't you gonna invite me in?"

"Hey, Ron," yelled Fiona, "go piss up a rope!"

He gave her the finger while braying, "Oh rare gem of mine, pearl of my heart. Will you be mine, dear Pearl, will you be mine?"

Despite Fiona's objections, Pearl ran outside. Finally, Ron's shadow stumbled into the streetlight. Pearl returned and climbed back into bed. "He wrote a song for me."

"Yeah, I heard. A real gem. What's it's called? "Muff Diving for Pearl?"

Pearl's other boyfriend was a full-time champion surfer and part-time entrepreneur, far too busy to pester them.

Fiona couldn't get back to sleep, Pearl in an expansive mood. Cuddling, they discussed the unmapped territory of their relationship. No rules. No role models.

"It's exhilarating, don't you think?" said Fiona.

Pearl told her she was being ridiculed by Ron and her co-workers.

"I think it's perfectly normal to love individuals of either gender." Fiona kissed Pearl's palm. "And it's only possible when you view them first as individuals, and then as either man or woman."

"I think you have your own definition of normal."

Raji's is a trip. To Marrakech? It was supposed to be Marrakech, or the inside of a sultan's tent, though felt more like a dungeon, the lighting so sparse. Fiona LaBand was to open for Candye Kane and the Armadillo Stampede, both groups congregating upstairs post-sound check. Soon the doors opened and fans began to fill up the place.

"Look," said Ted. "It's that guy from *Cheers.*"

"Woody Harrelson!" Candye tipped back the brim of her black cowboy hat, fringe on her white leather jacket swaying with excitement.

"Big whoop." Fiona continued applying lipstick.

Candye giggled. "Guess who's giving Woody a big, friendly welcome?"

Fiona turned around to see Pearl leaning against a pinball machine, smiling and chatting up the buff TV star as he batted away. *Just like this morning!* At the butcher shop, Pearl yakked with the proprietor so long Fiona was certain all the steaks in the place had started bleeding.

"She's soooo friendly. To everybody! How am I supposed to know who she actually likes?"

"Don't you worry about it, honey. She'll come around. Pearl just needs to grow up a little."

The pretty pluck of Candye Kane, her singular mix of carnal knowledge and homespun wisdom. Candye's shtick had gone through several permutations from country to burlesque swing to the blues. Flamboyant, larger than life at two hundred pounds, she had the "moves of a stripper and the voice of an angel." *Maybe that's her appeal.* Madonna and whore, all in one big, buxom bundle of joy. It seemed she and Fiona suffered the same problem, recording industry unable to pigeonhole them. They were always too something; Candye's mouth too foul,

Fiona's songs too dark.

Pearl snuck up behind her, pressing her hula girl hips into Fiona's bum, encircling her waist with her arms.

"Oh, I thought maybe you'd gotten a better offer."

"You know I love you."

"You have a funny way of showing it."

"I could say the same thing."

They'd agreed it was best to continue seeing other people, but sometimes entertained the notion of living together. It would mean turning their lives upside down, and Fiona had no desire to be part of the "gay stream."

"I don't care if it is politically incorrect. I can't abide rhetoric-spewing lesbians. And outing. How fascistic is that? I may be queer, but I am not about to march in a parade or play inane butch-femme mating games. How do they justify such behaviour? They emulate men, parody women, all the while disparaging lowly breeder heterosexuals. They abhor stereotypes, yet they ape stereotypes, which is cynical and hypocritical if you ask me."

Pearl concurred. "How does that constitute an alternative lifestyle?"

"Beyond gay," said Fiona. "Isn't that truly subversive? I refuse to label myself bisexual or anything else. I am not on a crusade. It's nobody's business whom I lie with."

Beyond male, female. *Beyond human?* Fiona felt like a creature in the throes of a sound and thorough out-of-body fuck. Not of this world. Though she was beginning to resent Pearl's thrusting her into the male role. Fiona could find no perks, except perhaps the surprising and newly found ability to empathize with men. She was learning to see through Pearl's feminine wiles. Still, Fiona was susceptible, often succumbing to her charms, cajoled into taking responsibility; making decisions about what to eat, where to eat it, and how to get there. Pearl claimed a southern temperament as justification, though Fiona suspected sloth. She may pay lip service to feminism, but Pearl was truly a princess at heart.

"I won't play Prince Charming anymore," she confided in

Shannon. "It's wearing me out."

★ ★ ★ ★

Forsaken as a shaggy poodle, Pearl hugged a pillow and moped.

"Why do you have to act like this every single time you're crashing on speed? Figure it out, Pearl."

"Why can't you be more considerate? I'm alone all the time!"

"Here we go again. I am not your husband, dearie."

"I know! But, I thought you wanted to make me happy."

"I do, don't I?"

Pearl's lower lip protruded further. "No. It doesn't make me happy hearing about life with Dennis. I don't like having it shoved down my throat."

"No one shoves it down your throat. At least he respects my privacy. Why can't you?"

"It's not like I have any choice in the matter."

"We agreed we wouldn't do that," said Fiona, contempt hardening her voice. "Be possessive. Demanding. Remember? I thought this was about living consciously, in the here and now. In the moment. You're afraid of the future. Afraid of living. Just like everybody else."

"Why won't you let me love you?"

"Don't be such a drama queen. You know I love you."

"You do not. You don't care!" wailed Pearl, plunging her face into the linens, smears of mascara detailing misery.

"It's never enough. And you just proved my point." Fiona heaved a long sigh. "Have some faith in me. Have some faith in yourself, for chrissakes!"

Pearl bolted upright, Fiona returning her entreating gaze with a glare. Pearl ran into the bathroom. *Great, now she'll sit on the toilet, bawling until I beg to be let in. Someone always has to punish me. Since day one. I must deserve it. Original sin and all that rot.*

Fiona raised her voice at the door. "Bottom line, Pearl, I can't live your life for you. It isn't fair to expect so much of me."

Though proud of her reasoning ability, and resolve, Fiona winced helplessly at the sound of Pearl's sobbing.

199

★ ★ ★ ★

Craig Lee called to set up an interview for an *LA Weekly* cover story.

"It's like a lope through the jungle with an Amazon," said Ted. "Playing music with Fiona."

I wonder how long he worked on that sound bite? Kit was his usual reticent self, but having nothing to say never stopped Floyd.

"That's right. Have no fear. Fiona is here!"

A Natural Woman

Unlike some post-punk divas, Fiona Larochelle is definitely on the calm, cool, and collected side, possessing an admirable degree of restraint, as guitarist Ted Orchardson notes. "The second time we played Club Lingerie," he recalls with a laugh, "El Duce from the Mentors came up and said, 'I like that girl. She don't whine. All these L.A. bitches whine, but not her!'"

It's true. Fiona Larochelle neither whines, moans, pisses, nor groans. She doesn't bark, growl, screech, yowl, pull at her hair, drink vodka out of a shoe, or flash her boobs while juggling chainsaws. But how will this woman ever get any attention? Larochelle may have the "longest legs in rock" but what really counts here is sound.

"Our music is structured a lot differently than most of the stuff around town," says Orchardson. "We avoid clichés. Our stuff is trance-ical. We create a groove, not fall-asleep fusion."

"Everything's intuitive," observes Larochelle. "We work hard to avoid contrivance."

Their music is smooth yet dark, setting up a hypnotic mesh of wandering guitar lines against Larochelle's low, breathy vocals. The songs reflect her concern about losing one's personal human values in a consumerist society. It may sound like a portentous theme, but Larochelle takes a down-to-earth approach, both literally and figuratively.

200

"I write from an intense nature, as opposed to culture, fixation," she explains. "My stories and songs originate in the backwoods of Canada. I didn't see the city 'til I was fourteen. My dreams are still populated with animals: owls, whales, bears. I think urbanites, even if they've never seen a wild creature, are haunted by past lives as hunter-gatherers, part of the natural world."

Larochelle takes the nature-culture contrast to absurdist extremes in "Party Animals": *Dumb animals don't eat Twinkies/Dumb animals don't carry guns/Dumb animals don't kill themselves/Dumb animals don't tell bad jokes/Dumb animals don't party 'til they die/Dumb animals rarely need insurance.*

"'No future' is over. I'm trying to convey something constructive."

Everyone was thrilled with the piece. Everyone except Kit. "They make you sound like Joan of Arc."

The *LA Weekly* ran the article with a photo of Fiona decked out in her black bolero hat, leather gloves, and cowboy boots, "walking" a stuffed coyote. The following day, Ted rang her up.

"RCA called! They're sending an A&R guy down to the Music Machine tonight."

Fiona climbed into the tub, stretching out her celebrated limbs, wriggling her toes under a rush of warm water.

"Woo hoo!" Her voice echoed off the tiles. "This warrants a shave."

Pearl was still a wild ride and Fiona missed touring, the boys in the band often unavailable. Oh well, she thought, going on the road with them is so much work. She wound up playing den mother. The band was pleased to be opening for Robyn Hitchcock and his Egyptians, her best girl Shannon flying in for a visit the same day. Night of, the green room was crammed with roadies, groupies, hangers-on, managers, and press. Fiona scarfed down some questionable cold cuts between taps on her shoulder and kudos on their set. Rampant rumours of a major label deal persisted. The *LA Weekly* Music Awards had nominated them for Best Pop Group, Ted upset they'd been listed under the Pop category. Another rumour held that a famous director was about to feature the group in his new movie. "She's gonna be big." Fiona heard it everywhere: in the wind, bouncing off the walls, whispered in her ear, intoned by fellow musicians to each other like a prophecy.

Security was so tight they wouldn't let Shannon in. Fiona had to go square it with the club owner, who cornered her after sorting out the confusion, contrite.

"Is there anything I can do for you, Ms. Larochelle?" He winked. "Anything you want?"

The myriad of possibilities gave her a charge. Fiona looked around to make sure no one was watching and followed him into his office to snort a few lines.

She rejoined Shannon, who quickly became frustrated, each of their conversations interrupted. Ted was high, droning on about the gestalt of production values, Yreina looking to the ceiling. Shannon flirted with Floyd. Chloe Chan and Melanie Bowman glided into the room, stridently beautiful as ever. They'd been showing up ever since the buzz began escalating into a roar, probably so they could say, "I knew her when."

"The right situation." *That's a new one.* Fiona shoved the Chrysalis Records letter into her thickening Rejects folder. How to market Fiona LaBand was her greatest challenge. They were too folk, too obscure, too this, too that. "We haven't heard that hit single yet." The most popular excuse was, "Female artists don't sell records." Women buy the most albums, featuring male artists, so the theory went. Geffen "expressed interest," but Fiona wasn't surprised when they finally reported, "We have enough female singer-songwriters on our roster." Geffen was known for their nasty boys, Aerosmith and Guns N' Roses, but Fiona had held out hope.

"Unfortunately, I'm not a dude with big hair and a repertoire of rude gestures," she griped to Shannon. "I can't figure it out! Our audience is growing, ditto for the good reviews."

> Fiona LaBand weaves a mesmerizing spell over the unwary listener with moody, passionate, impressionistic folk pop.

> Intriguing lyrics and cool vocals from the Jackie O of rock singers.

> Twisted guitar textures, atmospheric, windblown desert music from Fiona LaBand proves there's rock and roll beyond art.

> Sassy and spirited, Fiona Larochelle lurches along that jagged blade between pop and alternative, scuffing her elbows and drawing blood with "In the Flesh" and Virgin Marries favourite, "Everything Gets in Your Mouth." Fiona Larochelle is Annie Lennox with a quivering moan.

"Drawing blood" is right. At least some people appreciated her sacrifices.

One night, convened on the bed after their bubble bath by candlelight ritual, Fiona pulled out a pink vibrator, the most innocuous one she could find.

"Let's play."

Pearl blanched. "What?"

"Don't you use a vibrator? You masturbate, don't you?"

Fiona leaned against the pillows, splayed her legs, and demonstrated. Pearl propped her head on her hand, watching intently. Fiona soon abandoned the toy for Pearl's thighs, leaving a trail of pink lip prints advancing upon Pearl's swollen clit. Fiona adored clits, the way they reveal desire. She tongued it a little, then flicked in a gentle rhythm. She wet her middle finger and slid it into Pearl's anus. Pearl groaned gutturally as Fiona variously hooked, stroked, jiggled, and shook her finger inside.

"Oh, Fiona."

Fiona schemed. *Wouldn't a rear entry be lovely? I'd love to roll her over on her tummy, smack her tush until red hot, then fuck her up the ass with a strap-on dildo.* Immediately, the thought scorched her with shame. *It'll never happen anyway.*

Teasing her clit, diddling her bum, Fiona's tongue moved from gentle flickering to steady, hypnotic stroking. Pearl tensed, trying to dam the rising tide, but came and roared, roared and came, clutching Fiona's head with her thighs. Pearl was so responsive, so resolutely orgasmic it always astounded Fiona. Taking a breather, they sipped wine between wet, exuberant kisses.

"Here, you play with it."

Fiona dropped the sex toy into Pearl's hand. She held it like a microphone, like a reluctant lady of the church auxiliary, and soon handed it back. Fiona pulled Pearl's delectable ass to the edge of the bed. She warmed some lube in her hands and smeared the vibrator, Pearl eying her dubiously. Fiona went down on her before she could protest, caressing the delicate skin between vulva and anus. Light licking and hot breath soon loosened and lowered Pearl's legs.

"Turn over."

Pearl slowly rolled over. Her hesitation only fuelled Fiona's ardour. She pulled her up by the hips onto a pile of pillows so that Pearl's ass was high in the air. *Maybe I should have brought a butt plug. Nah. I want to see this thing go in her. It's little. It's lubed. What the hell. It's not like her hole hasn't been primed.* Mesmerized, savouring the sight of Pearl's plushy, dimpled bottom, prone and entreating, Fiona gently probed the puckering flesh, set the vibrator to low, and inserted it slowly and deliberately, instructing Pearl to relax. Pearl complied, phallus gliding in. *I am the first.* Pearl's involuntary moans and the wildly popping thoughts in her head animated Fiona as much as the reflection of the two of them in the mirror. *Beside herself, outside herself. This is what it's all about. No wonder men love to fuck.* She wrapped Pearl's hair in her fist, pulling her head back so she could watch Fiona pumping away between her butt cheeks.

"Look."

Pearl looked, glanced away. Fiona leaned over, stiff nipples grazing the small of her back.

"You okay? Do you like it?" Pearl said nothing. "I'll stop if you want."

"I'm okay," she mumbled.

She's done. Fiona could tell by the sounds emanating from the back of her throat. She gently pulled the thing out. Pearl turned over.

Licking her clit, reaching up to squeeze her nipple, Fiona teased for long minutes, creating an excruciating tension bordering on pain so palpable they could both taste it, Pearl squirming, pleading. Training her tongue on her clit, Fiona got a good rhythm going until Pearl wailed through another climax. Fiona waited for her breathing to slow, moved up to her mouth for a kiss. Eyes shining, Pearl smiled a grateful smile.

"Next time, fun with dildos. You can do me, you know."

Next time never came.

"You can't have it all, Fiona!"

"Why not? And who are you to deny me anything?"

The honeymoon was over. Fiona decided Pearl's resentment was destroying her morale. She was tired of the constant questioning of her motives and choices. *Who is she to judge me?* Things were fine as long as they didn't discuss the truth of the matter. Any matter. How does that constitute intimacy? *Ah, it's all a ruse. Pearl's just overwhelmed, can't assimilate it. Us. Sadly, she's the one driving me away, consciously or subconsciously, clinging at the same time, the way a woman on foreign soil clutches her purse. Maybe it isn't fair. Maybe I am a selfish shithead, unrealistic to think it could work, that we could be happy together.*

"We can work things out. Please don't leave!" cried Pearl.

Fiona stopped returning her calls. Pearl called her a vampire.

Bereft, especially of Pearl's booty, Fiona was miserable. For about two weeks.

I am a monster. Someone always opens the cage or proffers blow. What to do but wreak havoc along with all God's fiends, fan the flames, trespass against others, burn bridges, the maps that lead to treasure. If we are not freaks, surely we are flukes. Fuck ups. Lights so bright Fiona couldn't see their faces, their ghastly, forbidding faces. *Fuck 'em. Stand up. Strap it on. Grab the mic. Form a fist. I have always been malignant. Cold. Hot. I can't swallow! Shit. Why did I rub my gums with it? 'Cause he did. A high man is good to find. They were not lies to her. Pearl. Pearl, who became a boar, more tusk than roar. Woe to you. I have the power. I created this. This sound. This singular sound.*

Fiona descended stage left to a thumbs-up from Caleb Crowe, Dennis on her immediately.

"What's that asshole doing here?" Not surprisingly, Dennis hadn't forgotten the foppish producer they'd met in Mexico.

"He wants to record a new demo for us."

The band convened at Kit's place, an old storefront in an industrial area across from the Wonder Bread bakery, roof capped with a barge-sized loaf. Fiona observed the frosty air, plywood floor, little arm—a doll part—floating in a refurbished lava lamp filled with rose-coloured water. Kit's kitchen, cum bathroom, cum bedroom, though threadbare, was neat and orderly. She noticed a row of glitzy dresses hanging above a collection of stiletto-heeled boots and pumps. *Kit has a girlfriend?* He brought them beer. The Doucettes started harping.

"We need to play stuff that's commercial."

"Look, I'm not about to cash in my integrity."

Floyd shook his head, eyeing her with pity. "Fuck. How naive is that?"

"Okay, let's talk about naïveté. You really think it's that simple? We just compromise our principles and 'play stuff that's commercial,' then POOF, suddenly the majors clamour to sign us?"

Kit looked past her. "You do think you're Joan of Arc."

"She's right," said Ted. "There is no rhyme or reason. Do you actually believe we have control over any of this? The entire recording industry is a farce."

"Yeah!" said Fiona. "You do it because you love it. Play music 'cause it's who you are. Besides, you know, we hear rumours of some A&R guy in the crowd. How many times has that happened? Artful dodgers. At this point, I probably would pay somebody off if I knew who to give the cash, or the coke, or the blowjob to!" They all stared at the floor. Fiona jumped up. "I'm outta here. I mean, what else is there to say? And screw it! I'm calling Caleb Crowe tomorrow. He said he'd shop a demo for us."

Dennis was dubious, but the band seemed appeased. On the drive home Fiona wailed.

"Do the Doucettes really think I'm not doing everything I can to get us signed?"

"They don't have a clue," said Dennis. "They're in their own world. By the way, Kit's a cross-dresser."

"Wow! I knew he was weird. I just thought he was hypoglycemic."

Fiona was pleased to find a new job, by word of mouth, the best way to find a new job, relieved it was unrelated to the music business. She was the new curator's assistant at the Woman's Building Gallery.

Everybody was having babies. Ted and Yreina, Candye and Thomas, Floyd and his girlfriend. Even Pearl, according to the latest scuttlebutt.

Fiona examined her crow's feet. *Too late to die young now.* Minimal damage though. No sun bunny was she. Good genes, bone structure. Fiona cursed. Just when she'd finally quit feeling ugly, she'd have to worry about getting old. A big-shot record producer at a party advised her to start marketing her songs to other artists.

"If you haven't made it by now, forget it." He made a big show of taking her demo anyway. A week later he told Fiona she needed to fire everybody and get a new band.

Floyd gave her *Hit Men* to read, an exposé of the recording industry. *Wow, the music business is corrupt.* She was depressed enough, she told him. Couldn't bring herself to read it.

Fiona was so broke she drove around with a can of Instant Tire in the trunk of her beater. She might be reduced to busking, but hey, that's how the Violent Femmes got discovered. She'd blown it with Lost Angels and the majors were not coming through. The album that never was. The career that never was. But she did have a stalker. Some fan was leaving notes in her mailbox and on her windshield.

There'd been a drive-by shooting at a house across the street. Fiona slept with a baseball bat next to her pillow and woke to helicopter hullabaloo nearly every night, their white lights searing her room, turning her bed into a hot seat. *Time to move.* She'd been scouring Laurel Canyon, its rocky, treed hillsides providing a respite from sweltering concrete. It reminded her of Canada. She imagined the house on the hill with a grand piano to be Joni Mitchell's. The area was pricey, but Fiona was determined.

Six months later she found an affordable place on Lookout Mountain Avenue, a charming one-bedroom A-frame with a loft and stained glass windows. Dennis was vying to move in and she'd have to watch Evinrude closely; coyotes of the canyon feasted nightly on the resident fat cats.

The morning after the housewarming party, Fiona woke to songbirds and smiled. Inhaling eucalyptus, nursing a hangover with Gatorade and Alka-Seltzer, she picked up the remote and idly flipped through the channels. *Oscar coverage, all day, all night, whether you give a rat's ass or not.* She heard a noise outside, and ventured past the sliding glass doors to find a German shepherd and two young LAPD officers combing through the ground cover with long sticks. Up and down the street, cops and hounds sniffed through each yard. She asked them what they were doing. The female officer looked at her partner.

He shrugged. "We're looking for body parts."

"What!"

"Didn't you hear? A few blocks from here, on Wonderland. Drug deal gone bad. People killed. Dismembered."

Fiona peered into the creeping ivy. "I thought it harboured vermin."

Later, she heard rumours of a pornography mill, an implicated John Holmes on the lam, and a missing head. *Christ. And here I thought I was moving up in the world.*

girl with ratty hair

CHAPTER NINE

Fiona stood waiting, nervously squinting into a surveillance camera as she rang the bell. Once a sweatshop, Caleb Crowe's Silver Lake studio was situated between a notorious gay leather bar, the Back Door, and Bob's Market, a Korean grocery. Its display windows were painted over in machine-gun grey, graffiti's secret code gracing the dumpster and telephone poles like dog piss. A broad-faced Chicano teenager opened the door and pulled back a screechy, iron gate. Fiona slipped into the studio's long, cool shadows.

"Hi, I'm Hector."

She followed Hector through a large soundproofed room with hardwood floors, baffled-in drum kit in one corner, and gleaming white baby grand piano in the other. She caught a faint whiff of marijuana, then potpourri, a Glade Plug-In glowing in a wall socket. They navigated a wide serpentine river of cords and cables, making their way through a vocal booth and adjoining control room. Hector yarded on a solid steel door opening to a sleek, well-appointed apartment, ambient with Charlie Parker. Hector knocked on the bathroom door.

"Oh yeah, hi, Fiona!" Caleb shouted cheerfully. "Make yourself at home. I'm on the phone but I'll be right out."

Hector left to run errands. Fiona stood in the filtered air and gawked at Caleb's highly equipped kitchen; Cuisinart food processor, gas range, vintage chrome-based Osterizer blender, copper-bottom cookware suspended from a rack over a granite-topped island. *Wow. A man that can cook. A man that likes it hot.* A collection of chili sauces were displayed in a rack.

Out back, Fiona could see a patio and a serene garden of

jasmine, climbing roses, fig, orange and banana trees, the fence obscured by ivy and mauve morning glories. She paced about the living room, admiring the Persian rugs and neo-Yves Klein paintings. The library, housed within custom teakwood cabinets, contained a respectable number of classics. An ionizer rested on the shelf like a sated spider. Elegant art books graced the marble-topped coffee table. A pair of nun chucks and a collection of trophies had been jammed in one corner of the living room, Caleb a black belt in judo. Another corner overflowed with shiny fly-fishing rods and gear.

While listening to Caleb on the phone, Fiona snuck into his bedroom. In a nightstand next to the solid mahogany bed she found a fat wad of cash, held together by a silver money clip, a fearsome dildo, porno videos, and pill bottles. She shoved two Dilaudids in her pocket and tiptoed back to the living room. Fiona sat on the tufted leather couch and idly flipped through a foot-high volume of Van Gogh.

Caleb called out. "Can you grab us a bottle of Perrier please?"

She grabbed two bottles of Perrier from the fridge. "Got 'em!"

"Pass it to me, will you?"

Gawd. Do I actually have to go in there? Fiona was determined to keep things on a professional level. "Hey, Caleb, are you having a bubble bath?"

"No. Why?"

"Well, believe it or not, I'm a bit shy and would really rather not gaze upon the family jewels. Okay?"

Caleb laughed. "Hey, no problem. I'm hanging up." She heard water sloshing "Pass my robe, okay? It's on the back of my bedroom door."

Are those legs painted on? Fiona found a plush, white terry cloth bathrobe, and passed it to him. Caleb emerged from an immense bathroom with a stone floor, sunken tub, and skylight.

"Sorry about that," he said unapologetically. "I was talking to my mother. It's not like I can just hang up."

"Yeah. My mother always calls just as I'm running out the

door. To dump on me. I try not to hurt her feelings or I just feel guilty."

"Well, Catholic guilt is almost as oppressive as Jewish guilt." Caleb smiled and went into the bedroom. "My dad's retired. They live in Palm Springs now." He emerged in a rust-coloured silk shirt, black slacks, and Chinese slippers, redolent of bergamot. "It's definitely a mixed blessing for my sister and I, our mother being the quintessential JAP." He chuckled. "Know what a JAP is?"

"I've encountered a few Jewish American Princesses. Guess that makes me a shiksa, a term I believe is steeped in rancour."

"It's distasteful, I agree."

"No one likes being reduced to a cultural stereotype." She smiled. Though Caleb had brought it up, she sensed the subject might be a tad sensitive. "But hey! This place is an oasis. You'd never know it's here from the street."

"That's the idea. The musicians love it. We keep a low profile. It's a rough neighbourhood. I would have preferred West Hollywood, but the overhead is so low here, I can't complain." Caleb sat down next to her. "I really enjoyed your performance the other night. What a firebrand! You destroyed that audience."

She shook her head. "Thanks, but I feel like I haven't even hit my stride."

"That's a good attitude. Always striving. You weren't particularly shy either. Not anything like the sweet young gamine I met in Mexico."

"I'm not exactly me when I'm onstage."

"I don't enjoy performing. You're a natural."

"Performing's not 'natural,' but I live for those times when I can transcend, you know? Oblivious to everyone, everything, entirely and utterly immersed in the moment. In the music."

"See. I've never had that experience. Not onstage, anyway." Caleb moved toward an antique rolltop desk. "Want a bump?"

"Uh, sure." *Thought you'd never ask.*

Caleb pulled a tray of accoutrement from the top drawer, picked up a plastic cylinder and turned its crank as though sifting

213

flour, until a stack of blow the size of a baby's fist rested upon the mirror. Caleb formed four precise lines. Though physically formidable, he held his cigarette like a girl. An oddball, but an intriguing oddball who had his act together. Caleb passed the mirror and a brass tube.

"Ladies first."

She held her hair back, leaned forward, and snorted two lines. *Real ladylike.* "Thank you."

He followed suit. They discussed music, Caleb an unrepentant name-dropper, though she was impressed with his encyclopedic knowledge of jazz, R&B, and funk.

"That's me, a Jew boy with soul."

He put on a Tony! Toni! Toné! record. "These brothers play real soul."

Next, Caleb put his own EP on the turntable, though Fiona was more interested in hearing the bands he'd produced. *Who told him he could sing?* Caleb's guitar skills were exceptional though. She told him so. He beamed. Nice bass sound, horn arrangements bona fide, production slick, but none of it moved her. *Limp Steely Dan.* What could she say?

"Pretty good."

He pointed to the liner notes. "Best horn players in L.A."

Nice he can afford them. "Great backup singer."

"Latisha, yeah, she's exceptional. Touring with Luther Vandross."

"Luther who?"

Chuckling, Caleb put out more lines. Fiona admired the cover art. Quite noir, she told him, an evocative visage of a haughty woman reclining on a divan in the shadow of a full moon.

Caleb was bending toward her ear when there was a knock on the door. He got up and let in a middle-aged dude with long, stringy brown hair tied back in a ponytail. *Hippie handyman?*

"This is my partner, Lenny."

"His silent partner." Lenny laughed.

"Lenny's Canadian too, from Montreal. A fellow Jew. Probably why we get along. Tribe vibe."

"Since when do we get along?" said Lenny. He pointed to the clock. "It's one p.m. and you're not dressed yet?"

"Give me a break. My back is acting up again."

"You and your back. Doesn't stop you from partying, does it?"

Fiona interceded. "Dost thou think, because thou art virtuous, there shall be no more cakes and ale?"

"Uh oh. She's quoting Shakespeare."

"I know it's Shakespeare."

"Sorry. I don't normally quote Shakespeare. I'm attending night school."

"Good girl." Lenny fished out a Perrier. "Well, back to the old grind. Some of us have to work for a living."

Lenny disappeared through the back door. *Maybe he's the gardener.*

"Putz," muttered Caleb. "Not very silent, is he?"

"So, do you like living in L.A.?"

"The music business is stimulating. I do miss New York. Zabar's! Pastrami and bagels. My father the WASP used to run out for *The New York Times* on Sunday mornings and bring us lox, cream cheese, and fresh bagels. It's hard to find a good one in this town."

"I have. Brooklyn Bagel. It's not far from here."

"Really? I'll have to check it out. I was seriously considering having some FedExed."

"You know my music is probably more folk than the stuff you like. Think you can work with a white girl?"

"Sure. I love your music. I have eclectic taste. The only music I don't like is bad music."

"I'm getting discouraged. There's lots of 'major label interest,' but it never goes anywhere. Still don't have a manager or an agent. I'd like to record a bunch of new songs by Christmas, send a tape out and follow through. Aggressively. Track down the right contact person, make sure they come out to see us play. You know?"

Caleb snorted, sniffed, and passed the mirror. "Here. Not much consolation. But I do have some good contacts for you."

"Great!" She pressed her right nostril closed and sniffed deeply. "Ah. My optimism is returning."

"This is no time to give up. We have a lot of work to do though. You may have a unique sound, but there's a lot of discordance. You and Ted especially need to tighten things up."

"Okay. Well, I'm all in favour of that. Things have been disintegrating." *I shouldn't have revealed that.*

Caleb proceeded to dissect her voice, songs, career. Putting his money where his mouth is, she thought, inviting the band to rehearse at his studio.

Rory had announced a forthcoming visit to California, but Maureen actually showed up, miffed when Fiona refused to pick them up at the airport, insisting they take a shuttle to the Roosevelt Hotel. Easy peasy. Gary, Maureen's latest husband, was an irritating rube, but her niece, Emma, had matured into a bright and spirited adolescent, and an aspiring musician. Fiona pulled out her arsenal, providing Emma with a kalimba, tambourine, maracas, panpipes, and recorders.

They went out for Mexican food, Maureen gripping the dashboard, complaining about Fiona's aggressive driving.

"It's an aggressive town."

Maureen insisted on ordering a steak. Fiona tried to explain that Mexicans ate pork and seafood. It arrived tough, sinewy, inedible. "You'd still rather die than take my advice."

Maureen wound up sampling everyone's enchiladas, tostados, and tacos.

"Mo does L.A."

"Shut up."

Determined to make the most of whatever label interest remained, Fiona scheduled rehearsals in preparation for recording, but soon ran into resistance: Kit, via his usual mumbling, noncommittal self; Floyd fucking up, drinking a lot, blowing off rehearsals; and Ted too busy to get together. She worried that Ted was assimilating Dennis' resentment toward Caleb. Fiona tried talking to Floyd about his reckless, self-destructive behaviour. He told her it was none of her business.

Dennis was at her place nearly every day, which meant a fight nearly every day.

"I do love you. I'll always love you, and maybe someday I can even be what you want; your loyal, nice girl bitch. Just not now!"

Dennis slumped. He insisted he was her rock, her muse. Fiona stifled laughter.

"Look, right now, I need to sing, write, work. I can't be in love. It takes up too much psychic energy. We have to give it a rest."

She declared a three-month hiatus. Stricken, Dennis stood there, vacillating, and grappling with anger, hurt, humiliation.

"I need to focus. This is a critical time. Do or die! All this emotional turmoil is draining, compromising my productivity. I'm sick of it."

"Fine," said Dennis evenly. "I'm sick of it too. Maybe you're right. Maybe we need a break, but I have faith in our future, even if you don't."

"I do have faith in our future. You don't understand. I wanna live in the present!"

The recording went well, Caleb an adroit engineer, attentive and patient, though he had an irritating habit of disappearing. Often Fiona would turn to say something, only to find him vanished. She presumed he was taking smoke breaks or snorting cocaine. Certainly intent whenever he set out to "orchestrate," Caleb breathed quickly and sighed deeply, speaking rapidly of MIDI, SMPTE, emulators, master time code machines, automated mixes, and the horrors of the Steinberg DMP-7 program, laughing when Fiona told him it was giving her a headache.

He'd hired a backup singer; a robust young black woman

217

named Shayla Greene. She arrived at the studio, two kids in tow, wearing a blond wig and baseball cap obscured by buttons, one pin proclaiming "I amaze myself". She amazed Fiona the moment she opened her mouth, mightily navigating the harmony high notes of "Coral Aggression's" chorus. Caleb was pleased with the way the women's voices blended. The entire production had a quality of tempered boldness. *He gets it.* The boys were surprised and pleased with their efforts, synergy on the tape bonding the band members, long enough, she prayed, to get signed.

Caleb invited the band to his parents' vacant Palm Springs condo. The Doucettes declined, but Ted and Yreina were happy to partake of his largesse. They headed for the country club community of Rancho Mirage, Fiona startled that the condo was behind security gates and on a golf course. Plush carpets muted their boisterous arrival, soft neutral colours lending to the desert's tranquility.

"It's the biggest condo I've ever seen!" Ted stood drooling in front of an elaborate wet bar.

"Go ahead," said their munificent host. "Fix us a round of drinks."

"Oh God," moaned Yreina, "don't encourage him."

Ted laughed. "Palm Springs weekend, honey!"

"You know what they say," said Caleb, pulling matches out of his pocket. "Living well is the best revenge." The matchbook flipped into the air, landing at Fiona's feet. "Oh here, I'd better get that." Slyly grinning, Caleb bent to retrieve it, taking in her long legs. Fiona's nerves jangled. *He's cute. Sexy.*

She basked in a spot of solitude, the others at the store. The pervasive quiet made Fiona antsy. Only the rich can afford peace and quiet, she thought, din of choppers, sirens, gunshots slowly receding from her psyche.

After a dinner of grilled pineapple and mahi-mahi on the terrace, they cooked themselves in the Jacuzzi, sipping gin and tonics, and lolled by the pool, tooting coca between lackadaisical laps. Though she lived on the West Coast, Fiona rarely went swimming. *I must be moving in the wrong circles.* She worked on her breaststroke.

"You just need to get the rhythm down," offered Caleb. "And all God's children got rhythm. Especially you."

Fiona blushed, and it seemed so as they passed a guitar back and forth, warbling their favourite tunes, crimson sun bowing behind the San Quinto Mountains. The desert reminded her of Dennis. Fiona missed him terribly, haunted by their telepathy, his last words. "How will I feel about you in three months?"

The urbanites spent the next day exploring. Hiking the Andreas Canyon, they marvelled at caves and otherworldly rock formations. Take Nothing but Photos, Leave Nothing but Footprints; Americans and their penchant for signage, she thought. Such managed wilderness still jarring to her Canadian sensibilities. They rode the gondola to the top of Mount San Jacinto, 10,000 feet up. Swiss-made, Fiona hoped it was as reliable as their timepieces, swaying and crammed as it was with tourists. At the top, Caleb handed her a pair of binoculars. Fiona spotted a golden eagle. A large swath of windmills hugged the base of the mountains like a twirling vineyard. Caleb pointed out garages, motels, shopping centres, and schools, all designed by visionaries, Richard Neutra, Donald Wexler, Albert Frey.

"Modern is perfect in this environment. All that glass, concrete, steel, integrated with the terrain! A sublime wedding of design and geography."

"Are all New Yorkers so sensitive to architecture?"

Caleb laughed. "I almost became an architect. Studied at Princeton. Thought I'd meet more girls playing music though."

"But what kind of girls?"

"I doubt I would have met you at Princeton."

Rather a backhanded compliment, she thought. They spent another night stretched out by the pool, smoking, drinking, snorting lines.

"Look!" said Fiona. "I swear, the desert sky doesn't blacken. It really is violet."

Fiona caught Caleb gazing at her wistfully. She invited them all for a walk. The Orchardsons declined. An ebullient chorus of crickets serenaded Fiona and Caleb as they strolled together.

"I'm pretty blissed out. But hey, don't you live in dread of a golf ball flying through your window?"

Caleb laughed. "Free entertainment, my dad calls it."

Quack, quack, quack, quack fell into Fiona's consciousness like a soft rain. A family of mallards waddled by and tossed themselves into the pond. A coyote howled, how far or near, she could not tell. Fiona put her arm companionably through Caleb's. They listened to gravel crunching beneath their feet, limelight of a full moon lighting their faces. They stopped to fire up cigarettes.

"What's that?" Fiona pointed to a form silhouetted and cleaved to the limb of a ponderosa pine. "Is that a hawk?"

They walked softly, careful not to disturb the creature. Peering closely, they discerned a bare, red, creased neck and head protruding from a cloak of coarse brown feathers. The thing had a hooked, waxy, white beak and tawny eyes fixed upon nothing. Recoiling, Fiona screamed.

"It's a vulture!" She looked down at her hands shaking. "Christ. Why should that send me into a state of panic?"

"They are repulsive. It's understandable."

"It upsets my equilibrium I suppose. Or else it's just a shock coming face-to-face with such a fabled bird. Such a reviled bird."

Caleb put his arm around her shoulder, the way he had on the beach in Mexico. She felt little reassurance.

"Vultures are vital though. They make quick work of carcasses, which stops the spread of bacteria and disease."

"Still, an agent of death."

"And a fact of life."

"But what's it doing here? I don't see too many corpses lying around. Although, this is a retirement community, and scavengers are opportunists."

Laughing, Caleb pulled her close. Fiona rested her head on his chest. She thought she heard hooves pounding in the distance, or thunder. She raised her eyes to his, black in the shadow of the lone pine, Caleb's face white as bone. Choking on his musk, Fiona couldn't breathe. *He looks like Lucifer.* She regretted getting high with him. *He is Lucifer! Here to annihilate. My muscles are disintegrating.* Fiona felt weak, vulnerable as prey. *I must be losing my mind. Man! What if he slipped me something?* Long, heavy wings flapped, raptor ascending, tree trembling in its wake. Fiona smiled reflexively. Caleb leaned over, kissed her mouth.

They snuck into the condo, into his bedroom, starting in with cocaine and cocktails, Caleb rendering asunder, plumbing depths of Fiona flesh with a relentless cock, inordinately proud of his ability to delay orgasm.

"Withholding my chi."

Her challenge was to orgasm. *Maybe someday I'll be in a position to withhold, or ply, or temper.* Caleb gripped Fiona's waist so roughly, and finally succumbing to orgasm, she cried out in pain. The next morning she noticed scratches and bruises, and was so wrung out she doused her cereal with orange juice instead of milk. Unsure of how she felt, they agreed to be discreet. Fiona had not anticipated this, and there was Dennis to consider.

"Hey girl. I think I might be getting in over my head," she told Shannon. "Got high with Caleb. It was not a good trip. The day after the day after and I'm still having flashbacks to a bizarre scene I cannot figure out. Did it happen? He is such an enigma. I swear, just as the drugs were hitting my central nervous system, he morphed into Satan!" Shannon suggested it might have been a drug-induced psychotic episode.

"So I am crazy. Was I living out some long-repressed fear? Some Catholic supernatural bullshit? What if this is all some kind of perverse game, a mindfuck? Is that why he wants to get me alone? Is that why he asked if I told anyone about us? Ah, I'm just paranoid. Right? It'll wear off. Right?"

Caleb was an ardent suitor, wining and dining Fiona, buying her flowers and jewellery. Or calling. His raging lust was flattering, but she demurred.

"I've gotta get some writing done."

The lovers talked for an hour. There was scant uncharted territory within the boundaries of Caleb's sexuality, though he harped that all his zones, however feral, were strictly heterosexual.

"Doth the gentleman protest too much?" she teased. "Anyway, I think the anticipation is good for you."

"No it's not!" he cried. "It's painful. I'm getting a sperm-retention headache."

"Ha-ha! Poor baby. What about withholding your chi?"

"Chi, shmie."

"Say hi to Fiona!" Lenny shouted in the background.

"How do you know it's Fiona?" Caleb asked. He laughed. "Lenny just pointed to my hard-on."

"I'm coming over."

The first order of their day was a rigorous romp, then lunch at Cha Cha Cha, Fiona ordering jerk chicken and greens tossed with mango vinaigrette. Caleb pointed discreetly, surprised to learn that she knew of Herbie Hancock; he looked professorial in a spiffy suit, high-collared shirt and spectacles, wavy hair slicked back.

"Don't you know him?" she asked, only half in jest. "I loved that video for 'Rockit,' the one with the kinetic mannequin? It's so funky. Danceable. Beyond jazz. Is that fusion?"

"You could say that. Hancock's definitely a risk taker. Like Miles. He started out with Miles Davis. He's also a prolific composer."

"Handsome too! I like his demeanour. Very genteel."

"You sound like a groupie. Why don't you go say hi?"

"I beg your pardon! I could say the same thing about you."

Caleb lowered his eyes and nipped into his red pepper and fennel soup. *Why the petulance?*

222

There was something about their bodies conjoining that ensured everything got rubbed the right way. Fiona thought his cock was exceptional, its size and shape seemingly tailored to her anatomy; thick, slightly curved at the end, and it oh so sublimely prodded her G spot. It made her come, much to her astonishment. He made her come. Caleb was always up, with as much zeal as stamina, and they liked to take their time.

"I know this sounds crazy, but I've loved you since Mexico. Could not get you out of my mind. Then I heard that exquisite voice. My DJ friend Diego had your Virgin Marries EP. Such a coincidence. Of course, I fell in love all over again."

Fiona didn't think it was that much of a coincidence. "Well, you have such a commanding presence, I didn't forget you either."

Caleb pointed to his record cover. "That's you, you know. I found this movie still and thought she looked like you. That's why I used it."

"You're so romantic."

Each morning, they rode in on the same corybantic horse. Still, Fiona's ardour cooled as she struggled for clarity.

I do not intend to fall in love. I need to concentrate on my career. Such as it is.

Caleb's rapture was infectious, however, and they often talked for hours. Inventive, versatile, a dauntless explorer, he claimed to find joy in losing himself. In her. They thrashed out their desires, limits, and fantasies. Fiona felt approval. He understood that she was not a nice girl, that she could be rude, lewd, voracious. Bad. "The two of us can be bad together," she confessed to Shannon. Caleb loved to rouge her nipples, labia, mouth; all the better for watching her go down round his cock. Astounded she had so many orgasms Fiona lost count, couldn't imagine coming again, then—weeping once—did. The Big O had eluded her for so long; she recalled feverishly contracting her Kegel muscles, desperately aiming, always missing her mark.

"I was a female eunuch. You're the only one who's ever made me feel this way. Feel this much."

★ ★ ★ ★

A reproachful Dennis called to remind her that their three-month suspension-of-relations was nearly over.

"You know what?" said Fiona. "I've gotten some perspective on how much I've accommodated you. How much you've always made demands. I'm tired of it. And we were stagnating."

Though nearly as appalled as Dennis, she marvelled at her coldness. *Or is it boldness?* She could own her flaws with Caleb. Her pain. Regrets. He mirrored her unflinchingly. At first Fiona couldn't shower in the open floor plan of his bathroom. Exposed, she'd felt like a doe in the crosshairs, skin prickling with every shift of air. Lately, she sauntered around the place in the raw, inhabiting the full length and breadth of her body. No shame. No hesitation. *And I will take this feeling onstage.* The copious sex forced Fiona to reside in her body, to know its every curve, arch, contour. *Home at last.*

They could fuck, and often did, round the clock. Then he'd appear to her in charged, erotic dreams. She suffered separation anxiety when Caleb went to the bathroom, crawling into his arms the moment he returned. *Okay. I'm pathetic. I can't handle this. And he's wearing me out!* Late one night, exhausted after a marathon session, Fiona declared she needed time alone. Time to reflect and strategize, though everything seemed futile.

"I'm about ready to pack it in. My brilliant career."

But Caleb made her laugh. Come. Forget so well. Fiona was ragged, sore from fucking. He could be a bit of a brute sometimes. Returning home, she ruminated. *So much has happened! I don't want to fall in love.* She justified their pairing as it was spawned in friendship, a shared passion for music. It had to be a good thing.

I have to bear in mind the perils of working with a lover. It should be okay as long as we don't live together. Between bouts of sheer terror, Fiona was excited about the future. *But all I do when I'm with Caleb is be with Caleb.* And oh God, she was guilty, so guilty; missing rehearsals, away so much, Evinrude so lonely, she found him sleeping in her guitar case.

A Dennis dream. Dennis often weighed upon her psyche, which made her feel manipulated and resentful, as much as she was unwilling to lose him. Rest eluded her. Fiona woke, sweating, limbs loose with longing, mind taut. She tried to pin down her emotions. *Ugh. Love. Hasn't it chosen me? Ah, it's just an invention. A conspiracy. Against women. Gawd. I am not neurotic! I will stop agonizing over all this crap. Conserve my energy. Play music.*

They talked of travels together, Caleb bringing out the hedonist in her. Fiona cooked for him, one night a supper of forty-clove chicken roasted in his clay oven with winter fruit compote and mocha ice cream for dessert. She'd relished the marketing; wine, baguette, currants, figs, pears, vanilla bean.

She felt augmented, her spine like an electric eel radiating heat. They snorted, sipped, Caleb fondling an indolent Fiona into a trance. He rubbed her nipples with the tip of his cock.

"Suck it."

He encouraged her to use her hands as much as her tongue. No qualms letting her know what he liked, which Fiona quite liked. They shared a cigarette, snorted more lines. She squeezed rhythmically, his cock soon rock hard. Fiona took it in her mouth, bell end tapping the back of her throat. She could see the beauty of this cock. On Caleb's cock, sensations were so spiked, she soared, blinded, their voices faint.

He asked her to ride bareback. She asked about STDs. Caleb reassured her.

"Of course, I use condoms, and get tested regularly, results always negative."

The sun rose, Fiona shocked to learn it was Sunday. They drew the drapes and showered, Caleb insisting they take sustenance in the form of bread and cheese before indulging in more cocaine. He grabbed his works, engaged in the ritualistic crushing, chopping, and laying out of lines as Fiona nibbled. They talked in long, heady spirals, locking eyes to keep their heads on. He spread the powder on the shaft of his cock. Fiona called him a coke monster and licked it off. They shot Polaroids, Fiona on her knees, wrists bound at the small of her back, posing with his cock distended against the roof of her mouth. He framed Fiona from above, in her lacey black teddy, lying on the pillows, legs spread, dildo poised above.

"Nice pussy shot."

Clinical, absurd, or vulgar, names for human genitalia reveal a lot about human beings, she thought. Mainly, that we're pathetic. Caleb gently pushed in the dildo, lifelike, except that it was purple. A game to see how many poses they could get out of a box of film, they paused to snort more lines, Fiona confessing that men scared her.

"Hey, not all men are bastards."

"I didn't say they were. But there is such a thing as misogyny, though these days I find the male of the species more amusing than threatening. Well, except when they're trying to fuck me, or trounce me. For knowing too much. They want you meek. Malleable. Nice."

Caleb related the comment to the whore, Mary Magdalene, how she ignored scorn to wash the feet of Jesus in her tears and dry them with her hair.

"Women are brave," said Fiona. "Merciful. Powerful. Odd, a nice Jewish boy bringing up Mary Magdalene."

"My dad's a Christian, remember? I'm doubly indoctrinated, so of course, believe in nothing."

"Unfortunately, women are forced to play the role of confessed sinner," said Fiona. "The burden we bear, punishment for tempting poor old Adam into eating forbidden fruit in the Garden of Eden."

"A Judeo-Christian notion maybe, women as the source of human suffering, but I doubt there's anything in the Bible directly holding them responsible for mankind's expulsion from paradise."

"What are we punished for then? Oppression of women is fundamental to nearly all religious doctrines."

"You're gettin' your Irish up."

"Oh, I'm up all right! Why shouldn't I be? It's something I

have to live with every day. You don't know what it's like. There are times when I just want to be left alone. You know? Well, because I happen to have a vagina, I can't walk down the street without being harassed."

"You got way more than a vagina, baby. Look, they want you to get angry. They're trying to elicit just that response."

"Why can't they leave me alone?"

"You're right. I don't know what it's like. What am I supposed to do? I love women. Am I to be strung up by the balls 'cause I own a pair?"

"I'm not blaming you!" Fiona snorted a line and passed the mirror. "It's men who fear women. It's why they bully women."

He looked past her. She let it go. He changed the subject. Soon they were onto geography, taking great pleasure in looking up Belize in the Atlas. Another paradise he vowed to take her to.

Further banishing the banal, Fiona and Caleb ventured to Catalina. Enduring a loud, bumpy speedboat ride, Caleb indulged in ogling a gaggle of giggling teenaged girls. An hour later, they landed at the quaint, charming burg of Avalon, crime- and car-free, locals tooling around in golf carts. Caleb read from the brochure as they climbed to the hilltop Zane Grey Pueblo Hotel.

"'Grey only wrote to support his fishing habit.' My kind of guy! Hey, the rooms are named after his books."

"What a novel idea."

Caleb groaned. They checked in and were given the key to Western Stars. Fiona laughed.

"That's me, a legend in my own mind."

They stuffed themselves with sand dabs and grilled shark for supper.

"I think the sea air makes me hungry." Caleb winked. "And horny."

"You're always horny. You were born horny."

They retired to their room. Fiona gazed out the window,

watching the yachts and sailboats moored in the lee of a eucalyptus grove. A pod of grey whales passed, heading down to Baja, breaching, spy hopping, expulsions of breath from their blowholes rising like whirling dervishes. Enchanted, Fiona and Caleb talked and fucked into the wee hours. Lately he'd been on about anal sex, how it's an erogenous zone richly endowed with nerve endings, how to break the powerful taboo, blah, blah, blah. Feeling me out on the subject, she presumed.

They crashed. After a few hours of shallow sleeping, the pair managed to rise to spend the day on a charter boat. A few hours in, Fiona had caught more fish than a grim Caleb.

"I'd rather land a recording contract," she joked.

It was becoming a sore subject. Fiona thought the demo would have generated more interest; that she'd be able to capitalize on Caleb's contacts. She reminded herself that she was on vacation and went down to the galley to rest and read. The cheery, gumbooted first mate soon clomped in. They chatted as Ida's strong hands gutted a red snapper.

"Your boyfriend's tackle's too heavy. He should try a plastic lure."

Ida seemed obsessed with tuna pilfering sea lions. Brandishing a slingshot, suddenly menacing, she demonstrated how she beaned them in the head when the conservation officers weren't looking. The two went back up on deck to tight lines and set jaws. Caleb waved, gesturing at the depths below, manhood vindicated as he battled a huge swordfish, much to Fiona's delight. Just as she decided Ida was delusional, Fiona spied two sea lions, keenly interested in what Caleb had on his line. Fiona watched its dramatic aerial acrobatics and thought that surely the great fish must be tiring. Grunting and whooping, Caleb slowly and steadily reeled it in. Nearly thirty minutes later, Ida helped pull the fish on-board and gaffed it on the head, its vertical lavender stripes fading with each gasp. The math professor from San Diego insisted Caleb had just hauled in a marlin.

"Swordfish are more fierce," he said, citing as an example the one that attacked Alvin, the Woods Hole Oceanographic

Institution's submarine.

"Fierce!" Caleb muttered below his breath. "I'll show him fierce."

"Yep, it's a marlin." Ida pointed. "See the dorsal fin. It's low. Swordfish got taller dorsals, longer bills"

Caleb was angry.

"I don't understand why the distinction matters," said Fiona. "It's an amazing catch, 'a formidable angling achievement.' I'm proud of you!"

He smiled. They headed back into Avalon. "What would you like to do tomorrow?"

She peered at several species of fish below, due no doubt to Catalina's serious anti-dumping and pollution laws.

"Diving. Let's go diving!"

Amid rocky underwater coves the next day, they came upon groupers, opal eyes, black sea bass, octopi, and lobster trekking across the ocean floor like mottled clowns on stilts. They saw toothless leopard sharks, great forests of kelp and glowing orange Garibaldi that appeared misplaced, like runaways from the tropics. Fiona was most enthralled with the dolphins.

On their last day they toured the famous Avalon casino. Twelve round, white stories high, it encompassed a theatre, a ballroom, and art deco chandeliers that looked like giant poppies of frosted glass.

"Count Basie and Xavier Cugat played on that stage," said Caleb, stretching out his arms as if to soak up the vibes. "Let's get married here!"

Fiona ignored the comment. He bought her a pair of black pearl earrings and a fluorescent green Sharky's Beach Club T-shirt. They dined on scallops and calamari steak. Fiona thanked Caleb profusely for the idyllic weekend, impressed with his *übermensch-ness*. She dreaded her return to smog and the inevitable showdown with Dennis.

He liked to braid her hair. Fiona was growing it long for him, much the way she left the house commando so Caleb could fondle her pussy in the car or under the table in restaurants.

"I used to braid Carrie's hair, when she was a little girl."

Fiona reclined, languorous as a sated lioness. Caleb leaned over to squeeze her tits, bite her neck, nibble her earlobes. He turned her over onto her belly, tugging on her pigtails, steadying her hips. He thrust wildly, Fiona rising to meet his rhythm. At last, Caleb came, each spurt of jizz spurring her to yowl.

Each time Fiona started to crash, Caleb disappeared and returned with more cocaine. *Über* Coca Candyman. They lounged, sweat seeping into the sheets. He jumped up to demonstrate how karate moves differed from judo. Ten p.m. Sunday, Fiona gratefully ingested the Valium he proffered. Still, it was difficult to fall asleep with Caleb's cock cradled against her ass.

Monday morning, enfeebled, Fiona felt certain the chain-smoking had seared holes through her lungs. She blew her nose, smears of coral-red blood on the tissue, nostrils raw. He showed her how to flush them with a warm saline solution. An antidote for everything, but Fiona only felt sad and guilty, especially from realizing she'd missed another rehearsal. She called Ted with a lame excuse, the taste of coca at the back of her throat. *More. I always want more.*

CHAPTER TEN

Four months in, still fucking like rabbits, Fiona contracted one bladder infection after another. Caleb took her to see Miles Davis at the Hollywood Bowl. The man really did play with his back to the audience and surprised them with a cover of Michael Jackson's "Human Nature."

Fiona vainly tried to dodge the inevitable relationship discussions. Caleb needed Dennis out of the picture. Though weary of feeling torn, of appeasing Dennis, she hesitated to alter the status quo.

"Do you really need another lover?"

She gave Caleb her spiel. "I'm not sure monogamy is possible or if it even matters. I'm not monogamous by nature. I don't think any of us are."

This only made Caleb more determined. He stepped up his campaign, taking her Christmas shopping, indulging Fiona with designer perfume and turquoise earrings. She revelled in the garters he bestowed, the stockings and corsets, the way they made her feel utterly female.

"No one's ever bought me lingerie."

"You need lingerie, with a body like that. Obviously, they're a present for me too."

He fucked her on the kitchen table. They engaged in the most acrobatic sex, birds driven from the trees with their yelling. Nearly all the Polaroids depicted her sucking cock, joyously sucking cock. 'Tis the season.

It is me. Fiona didn't recognize herself at first, shocked by the lasciviousness in the photographs, determined nonetheless to embrace the wanton lass portrayed thusly.

★ ★ ★ ★

Caleb, in parrot-motif surfer shorts and an "I'd Rather Be Fishing" T-shirt, leaned over a mirror, scrutinizing a marble-sized chunk of cocaine. He leaned in and began methodically crushing. Pressing his left nostril, he snorted loudly, then serviced the other.

"Ah . . . " Beaming, Caleb sat back, lit a cigarette, and passed the blow over to Fiona.

"So, who popped your cherry, babe?"

"Oh, it was typical. Sordid. Sad. A house party in town. A cot in the basement with my best friend's boyfriend. We didn't even take our clothes off; he just pulled my pants down and stuck it in. He and Lori had broken up, like they did every other week. I wanted him so bad though! Desperately, because that would mean I was in with the in-crowd. It was humiliating. I cried."

"Did he have a big cock?"

"I don't know. Didn't even see it. Guess so. He stood six foot two and it certainly hurt enough. Blood everywhere."

"You didn't see it?"

Caleb snorted up another line. She followed suit, Caleb fidgeting, puffing a cigarette, knee bouncing.

"I probably didn't want to," said Fiona. "I was scared! Fourteen, the last of my crowd to do it. I was so embarrassed . . . "

"Was he good-looking?"

". . . to still be a virgin. Yeah. He was. Tall, blond. Rebel boy. Sexy. Okay. Your turn."

Looking past her, eyes bright, Caleb launched into a long, animated tale, fondly recalling a family skiing vacation in Connecticut, fucking his thirteen-year-old girlfriend against a tree, bending her over, sliding an icicle into her asshole, then his cock. Simultaneously repulsed, fascinated, amused, Fiona noticed he was getting an erection. Caleb liked discussing sex almost as much as having sex.

Caleb ran out to Trader Joe's for supplies: beer, wine, cheese, crackers, macadamia nuts. *Five basic food groups around here.* Fiona indulged her inquisitive nature. Taking the opportunity to snoop, she uncovered photographs of Caleb's ex-wife and old girlfriends; some pretty, some plain, all young and squeaky clean. *Christ. Am I the first woman he's been with? Is that how I constitute "a challenge"?* Her ears pricked, listening for his car. Who's this? wondered Fiona. The aspiring filmmaker? Angela? The girl in the photograph was almond-eyed, hard-bodied. *I have better hair though.* Fiona jumped at the sound of the air conditioner grating. *This must be Danielle, the cocktail waitress.* Fiona wondered why Caleb bad-mouthed her so much, going on about how fat and neurotic Danielle was, how poorly she was aging. Fiona had refrained from mentioning the tire beginning to inflate around Caleb's middle. She thought Danielle actually looked very small-boned. *I gotta get out of here!* Fiona looked for a pen and paper to leave a note. She went to the desk, rummaging through drawers. She could hear children playing in the neighbour's yard, and marvelled that people raised children in this environment; more concrete than playgrounds, more X-rated theatres than parks.

Fiona opened a cupboard door. She had to blink several times before focusing on a shiny, silver scale sitting on a shelf with several large stainless steel mixing bowls of white powder, one containing rocks of cocaine, iridescent, glinting like abalone, large spoon resting, apparently mid-job. *Caleb is moving pounds!* Fiona stared in disbelief, never having seen so much contraband. *I'm getting high just standing here!* Heart thumping, she snatched a pea-sized chunk of pure cocaine and bolted.

The next day, still freaked, relieved to be home, Fiona tried to figure out how to break up with Caleb. He called.

"I'm wasting my time," she said. Caleb was wounded. "I have to get out there and face my challenges. Find my voice." She heard him snigger. "Quit hiding. Being a coward."

"That's certainly not the impression you give."

"It's a facade. A well-cultivated facade. Okay? And I'm getting a chronic bladder infection from all the fucking. I have to abstain. At least for a week."

She knew she couldn't stay away. Fiona held out for three excruciating days, then called Caleb and went over.

Fiona pointed to the cupboard. "So, is the studio just a front?"

Caleb's eyes flashed as he considered a stance of outraged indignation, then he slumped his shoulders.

"No. I don't usually sell cocaine. This is the last time. I've been in dire financial straits, but I'm working everything out."

"Jesus, Caleb."

"Hey, I don't deal on the street. None of this low-life gram bullshit. I break it down quickly and sell it out of a hotel room in one afternoon."

Since the coke was out of the bag, Caleb hired her. Fiona ran errands, helped with studio administration, counted the piles of cash, and even made the occasional delivery.

"But don't ask me to be your mule."

He looked at her, aghast. "I'm not a smuggler!"

He showed her how to spot counterfeit twenties, Fiona slipping the genuine article into her bra those times she was short of cash. Like the gallery, Caleb didn't pay enough.

Dennis came over to deliver the bad news. The other members of Fiona LaBand were unhappy with her "unprofessional conduct" and Floyd had officially given notice. Kit had confirmed his commitment, but Fiona worried he might follow his brother's lead.

Pacing the room, Dennis refused to look her in the eye. He must be drunk, thought Fiona. "What's the matter with you?"

Dennis turned abruptly, walked over, and picked her up off the floor.

"What the fuck? Put me down!"

Dennis put her down. "I'm going to Vancouver. Come with me."

"Sure. Right when I'm on the verge of getting signed."

They argued. Shouted. "I've never made any promises! Remember?"

"Are you fucking that Caleb creep?"

"It's none of your business." Fiona opened the door. "Now get the fuck out!"

"My mother's an artist, an extremely talented sculptor, but she bought into that whole June Cleaver motherhood trip, you know, or 'trap.' She likes to remind us how she sacrificed her career for her family. Of course no one asked her to, but we've paid the price. My father's a brilliant underachiever. At least I come by it honestly. A drone for IBM since forever. He's well-meaning, hard-working, and utterly pussy-whipped."

"Maybe he likes pussy."

Caleb chortled. "At any rate, Mom supports me in my musical endeavours, but would rather I'd become an architect. It's so much more prestigious, not to mention, lucrative. At least Carrie's successful. Fine art photographer. Real art star. She owns an amazing Neutra house up in the Hollywood Hills. And it's obvious Mom is living vicariously through her daughter." Caleb turned to make eye contact. "I am very devoted to my mother though, and you must never say anything against her. Or my sister."

"Okay. Okay. Christ. I haven't even met them."

Maybe she could ask Carrie to do her new headshots, thought Fiona, though it might be a little soon to be asking favours. "I've heard of Carrie Crowe. She's hot."

Caleb laughed. "I'm hotter."

They boarded the Amtrak to San Francisco for a long weekend. *All aboard!* They rarely left the snug berth of their deluxe compartment. Caleb relished being waited on and kept the porter busy. How is it the rhythm of the rails is so conducive to lust? It thrummed her clit, climbed her spine, Caleb's tongue matching the tempo much of the way up the coast.

They arrived the next morning and checked into the Miyako Hotel to sip hot sake and get high while soaking in the deep, sunken tub. The rooms were appointed with rice paper lamps, screens, tatami mats, sliding Shoji screen doors, austere white linens, and cherry wood tables. They fucked languidly in the hot water. Caleb whispered in her ear.

"Wanna be my sex slave?"

"I am your sex slave. What have you got in mind now, you naughty boy?"

Caleb indicated a razor on display. "Let me shave your pussy."

The proposal landed on her like a punch. Fiona nodded, smiling. Caleb led her to the counter and helped her up. She reclined, as uneasy as a gynecology patient. Dr. Crowe pulled out a small pair of scissors, spread her legs, and went to work, trimming Fiona's pubes closely. It was excruciating, her thick curls cut, but Caleb was meticulous, effectively employing the comb as a barrier between flesh and blade.

"You do enjoy ritual, don't you?"

Smiling, Caleb nodded as her blood surged, nipples rose, clit swelled. Generating foam in a mug with a jade-handled, camel-haired brush, Caleb swabbed the warm lather onto what remained of her bush. He rinsed the razor under hot running water and shaved laboriously until finally stepping back to admire his handiwork. He held up a mirror.

"Mademoiselle, you like?" he asked, invoking an effeminate hairdresser.

"Wow! I've never really seen it before."

Caleb couldn't contain himself and pounced upon her exposed labial lips.

"Gawd. It feels amazing. It's so sensitive! Almost too sensitive."

Caleb lifted his head.

"I said almost."

She was beginning to think Caleb was obsessed with sex. Compulsive.

"I had to get it out of my system. That whole brown sugar thing, you know."

"Where did you meet her?"

"Some dance club. I loved banging that African shelf of hers with my big, white cock. She loved it too."

"Racist."

"Realist."

"You were using her."

"Yeah, well, she was using me too. I was her Great White Hope. She wouldn't stop calling. It's a good thing I moved."

Gawd. The glutinous blood and gunk coming out my nose! Fiona tried not to think about the brew of chemicals going up their nostrils each day: hydrochloric acid, ether, acetone, ammonia.

Caleb's sister Carrie came over to meet Fiona, presenting her with an extravagant bouquet of yellow roses.

"Here she is, my significant other, my gorgeous partner in crime." Caleb winked. "Fiona Larochelle." He rolled the r, imitating a bad French accent.

A few hours into their visit, Fiona was enjoying Carrie's company, though she found her irritatingly hyper-feminine and boy crazy despite her claim to only care about her art. It appeared Carrie had recovered from anorexia, designer duds draping a thin, rather than bony carriage, long hair dyed raven-wing black, nails and makeup elaborate. She spoke of her parents with contempt, seemed compelled to impress Fiona.

"Get this. One of my dearest friends, Emilio, and his lover David had the most hilarious fight. David was driving Emilio cuckoo with his new beeper. It kept going off in the middle of conversations, or God forbid, while they were in bed. One night after margaritas David passed out and Emilio shoved the beeper up his ass."

Caleb laughed heartily. Fiona groaned. Carrie smiled, lifting her artfully plucked eyebrows.

"Wait. This is the best part: So David wakes up in the morning, searches the house, but Emilio doesn't say a word. Finally, somebody calls. David hears the beeping and thinks it's the smoke alarm!"

"Come on, you mean he actually didn't feel it? How is that possible?"

Exchanging conspiratorial looks with her brother, Carrie smiled wickedly. "Believe me darlin', it's possible."

"It's eighty per cent pure!"

In high school chemistry teacher mode, Caleb demonstrated several purity tests, precisely weighing out a sample of cocaine on his precious pharmaceutical scale. He placed several crystals on a square of aluminum foil, and then heated them with a flame, explaining that pure coke bubbled, while cut turned black and lumpy.

"But this is the true test." He snorted up a long fat, line. "The best stuff doesn't freeze your nose."

"She used to beg me to beat her."

"So you obliged?"

"With a belt, usually. Until my arms ached."

"Well, a sadist would have said no."

Caleb grinned. "You know, it might have been fun, but it was in the last days of the relationship, when I felt nothing. Contempt, maybe."

Fiona began to dread the prospect of recording yet another demo. She'd need to work on graphics for a new j-card, invariably frustrating. Another Hollywood's Best Kept Secrets showcase at the Coconut Teaszer came and went with the usual anticlimactic letdown. And after all the effort, expense, and preparation, all she felt was, so what? They did get a good video out of the show.

"At least we'll have something to show the grandkids," said Caleb.

Fiona wept. Performing was a rain dance, no end in sight to the drought.

"I didn't know you could do that. Get a fist in somebody's ass like that. I used lube, but still! I'd raise her legs up high in the air, stick my thumb in her asshole. Then a finger. She'd arch her back, loosen her muscles, take in more, and more, slowly all my fingers, one by one, until I had my whole hand in her ass and she'd groan. It was amazing! I'd just stand there and watch my arm disappear into that pretty, pink butt hole, practically up to my elbow. She loved it. Her nipples'd get hard and she'd ram her body against me, screaming in Japanese the whole time."

"You told me," said Fiona weakly. "And I've been wondering how she—you never did tell me her name—had the presence of mind to speak?"

"Junko was incredible. It was so funny." Caleb launched into his impression of the Japanese exchange student his parents had hosted. "The way she'd say, 'Fuck me! Give it to me hard!' in that accent."

"She'd spread her cheeks, yell, 'Fuck me! Hard! Harder!' I'd pump her ass until she was wailing. She woke up my parents a couple of times. We told them we were practising judo."

One evening Fiona nearly lost her heartbeat. "I think I'm too high. I can't breathe."

Brow furrowed, Caleb placed two fingers on her neck. "Are you okay?"

Am I? "Am I Blue?" She laughed at the irony, Chet Baker, in the background. "Am I blue?"

Am I dying? I don't feel anything. Fiona couldn't move, her body as heavy as if she had mercury for blood.

"I wanna soak in the tub." She imagined the water coming up over her head like a sheet. "Christ. I'm supposed to go to work tomorrow. All this debauchery is wearing me out."

"Quit your job. Focus on your music. Move in with me. Save your rent money."

Fiona was apprehensive, Caleb already taking her for granted, expecting her to drop everything and come running whenever he called.

Ted unceremoniously announced he was quitting.

"You two are like one of those ventriloquist acts. Caleb decides something and it comes out of your mouth."

"Are you calling me a dummy?"

"No, I'm calling you late for supper. Yeah, I'm calling you a dummy. That's how you're behaving. Earth to Fiona. He's fucking up the band! Our sound."

"You're jealous. You can't let go of the status quo."

"He's trying to funkify it, infuse his production values on our music, impose his sensibilities. Good example, hiring backup singers, insisting they be black."

"He doesn't insist they be black."

"I know, it's a coincidence. Fuck! He thinks he's Quincy Jones! He's actually talking horn section. He'd hire Tower of Power if he could afford it. And you'd let him!"

"You have to give the changes some time. A chance to evolve. What's wrong with experimenting?"

"Hey, if it ain't broke, why fix it? Bottom line, Fiona, it's not you up there anymore."

"How would you know?"

"I didn't sign on to back up that asshole. Our music is way better than that retread, neo-funk garbage he plays. Or at least it was."

"How can you talk to me like that?"

Eyes welling, Ted gently placed his Strat in its case and strode toward the door. "See you on MTV, Fiona."

"Let him go," said Caleb over dinner. "We don't need him. I'll back you."

She gave notice, moved in with Caleb. They celebrated with a magnum of champagne and an eight ball of cocaine. He toasted her.

"We belong together."

She recreated her Catholic schoolgirl uniform. Caleb delighted in bending her over his knee, lifting up the tartan skirt, pulling down the white cotton panties and spanking her bottom. Lips bruised and swollen, body covered in marks from the clamps and whips, they spoke of the fine line between pleasure and pain, though she'd learned long ago, probably better than Caleb, pain is better than nothing.

They quickly settled into domesticity, though Fiona soon discovered several of his annoying habits. Caleb was a control freak and monopolized the bathroom, sitting on the throne for hours. *Doesn't it occur to him I might be waiting? Why do men do that? Use the loo for a library? Like Henry Miller says, taking a dump might be your only moment of bliss all day. Why not revel in it?* Then Caleb showered for half an hour every morning, masturbating. What a waste of water, she thought, and in the middle of a drought.

She ran the errands, did the cleaning, laundry, grocery shopping, and cooking. Caleb worked diligently, often staying up all night, mixing, struggling to integrate a new automation program with the control room software. They were to split the profits. She wouldn't get rich, but Caleb did agree to pay for an orthodontist. Fiona had more time for music, though she missed Laurel Canyon, often uneasy in Silver Lake. Standing out front of the studio one night chatting with their clients, Frantic Planet, a carload of fag-bashing yeehaws roared by yelling obscenities and throwing beer cans, assuming they were patrons of the neighbouring Back Door.

"How do they even know it's there?" said Fiona. "The place is so inconspicuous."

"I've lived here for two years and never been inside," said Caleb.

"Afraid?" asked Frantic Planet lead singer, Joel Perkins with a smirk.

"No," spat Caleb. "Heterosexual."

Tiring of his porno collection, Caleb persuaded her to go to the X-rated video store with him.

"I'm very ambivalent about pornography," said Fiona.

She told him her first exposure was through babysitting. Fiona recalled unearthing a collection of adult books stashed under the couple's bed. Titles like *Slave Girl* and *House of Discipline*. She'd found pornographic Polaroids of her charge's parents, shocked by the images, even as a part of her understood exactly what they portrayed. Fiona repeatedly dug out the trashy novels, the heat between her legs becoming familiar, reassuring.

The first one they watched together starred an all-female cast; *Back Door Bitch* featured a gnarly sleaze queen holding court, slapping a girl's face with her tits.

"Well, none of them are my type. Gawd. Such tacky production values."

"Ignore them."

"I can't. I'm an aesthete."

"Get over yourself."

"How you can abide that sound track, that generic seventies rock music with the cheesy, incessant wah-wah guitar? This is tedious. Predictable."

The inherent hypocrisy irritated her, actresses remaining pretty no matter how grotesque the acts. Fiona found herself aroused at the sight of a flogging, the woman's arms tied overhead.

"How can I respond to that? I was physically abused."

"Give yourself a break. It's possible that's precisely why it turns you on. You think too much. You need to free yourself of all these third-party standards, your own misconceptions." Caleb took her hand. "Look. Being human's all about contradiction, complexity. Let go. Surrender. That's liberation." He pointed to the screen. "Nice tits, huh?"

"They are. Everybody loves tits."

Caleb brought up Desmond Morris' theory that women's breasts were inordinately large in order to resemble the buttocks that had beckoned males when humans were quadrupeds.

"Hey, we're still on all fours, as far as I'm concerned."

"I thought you liked it doggy style?" He leaned over to smack her bum. "Woof."

"I still need my imagination engaged. We fuck with our minds after all."

"If you enjoy watching people kiss, why can't you watch people fuck?"

"Kissing is sublime."

He groaned and played the arty video Fiona had selected. It nearly put them to sleep.

"Okay, you proved your point. Porno is better when it has no pretensions. Which isn't saying much." Fiona ejected it and put in *Rookies*, a men-in-blue romp. "Look. Gay porno." *Was it a mix-up?* Did the clerk give it to them accidentally on purpose? "They really like playing the race card, don't they?"

"There you go, thinking again." Caleb laughed. "Look. The white guy's dick is bigger! Smashing racial stereotypes. See?"

He fast-forwarded through a fleeting montage of fervid fellatio, to the white guy fucking the black guy. "Raise your legs bitch!" Bottom's face grimacing, hole rammed. *Or, is it reamed?* Caleb's eyes widened, riveted to the punishing ass-fucking, scrambling to cover his quickening cock with the sheet. No safe sex, no condoms. Caleb flipped it off.

Of course, now he wants to fuck me up the ass. She'd tried it with Emmett once when they were drunk. It wasn't awful, but it wasn't all that great either. *Let him think I'm a virgin.*

"Like it?" Caleb asked huskily, nipping her earlobe.

Fiona nodded.

"Tell me."

"I like it."

"Say it again."

"I like it."

"Again!"

"I like it."

"Say, 'I love it when you fuck me up my ass with your big cock, Caleb.'"

"I love it when you fuck me up my ass with your big cock, Caleb."

Three months later, they drove to Palm Springs to meet Caleb's parents, father Derek as reserved, homely, and sartorially challenged as mother Mitzi was plucky, attractive, and stylish. As an audacious young woman, Mitzi Goldsmith had enrolled at the National Academy of Design, winning numerous prizes. She met Harvard Business School graduate, Derek Crowe, at a Young Democrats convention.

In the tone of an oft-stated view, Mitzi said, "He was my best friend before we fell in love. That's a solid foundation for a marriage."

She tried to suss out the degree of Caleb and Fiona's involvement. Apparently it was irritatingly crucial to Mitzi whom Caleb dated, fucked, married. She doted on him, suffering Fiona like an encroaching virus.

"I hope Caleb doesn't marry again. It was frightful, what he had to go through during the divorce. He tried so hard to understand Barbara's dysfunction. Awful word, isn't it?"

If only they knew. To them, Caleb was an ingenious, savvy entrepreneur, a self-made man. He wasn't about to share the news that bookings at the studio had slowed and they were forced to rent out rehearsal time. Carrie knew, recently revealing to Fiona that Caleb had lied.

"All those bands he produced? He's just a drug dealer." Questioning Carrie's motives, Fiona wasn't sure she believed her, but feared pressing Caleb on the subject.

They returned from dinner to lounge around the pool, sat discussing politics. She could see why Caleb called them bleeding hearts, though Mitzi was disdainful of feminism. They praised Canada's universal health care system, bemoaning the lack of affordable health insurance in America, the injustice of it all, Derek expounding through perfect pearly whites.

"Dental health is such a big factor. Consider what happens when a person doesn't have access to dental care. How can the body be sound?"

Fiona didn't mention her first trip to the dentist as an adolescent with an abscessed tooth that was promptly and ruthlessly extracted.

"You're not going out dressed like that, are you?"

"Christ, Caleb. You sound like my father. You said you liked my style."

"I do. But that skirt is too short. And don't talk to any men."

"I'm going babysitting!"

That evening she returned home an hour late, Caleb pouncing as she entered the apartment. "Where have you been?"

"I was at Candye's. Taking care of Tommy. I told you. She was late getting back. We chatted a bit."

"Why didn't you call? You didn't leave the number!"

She pointed to the Rolodex. "It's right in there. Under K, for Kane."

"I was worried!"

"Maybe you shouldn't worry so much."

"Are you calling me a neurotic Jew again?"

"You are a neurotic Jew. When you're not being a neurotic WASP."

Caleb lifted his arm and smacked her across the face with the back of his hand, Fiona's skull cracking against the wall. She thrust her right fist reflexively, Caleb snatching it mid-air. Fiona raised her other fist. Seizing it, Caleb pulled her arms down, gripping them by the wrists. She kicked him in the shins. He yanked her to the ground. They grappled, rolling on the floor as Fiona desperately tried to connect her fist to his throat, or knee to his balls. He pinned her, Caleb's uncanny strength confounding Fiona's fury.

"Caleb! Get off me!"

Caleb got off.

"I'm sorry. Fiona, I'm sorry!"

"How dare you?" she roared.

"Look, I was out of my mind with worry. I drank too much. You shouldn't buy that wine I like."

Weeping, Fiona crawled into bed, wouldn't allow him near. He made tea and toast, begged forgiveness. Exhausted, she eventually allowed him to sit on the bed, then next to her. He stroked Fiona's hair. She let him cautiously and reverently undress her. He kissed her toes, knees, thighs. By the end of the night, Fiona dutifully pitied Caleb, having been reminded of all he'd done for her.

They sat together sipping wine, snorting coke. Caleb had taken to wearing Malcom frames and his face was getting wider, rounder. She thought he looked like a basketball with glasses. Smiling inwardly, Fiona pointed to a sparrows' nest perched precariously atop a bundle of two by fours leaning against the building, the birds' peeping a familiar, heartening sound.

"I've been witness to the entire process! From the construction, to the laying and hatching."

"Great," grumbled Caleb. "They're shitting all over the wicker." He lit a joint. "Hey, I noticed a Jeep parked out front last night. Rocking up and down. Naked people inside. Two men and a woman. Then I saw her penis. Drag queen or something. They had its dress hiked up, spanking its butt. So, the guy in the leather chaps sucked off the she-male while the other guy fucked her up the ass. Then they drove off, still naked."

"Wow. What were you doing? Did they know you were watching?"

"I'm not sure. But they wouldn't have cared."

"Like I always say, we fuck with our minds."

So that's where he disappears to. She called him a voyeur. Caleb got defensive. They argued. He grilled her, having heard Dennis was in town.

"'Cause a bi slut like you will fuck anything that moves."

"I prefer to think of myself as a polyamorous sexual being." She couldn't help but goad him. "My dad used to call me a slut. It's just as pathetic a ploy coming out of your mouth."

Caleb grabbed Fiona by the neck, lifting her off her feet and slamming her body against the wall. Fastened, flailing, fluttering, feet thrashing, arms dangling like meat, Caleb steadily squeezed Fiona's throat, slowly forcing air from her windpipe. *This is it.* Eyeball to eyeball. She glared. *I'm going to die.* Grunting, sneering grotesquely, Caleb compressed her neck even harder. Then, abruptly, released her. Sputtering, Fiona briefly bent her head down, then rose up, pounding his chest with her fists.

"You fucker! Think you can scare me?"

Later that night in a long-sought quiet moment, Fiona thought surely she must harbour a death wish, finally admitting the cocaine was fuelling their madness. Once again, she resolved to get out.

I can take it up the ass, just not every single time. Fiona began sleeping with one eye open, Caleb finding fault with everything she did lately, agitated if she selected a CD or answered phone calls.

"You're getting a little ample. I want her back." Caleb indicated a photograph of Fiona on the fridge, held by a Catalina Island magnet. "You should indulge your passion, not your sweet tooth. More sex, less food."

"More sex? I don't know how that's possible."

"It's been dropping off."

"Oh yeah. Down to twice a day instead of five. What do you expect? We can't keep up that pace and get any work done."

"Well, maybe you should work this off." He smacked her bum.

"Why should I even care about the opinion of someone so shallow?" she wailed to Shannon over the phone.

A pattern had emerged. They went on binges, then laid off for as long as ten days. *At least Caleb wasn't dealing anymore.*

"You have no respect for my limits."

"What! Now you're crying rape? That's not what you said last night. Whatever happened to consenting adults?" Fiona tossed the strap-on dildo onto the bed. "You said you loved it."

She had loved it. Fiona recalled wielding it, brandishing it, imagining herself as male. Hung. Watching her "cock" disappear inexorably into flesh. His flesh. Caleb raising his ass, moans, drowning out the music. In awe of his capacity for surrender. In awe of his faith. In her. Beyond gender. Beyond fear. Beyond flesh. It had bonded them, perhaps even mitigated Caleb's aggression. But that was yesterday. No flying his freak flag today. Caleb picked up the video and threw it against the wall, walked over and ripped the tape out of the casing. Insurance.

"You ever tell anybody and I'll make you sorry you did." He lunged for the dildo. "Your turn!"

Revenge, not reciprocity, Fiona too weary to point out she had the ability to lead or follow, fight or switch, submit or dominate. All avenues to ecstasy. Too demoralized to remind him that it was he, who so demanding of trust, claimed sadomasochism as a bid for true intimacy. He's a dilettante, she thought, a hypocrite. Fiona disappointed, again. Caleb must remain in control. Always. She'd have to accept she was alone, however much deviancy they'd shared. *I shudder to think of all the misery in the world caused by fools like Caleb. Fools like me.* She bent over.

248

★ ★ ★ ★

One clement Sunday of light, warm, embracing winds, Fiona and Caleb relaxed post-rehearsal, nibbling at supper and reading. Fiona placed her novel down and found him taking a siesta. She went into the garden, Evinrude basking in the sun, purring. Into the catnip again. Fiona breathed in the sticky scent of orange blossoms. A blimp hovered: The USO's 50th Anniversary Commemorative Coins. She repotted a fern and pruned her climbing pink roses. At times, their life together was serene. The sun began to set. Fiona kept glancing at the basement door. Caleb had warned her repeatedly not to go down there, that it was full of junk.

She opened the door with the key he kept stashed in his filing cabinet. A helicopter passed overhead. *Are they spraying again?* Nope, it's the LAPD. Eye in the sky. The distinction between surveillance and voyeurism seems to be blurring, she thought. Entering, Fiona ducked beneath the low doorway, pupils adjusting to the dark, dank coolness. She found an easel with a broken leg, forsaken tennis rackets, stacks of clay pots, cardboard boxes, and old tires, a well-worn path through it all. A dazzling light emanated from the crack of what appeared to be a large closet. *I should leave.* Fiona opened the door to a thick maze of marijuana plants, hundreds set in cubes of Styrofoam, rising out of white plastic trays of water, dense with buds oozing cannabis, silver ducts and ballasts of high-powered lights suspended from the ceiling. *Lenny is the gardener!* Like drones, oscillating fans stood guard, heads turning accusingly at precise intervals. Fiona stood, paralyzed for a moment before turning to flee, stumbling through the muck and mishmash back to her flowers and tomatoes.

Caleb will be furious. She agonized, as angry as she was frightened. *Should I pretend I never saw it? I could get busted too! Go to fucking prison for twenty years in this bloody country with its draconian drug laws. Why didn't he warn me? That prick! Some partner.*

For days Fiona said nothing, worried that Caleb must suspect; she was so jumpy. Finally, she couldn't contain it any longer and told him she'd discovered the grow op. His face turned ashen. He put his fist through the wall next to her head.

"How dare you go down there! I told you to never go down there!"

"What else are you keeping from me?"

Caleb and Lenny both reassured her, explaining the odds were greatly against getting busted. They put her to work, feeding, watering, clipping, and bagging at harvest time. After a few all-night sloggers, Caleb started talking marriage again, stating that a wife can't testify against her husband.

"I woke up and she was trying to take off my Rolex!" Caleb described spending a long night with a whore, and, "taking her," to punish her.

"That's rape, Caleb!"

"No. She loved it. Believe me. Got in over her head. Women generally aren't smart enough to know what they want."

The exchange escalated into an argument, erupting into verbal attacks, the "fuck yous!" flying. Hours after the storm passed, Caleb exhausted and contrite, got down on one knee to proffer an emerald ring.

"Actually, I think this would be a good time to break up."

Caleb raised his fist but managed to restrain himself.

"I can't live without you Fiona."

Within two days he'd convinced her to stay.

She called Shannon. "Lake Tahoe. December. A white winter wedding."

"To Caleb?"

"Yes!"

"Why?"

Sighing, Fiona explained it was partly because she was tired of being an illegal alien. "I can get a green card. And I do love him."

"He's such a spaz." But Shannon agreed to be her maid of honour.

"They don't like you, you know," Carrie told Fiona in the car on the way to their lunch date. "My parents. They think you're marrying Caleb for our money."

"Hah! You'd think you were the Rockefellers."

Carrie laughed. "My parents act like we're the Rockefellers."

Carrie dropped another bombshell as they sipped their Chardonnay. Caleb had been molesting her since the age of eight.

"My mother knew. She walked in on us once, turned around, and walked out! Didn't want to believe it."

Carrie swore Fiona to secrecy. Shocked, appalled, she immediately confronted Caleb, who didn't deny it, but said it happened only because he'd been acting out after being molested by Uncle Harold.

"I was just a kid. All that abuse ended years ago." Caleb refused to discuss it further.

And I thought my family was weird.

Fiona hunted down a white faux-fur coat, stockings, gloves, and lingerie, discovering it was nearly impossible to find white shoes post-Labour Day.

"Wearing white to coordinate with the snow," she told Shannon. "You know, the various textures of white-on-white thing."

"Certainly doesn't have anything to do with purity."

"So, I drifted."

The big day was less than a month away, everything under control. Though she'd lost touch with a lot of friends, Fiona was surprised to receive thirty RSVPs, considering that attendance involved traipsing off to the High Sierras. None of Fiona's poor relations could make it. Fortunately, Caleb's parents were paying for the reception. After a fitting with Yreina, The Dress was under construction. She had designed a minidress of white velvet with a sweetheart neckline, trimmed with marabou. The white lace of Fiona's stockings would provide a hint of tradition. Screw the veil. *I'm a minimalist.* Yreina suggested gardenias in her hair à la Billie Holiday.

"Thanks so much for doing this! Please say hi to Ted. I wish you two were coming."

"So do I. He usually isn't this stubborn, but he's not over the band breaking up."

"Neither am I."

"So who's the best man?"

"His dad, Derek. I don't think Caleb has a best friend. That would be me."

Lenny agreed to take care of the studio while they were away, joking about missing the wedding of the century. Their bigoted friend was also a level-headed, industrious, meticulous craftsman. He smoked pot, but never seemed high, so street-savvy and benign in appearance, he'd never been arrested. Lenny listened to police calls on a CB radio, parked five blocks from the hydroponics store, entering incognito. She used to think him paranoid, but had come to trust his instincts. He was the main reason she hadn't been living in complete dread of a bust.

Her braces were coming off just in time for the wedding. Fiona was excited, even happy. Upon seeing an enormous thalidomide baby-woman with flipper arms, wide and wiggly as a truck of Jell-O, Fiona thought, I don't have any problems.

She did suffer cold feet. They'd attended a party at Carrie's to meet her famous Hollywood director friend, Ted Maguire. Brash, witty, wicked, Maguire reverberated with manic energy. Flirting outrageously, he slipped his hand under Fiona's shirt to fondle her breast, Caleb a few feet away. Amused, aroused, Fiona relished hearing how beautiful and how sexy she was, how much he needed to fuck her.

"A rendezvous?" whispered Maguire.

Tempted, Fiona was also acutely aware of the pointlessness of such a scenario and demurred. "I'm getting married. I'm in love."

Marriage? To Caleb? It's natural to feel trepidation. She'd managed monogamy a decent length of time, though lately had been troubled by fevered erotic dreams, a persistent aching, yearning for Pearl, all the while flirting with the studio's studly young players.

"How do we stand any chance of a life together?" she wailed at Shannon, repeating the sentiment to Caleb after their last row, two nights previous.

"I want out!"

"Are you crazy?" said Caleb. "We've been planning this wedding for six months! Friends and relatives flying in from all over the globe."

Then, more family bullshit, brother and sister engaged in some sort of nasty dispute, Carrie claiming Caleb didn't want her at the wedding, which he denied.

"She's jealous," he said.

The trip north was hairy, roads icy, treacherous, goosey Caleb nearly driving off the highway several times before stopping to put on chains. They arrived at Lake Tahoe after eleven hours of forging through heavy snowfall, a bleak landscape, the lake indistinguishable from a wall of fog. It seemed fitting, getting married in a storm.

They greeted Shannon, Mitzi, Derek, and Carrie at the cabins, Fiona relieved the family had resolved their differences. Shannon groused about an eighty-dollar cab ride and hoisted up her sack of booze. Jeremy, Caleb's cousin from New York, arrived graciously bearing groceries, and dinner, his good humour startling in contrast to Caleb, who made a sour face as Jeremy placed a loaf of pre-buttered garlic bread in the oven.

Several friends couldn't make it after all. Mitzi grumbled. She agonized over which dress to wear and fussed over Derek's suit. Shannon read from the brochure.

"All wedding ceremonies include the chapel, minister, and live music. Our world-renowned Gazebo, Lakeside Chapel, and historic Indian Room are reserved exclusively for our guests. A wonderful place to celebrate the magic of your wedding."

"Gag me," said Fiona. "The place is fascinating though. Sinatra owned it for a while. They think Marilyn Monroe rendezvoused here with President Kennedy."

Her future in-laws left, Fiona's neck and shoulders loosening immediately. The cabin filled with drink, talk, music, laughter, pot and cigarette smoke. The alarm squealed. Scrambling, Caleb grabbed a chair and disconnected it.

"Well, what do you expect?" shouted Fiona. "There's no ventilation. Open a window!"

Jeremy jumped up. "The garlic bread!" He opened the oven door. Smoke billowed out. "Oh my God!" He held up a charred, black object resembling a snowshoe.

"Good," said Caleb. "I didn't want to eat that thing anyway."

By morning, storm over, sunlight filtered through a stand of ponderosa pines, feathery mist hovering along the shaded shoreline. Yesterday's roiling waters were calm, a band of powdery snow muting sound. A wooden sloop rested atop a rock pile, soft and white, as though dusted with icing sugar. Shivering, Fiona ventured down to the edge of majestic Lake Tahoe. She watched a dark blue blemish rise to the surface from a deep undulating current. *What am I doing?*

Shannon called to her. Fiona waved and walked over to meet her at their cabin. She made breakfast, then swung into several hours of frantic preparations, ripping her stockings the moment she put them on. Shannon was actually wearing lipstick. They smoked a little pot with Carrie, Fiona gulping down a Valium with her champagne. Fifteen minutes later she still felt wired.

The flowers arrived. Carrie photographed the "exquisite"

bouquet of reeds and pussy willows, white daffodils and tulips bound with ivory ribbons against the snow. Shannon delivered the boutonnieres to the men's cabin. Finally, they were ready and drove to the chapel. Wedding coordinator Melinda parked the bride and maid of honour in the Indian Room, then herded the guests inside.

Shannon paced. "I'm more nervous than you are!"

Fiona bit her nails, polish bitter on her tongue. The girlfriends waited beneath the immense beams, walls of mounted animal heads rapidly becoming familiar. A musty, baleful buck stared as they scrutinized a thick white line painted down the middle of the stone fireplace, demarcating California on one side, Nevada on the other. Inveterate gamblers in the casino gawked, Fiona tempted to grab a drink from the bar. Melinda returned to escort them down the icy stairs and opened the door. *Wow. Live music. Something cheesy on the organ. Not registering.* From the corner of her eye, Fiona noticed a Christmas tree bearing white doves. Caleb was beaming. Kit stood up to escort Fiona down the aisle.

She rushed forward, head down, avoiding the guests' radiating smiles, descending sun distilling the light. Shannon bawled.

"You look beautiful," he whispered.

Caleb didn't seem anxious at all. *What's he on?* A squat, mustachioed justice of the peace, more nervous than bride and groom, ran over the words, none of them audible. Fiona tried to focus. Voice faltering, she made a concerted effort to recite her self-penned vows. Caleb confidently recited his, though fumbled for the ring. The solemnity of the moment, the significance of the act, the enormity of its consequences . . . ah! Fiona resisted assimilating any of it, relieved when the ceremony finally ended. Breathless, the newlyweds managed a kiss. Melinda directed them to a slippery balcony for a photo session, Carrie snapping away, Lake Tahoe and towering pines providing a fantastic backdrop.

"We made it!" yelled Mitzi.

Everyone raised their fists and cheered. The wedding party

headed to the reception, amid much confusion, bride and maid of honour winding up in a taxi with Carrie. They tooted several spoons of cocaine on the way to the restaurant, only to find a mix-up over the starting time.

Shannon patted Fiona's hand. "Don't worry. We can wait in the lounge. Let's have a drink."

Fiona requested a glass of wine.

"Oh, come on, let's have a real drink!"

Fiona ordered a vodka martini. "I shouldn't have this on an empty stomach." Discretely, she pulled out the coke and shared another toot with her best girls. *White on white.* They savoured their cocktails, gazing at trees silhouetted against patches of mauve sky. As if to console the languishing Canadians, the bartender informed them that the lake hosted a species of Kokanee salmon, escapees from a former hatchery.

Caleb popped in and out of the bathroom with Cousin Jeremy. Finally the guests were all seated in the cozy dining room, done up like a Provençal *auberge* with copper pans and garlic braids gracing the plaster walls, wood crackling in the fireplace. After a few bottles of wine, Carrie climbed onto chairs to shoot the various couples' lip-locking from above. Amid the hubbub, the bride and groom barely spoke, until meeting up to cut the cake. The best man feted the newlyweds. Caleb toasted Fiona.

"To my sweet, darling, precious, beautiful Girl from the North Country!"

Later, bride and groom snorted lines until five a.m. Shannon arrived at their cabin at eight to say goodbye. She carved the newlyweds' initials inside a heart in the sand on the beach, then departed for the airport. By ones and twos, the guests departed. Relieved to be alone at last, Fiona and Caleb slept all afternoon, rising to party and gamble all night. Caleb lost most of his bankroll, delighted by Fiona's steady winning. *I still have the knack!* Like a hooker hiding hard-earned cash from her pimp, Fiona slipped five one-hundred-dollar bills into her lovely, new white shoes.

CHAPTER ELEVEN

First anniversary. Fiona delivered a glass of champagne to Caleb soaking his bumps and bruises in Epsom salts, post-sparring with the Everlast bag. "Let's do it in the tub."

She declined. Nostalgic for the good old days, days that included foreplay, Fiona thought. The supposed deviant didn't deviate from his pattern much anymore, bondage no longer a game or playful at all. Caleb hauled himself out, calling her a malcontent.

"You are never satisfied, Princess."

"Oh, yeah. Look how extravagant I am," she said, indicating her decidedly worn slippers.

"The truth hurts, doesn't it?"

"You want the truth? You don't have a monopoly on truth. The truth is nobody hires you because you're an asshole."

Caleb raised his fist Ralph Kramden-style. "Fuck you, Fiona! Who's going to hire you, huh? Why don't you get a fucking job?"

"I have a job! I've had a job since I was twelve years old. You convinced me to quit my last one so I could come work for you, remember?"

"Oh yeah. I really had to twist your arm."

"I can't win! I get zero respect. You don't provoke Lenny or insult him. You don't 'put him in his place' or feel the need to. Why are you so disrespectful of me?"

Next morning, Fiona woke on the couch to the smell of sun-ripened beer backwash, birdsong striking her as ludicrous. Her bum was sore, hair a rat's nest, Evinrude asleep on her legs. He stared as she slowly hauled herself up and shuffled about the room. *Shit. I forgot to feed him.* The household's humans had been subsisting on take-out or delivery pizza, when and if they got around to eating. Fiona filed away the albums invariably pulled out when they got high. She'd been looking for the song "Jezebel" after discussing the Controllers' mind-blowing rendition. She wiped coke residue off the mirror, rubbed her gums, and threw open a window to air the place out. Carrie was coming over for lunch, solo, thank God. Last visit with her mother-in-law, Mitzi kept glancing at Fiona's tummy, worried she might be pregnant, which, God forbid, would make her a grandmother. Mitzi had thrown a hissy fit, reprimanding Derek for never supporting her artistic career, how her apprenticeship with Hans Hoffman was doomed, he and the children sabotaging her efforts. Then she stood at the window, staring out, refusing to speak to anyone. *Menopause?*

What did we do last night? Or was it the night before? Fiona cringed, recalling long hours of deliberations and recriminations. Talking had waxed as sex waned. She remembered: She'd told Caleb she wanted a divorce, threatening to sue for involuntary servitude. He laughed.

"You treat me like a whore."

"You are a whore."

"So, what does that make you?"

Caleb proceeded to smash things; many things, a chunk of a cup flying up and hitting Fiona near the eye. Then he locked her out of the house, in the nude.

Gawd. Carrie! I'll have to be nice to the wretched thing. Fiona loved her sister-in-law, but Carrie's whining drove her nuts. She seemed desperate and needy, recently embarking upon a pitiless health regimen. *Why did she have such a persecution complex?* She'd been running after the DJ from neo-funk band Wilderness Family, described giving him a blowjob while his buddies partied down the hall. When he hadn't called, Carrie felt "humiliated." *Jeez, did she think that meant he liked her?* Fiona was surprised that her tough, mouthy sister-in-law could be so gullible.

Fiona went to the bathroom to brush the crud off her teeth, gasping as she closed the medicine cabinet door, a humungous,

258

blue shiner sprawled over half her face. *Jesus Christ! How am I going to cover that?* She recalled being throttled and sure enough, found bruises on her neck. *It's not like I can dial 9-1-1 when he's on top of me.* Fiona had tried to grab the phone, but Caleb threw it across the room.

"What the fuck are you doing? Calling the police? That's brilliant! You wanna get busted? You stupid bitch! If I go down, you go down. I can't believe how fucking stupid you are!"

Fiona brewed coffee, and rifled through cupboards and closets seeking stray Halcions. She came across an old band photo of the Virgin Marries, collapsed at her desk, and wept, then moaning and stretching, dragged herself upstairs to a stinking, snoring Caleb, television droning, Rosalind Russell as Australian nurse Sister Kenny. Too antsy to rest, Fiona flipped it off and went back downstairs, Evinrude stretched out, seemingly listening to Frank Sinatra's "Silver Bells." She turned off the stereo. A small spruce leaned against a wall in the corner. *It will dry out before we ever trim it.*

They'd decided to split up, which is what usually happened at the tail end of a binge. He'd commanded her to leave, threatened to change the locks. Fiona began packing. Caleb begged her to stay. The evening had begun auspiciously. They'd actually left the premises, and gone out to see a movie. Afterward, they went by the Dresden for a drink, running into several friends from her past life, Evelyn and Kaye and frequent billing mates, the Apache Dancers, Terry, and Bernadette. Caleb groused about her "working the room."

"I know a lot of people in this town, okay? Or did."

Fiona could find no drugs. She'd have to let Thelonious Monster in for rehearsal, hoping their erudite and charming bassist, Jon Huck, arrived first. Jon arrived and the two chatted. Caleb got up. It was as if he had a testosterone sensor indicating any Fiona interactions involving males.

Caleb announced he was jonesing. She tried to snap him out of his funk, but the only thing that cheered him up was a call to connection, Rango.

"This is the last time. I swear. We'll have a healthy spring.

259

Buy those mountain bikes, okay? Go camping. Fishing. Eastern Sierras. Catherine Lake. Okay?" Caleb smiled as she walked out the door to score.

Caleb refused to go out to see or hear Sonic Youth, choosing to stay in and cocoon. He belittled her friends and relatives, barely civil the rare times he encountered any. Caleb complained about his friends too; they were leeches. One afternoon, Fiona's Lost Angels cohort, Bradley, called with an invitation to visit him at Sunset Sound Studios where he was recording. Bradley's famous British drummer friend was in town and had asked to see her again, the same famous British drummer who said he'd call after they slept together, and never did. Fiona didn't mention that part to Caleb, only her cabin fever.

"Bradley and I are just friends. He's gay."

Caleb insisted she stay home.

The music industry was atwitter with the Penny Muck lawsuit against Geffen Records. Apparently, Muck's boss liked to jerk off in front of her. Funny how truth, like a law of nature, like a scumbag's dick, ultimately rises.

Candye called, requesting Fiona accompany her to Austin to sing backup on her recording of "These Boots Are Made For Walkin," for her new album, puzzled by Fiona's reaction, a rueful laugh. They managed to convince Caleb it was a good opportunity—Candye could be very persuasive—but the day before Fiona's departure he contracted a virus. She had to cancel, run the studio.

Another binge, two days in Caleb declaring, "Blue balls," and demanding, "Suck me." Fiona worked feverishly, moving her hair off her face, affording a better view. Eighteen minutes later Caleb climaxed. She slumped to the floor. He soon rolled over and dozed off. Fiona dragged her ass into bed. She tried to rest despite the pain that pierced her chest relentlessly. After some time, it evoked a loud, involuntary cry, rousing her husband.

"I can't breathe! I feel strange. My heart's pounding."

"Is your arm numb?"

"Yeah. I'm scared, Caleb."

He sat up, grabbed the remote, and turned on the television. "If it doesn't stop in ten minutes, I'm taking you to the hospital."

The next day, a Cholo rap band left without paying, absconding with several microphones.

"We have to be more discriminating," said Caleb, "demand to see ID. Require new clients to sign a rental agreement."

Ray of hope: Fiona was thrilled to hear from legendary entertainment lawyer Seth Applebaum, though his advice often consisted of tangle-tongued mixed signals. Still, she felt optimistic while driving to Santa Monica for their meeting. A pleasant day, same as any other, when suddenly some unknown force buffeted the car. Palm trees swung wildly in widening circles as Fiona maneuvered into a parking space, the ground undulating as she crossed the boulevard. Lurching into the building, Fiona opened the office doors to barely stifled pandemonium. One of the suits noticed her puzzled expression, asked if she'd felt it.

"Fiona Larochelle to see Seth Applebaum, please."

"Sorry," replied the slim receptionist in a severe updo. "He left. The earthquake really shook him up."

Studio nearly bankrupt, last marijuana crop failing due to a series of power outages, Fiona was pounding the pavement as Caleb considered teaching guitar or judo. He moaned to Mitzi on the phone, then hung up.

"Funny how assurances from one's mother only make you feel worse."

He berated Fiona for a bit, then took off as she had hoped,

to Rango's, probably.

"I'm just about done with this charade we call a marriage," she reported to Shannon.

Where once Fiona fantasized about big tits and dildos, she was now lying in bed devising murder plots. She could cash out the credit cards, fly off to Portugal long enough to convalesce, spend a year traipsing around Europe, ride a gondola, swim the Aegean, drink rosé in Provence, finally learn to speak French.

Caleb returned late in the afternoon, stoned, inebriated. He stood in the doorway swaying, glaring as Fiona chatted on the phone with Kaye Shutter. She turned around. *Uh, oh.* Caleb charged. Ripping the phone from her hand, he lifted Fiona by the neck and flung her onto the couch. She screamed. Caleb gripped her throat with both hands and squeezed tightly. She could hear Lenny's car driving off, Kaye yelling through the receiver, "Fiona! Fiona!" She tried to knee his back, eventually managed to break his hold, pushing her arms up and through his. Fiona bolted. Caleb reached out and grabbed her arm, flinging her to the ground again. He stomped on her chest. Fiona felt the breath leave her, astonished that she could feel her ribs cracking. She pitched her arm into his legs to trip him, rolled away, and dashed from the apartment to Bob's Market next door. Hiding behind the counter, she called Kaye. Relieved Caleb hadn't followed her, Fiona was grateful that Kaye arrived quickly to rush her to the hospital. Her right lung was pierced and had collapsed. Kaye insisted they report the assault, but Fiona refused.

"He could have killed you! Why didn't you call the police?"

She only told Kaye that Caleb never let her near the phone. She never told anyone everything.

Hospital stays provide time to reflect. *Why, oh why do I allow myself to be sacrificed upon the altar of Caleb's self-loathing?* It seemed any success for Fiona parlayed into failure for Caleb.

"And I wish he'd give up the idle threats and finally blow his brains out."

Kaye laughed. "Just do it? Well, that way we wouldn't have to kill him."

"I don't know what I'm gonna do. I have nothing! He won't pay me what he owes me and I refuse to beg."

Thank God we don't have kids. Small, bittersweet consolation. She would stay with Kaye for a while, regroup. Caleb soon showed up, however. She refused to return to the studio. He balked. Fiona threatened to press charges. She had a doctor's report, and photographs of her injuries. He begged forgiveness; she begged him to leave.

"I'll be back," said Caleb, invoking Schwarzenegger's killer cyborg from *Terminator*.

She had to laugh, though waited until he was out of earshot.

A few days after discharge, a hinky Fiona had gone out for drinks with Kaye and spent the evening nervously glancing at the door. Kaye pestered her to get counselling, join a battered women's support group; Caleb called incessantly.

"Fiona! Don't hang up. Look, if you'll just talk to me, everything will be fine. We can work this out."

"I'm tired of talking. I'm tired of the blame game. I'm tired of being pushed around. I am so tired! Sick and tired."

"Fiona! Please. I love you. I miss you! Please come home. Come on, we've got too much invested in this marriage to just throw it all away."

Again, Fiona refused. Two days later, Caleb snuck in to Kaye's place while they were out and affixed a note to her mattress with a butcher knife.

Thank you for everything, Fiona. Thank you for leading me along with the hope that I could create something with you and support you in the pursuit of your dreams. I guess they're last year's dreams. I've never cried with a deeper bitterness, while you lie in comfort with Kaye. I'm sure you're telling her what a shithead I am. Thanks a bunch babe, for all your consideration.

Love, Caleb

Furious, Kaye called the police. They came around, but claimed they couldn't do anything without a restraining order. Again, Fiona promised to file one. Caleb vowed to go to NA.

"He's never said that before."

Kaye shook her head. "He's never had to. Fiona, he would have changed by now if he were capable of change. He's desperate."

"You're right. He's lonely. He can't stand being alone."

Caleb had provided an escape from the pressures of the music business, she thought. In the beginning. Now, Caleb is the pressure. *And we're both in a downward spiral. I'm not going to let him take me down with him.* He called the next day, threatening suicide.

"Fiona! I love you. I can't live without you!"

She tried to console him, and get off the phone.

"I'll come over there and kill you both."

"Don't you dare answer that phone anymore!" commanded Kaye. "I'm taking you down to file that restraining order tomorrow morning."

Fiona filed the restraining order. Five days later, Carrie called. Caleb had been in a car accident.

"Jesus Christ! What happened? Is he okay?"

"He broke his arm. Some kind of internal injuries too. I don't know much more than that. I'm on my way to the hospital. Shall I pick you up?"

Broken wrist, not arm. "I may never play guitar again," Fiona imagined him whining. Caleb had T-boned a Mercedes. *Up go our premiums.* Much to Kaye's dismay, Fiona returned to the studio a few days later.

"I'm sorry. But it's my business too! We're partners. I can't let it go down the tubes."

Fiona let herself in, nearly gagging from the stench of sun-dried urine in the building's alcove. *Men.* Unzipping, whizzing wherever and whenever they felt like. Just because you can do something, doesn't mean you should. "It smells like Paris," Caleb always joked.

She found blood on the walls, dining chairs busted, pieces piled in a heap. Contrite, miserable, Caleb welcomed her with a long embrace. Their car battery had been stolen, again, Bob's Market robbed, again.

"And I saw a prowler on the roof yesterday. More graffiti too."

"Well, we do live in Rampart. It only leads the city in homicides."

They installed security lights and closed the blinds as soon as it got dark. Caleb warned her that Aurora, the woman who ran the barbecue joint up the street had just been raped.

"Good thing I'm here to protect you."

She had to laugh.

Caleb's injuries gave him licence to whine and make demands more than usual, though he tried to make amends by working on arrangements for a couple of new songs.

Fiona was permitted to attend Yreina's baby shower, phone ringing as she arrived, girlfriends giggling. Yreina handed her the receiver. It was Caleb, frantic she hadn't been there the previous two times he'd called. She managed a lovely visit with old friends over mimosas and cake, revelling in several hours of pure girl talk. Driving back through her old stomping grounds, Fiona wondered how she'd arrived at this hell now called home.

"Who was there?" Caleb put out four lines of cocaine. "Did you tell them anything?"

A few days later, a friend of a friend called to ask Fiona if she'd like to appear on *The New Dating Game*.

"Sorry. Can't. I'm married. Is the city short of bachelorettes or something?"

Caleb came upon her a few minutes later, working at the computer. "Who called?"

She lied, saying it was a wrong number.

"Right." Slightly switching gears Caleb said, "You better quit frowning, Mrs. Crowe. You're going to get wrinkles."

I must be the only one aging around here, she thought. Or maybe Caleb has a portrait stashed in the attic. *And I'm not about to look.*

Odd how Kit remained with the band and male-bonded with Caleb, who had little patience for his bouts of depression. Surely Caleb could conjure up a little empathy, considering how black his moods got. They resumed rehearsals, which provided relief and hope. Fiona set up the PA. Shayla arrived, then Kit. Shayla yawned throughout the afternoon, but it was Fiona's vocals that were flat. Halfway through the first song, they were besieged by feedback. Cursing, Caleb made adjustments. Fiona dared to inform him that the levels were still too low in the monitors. He began slamming stuff around, then stalked out of the room.

Kit started in. "Can't you try to be a little diplomatic?"

"Christ!" replied Fiona. "What did I say that was so out of line? It was an observation. Input. He's overreacting. It's not my fault the PA fucked up. I didn't lose my temper and walk out."

Kit walked out. Fiona cried. *I will walk out, I swear! I'm just about done being the girl singer around here.* Shayla tried to console Fiona, but was visibly relieved to go home.

It hit her. She'd been dressing in the dark, feeling fat and ugly despite working out every day.

Fiona had begun to dread singing. Performing. Several hours were required to psyche herself up for it. She felt cursed. Still, Fiona held out hope they could get a gig at the prestigious China Club.

Reading in bed one afternoon, she overheard Lenny and

Caleb. "We're not addicted! We're psychologically habituated. Maybe. We can quit if we want."

"Oh come on," said Lenny. "Don't tell me there's no physical dependency. The amount you're consuming constitutes abuse. You're developing tolerance. Don't you need more to get high?"

"How do you know how much we do?"

"Hey, I'm your partner. I know everything."

"Bullshit. We go for weeks without getting high."

Lenny moaned. "Come on! A week, tops. Maybe."

Fiona knew how it worked. The crash began before the coke ran out. Feeling more morose watching the pile diminish, she'd wish Carrie would leave so the drugs would last longer, always hoping there were Halcions when it did. *I always have hope.*

"Make me come. I've got blue balls."

Bluebeard and his precious blue balls. Caleb's priapism used to be flattering, now only tedious. Quickly, he became infuriated with her efforts, as though fatigue was a betrayal. Fluey, Fiona ignored her tender kidneys, aching muscles, and sucked Caleb's cock. He came at last, but instead of passing out, insisted on going for another round. Caleb had a gram stashed, much to her relief, and dismay. He began talking babies again as he chopped up the cocaine.

"You focus on my doubts instead of your own. There'd be laughter with a child around."

He will say anything, she thought. A cheap ploy, Caleb brought up the subject despite her ambivalence, whenever he sensed she might be plotting to leave. She'd tried unsuccessfully to ignore her much media bandied "biological clock." Too late perhaps, Fiona had decided family and friends were more important than record deals. *Fuck my brilliant career. I'm jinxed anyway. But how to be a mother and an artist? Maybe it's the same goddamned thing.* Once again Fiona and Caleb agreed to prepare to conceive, to quit drinking and drugging.

Caleb turned thirty-two. Life ground to a halt as they celebrated at a little Italian place with his family, several studio clients, Lenny, Kit, Shayla, and Japanese colleague and cokehead-record producer Kazuki. Fiona marvelled at her husband's charisma despite him being a sociopath, or perhaps because of it. Shayla gave him a troll doll. *How apropos.*

Lenny tried to bestow Caleb with a handgun, a 9mm Luger. Priding himself on his martial arts abilities, Caleb recoiled.

"Handguns get used on their owners," said Fiona. "It's a fact."

She recalled seeing a map of L.A. County, numerous indoor pistol ranges marked along with the city's tourist attractions. Still, Fiona knew gun owners who had never fired a round.

"You have to be prepared to shoot someone if you have a gun in your house," said Caleb. "I'm not sure I could. I doubt Fiona could."

"Speak for yourself. I've been feeling particularly vulnerable, but I don't want a gun in the house either. We might use it on each other."

Caleb scowled.

"Arm yourselves with a shotgun. Anybody can use one." Lenny delivered the tired old saw. "SHIK-SHIK. That's a sound every bad guy knows." Disgusted, he left.

Caleb sat down in his swivel chair at the soundboard in the control room, demanding a blowjob for his birthday. "Right here. Right now."

"Christ, it's not as if I don't give you blowjobs every fucking day." Fiona sighed. "Okay, okay. When you're happy, I'm happy."

Later Caleb chuckled, describing the birthday blowjob Danielle had delivered despite her distaste for fellatio; how he deliberately came all over her new black dress, "Just to piss her off."

"You mean, just to further humiliate her?"

"Tough girl, aren't you?"

Have to be.

★ ★ ★ ★

Caleb loved to videotape.

"Leave it on! They look better that way. Leave the bra on, but pull your tits out."

Carrie complied. Caleb reached down and removed a comb from her hair so that it fell loose. He demanded a shot from above, of Carrie sucking Fiona's nipples.

"Now move your mouth down to her pussy. Slowly. Little kisses along the way."

Next, a close-up of Fiona's tongue, tightly curled, stuck out, pressed against Carrie's clit. He tossed over a pair of stilettos, instructing Carrie to put them on. She protested they didn't fit.

"Put them on anyway." Caleb directed Fiona to rub her nipples against Carrie's. "Now, straddle her face. Sixty-nine."

He threw Sly Stone's "It's a Family Affair" on the stereo. The girls giggled.

"You're sick, bro!"

Caleb hiked Carrie's ass high into the air and handed Fiona the strap-on dildo, commanding, "Fuck her."

Fiona obliged.

"Not her cunt," he seethed. "Fuck her ass!"

Fiona hesitated. Carrie nodded. "It's okay."

Caleb tapped his toe while Fiona lubed her up. They watched the monitor, Caleb zooming in on the black cock gliding in and out of Carrie's anus. Soon tiring of that, he leaned back, camera in hand, indicating his erection. They were to suck and lick his cock simultaneously. Carrie lapped at the head of his penis, moving down, stroking the shaft with a pointed tongue, just the way he liked.

"I think I've died and gone to heaven. Come on, Fiona. You don't want to be outdone, do you?" Shoving her nose up into his ball sac, Fiona licked, delineating first the right, then the left testicle with her tongue. He clutched her hair, moaning, "Ah, you teabag so nice."

269

They joked about sending the tape to Mitzi for Mother's Day. Caleb pleaded blue balls once again, demanding that Fiona and Carrie take turns sucking him off. Finally, he blew. The trio lolled about smoking hash until Caleb crashed. Giggling, the girls retreated to the living room. "While the cat's away . . ."

"Bring me those luscious tits of yours." Fiona draped herself on the couch.

Carrie dangled her formidable breasts in Fiona's face. Fiona squished them together, suckling, nibbling, gorging. She sat up, and slowly applied clamps to Carrie's nipples. Carrie squealed.

"Shhhh! He'd kill us, you know."

Carrie laughed. "Fuck him!"

"Do you?"

"No! I never let him fuck me. It was the other way around." Carrie got up, ran into the bedroom, and returned with the dildo, smiling slyly. "Your turn!"

Kit finally quit. Fiona spent a few days moping before deciding to regroup yet again. She longed to work up some new songs, but Caleb wasn't in the mood. He lit a joint and poured a glass of wine.

"I might be, after a run to Rango's."

"Well if you don't want to record, let's go out. We said we were going to start going out on Sundays, remember? Will Rogers Park, hiking the Malibu hills, the Getty. See all the things we haven't seen, do all the things we haven't done."

Caleb groaned. "Soon. I promise."

He called his mother. They argued. Caleb hung up, complaining that his parents didn't take him seriously. "And she's mad because we don't visit often enough."

"Why should we? You know what she said to me the other day? 'Children would exhaust you at your age, Fiona.'"

"I can't eat tuna salad without potato chips!"

She'd forgotten, apologized. Fiona dared bring up another sore subject, working up a new act, independent of Caleb.

"Which you could produce if you like." He scowled. "The thing with the backing tapes isn't working out," pleaded Fiona. "It's too much hassle. Far too time-consuming. This way you can concentrate on producing and film-scoring."

Caleb called her an ingrate.

News Hour. Line in the sand. Brink of war. Fiona pointed to the television, old gunfighter Saddam. Lenny cursed.

"Why hasn't the CIA taken that bastard out?"

Caleb cranked the volume. President Bush was addressing a joint session of the U.S. Congress, going on about Iraq withdrawing from Kuwait and "a fifth objective, a new world order, free from the threat of terror, secure in our quest for peace."

"Yeah, right," said Fiona. "Read my lips, you war-mongering old coot. We know you're only interested in oil and 'protecting your interests abroad.'"

Caleb rolled his eyes. "You mean our interests."

The news kept them up all night, CNN coming up with a logo and corresponding jingle—"Operation Desert Storm," which pissed her off.

"Actually, it's officially the 'Persian Gulf War.' Assholes!"

Or, invasion.

"Saddam may use chemical warfare. Another Vietnam. Great unease spreading over the nation."

Tension permeated the studio as well.

"Where's that invoice I made out for Wilderness Family? Did you throw it out?"

Here we go again. "How could I throw it out if I haven't seen it, Caleb?"

"So, did it grow legs and walk out?"

Fiona put her guitar aside. "I'll help you look for it."

Cursing, Caleb slammed a paperweight down so hard it

dented the teak desk, infuriating him further. In a blind rage, he yanked drawers open and banged cupboard doors shut.

"You better find it! You better find it fast!"

"Did you look in your jacket?"

Grumbling, Caleb went to the closet and fished through his pockets, glaring at her as he pulled out the invoice. Quickly switching gears into nonchalance, he turned on his heel and left. *Asshole.* Later in the bathroom, Fiona swapped his toothbrush with the one she used for cleaning grout.

Next morning, Caleb woke in a hideous funk, feeling discouraged, like a failure, he said.

"It's been a tough winter, honey. Things will get better."

He might drive her crazy, but Fiona still hoped things would work out. Somehow. They talked amiably.

"You're not a failure until you stop trying," he said, parroting Mitzi.

"Maybe we don't live long enough to be anything but amateurs. By the time I figure shit out, it's too late and I'm too old."

War, faltering economy, business slowing, Caleb frequently employed the "B" word—bankruptcy—which made him cranky. They routinely had an argument for breakfast. Keeping quiet wasn't safe either, her silence an affront.

Jeanette began calling often, agitated. Boyfriend Bernie had so many DUIs he couldn't drive her to the doctor. Maureen called to gripe about Jeanette.

An hour later, another argument with Caleb ensued, about whether or not to arrange a meeting with a band interested in recording. He claimed fatigue.

"Then don't whine that you don't have enough work. You think you're too good for them. You're the prima donna."

Caleb brandished a fist as he made a call to Rango. Too drunk to drive, he sent Fiona to score. *I shouldn't be driving either. I shouldn't be doing a lot of things.* They sat up all night snorting coke, Caleb ranting about his angst, his torn identity, how he was a Jew-light.

Operation Desert Storm raged on as the studio and grow op

272

endured some of southern California's worst rainstorms. Rain equals mudslide in Los Angeles. The sump pumps they placed on the roof chugged away round the clock. The water had to be drained off by hand on the hour, every hour, or it would leak into the control room. The basement flooded. The plants seemed to be holding up, but the change in humidity was wreaking havoc, and Lenny was threatening burnout.

Jeanette suffered a stroke. "I have to go see her, Caleb!"

He insisted Fiona wait until the floods subsided. They had four bands in that night, Hole to arrive at eight p.m. Hole. She'd laughed the first time she heard their name. Now it only struck her as ironic. *That's exactly where I am. In a hole. An abyss. Courtney's getting signed and I'm not.* Courtney's caterwauling oddly worked to diminish Fiona's despair. *At least somebody's making it.*

Terribly broke, they accepted Rango's invitation to come over and get high with him; always a bad sign according to Caleb, hanging with your connection. They returned home the next afternoon. Caleb flipped on the television reflexively as they crawled into bed, puzzled by a news item featuring a home video. LAPD officers were swarming a large black man prostrate lying on the ground. Repeatedly, they delivered silent, lethal blows. The man too feeble to cover his face, jackknifed and flopped around like a rag doll. Batons found their mark unerringly, cops kicking and clubbing him about the head, while more officers lurked.

"Oh my God!"

"They're made of steel, those billy clubs of theirs," said Caleb. "Exclusive to the LAPD, of course."

They turned it off and tried to sleep.

A Letter from Craig Lee—*LA Weekly*. "Treasure life. Don't abuse your bodies and souls. And the next time some girl with ratty hair is screaming her lungs out playing three chords on an out-of-tune guitar, know that I'm there in spirit, cheering her on. Thanks for all the beautiful music."

She called Kaye. "I feel like an utter shithead! I didn't know how bad it was."

"It's okay. He wasn't receiving visitors at the end."

"Man! He was always so supportive."

"It's the end of an era, isn't it?" said Kaye. "I miss you. How are you doing?"

They vowed to meet for lunch.

Fiona caught a virus, not surprising with her feet perpetually in cold water. Homesick as well, she actually longed to see her mother, and found herself watching *The Kids in the Hall*, who reminded her of every guy she went to high school with. *The year is improving though.* Caleb had been discussing the possibility of getting into audio post, which was far more lucrative than recording and far less stressful, but he needed new equipment and software.

Jeanette called from the hospital, baying, "I want to die!"

She had to get to Canada. Fiona got a nurse on the phone, who explained that there was a large blood clot in her mother's arm. "It's atrophying. She's in a lot of pain. She'll need surgery, and an amputation." Fiona shuddered. Gazing out the window at a drab sky, she recalled a song she'd penned the previous month. "Phantom Limb." *Synchronicity?*

Fiona woke to grotesque noises; walls groaning, floors heaving. *The Big One?* She and Caleb rose together. They ran and stood in the door jamb, the soles of her feet pinched between the bathroom's honeycomb tiles and the bedroom's wooden floorboards. Mother Earth, a dog shaking off fleas, Fiona, falling, bawling, Evinrude yowling from beneath the couch.

Caleb, from behind, squeezed her tits. Fiona braced herself, gripping both sides of the doorframe as the building pitched to and fro. He grabbed her hips. Entranced, Fiona watched her necklaces, pendants, and beads rock back and forth on a hook. Caleb thrust in his cock. They moved in tandem with the earth's seesaw motion, a black blur of crows screeching past the window, quake a ruse neatly diverting husband and wife from a mouldering paperback marriage.

Radio newscasts announced this latest quake measured 4.5 on the Richter scale, the epicentre near Whittier. Tremors subsiding, Fiona ran out to score another gram. Rango buzzed her in. She found him, arm tied off. He indicated a grimy loveseat, asked her to tighten the band around his bicep. She did so efficiently, determined to get out quickly.

"Thanks, doll."

Rango surveyed the carnage, what was left of his veins, knotted and purple against mocha skin. Gently, he guided needle to flesh. His head jolted backward. Rango swayed in sideways rapture for a few moments, nearly toppling off his stool. Moaning, he slowly removed the syringe.

"Hey, girl," he said, opening his eyes with effort, smiling beatifically.

"Hey, Rango."

He slumped and breathed for a bit, then tossed her a bindle. "You're wasting your money doin' it like that. Missin' out on a whole other dimension."

"I don't think I can handle another dimension."

He sat dead-eyed, quivering. Lonesome Rango didn't want her to leave. Begging Fiona to stay, he set a pistol down on the coffee table between them. She was more aggravated than frightened. He put out a line for her. They talked of Rango's hard life, Rango unable to distinguish clients from friends. I'm stuck, she thought. Oh well, Caleb will call soon. When he did, Fiona said under her breath to him, "Call Rose."

Rango's prostitute mother eventually stumbled over from across the street, heavy-lidded and annoyed, scolding him like a little boy who'd pushed a playmate off the monkey bars.

275

"Rango! Put that gun away."

Fiona slipped out. Furious, Caleb threatened to throttle the truth out of her, insisting she was lying, that she'd chosen to stay and party with Rango.

CHAPTER TWELVE

Latest home-front news: Mo went postal, attacked a co-worker, walked out on Gary, packed up her stuff. Taking television and cat, leaving daughters Emma and Brianna, she fled to Cloverdale.

"I guess the borderline bitch has had enough of border-town living," Fiona told Shannon.

Fiona couldn't sleep for worrying about her mother, her hand tingling as if in sympathy. Jeanette's surgeon, Dr. Palmer, called. She was in the Intensive Care Unit, several of her fingers black. Her hand would have to be amputated. Soon. Fiona persuaded Caleb to let her go. She booked a flight. They got wasted. It felt like a celebration and who knew when, or how, she'd get high again.

Caleb delivered her to the airport, griping about the expensive parking, and how he was going to have to run the business all by himself while enduring aftershocks. Double sulk: Fiona wouldn't allow him to videotape her with Carrie anymore. He escorted Fiona to pick up her ticket and check her baggage. *Christ. May as well still be wearing cuffs.* They arrived at her gate.

"I love you!" He kissed her fiercely.

I am not coming back. She worried he might guess. "I have to go, Caleb! I'll miss my plane."

Fiona requested a window seat, nearly collapsing with relief, though didn't fully release her breath until after takeoff. She grabbed the inflight magazine, ordered tomato juice, and chatted with the sexy cowboy seated next to her. *Caleb would kill me.*

Fiona vacillated between fear and exhilaration. Five hours later, gladdened by the sight of the Rockies, she landed in

Calgary. *Nation of nerds.* Strange being back, confronted with Canadian reserve, though in this neck of the woods they said "eh" and "excuse my French" after cursing. They drove drunk to Tim Hortons on skidoos. They bloated their landfills with bottles and cans. They wasted water, faucets blasting as they idly brushed their teeth. *They. And fuck it's cold! In June.* Fiona sat in the bus station cafeteria, eating chips with gravy as she waited, quaffing a Labatt Blue, feeling conspicuous. Several hosers sitting across the way were farting and belching rude remarks. *Hmmm, maybe I don't miss Canada. Certainly don't miss Canadian men.*

Arriving in Taber, it appeared that half the citizens resided in trailers, the rest in trailer-like bungalows. Fiona watched a family of Hutterites pile into a sporty Chevy pickup truck with their funeral garb and antediluvian manner. She pitied them, certain they were driven by fear, vainly and arrogantly attempting to control time, the natural order of things. Fiona walked about freely, though feeling out of sorts. *Like I've lost a limb? Christ. I don't miss him, do I? No, I miss L.A. My friends. Home.* Everywhere she went, the locals stared. The population of Taber, Alberta, may be 5,662, but you have to wonder about people suspicious of a woman wearing red lipstick.

Fiona arrived at a Lethbridge hospital late in the afternoon, reluctantly venturing down a long, dim hallway, peeking into patients' rooms, stealing glimpses, hoping to find her mother asleep. The hand was coming off any day. The right hand. Ironic, because Jeanette would have been a southpaw if the nuns hadn't beaten it out of her. 'Tis the sign of the devil, after all.

The staff resignedly wheeled trays past her, Fiona colliding with a blond, big-boned nurse not once, but twice. She seemed relieved to direct Fiona to Jeanette's room. Delivering herself like a Thanksgiving turkey, Fiona found her mother's bed concealed behind a blue drape. She peered in to find Jeanette lying atop the covers, lost in reverie. *I think it's Jeanette.* The woman in the faded floral gown was a mere husk of the woman who used to shake the house with unholy rages. Cheeks sunken, her oddly shaped nose was more prominent. Equally dismaying were the broken capillaries and grog blossoms all over her face. Fiona moved to place herself in Jeanette's line of vision.

"Fiona!" she sobbed, thrusting her arms up into the air like a toddler.

Fiona rushed over and sat on the bed gently, leery of capsizing her. Pulling her mother close, she rocked her back and forth, woozy at the tables having turned so irrevocably. Scarred, emaciated, frail, Jeanette smelled of decayed tooth. The swollen fingers of her hand were a deep, menacing blue. She called Fiona "Rory" and demanded a cigarette.

"You're not allowed to smoke."

"Then get me a chocolate bar."

Jeanette wasn't allowed chocolate bars either. She cursed.

Two days later, Fiona still had not consulted with Jeanette's physician, though she'd been flattening out on morphine. And she was agitated. It seemed just as she finally dozed off, a nurse would charge in to check her vitals or administer a shot.

"Can't you let her rest?"

They ignored Fiona's pleas. Jeanette started calling the nurses Pokey. When Pokey arrived for the third time, Jeanette cried pitifully.

"Come on!" protested Fiona. "You're breaking my heart here."

Pokey ignored Fiona and inserted the syringe. Jeanette groaned, nearly fainted.

"What is that anyway?"

"You'll have to talk to Dr. Palmer."

"Okay. Sure. When?"

"When he comes in."

"And when will that be?"

"Soon."

Why the hell would anybody want to be a nurse? They do all the dirty work and don't have nearly enough time to provide the kind of quality care a patient needs to heal.

Fiona anxiously awaited Rory's arrival. Navigating the grand ole' prairie without a car was nearly impossible. Fiona bought Jeanette a stuffed pink pig and a deck of cards. They played gin rummy and admired the roses from Uncle Stephen. Fiona wished she could shut out the moans and cries broadcasting down the corridor.

Caleb phoned again, complaining about water rationing, his loneliness, and the recession. Their car battery had been swiped again.

"How are the girls?" she asked, code for the pot plants, females bearing the most THC.

Soon the couple was bickering. "You know what? I'm staying. I am not coming back! I'm going to Vancouver after Jeanette recovers, and find a job."

"You're disgusting!" shouted Caleb and hung up.

Jeanette had no regard for anyone or anything. Unable to sit still, she banged her bad hand repeatedly, regularly falling out of bed. The nurses refused to put the bars up, but kept bugging her. Jeanette spoke nonchalantly of dying. Fiona wept. Pointing to Fiona's crotch once, Jeanette said, "Remember when I pulled out every one of your hairs?" The look in her eyes transported Fiona to the past at a dizzying rate.

"Bill's not your father, you know."

"Are you kidding?" Fiona focused on the floor, trying to assimilate the information.

"No."

"Well, then. Who is my father?"

A nurse bustled in. Jeanette averted her eyes. Soon, she was out cold. Next morning Jeanette characteristically refused to acknowledge the bomb she'd dropped, or its fallout.

"Who's my father? Does he even know I exist?"

Jeanette would not, or could not answer. *The slut. Well, it explains a lot.* Why people always asked if Fiona was adopted, why she felt no kinship to the Koretchucks, or KoretFucks, as their schoolyard tormenters called them. Why Fiona chose to adopt her mother's maiden name. It explained the bouts of estrangement between her sisters—half-sisters—what little common ground they shared now divided in two. Why Grandma Koretchuck favoured Rory and Maureen. She must have harboured suspicions. *Why I always felt like a freak! Christ. Who needs this crap? Especially now.*

Rory showed up with a heart-shaped music box playing "Make Someone Happy." Fiona had always envied Rory's easy grace, charm, and confidence despite the state of terror the sisters had resided in. The only popular Koretchuck girl, Rory instinctively knew how to befriend people. Fiona brought her up to speed.

"Jeanette's really out there. And don't let me near the window. I'm about to jump!"

Their mother cried out, "Rory," and then, "Don."

Fiona shrugged. "We have to watch her closely. I'm not kidding. I wish they'd get the damn operation over with."

Jeanette flirted with the doctor, kissed the nurses, punched Fiona and Rory, and frightened children in the visitors' lounge. She talked to her mother, Riva, as if she were in the room and demanded to phone her long-deceased sister. Jeanette pointed at Rory.

"Doesn't she look like Rory?"

"Has the doctor discussed the dementia with you?"

"No!" said Fiona. "I don't think he knows. How could he? He's never here for more than five minutes."

They retreated to a Chinese restaurant, grateful for the restorative wonders of won ton. The sisters reminisced, sort of, Rory insisting she remembered practically nothing of their childhood. *God only knows how much I've blocked out.* They had all learned to disassociate at will and in tandem, Fiona's strategy to induce a trance, spooking Jeanette, who like any good Catholic, believed her daughter to be possessed.

Retreating to their motel, Fiona listened to several frantic messages from Caleb. A 5.8 earthquake, Sierra Madre its epicentre, had hit Los Angeles. Fiona called, relieved to hear that everything was still standing.

"Fiona! When are you coming home? I miss you so much. I need your titties."

"I told you, Caleb. I'm not coming back." She hung up.

She hadn't had much opportunity to reflect on her farcical marriage, but one hospital-bedside morning, it occurred to Fiona that Caleb and Carrie were the true partners in crime, and she, their dupe.

The hour-long drive to and from the hospital each day in Rory's chinook-battered Toyota quickly became monotonous. Fiona shared Jeanette's comment regarding her paternity, or paternity fraud. Rory said nothing. Fiona did the math. Jeanette must have conceived during a trip home to visit Riva on her deathbed. Fiona's roots truly were Québécois, in Quebec, with the Larochelles, the Donegans, and God only knows who else.

They bought Jeanette slippers, nightgowns, a robe, and flowers. She was still highly ornery, but Rory could make her laugh. Jeanette pleaded with the nurses to spike her orange juice. One morning, she picked at her food, then flopped on the bed.

Squirming, she reported, "There's something between my legs and it's not a cock."

Rory pointed to the catheter. The girls giggled. Jeanette tossed toast at them. Dr. Palmer arrived at last to inform them that gangrene was setting in. They'd be operating on Monday. He would decide then whether to amputate at the wrist or the elbow.

"We wanted to avoid another operation," he said. "It's tricky, given the complications: diabetes, heart condition, stroke. Her body is twenty years older than her chronological age."

Good goin', Ma.

Brianna visited, their young niece amiable, unruffled. It must be hard to witness her grandmother in such a state, thought Fiona, but the girl had insisted. She missed her mother. Fiona cursed Maureen under her breath.

★ ★ ★ ★

"I want a wedding before I die!"

Fiona held Jeanette's good hand. She'd ripped the patches and tubing off, nearly pulling a monitor down on their heads. Rory helped the nurses calm her.

"It's a good sign," said Rory. "Maybe she's got enough spirit to survive."

"It's dementia. Remember?"

Sunday morning, the doctor called. Jeanette had an episode, they should come right away; respiratory problems and she might be too weak to undergo surgery. They arrived at the hospital, doctor having decided to operate immediately. The sisters perched on hard plastic chairs, breathing in sour, antiseptic air, staring at the obscenely trivial headlines of tattered fashion magazines. *Celebrity Weddings! Healthy, Beautiful, Sexy You!* Several torturously long hours later, the medical team emerged, Jeanette's gaunt frame outlined upon a gurney. Dr. Palmer's face revealed little as he strode toward them.

"She seems fine. We removed her hand at the wrist. Now we just have to make sure her lungs and heart do their work." He laughed and told them Jeanette had called the Australian anesthesiologist a "Limey."

She was still under the next morning, but her vital signs looked good. Jeanette would pull through. The sisters bought groceries, distracting themselves with cleaning and cooking. Fiona popped one of the Ativans littered throughout her mother's house. Still edgy, she laid down and tried to rest, irritated with Rory for chain-smoking and leaving the television on. They'd been close growing up. Too close. So close in age they fought over clothes, boyfriends, and who got the most attention. As adults, there was little to discuss. Fiona counted grain elevators and scanned the landscape for pronghorn antelope during their long drives to visit Jeanette.

A bellicose Caleb called to complain. "Do you still love me?"

Fiona's response of "I don't know" enraged him.

No time to consider such things, though she missed their big bed. The gym. Palm trees. Tom Kha Gai soup. Napa reds. Grilled yellowtail. Cocaine. After long days of jonesing, Fiona dreamt about cocaine at night. *What a way to detox.*

The whiner and the wiener. Brother-in-law Gary was also under the impression that Fiona was on holiday, "Don't worry, be happy" his mantra. He steadfastly refused to acknowledge his children's suffering; that they'd lost their mother, no one allowed to be unhappy.

"It's unconscionable," she told Shannon. "And nearly impossible to ignore his despotic cheerfulness."

She had to admit he provided a respite from Jeanette and the hospital though. Gary could be kind and considerate, when inclined. Teenaged Emma was buoyed by her pack of pals, but Brianna clung to Fiona. I must provide a poor substitute, she thought, distracted with Jeanette and Caleb.

The sisters stared. Jeanette had not acknowledged the missing hand—the stump—though it was swollen, ghastly looking, and surely the cause of much pain and discomfort.

Fiona went to visit Brianna and prepare dinner. The first time she opened Gary's cutlery drawer, a rust-coloured moth fluttered out and they laughed. Sitting on the veranda, the peculiar prairie light made Fiona nostalgic, for what, she wasn't certain. Brianna spied a doe with its fawn. A few minutes later she was bouncing and whooping at the sight of a rainbow straddling a bank of popcorn clouds.

"Brianna," said Fiona. "You see!"

Next morning, weak and nauseated, Fiona craved carrot juice. Brianna donned her Beetlejuice mask as they tried to make some in the blender.

"Beetlejuice meets carrot juice!" cried Brianna, declaring, "I hate carrot juice!" before running to the bathroom to spit it into the toilet bowl.

Fiona bought Brianna a set of animal rubber stamps, Magic Markers, and a cassette featuring Robin Williams as Pecos Bill. They played it in the car while driving to Writing-on-Stone Provincial Park's hoodoos and petroglyphs. Fiona sang to her and read bedtime stories, including their favourite, Winnie-the-Pooh. Gary reported that his daughter's nightmares had subsided. Fiona adored her niece, the way her little girl frame fit neatly into her arms.

"I'd spirit her away if I could," she told Shannon. "I'd be happy with a child half as wonderful."

"I think it's good you still harbour such a hope."

"Guess I do. I'm fucked, in that case."

Jeanette was to be discharged soon, too soon it seemed, but she had improved. Still whining for cigarettes and refusing to discuss the issue of Fiona's paternity, she snatched a Player's Filter from Rory, snapped it in half, and flung the tobacco into the air. They took her downstairs to get her hair done. Jeanette went on a telecommunications binge, calling her brother Reggie in Winnipeg, and boyfriend Bernie in Quebec. Her stuffed pig had been stolen so they bought a Bee's Knees teddy bear. Suddenly their mother coveted stuffed animals.

"Regressing to an infantile state, I guess," said Rory.

"Actually, I think that's where Jeanette's been residing most of her life."

They drove her home, Jeanette in good humour for a few hours before demanding to be taken shopping. They packed her up and went to Zellers. Jeanette tried on several pairs of shoes and demanded fifty dollars. Fiona had no money. Jeanette grabbed a shopping cart and attempted to stuff in an eight-pack of toilet paper. It was amazing how much she could do with one hand. When Fiona insisted they leave, Jeanette threw a tin of coffee on the floor and stomped away.

The daughters needed to sort out their mother's myriad of bills before she lost or bestowed more of her meagre funds.

They arranged an appointment with her GP. At last they could get the medications straightened out. Jeanette had been dosing herself with outdated prescriptions. They worried about drug interactions. It had become a compulsion to unwrap the stump, especially with people around. The sisters feared infection. There was no reasoning with Jeanette. Each outing was a trial, each day as taxing as three.

One afternoon, after Jeanette mercifully settled down, Fiona was able to drive Brianna home. Gary was at work, and his brother Ralph showed up completely hammered, waving a pistol. Apparently, Gary had given him ammo and beer earlier in the day. Ralph had run out of both.

"Hey, Blooooondie!" he leered. "Yer lookin' gooooood!"

Fiona and Brianna fled to her room. *What is it with this country?* Toronto wants to be New York, B.C. wants to be California, Alberta wants to be Texas, though Canadians are as rabidly anti-American as the rest of the world. She'd never felt any desire to become a U.S. citizen, revelling in her status as the girl from Canada, though Fiona hadn't been feeling particularly Canadian either. *Fuck borders. I'm a citizen of the world. At least I'm not stuck here in Bumfuck, Alberta.*

Downstairs, Ralph plundered the house. To their great relief they heard the door slam, and watched as he stumbled to his Barracuda, tossed in his loot, and sped off. Gary's mother called him at work to inform him that Ralph was in his backyard firing off rounds, and that someone had called 9-1-1. When Gary arrived, an RCMP Emergency Response Team surrounded his brother's house, their guns drawn, eyes trained on the door. Gary convinced the police to let him go inside, entering to find Ralph passed out on the couch.

When Fiona finally returned to her mother's house, she found Rory and Jeanette conked out, and promptly got Shannon on the phone.

"Kee-rist! Get me out of this hillbilly hell! I can understand why Mo left, but why did she come here in the first place?"

She had to hang up, check Jeanette's pulse. Exhausted, Fiona reclined on the couch. Jeanette soon awakened to make coffee and watch *Scooby-Doo*. She poured milk into the kettle and clicked on the empty toaster. Sometimes Jeanette thought Fiona and Rory were nurses and recoiled in fear. She gave her mother some warm milk and got her settled down again. At seven a.m. Fiona woke to find Jeanette gone. She yelled at Rory. They drove to Gary's house. No Jeanette. They returned and soon received a call from Pete at the PetroCan. Penniless, drenched, and in her bathrobe and slippers, Jeanette was banging on the counter, demanding cigarettes. The girls picked her up, while she ranted and spit profanities. Jeanette demanded to be taken to Gary's. They went to Gary's, Rory calming Jeanette as Fiona prepared breakfast. Brianna insisted on dousing her scrambled eggs with ketchup.

"I wish my mom would come back."

Fiona and Rory exchanged mournful glances. Gary said nothing. No one knew what Maureen was doing and she certainly wasn't about to tell any of them.

"I know she misses you too, honey," cooed Rory. "You'll be seeing your mom soon. I'm sure that after Grandma feels better, we can all get together."

They went to see about a prosthesis, uncertain Jeanette would deign to wear one, or live to use it. There were several styles, ranging from a menacing hook to a nifty $10,000 electronic hand. Rory selected the most practical unit, handsome Dr. Russo assuring them the cost would be covered by Social Services. The sisters spent several days on the phone in a vain attempt to track down said resources. Nor did Jeanette qualify for counselling for the trauma of limb loss.

"This fucking province! All their cutbacks and reforms. They're like Americans, always bitching about taxes."

"Let's get out of this dump," said Rory. "Head to the coast."

With only one hand and half a mind, Jeanette had indeed

regressed to an infantile state. Fiona was grateful Rory had taken on the task of injecting her with insulin. When Jeanette wasn't twitchy or combative, she slept fitfully for short periods, weaving in and out of lucidity; mostly out. She was incontinent, so they'd need to buy geriatric diapers for the trip. The prescriptions were still a mess. Jeanette persisted in removing the bandages, her daughters cringing as she poked the stump with scissors in a frenzied attempt to relieve unremitting pain.

"I will go mad!" Fiona longed for her mother, the mother she'd loved as fiercely as she dreaded.

"You're my favourite," Jeanette had often whispered, allowing Fiona to watch television with her after her sisters fell asleep. Fiona was nostalgic for the stories Jeanette used to tell, the way she made them laugh, the way she welcomed friends and neighbours, sharing what little they had. Highly intelligent despite being ill-educated, Jeanette laboured under the belief, perpetuated by Bill, that she was stupid. Fiona had always longed to reassure her.

They drove Jeanette to the hospital to check her blood sugar before hitting the road. It was fine, but she threw several nasty fits, again demanding to be taken shopping. Her daughters refused. Caleb called during their standoff. He capably consoled his wife, but the subject soon reverted to his favourite subject.

"I'm so lonely! I don't know what vitamins to take. I'm watching too much TV. I've got on *Blood Vows: the Story of a Mafia Wife*."

She visualized him lying on the bed, cradling his guitar. "Caleb, I have to go."

He was having nightmares; dreamt Fiona was fucking someone else. "It was horrible!"

"I'm sorry to hear that Caleb, but I'm living a fucking nightmare! Okay? We can talk when I get out to B.C."

Jeanette relented. The sisters shut up the house and were finally ready to depart when Fiona accidentally locked Rory's keys in the car. It was Sunday, the wait for CAA interminable. Post-fiasco, they finally loaded up and were down the road a mile when Fiona remembered she'd forgotten her retainer.

Sweet, long-suffering Rory made a U-turn so Fiona could run into the house and retrieve it, yelling after her to grab something to drink. Finding nothing in the fridge but prune nectar, she got in the car and handed it to Jeanette.

Rory freaked. "It's gonna loosen her bowels!"

"I am losing it!" Fiona leaned her head against the cold window, quietly weeping, listening to Jeanette's rattled breathing.

They made it to Lethbridge, Jeanette whining for a milkshake the entire way.

"Hey, Rory, I think we may end up carting back a corpse. Or two."

Wendy's. Jeanette insisted on going inside instead of driving through the drive-thru. She needed to use the washroom. They ordered and sat, knowing Jeanette wouldn't eat much, if at all. Fiona worried that her mother might topple over or stop breathing. Instead, Jeanette started to choke on a hamburger. They pleaded with her to drink some water. She couldn't speak, kept choking. Fiona leapt up, got behind her, and attempted the Heimlich maneuver. Jeanette's body, like jelly, kept slipping from Fiona's grip, though she managed to place her fists above Jeanette's navel and deliver several sharp thrusts to her abdomen. People stared. She didn't care. Rory was about to run and dial 9-1-1 when Jeanette spewed forth a huge, slimy chunk of ground meat. Several customers got up and left.

"I don't want my hamburger, Mommy," mewled the little girl in the next booth.

Dazed, Jeanette refused water or to go to the bathroom. They slowly maneuvered her into the car and drove off, relieved to contain her mania. Rory promptly got lost in a city park. As they spun in tiresome, frenzied circles, Fiona realized her retainer was sitting on the table back at Wendy's, wrapped in a yellow napkin. Rory glared at the windshield.

"It's worth three hundred dollars. Three hundred *American* dollars! Caleb will kill me."

They located the highway, then Wendy's, Fiona dashing inside to find their table had been cleared. She asked one of the adolescent employees where the trash was. The girl stared at her.

"Trash!" screeched Fiona. "Where's the trash?" The frightened girl didn't move. "I mean garbage! I lost my retainer. You know what a retainer is?" Fiona glanced out the window at her mother badgering her sister. "I gotta do this quick!" Fiona rushed into the kitchen, sought out the trash cans, and demanded rubber gloves. "Hurry!" She flung Styrofoam cups, napkins, plastic forks, and knives behind her, cursing, "Goddamn hicks and Hutterites. Cowboys and yahoos. Farmers and rednecks. Truckers and guns and yokels and horses and cows and quacks and crackpots and dinosaurs and FUUUUUUCK! I'll be so glad to get out of this hell hole!"

"Is this it?"

Fiona looked up to see the girl holding the retainer. "I could kiss you!"

Instead, she grabbed the cursed thing and ran past three dutiful employees standing in a row, hands hanging by their sides, mouths agape.

They crossed the border into B.C., Jeanette whining, but a little less belligerent, shoulders dropped instead of hunched. Fiona was shocked by the growth of the Okanagan Valley, the once-sleepy Kelowna overrun with housing developments, billboards, drive-ins, and strip malls. *Christ. It looks like L.A.*

Doll Hospital, Realtor on Duty, Inniskillin Vintners.

"B.C. has a wine industry now?"

"Some of it's really good too," said Rory.

"Too bad it's been Napa Valley-ized."

South of Summerland, the countryside began to resemble the Okanagan she remembered. Sixteen hours on the road. Jeanette still refused to sleep. They arrived at Rory's house in Langley at three a.m., relieved and exhausted. The next day they drove their mother to see Rory's GP, who informed them she was suffering from Ativan withdrawal and psychosis, and should have been provided with a medication schedule.

"Ha!" said Rory. "Are you going to help us with the malpractice suit?"

Maureen pulled herself away from work, arriving with flowers and gifts, on the defensive, worried she might be called upon to take care of their mother. Mo went on about her new boyfriend, house, job, life. Fiona felt like smacking her.

Caleb called. "How's Jeanette? I hope she's improving. Wish I could be more helpful. I don't know what to say to make things better. All I can say is, I love you, Fiona. I hope it helps."

"It helps."

"I'm here for you, babe."

Thanksgiving. Despite her foul mood, Fiona volunteered to cook dinner, roasting a huge bird with all the trimmings, appalled when no one sat in the dining room to eat. They filled their plates and retreated to their corners, Rory in the kitchen reading a *People* magazine, her husband, Roger, proud owner of a new satellite dish and purveyor of over 100 channels, in the living room. No wine, no ceremony, no toasts, no thanks. Fiona brought some food to her mother. They ate in the bedroom in front of the other television.

Caleb called. "I miss you!"

"I miss you too."

"Come home, babe. Let's have a baby."

She had to laugh.

"We can do it. I know things have been rough, but I promise, they'll get better. Hey, I got a gig! Playing guitar. Toyota commercial."

They talked a long while. They could finish recording. She was homesick, as fucked up as things were. Caleb had arranged and charted three Fiona LaBand songs and was working hard around the place, cleaning, repairing, organizing. He would book a flight for her. She agreed, sisters upset at her impending departure.

Three days later Fiona was packed. She bought souvenirs: 222s, maple syrup, smoked salmon, and a bottle of Alberta Springs Whiskey, so dark and syrupy it resembled bourbon. Caleb would love it. She flew to Los Angeles. They made Canadian-style mint juleps to celebrate her homecoming, Caleb careening between charming and crusty, eager to re-establish the status quo. Fiona found the studio walls dented, cigarette burns on the carpet, a wastebasket brimming with the shattered remains of their wedding pictures, patina of grime covering everything. She was appalled to discover he'd hired illegals to do most of the work he so proudly laid claim to. Fiona was alarmed by the extent of his paranoia, Caleb convinced the studio was under surveillance, once refusing to put his key in the ignition, certain it was hooked up to an explosive. She lured him inside with the promise of a massage, encouraged him to take a Valium.

Why did I ever think he had an intellect? She'd noticed the books, not the dust upon them. If Caleb read anything, it was *TV Guide*. Nearly every conversation disintegrated into a quarrel. Once he'd said, "grammerical."

Fiona had laughed. "It's *grammatical*."

He would get drunk early in the evening, Fiona catching up, the night usually ending with a brawl. More announcement than confession, Caleb revealed he'd slept with Jill, a friend of a friend. He'd "needed some strange." Fiona was forced to feign outrage and moral indignation.

Weary of cancelled sessions, nagging and cajoling, she placed an ad in *BAM Magazine*, seeking collaborators, infuriating her husband.

"You don't take it seriously. You show no enthusiasm! Why should you care if I work up another act? What am I supposed to do? Give up? Like you?"

He slapped her hard across the face. Fiona clasped her jaw

and shut her eyes, as if to keep her head on, eyeballs in.

"You know what? It doesn't hurt anymore. And I'm leaving!" Fiona headed for the door.

"You stupid bitch!"

Caleb grabbed her arm, twisting it up behind her back, while shoving her into the counter. Skirt pulled up, panties ripped down, parting flesh with a sideways hand, Caleb drove in his cock. Fiona stared at a paint-by-number desert landscape Dennis had given her. An inside joke. She'd protested its turquoise sky. "Desert sky is purple. Remember?"

Caleb pulled out just before coming, pausing, lingering, cobra cock weaving over Fiona's backside. Gripping her hips tightly, he rammed it up her ass.

"So, bitch! Does it hurt?" He fucked her hard and fast. "Tell me you love it!" He pulled her hair, grunted and came.

She turned around, found him weeping.

"Fiona! What happened to us?"

He reached behind her to grab a butcher knife off the magnetic bar. Fiona sidled left. Gripping the handle, using the blade as a pointer, Caleb emphasized key words.

"You are *not* going back to Canada. And *forget* school. We *will* save this business. We *will* save this marriage. You are staying *here*! We're going to *do* what we set out to do. *Understood*?"

Fiona schemed all night. Urinated in his beer, taking great pleasure watching him guzzle it down. *You want intimacy? I'll give you intimacy.*

CHAPTER THIRTEEN

Judgment Day. Another slap in the face. It was incomprehensible the Simi Valley jury didn't see excessive force on the George Holliday tape.

"Caleb, I need to go home. Jeanette is dying!" Her mother had suffered another stroke.

"Forget it." Caleb pointed at the television. "Rioting in the streets, my dear. L.A. is sweatin' bullets."

Flash point, Florence and Normandie, South Central L.A. Fiona's guts lurched at the sight of pumped-up homeboys hurling rocks at passing cars, all non-black and hapless motorists wrenched out, beaten, robbed. This is the Big One, she thought. Fiona had never been to South Central. She went to Marina del Rey once, Long Beach twice, for a DOA show and to tour the Spruce Goose/Queen Mary with out-of-towners. The 405 Freeway had taken them through Inglewood, Torrance, Compton, exiting the wrong off-ramp, something most white Angelinos dreaded. She recalled a trek to Watts once, with her Lost Angels tribe, to attend the Day of the Drum Festival, awed by both Italian immigrant Simon Rodia's Watts Towers, rising from the urban terrain like extraterrestrials, and new friends, Flea and Anthony of the Red Hot Chili Peppers.

"Where are the police now?" Caleb shouted at the television. "Now that we need them."

"Apparently they hightailed it out of there hours ago. They may very well be praying in vain. Like the rest of us." Fiona's stomach flip-flopped watching an attack on a diminutive señora. "Don't people know what's going on? How can that poor woman be mistaken for the oppressor? Oh yeah, there was one

Hispanic on the jury."

Grimacing, Caleb opened the sliding glass door to the deck, gesturing toward a horizon obscured by white smoke, which was raining black cinders. Helicopters blundered through the haze like buzzards spitting up video bites of the violence.

"It's a war zone." He paced while lighting a joint. "Beirut, right in our backyard."

Looting rampant, L.A. is a new pair of shoes. A demonstration escalated into a riot at Parker Center, LAPD's central station. Brawls and fires were scattered across the megalopolis. Fiona winced at the sight of a bookstore in flames, bedlam and arsonists steadily creeping north along Vermont Avenue, three blocks from their studio on Hoover.

"It won't come up this far! Will it?"

Caleb shrugged. They dashed out for gas and food, supermarket crammed with panicked shoppers in grim survival mode.

Shayla called. She'd been trying to talk her husband out of going to the First African Methodist Episcopal Church to attend a peaceful demonstration. She yelled at him, "What, are you a Muslim now?" Shayla being so light skinned she'd been mistaken for Caucasian, gangbangers had jumped in front of her car. She'd protested, but they refused to listen until her decidedly African-American sons popped up in the back seat.

Fiona watched news coverage of a black man and white man fighting over stereo components. "It's really a situation of the haves against the have-nots. A class war."

"Now you sound like a Marxist," said Caleb.

"Yeah, what do I know? I'm a Canadian. A shiksa. A white girl. Hey, I need to extract some meaning from all the madness. I can understand these riots. Their rage is legitimate."

Caleb shook his head. "Listen, Fiona, you'd better not push my buttons right now. Just shut up for a change."

★ ★ ★ ★

Siege mentality setting in, Caleb informed her they were to patrol the rooftop in shifts. He handed her the binoculars.

"Why didn't I think of that? Probably because I associate binoculars with birding."

A large plume rose from the vicinity of 40th and Hoover. They worried Bob's Market would be torched, the studio along with it. No police. Firemen being shot at, in retreat. She steeled herself, tried to remain calm. The wrong decision might be fatal. She feared losing her ability to reason.

"Don't be afraid," said Caleb.

"I'm not afraid. I'm terrified."

★ ★ ★ ★

Infotainment. They were riveted to the television set, the L.A. Riots show on every channel. A young black woman from South Central, distressed over the destruction of her neighbourhood, said, "I'm so ashamed! People here been buildin' it up for a lifetime, educatin' their children, workin' so hard."

A hulking black man ran up from behind to yell into the camera. "No justice!"

"You dumb nigga!" she shouted after him. He got in her face. She did not back down despite his menacing girth.

There was much talk of an exodus to Orange County to buy ammunition since Mayor Bradley had issued a ban on sales in L.A. County, along with gasoline.

"The looting is absurd," she said to Caleb. "Unreal! Hey, we can watch the poor redistribute the wealth." Some people stole bananas or baby food. Many stole beer. "How is this worse than white-collar crime? Embezzling, fraud, the S&L Crisis. Billions lost! They make looters look like amateurs."

Caleb glared. "Fiona. I am not in the mood."

Live breaking news: Homeboy ramming storefront security gates with a stolen van, young Hispanic man sprinting down the street, dining chair on his head like an oak veneer hat. A Toyota hatchback careening down the avenue, couch perched precariously on its roof. Windshield obscured, the driver was leaning out the window to navigate. Father and son emerging from a sporting goods store loaded down with Thigh Masters. Much was being made of Latinos gleefully plundering the stores, *niños* in tow. *The family that loots together, stays together.* Smashing windows, people dashed inside the Gap or Payless Shoes, fighting over sizes and styles, stopping occasionally to smile and wave at the camera.

"So much of this is about the camera. Such images!"

One man bravely tried to douse a blaze with a bucket of water, while a citizen in another part of the city—burning broom in hand—set fire to a giant oak tree.

"Hey, I'm rooting for the tree. Is it a white tree? Maybe it's a Korean tree. Or a Mexican tree. In any case, it certainly provides a convenient whipping post."

Caleb glowered. A pair of palm trees abreast the Harbor Freeway was set ablaze. A man dressed as Bozo the Clown held up a crude sign. *Daryl Gates is a Stupid Clown!* 9-1-1 lines jammed, cries for help put on hold.

"I hope our power doesn't go out," said Fiona. "It's too dark now. Hey, Caleb, what's the LAPD's motto?"

He shrugged.

"We treat you like a king!"

"That's not funny."

"Sure it is. In a sick way. It's a sick world we live in. And you know my motto: if you don't laugh, you'll cry. Might as well laugh. Come on, you have to laugh. Nothing's sacred."

"Yeah, well," said Caleb, "maybe we'll all die laughing."

With a new fire ignited every three minutes, they could taste smoke. Their eyes burned. Governor Pete Wilson declared a state of emergency and sent in the National Guard, "outraged" by the verdict, as was Mayor Tom Bradley, who'd been pressuring Gates to resign. But that would cut into his book sales.

Caleb lamented the dearth of drugs, went next door to Bob's to buy beer. Fiona called the hospital again to see how Jeanette was faring. The doctor didn't give her much to go on.

"We don't know. She could die in an hour, or she could hang on, recover, and live for years."

"I need to go to her!" shouted Fiona.

"You can't go anywhere!" replied Caleb. "Which word do you not understand? You can't go driving around this city. You're too goddamned white! Besides, I need you here."

Wednesday night roared into Thursday morning, sleep nigh impossible, fear shoving all common sense under the bed. They received one frantic call after another, from parents, sisters, friends, and cohorts in far-flung places, Shannon in New York, Kazuki in Tokyo.

"I appreciate your concern," was all she could say, unable to reassure anyone.

Toy soldiers, she thought, Wilson sending in two thousand more National Guardsmen. Kent State came to mind.

"Send in the Marines," said Caleb. "The professionals. Is there anything more dangerous than a scared young male of the species brandishing an automatic rifle?"

"One who isn't scared."

Eleven hundred fires burning. Pulling a Nero, Gates the megalomaniac ran off to Brentwood for a fundraising dinner just as all the shit came down. Humvees prowled the streets. Amid the all-macho posturing and talk of leadership, chaos still reigned. Politicians! she thought. They're like eunuchs.

"I feel like I'm from another planet, being from a civilized country."

"Right. You have hockey riots."

"Well, at least we have our priorities straight. Beer, hockey, education, health care."

Caleb threw up his arms and headed for the roof. Fiona turned back to the television. *Mob rule*. A mob must be as difficult to document as a hurricane. Broadcast journalists interviewed riot victims anywhere, anytime. Jodi Baskerville, described by the *Los Angeles Times* as a "Valley girl choking on her own adrenaline," had a fit as a squadron of guardsmen stampeded past, daring to refuse her interview. Laurel Erickson shoved her microphone at a young Korean woman who was sobbing just after she'd been commandeered off the freeway by the CHP, only to be robbed at gunpoint by gangbangers. Face hidden behind a curtain of hair, Erickson actually touched the woman, reaching in to pull her hair back, yelling, "Tell our audience what you just told me!"

Bloods and Crips together. Black-Owned Business spray-painted on many storefronts, many torched despite the pleas for brotherhood. Koreans stood guard on the roofs of their shops, armed with rifles, appalled their taxes weren't providing police protection. Black people didn't expect police protection, the tension between Koreans and African Americans having escalated in recent years. They complained that Koreans were arrogant and unfriendly, and that they followed them around in their stores, taking their money, refusing them jobs.

Up on the studio roof, sitting duck-like, Fiona dampened the building with a garden hose. *Suddenly, I'm part of the food chain.* She bitterly regretted not buying a shotgun as Lenny had advised, though still believed "live by the sword, die by the sword." *Christ, here I am wishing for a gun. Gawd! I have been in the U.S. too long.*

Gangbangers cruised by in a variety of hot cars, Bob was barricaded inside his store, crouching behind the Spider-Man pinball machine, clutching a .45 calibre. A white van slowed down to case the place, driver with beer in hand. Looted beer? Bob emerged to ask if he lived in the neighbourhood. The guy claimed to work for the police. Yeah, right. Even the police don't work for the police tonight. Thank God Bob doesn't sell hard liquor. The place probably isn't worth trashing. *I hope. All I have is hope.* Bob decided to go home to his wife and kids, bestowing Fiona and Caleb with a baseball bat and a machete.

I want the gun. And I am going to get my lily-white ass out of here. Somehow.

Evinrude was perched on the fence, Fiona afraid to go outside to feed him, gunfire increasing, drawing closer. She flinched at each report, Caleb warning repeatedly, "Stay down! Keep down." Her stomach hurt. Fiona kept trying to convince Caleb to head for the hills, though he viewed such statements as treasonous. He was right. Driving over to Carrie's place would probably be more dangerous than anything that might ensue at the studio. They planned an escape route, just in case; they'd sleep in their clothes, ready to bolt. Fortunately, Hoover Street was a bit off the beaten path. Fiona went to the kitchen to make sandwiches. She found a ladybug in the romaine. *Ladybug, ladybug, fly away home, your house is on fire, your children are alone.*

Charcoal Avenue. History repeating itself? Surely these riots must seem like a flashback to survivors of the Watts Riots. This is different, no neighbourhood is untouchable. The spark may be the same, but in 1992 Los Angeles is on fire, the entire metropolis, including Hollywood, Culver City, and Long Beach. Even the residents of Beverly Hills had a scare put into them despite their remote-controlled security gates and private parking lots.

"Nothing changes," claimed one weary old black woman on Channel 12.

These riots would not be contained. Fiona pondered looting as a political statement. Why are they tearing up and burning down their own neighbourhoods? All those lost jobs. Where are they going to buy milk and toilet paper and prescriptions? The power is out. They're losing the food in their freezers.

Fiona heard a shout from across the street. Some jerk had torched a palm tree. Caleb ran out with a fire extinguisher, Fiona heartened to see neighbours dashing to the scene.

The couple speculated endlessly, trying to get a grip on exactly what was happening out there, gleaning useful information from non-stop TV news futile. Fiona entertained herself by observing each network's angle. They were all out for blood, none gathering many facts. Flubbing and spitting and tripping over their condensed version of the events, the networks relayed the same images over and over again.

Defenses and testosterone up, Caleb announced, "We will continue guarding our home and property."

The man of the house was getting a hard-on. By midnight it was difficult to summon any presence of mind. Fiona talked to Shannon, Kaye, Candye; anyone she could reach on the phone. Oona called from Vancouver.

"You got to get out of there! You can always buy a new couch."

"It's not that simple. Everybody was completely unprepared for a not guilty verdict."

I am naive, she thought. The truth does surface, ultimately, but in the meantime people flee it like a turd floating in a swimming pool. Including me; life with Caleb a sham, the rage onscreen reflecting the rage simmering inside our home. Jury out, vultures circling, King's attorney warning everyone to get out of Dodge. It was too late now. She was stranded.

"Good night, Oona." Fiona hung up.

"What does she know?" said Caleb. "She's a Canadian."

"Oona's just concerned. She's not the only person urging us to get out."

"We're not going anywhere!" he shouted.

"No kidding!"

"This is our home. Our livelihood! We've worked our butts off building this place up. I've invested all my money and time."

I could leave and never look back. Fiona's eyes followed him around the room.

"I'm inured to violence," trumpeted Caleb. "I'm standing my ground!"

"I don't want to get used to it. What am I saying? I am used to it! Numb, in fact."

Bush was on the bandwagon, vowing to stop the violence by sending in the Marines. The National Guard was playing hide

301

and seek, their numbers changing every hour, depending on which politician was taking charge or setting the record straight, jumping from two thousand to six thousand. Then eight. The RTD shut down all service at six p.m. The FAA shut down LAX, police helicopters fired upon.

At 5:42 a.m., Fiona, still wired, felt a sharp pain in her chest. *Will this ever end?*

Caleb summoned her to the bedroom. She found him sneering, holding the phone as if it were contaminated.

"You have a long distance call."

"Thanks." Caleb handed her the receiver and lingered. "Hello?"

"Fiona! It's me Dennis. Are you okay? I can come down."

Caleb tread the carpet. Fiona smiled. "It'll all blow over."

She longed to tell Dennis she was grateful for the call, wished she could see him. Caleb drew a finger across his throat. "I have to go."

Caleb moved in closer. "Tell him you're fine."

"I'm fine."

"Tell him goodbye."

"Goodbye, Dennis."

★ ★ ★ ★

She dreamt of Canada. Home. Snug inside a tiny seaplane gliding over a deep, shimmering lake, Fiona reached out to touch the top of a Douglas fir. There was a time she'd enjoyed being an expatriate. All these tests. One after another. *Why did I come back? All my forces on this front now.* Police state. Stuck, like being put into a straitjacket for your own good. Martial law. There go their sacred civil liberties. The curfew was having a lot of impact, and according to the latest bulletins, working to highlight criminal activity for the police. Patrols had finally been deployed to protect firefighting units.

No Rango. Withdrawal. Fiona ransacked the place, hoping to find a lost bindle or forgotten stash. *Shit. Beat me to the punch.* Caleb had scraped the grinder clean.

Rage. Horror. Dread. Terror. *Four seasons around here.* Fiona couldn't watch it anymore, footage of the brutal assault on truck driver Reginald Denny, as excruciating to bear witness to as the King beating. They threw bricks at his head, bashed in his temple with a fire extinguisher, kicked and pummelled his limp body, leaving Denny's long red hair matted with blood, his face a pulpy mess. *Enough!* They would not stop. One attacker flashed a gang sign and danced a victory jig. Some guy ran over and stole Denny's wallet. Surely the perps will be identified from the video, though justice will be as elusive for Denny, she thought. Huddled on the bed, Fiona watched Rodney King's stammering plea for compassion, which was drowned out by the din. Life as an icon. Clearly, the speech was painful, injuries still evident though King finally appeared human in contrast to the puffy, stitched up, distorted monster projected via television for months.

"Come here." Caleb was hard.

He is aroused by the violence.

He fetched the stilettos from the closet, tossed them at her feet. "Leave the thong on. Take off the bra."

Fiona removed the bra. He came up from behind, clutched her breasts in both hands, pushed her to her knees, and slapped her ass.

"Turn around." He thrust his cock in her face.

God, he stinks.

"Suck me."

Nothing makes me gag anymore. He instructed her to lie back on the bed. Oddly, Caleb insisted on doing it the old-fashioned way. He's drunk, the cock ring won't come off. *It's going to be a long, sooty fuck.* Bile rose in the back of her throat. She peered into his pupils, bottomless, distending as he climaxed. Eyes of an adder. *So, what does that make me?* Fiona swallowed tears, and perversely, barely reined in laughter. Caleb rolled over and passed out.

303

Get out. *I have to get out.* If it isn't here, I can't come back. No one will ever know. They'll think the arsonists did it. War zone after all. *I'll set a fire under his ass.* For the last time. The riots, catalyst to freedom. What a great cover. She'd take the car. *Then he can't come after me.* The videotapes. The Polaroids. Fiona retrieved them from his hiding spot along with the Rolex. She returned upstairs to find Caleb asleep, listening to his breathing as she tugged the wallet from his jeans and removed the bills. She'd need to hit a bank machine right away, before he had a chance to call Visa and shut down her account. It would be all the money she'd have to live on for a while. At least the tank was full, enough fuel to get her well out of the city.

Fiona loaded the car with clothes, toiletries, camera, photos, guitar, amplifier and a few books. She grabbed her microphone and one of his precious Neumanns, planning to pawn it when the time came. She couldn't find Evinrude, calling softly, but frantically as she packed. Finally, she heard a piteous mewl emanating from beneath the far corner of the couch. She managed to coax him out and put him in the pet carrier.

"He likes his cage. It makes him feel secure. Like me?" *Gawd. I'm talking to myself.* "And if Caleb wakes up, I'll kill him."

Fiona tiptoed back to the bedroom to check once more, watched her husband's chest rising and falling. *Asshole. Sleeps through earthquakes, and Hole, after all.*

She put Evinrude's carrier in the car and returned to the basement. So, if those thugs had come along and set the place on fire, how would things appear? They're using Molotov cocktails, judging by the news. Fiona wondered if they were breaking into the buildings or torching them from the outside. The news choppers hadn't gotten close enough to reveal those kinds of details. Both, probably. Keep moving. Fiona found kerosene, walked through the studio to the front of the building, poked her head out, relieved to find the street deserted.

"Do it. Do it. Do it."

She constructed a pyre of newspapers, wood chip mulch, and

dried lawn clippings. Fire by design. Fire by Fiona. She hesitated, stared down at her shaking hands. *This place is killing me.* She looked around. Dumped the kerosene. It glugged out, splashing all over her shoes, intoxicating fumes overwhelming her lungs. She pulled out a box of Redbird Strike Anywhere Matches. *Anywhere?* 250 wooden matches. Caution: Handle With Care. Fiona struck a match, held the match, an eternity passing. "Ouch!" She lit another, breathing in the pungent fetor of dead wood and sulfur.

"Dead meat. I'll be dead meat." *Not anymore.* Fiona dropped the match and listened to the gasp of its conflagration taking in oxygen.

WHOMPF.

Wow. All that bushwhacking with the old man finally pays off. A pulsating pillar of flame roared upward, pausing as though to pose, flaunting its terrible splendor before heaving itself against the building. Fire number 2,508.

"Oh my God!"

Fiona loped to the car, jumped in, and booted it. *Adios, motherfucker! Do not look back. Can't! Gotta keep an eye out for gangstas.* Into the fire. Horizon crimson. Like a war movie. The future. *My future. There. On fire!*

It was past curfew, and though the studio was only a block from the 101 Freeway, Fiona realized it might be closed. *Maybe I can get on it somehow.* She raced down. Stop. No entrance. CHP with shotguns. *Maybe I should beg. Puleeeze, officer! Let me go home. My house is on fire and my mother is dying alone.* He didn't look too receptive. Fiona turned around. *Where the fuck am I gonna go?*

She closed her eyes, trying to envision an escape route. She'd head north, most importantly, north and then east. That would get her to the I-5. She could be out of the worst of it in twenty minutes. Fiona turned right onto Virgil, left onto Temple. *Not too bad. Shit. I still have to get past Vermont.* She cruised by burned-out buildings—charred steel frames suspended like ebony skeletons—portrait of Martin Luther King hanging from seared iron security bars. *Keep moving.* Cars sped down the street, some careened out of control. Looters waded through a sea of shards.

An overturned Volvo, incinerated black, rested across the street from the Silver Lake Dry Cleaners. Thunderous, close, incessant gunfire. Fiona found Vermont jammed, hordes descending, screaming, smashing glass, hurling bottles. The street, a river flooded with bodies, burning buildings on either side like blazing riverbanks. Impotent policemen guarded faceless firemen, hoses flaccid in their hands or lying on the ground. *Yea, though I walk through the valley of death.* Fiona crossed herself. *Stay in the left lane.* She kept her eyes on the road, praying her cap and high collar would conceal her whiteness. Fairness. *Hah!* She locked the doors and windows. *God, it's not bulletproof. Why do I think my car will keep me safe? Livin' in L.A. too long all right. Keep moving. Don't stop! Don't stop for anything. Anyone. Even the looters. Especially the looters. Crazy motherfuckers.*

Narrowly missing several people dodging her car, Fiona caught her eyes as they flashed in the rear-view mirror. Carloads of disaffected youth cruised the block, screeching to a stop every few minutes to casually smash a store window, tossing in a homemade bomb. Traffic lights out everywhere, absolutely everything in flames—street signs, mailboxes, parking metres. *Which is safer? Sunset or Santa Monica? Sunset. Surely Sunset will be spared.* Fiona cruised, head low, past Circuit City—hot spot—the goods inside so coveted. She watched a short, muscular, barefoot homie struggling to carry two television sets and a huge handgun. He dropped a TV. Determined not to lose his booty, he set the other one down, shoved his revolver into the front of his jeans, then heaved both televisions into his arms. *Yeah, pick 'em up, asshole. Then you can't shoot me.* It occurred to Fiona that she could swing by Rango's. *Bad idea. Still tempting though. Man, I've got it bad.*

Suddenly, a massive, cream-coloured Chevy Impala appeared, the driver yelling, jeering gangbangers speeding up to pull alongside her car.

"Get her!" An enraged black man leaned out the window, levelling a .45 at Fiona's face.

Duck! Fiona ducked and threw the car into reverse. "Get the fuck outta my way!" she screamed. "Goddamn muthafuckas! I will run you down!"

BAM. CRRRUNCH.

Fire hydrant. *Goddammit!* The Impala pulled away. An arc of water sailed over her car, dousing the mob, causing it to disperse. Somewhat. Shaking their fists, they cursed her. Fiona threw it into drive. "Move car. Move car. Move car. Please car! Please car! Pleeease car!" Her trusty old Valiant lurched forward, bumper still gripping the gushing hydrant. She revved the motor, freeing the bumper with a loud scraping sound, and steered through the throng, roaring, "Get outta my way!"

I could kill. Oh my God! Caleb. What have I done? I better go back. Fiona managed to be heading north. *Yes! North, all the way to Canada. All the way home. I hope!* A camouflaged army truck idled in front of the Vista Theater, Queen Ida blaring from a burrito stand. She wondered if queer friends were still cruising Griffith Park. *Must add to the thrill.* Fiona searched frantically for a freeway on-ramp, helicopter hovering. All Exits Closed. *I hope nobody stops me.* A CHP cruiser pulled up behind her.

"Don't pull me over."

He pulled her over. *Christ. Don't arrest me!* No due process. How long would she be holed up? Cop approached cautiously, probably relieved to find a white girl flying solo.

"Don't you know there's a curfew?"

Christ. I smell like kerosene. Fiona summoned tears. "I'm going home!" she stammered. *Can he smell it?*

"Home! Why did you leave home in the first place?"

Trick question? As much as she loathed being perceived as a dumb blond, Fiona always knew exactly when to bat her eyelashes.

"Please, officer! We need milk for my son. I'll go straight home. I promise." Fiona bit her tongue to stop from asking for help, from blurting, "I don't know where, or what home is. And I may have just killed my husband!" *Self-defence. I'll plead self-defence.*

The cop let her go. There were army tanks everywhere, National Guardsmen bearing M-16s standing at attention. Fiona kept moving, heading north. *Screw Sunset, I'll take Los Feliz through*

307

Atwater to the I-5 entrance. The interstate must be open up there and surely Atwater is quiet. Atwater was quiet, to the point of eerie. Streets were lined with softly swaying jacaranda. She would miss their showy lilac flowers, black trunks. Another transplant, from Brazil, apparently. Farther on the police presence thinned. People moved about freely, though their eyes were trained on their destinations. For once, Fiona was grateful for the I-5, breathing a huge sigh of relief upon seeing the sign, and entering the on-ramp.

Ah, so the entire world isn't in flames. Fiona gripped the steering wheel and leaned back. She derived much pleasure from driving, relishing her mobility, freedom. This drive was exhilarating, even while stuck behind a truck hauling a load of carrots that looked like giant orange dreadlocks. *Not for long.* Gunning the engine, cranking her tunes, Fiona pulled out and passed.

As home burns. She kept moving, driving until it got dark, checking into the Journey's End Motel just outside Santa Barbara, tempted to call Dennis' folks. Jumpy, torn, lonesome, dismayed at how far she still had to go, Fiona couldn't sleep. She paced the room amid the drone of television news, agonizing over Caleb and the studio. She ordered a pizza, ate a slice, had a shower, and slept fitfully. Leaving early without seeing anyone, she drove. And drove. And drove, listening to news of the aftermath on the radio. A rush of volunteers was cleaning up the mess, actor Edward James Olmos sweeping sidewalks; walking it like he talks it, she thought. Death toll up to fifty-three. White exodus. *White trash exodus in my case.* Tired clichés about healing and recovery.

A familiar road trip, after two more wretched nights of sneaking her cat into cheap motels, Fiona made it to Washington State, driving straight through to the border, crossing into Canada with no problems. She passed small white crosses tacked onto telephone poles near White Rock. Spooky, roadside memorials, *descansos* in Spanish, common down south, much in the tradition of Dia de los Muertos. She'd never seen them in Canada. Must be due to the country's expanding immigration policy; emphasis on ethnic diversity. Memorials. *What difference does it make?* People die. They die the way they do in stories, in ballads; the way they have for eons, in catastrophes, murders, plagues, car accidents.

She didn't make it in time, Jeanette dead and gone by the time she arrived; cremated, Rory in possession of her ashes. Three daughters and none of them with her during her last hours on earth. Jeanette would have died alone if not for good old Bernie. Her sisters refused to have a funeral.

"I need it," said Fiona. "It's unreal! I didn't see her body. I can't feel anything. I need to mourn. Please!"

Still they refused. Rory felt badly though, and offered to take care of Evinrude until Fiona could find a job and a place to live.

CHAPTER FOURTEEN

Home sweet home; in a fugue state, Fiona wandered, or fought panic. The Rolex a was a fake, pawn shop clerk amused.

"I'd be laughing too if I wasn't so broke," she wailed at Shannon, who kindly sent $250.

Fiona asked Bill for a loan. *A long shot.* Sure enough, he begged poverty. Neither did he have answers about Jeanette's paternity fraud, but did say that he'd never have married her if he'd known. *Thanks, Dad.* Maureen's reaction: "Hey, that means I'm the youngest!"

Though fraught with anxiety, Fiona revelled in her liberty. *I am my own bitch. At last.* She trashed the videotapes, but kept some of the Polaroids, culling the most graphic, the ones Caleb favoured. She cut them with kitchen shears and lit them, the act of burning providing a release, though she feared the fumes might be toxic. Fiona stared at her diminishing face, searching for some sign of herself. Many shots were candid, the majority posed, most invariably with his cock far down her throat. She tried to think of his cock as Everyman's Cock, but the rest of Caleb filled every frame. *Burning city. Burning man, burning husband, sphincter for a heart.*

"He's alive!" she told Shannon. Rumour had it Caleb had survived just fine, informing everyone that he was exiting perdition to go to her, to save their marriage.

"Guess my fire fizzled out. Christ. He is the Terminator. I pray he doesn't find me."

"I'm gonna call that prick, tell him to leave you alone!" said Shannon.

"Thanks, but it won't do much good. Besides, I think it's a

bluff."

Relying upon her engine of anger, Fiona strove to anticipate Caleb's next move.

Early one June morning, Fiona looked out Oona's window, startled by the sight of her big blond love bone pulling up in a red pickup. Knees buckling, she waved. *How did he find me?* She'd been couch surfing for weeks. Dennis jumped out of the truck, grin intact. Still unbridled. A relief, she thought. Trembling, Fiona opened the door. Dennis pounced and threw his arms around her. She peered outside, wondering if he'd been followed.

Succor of their reunion, Fiona made jasmine tea. The pair sat in a patch of kitchen sun and talked amiably for hours. She told Dennis about her shock regarding the paternity fraud.

"I think Jeanette's lies only emerged because of her dementia. She intended to take that secret to her grave. I'm trying to mourn, but can't think about her without feeling angry."

"It was a betrayal. You're entitled."

"I look in the mirror and wonder whose DNA I am carrying. My life is a farce! It's a shock finding out that something you believed your entire life is a lie."

"I'm sorry, Fiona. That's gotta be tough."

"How could she lie to me like that?"

"She was lying to herself. She must have believed it, that Bill was your father."

"Oh yeah, I'm sure she convinced herself. She's always been delusional."

Dennis gently took her hand.

"I'm kicking myself for not getting the truth out of her before she died. But I couldn't believe anything she said. And I was so worn out. Trying to deal with her and Caleb, and Gary and Brianna. I didn't want to believe it. I didn't want to believe she was dying either."

"Don't be so hard on yourself."

"Maybe she didn't know him. I remember when I was a teenager, both of us drunk, she described a rape. In the woods. Her clinging to a tree, the guy throwing her to the ground." Fiona wrapped her hands around her mug. "Or, she might have told me if I hadn't run away. Abandoned her."

"Like you said, maybe she didn't know his name. And you are not your mother's keeper. Do I have to repeat myself? Don't be so hard on yourself, Fiona. You did the best you could. So did Jeanette. Come on, small Catholic town, Quebec in the sixties?"

"You know what else really sucks? She wasn't allowed to be Québécois. Neither were we. Not with Bill around. He's such a bigot. She became completely assimilated." Fiona sipped her tea. "Christ. How am I ever going to find my real father?"

"You might never find him. You're just going to have to accept that. And yeah, I know, it sucks. "

No contact for a month. What a relief. *What am I afraid of?* That asshole can't connect with anyone, no matter how many people he surrounds himself with. Friendly neighbourhood sociopath.

Shannon had diagnosed her with PTSD, urged her to get counselling, but Fiona was beginning to breathe all on her own, easing out of acute withdrawal, slowly subduing her inner predator. *Perhaps it's mercy, letting me go, leaving me alone. If he's leaving me alone.* She hoped her dance with the devil was over. *I always have hope.* Still, Fiona found herself reluctant to hold hands with Dennis in public, certain Caleb was watching. As if such a precaution could save her.

"Come on, we're gonna hit the road. Go down home. Matapédia. Take your ma back." Dennis held up a square brass tin. She'd only seen it once, briefly.

"How did you manage that?"

"They took a little bit of her and let me have the rest."

"Oh, you charmer you. But then, my sisters like you better than me."

Nice tin. She had to look. *All that's left.* Fiona revealed the ashes to Dennis.

"That's how I feel. Haven't you had enough of the road? Enough of me?"

"Come on, it'll be like the good old days." Dennis grinned. "Actually, I think we should fly. Via New York, go visit Shannon."

"Yeah! Let's go see our girl. I miss her so bad." He tries so hard, she thought. "You know I'm on the rebound. Apparently, I 'need time to heal'."

"That's okay. I'll wait."

"Aren't you tired of waiting?"

"I haven't exactly been miserable, you know."

"Good. That's my job."

"Not anymore. You're fired."

"What about our painful history?"

"I forgive you."

She smiled. "You don't understand. I don't know if I'm capable of a normal relationship."

"Who wants to be normal?"

She tried to imagine Matapédia, what to do when they arrived. How much ceremony should be involved? Maybe it would be enough to go down to the river and scatter Jeanette's ashes. They spent the first day visiting old haunts and relatives, cruising the back roads of the quaint Matapédia Valley. They drove across covered bridges, past cathedrals, salmon fishermen, and fat, round hay bales squatting upon freshly mown fields. Old man Ferguson still has that mule. *A relic, like me.*

She asked many questions about Jeanette's past. Fiona listened to familiar family lore, but no one could remember much else. Jeanette's maternal family, the Donegans, had a house that was still standing, albeit desolate and overgrown. She fantasized about living by the river the way her mother had. Fiona felt a persistent tugging at her roots, a notion she'd previously dismissed. A few cousins and old family friends showed up for the memorial, many commenting on her resemblance to Jeanette, which made her cringe, then feel ashamed. Sad. Everyone kept asking after her sisters and their children.

"Ah, *mon ami.*" Mother tongue. Frustrated at losing what little French she'd had, Fiona's efforts were graciously accommodated. After a short service in the church, Fiona and Dennis proceeded down to the river. The Matapédia. Jeanette always got misty talking about the Matapédia, how happy she'd been there. A consummate swimmer, she'd saved more than one cousin from drowning. It wasn't hard to imagine those powerful arms slicing through the currents.

At the river's edge, Fiona and Dennis exchanged looks. Tossing a rose to the rapids, she stood a long moment watching it disappear, staring into the swirling water. Dennis passed the tin, steadying her with a resolute gaze. Fiona removed the lid carefully. Balanced precariously, one foot on the bank, the other on a boulder, a soaring hawk abruptly appeared, screeching, swooping down, fiercely grazing Fiona's head. It flapped away, several strands of hair caught in its talons. Fiona screamed, slipped, and stumbled into the water, Jeanette's remains spilling all over her skirt.

"Fiona!" Dennis grabbed her arm and yanked her out.

Bawling, Fiona climbed the bank and seriously considered tossing her ash-caked cipher's carcass back into the river. She hurled the empty tin instead.

"I am such a *fucking* loocr!"

Fiona fell to her knees, burying her face in her hands.

Dennis knelt down next to her. "Look." He lifted Fiona's chin, directing her gaze to a formidable nest resting high in the boughs of a maple. "Don't take it personally."

She had to laugh.

Acknowledgements

I am grateful for the support, encouragement, inspiration and various contributions of Lucas Haley Raycevick, Josef Roehrl, Michael Raycevick, Peter Haskell, Saint Teresa Stone, James Zink, Peter Draper, Art Bergmann, Mi Sook Burns, Jhim Pattison, Byron Baker, Craig Smith, Carol Cram, Victor Bonderoff, Derek von Essen, Gabor Gasztonyi, Peter Trower, Jenn Farrell, Scott Beadle, Mark Deutrom, Andy Flaster, Frank Scoblete, Chris Walter, Penelope Bacsfalvi, Bev Davies, Yvonne Yule, Vanessa Larochelle, Kyle Thiessen, Jason Armstrong, Ashley St. Jean, Heidi Rona Heer, Emily Kaily Heer, Jim Jacob St. Jean, Lisa Wallace, Katherine Wallace, Thom Burns, Kim Jones, Gloria Ohland, David Henry Sterry, Terry Jordan, Sage sisters Julianna McLean, Michelle Greysen, Sharron Arksey, Gwen Matyas Smid, soul sisters Cathy Cleghorn, Debra Margolis, Julie Vik, Gretl Rasmussen and my agent Drea Cohane. I am indebted to Davina Haisell for saving the (copyediting) day. Thank you to my fellow musicians, especially bandmates Jon Wrasse, Mark Francis White, Jeff Moses, Paul Eckman, Candye Kane, Christine de Veber, Jane Colligan, Conny Nowe, John MacAdams, Jon Huck, Randy Rampage, Brad Kent, Karla du Plantier, Roderick Shoolbraid, Chris Coon, and all my friends and family. Your love sustains me.

About the Author

Trailblazing poet, author, musician and media artist, Heather Haley, pushes boundaries by creatively integrating disciplines, genres and media. She was an editor for the *LA Weekly* and publisher of *The Edgewise Cafe*, one of Canada's first electronic magazines. With work featured in many journals and anthologies, Haley is the author of poetry collections *Sideways* and *Three Blocks West of Wonderland*. She has directed numerous videopoems, official selections at dozens of international film festivals and toured North America and Europe in support of two critically acclaimed AURAL Heather CDs of spoken word song, *Princess Nut* and *Surfing Season*.

www.ingramcontent.com/pod-product-compliance
Lightning Source LLC
Chambersburg PA
CBHW070217260626
47160CB00002B/579